The Alpha Group Trilogy

Maya Cross

Publisher: Maya Cross via Createspace
City: Sydney

ISBN-13: 978-1492326571

Dedicated to C.

For putting up with an awful lot.

Book One:
Locked

Chapter 1

It was nearly one in the morning when I realised that I was about to do something stupid. Ordinarily, I'm not someone who is prone to random acts of mischief. By day I'm as straight as they come. But get a few glasses of red into me, and suddenly that little devil on my shoulder starts sounding a whole lot more reasonable.

And tonight was definitely one of those nights.

I was sitting in a shabby little bar with two friends, celebrating Louisa's engagement. We'd only been there an hour, but the empty glasses were already starting to accrue in embarrassing amounts on the table in front of us. Our attention was focused on a finely dressed couple who were walking through a doorway at the back of the room.

"My money's on...international drug lord," I said.

"I'm going to go with local mafia," Louisa replied. We both looked expectantly at Ruth.

"Billionaire men's underwear mogul!" the other woman declared grandly, swaying a little in her seat. The three of us dissolved into giggles.

We were no strangers to a drink or two on a weeknight, but given that it was a special occasion, we'd wanted to take it up a notch. I'm not sure who actually uttered the words 'pub crawl', but all that mattered was it was said. Before I knew what was happening, we'd set off on a merry trek around Sydney. Five hours and four bars later, I was well on the way towards a killer hangover.

The bar we were in was not one of our usual haunts, and for good reason. It was the sort of place that might kindly have been described as 'a renovators dream,' or 'full of character.' In other words, it was a bit of a shit-hole. The angular metal tables looked like they'd been dug from some Soviet Cold War bunker, and the floor sloped away dangerously to one side, as though some of the foundations had simply given up and headed for greener pastures. The only wine they sold was a rather dubious house red, and it came served in the same squat, slightly grimy tumblers as every other drink on the menu.

If it'd been a normal night out, we'd never have considered visiting a place like this. It certainly didn't look like the kind of establishment that would be particularly friendly towards a couple of high spirited, professional women out on a bender. But the booze that was swilling around in our stomachs made us bold, and rather than continuing on our way, we'd found ourselves giggling and making a beeline for the entrance.

In retrospect I was rather glad we did, because there was something intriguing about the place, something that wasn't evident from first glance. Most of the other patrons were what I'd expected; sullen, rough looking, and wearing tradesman's clothes, they eyed us over their foaming cups with a kind of resentful curiosity. But shortly after we'd arrived, an unobtrusive doorway on the rear wall had opened, and a security guard had taken up position in front. Gradually, new people began to trickle in and disappear into the back, people that clearly didn't belong in a dump like this. None of the regulars seemed to care, but that little mystery had set my mind wandering.

"What about the girl?" Louisa asked.

Ruth snorted. "Professional trophy wife?"

"With a Ph.D in Pilates," I added.

"Who also happens to be the next Elizabeth Taylor, if only someone would give her a chance," Ruth finished.

Louisa chuckled. "We're such bitches. For all we know she could be perfectly lovely. It's probably a bloody banking conference or something."

I shook my head. "Bankers don't meet in strange rooms up the back of no name bars." My eyes were firmly fixed on the doorway now. To the casual observer, it might have looked unremarkable — just your everyday corporate gathering — but something about the whole situation struck me as strange. Maybe it was just the alcohol catching up with me, I don't know, but my curiosity was piqued.

None of the bartenders were any help. All they'd say was it was a private function. I couldn't even get a company name out of them. It didn't make any sense. Who were these people that their meeting was such a secret? And why hide it away back here in this place?

"Well, unless you plan on flashing the guard a peek at the girls so we can sneak in, I doubt we'll ever know," Ruth said.

"Don't give her ideas," Louisa replied, now staring at me. "She's got that look in her eyes again."

"What look?" I asked.

"The look that says, 'I'm preparing to make a giant, drunken ass of myself again.'"

"Now when have I ever done that?" I replied, unable to contain my grin. In truth, I did have something of a history of getting a little crazy on big nights out. Being an attorney is hard work. Eighty hour weeks, mounds of paperwork, Partners constantly hounding you; half the time I felt like a worn guitar string that was just a few strums away from snapping. So on those rare occasions that I did get some R&R, I tended to cut loose more than I should. It felt good to just put Professional Sophia in a box for a few hours and forget about her.

Louisa didn't look amused. "Come on Soph, why ruin a perfectly good night by getting yourself kicked out?"

"I haven't said I'm doing anything yet!"

"But you're thinking about it."

My grin widened. "Maybe."

Louisa sighed. "One of these days you're going to get yourself into actual trouble, you know."

The sensible part of me agreed with her. It wasn't exactly lawyerly to be getting tossed out into the street on my ass at one in the morning. But on the other hand, the situation was rather mysterious, and my brain had been marinating in alcohol for hours. I felt restless, energetic, daring; daring enough to do something I might regret later.

I watched as another couple slipped casually into the bar and headed for the back. Whoever these people were, they might as well have had dollar signs printed on their foreheads. Armani, Gucci, Louis Vuitton, Prada; it was like Milan Fashion Week.

Most of the visitors were men. Suited and broad shouldered, they all exuded that kind of arrogant confidence that comes from a lifetime of getting exactly what you want. Some had partners on their arms as well; slim, rouged, perfectly varnished girls, many of whom looked barely out of high school. By glossy magazine standards they were probably attractive, but to me they just looked fake, more like ornaments than real people.

"Come on," I said, "where's your sense of adventure?"

"I'd hardly classify sneaking into some la-di-da business function as an adventure," Louisa replied.

4

"Hey, if she wants to try, I say let her," Ruth said. "Who knows, maybe she can bring back a couple of the suits for us. There were a few I wouldn't kick out of bed."

"A lot of good that'll do me," Louisa said, pointing to her ring.

"Hey, what he doesn't know can't hurt him," Ruth replied. "It can be like... Soph's engagement present to you. A little bon voyage to the single life!"

I couldn't help but grin at Louisa's indignant expression. Sometimes, I still wondered how we were such a tight group. Louisa was as reserved as Ruth was free spirited, and I worked too hard to be much of either. But nonetheless we'd been friends since university. Somehow, we just clicked.

"I haven't been single for four years," Louisa said.

Ruth giggled. "Oh lighten up Lou, I'm just messing around. Obviously they'll both be for me."

At that moment, the front door of the bar opened, and another sharply dressed man walked in. It took me a few moments to realise that I recognised him.

"No way," I said, my eyes flicking to my friends. They were both staring at him as he crossed the room, mouths hanging slightly open. After a quiet word to the guard, he vanished into the back.

"Did one of you spike this with a little something extra when I wasn't looking?" Ruth asked, glancing down at her drink. "Because I swear that was Chase Adams."

Chase Adams was one of the biggest stars in Hollywood. A home grown Australian hero, he'd had a string of high profile hits in recent years, although he was known more for his washboard abs, axe-blade jaw, and baby blue eyes than any kind of real acting talent. I'm not really the sort of girl who lusts after celebrities, but his presence made things even more interesting. Before, I'd assumed the event was something corporate, but now, I didn't know what to think. None of the other guests had been familiar. Were they minor celebrities I just didn't recognise? Or perhaps Chase was just there as a friend? My head was swimming with a million questions.

"Nope," Louisa said, "I saw him too." She gave her lips a little involuntary lick. "No date either."

"Such a pity you're not single anymore, hey?" Ruth replied with a smirk.

Louisa shot her a withering look, but she couldn't maintain it long.

"So Lou," I said, "still not even a tiny bit curious?"

She glanced at the doorway once more and then sighed. "Maybe a little. But that doesn't change the fact that it's crazy to try and do anything about it." She nodded at the gargantuan man who stood guard in front of the door. "That guy looks like he eats a bowl of nails for breakfast each morning. We're not going to just giggle and bat our eyelashes past him."

I glanced over once more, sizing him up. She had a point. He looked like a secret service agent from some sort of presidential thriller movie. Clean shaven and unsmiling, his barrel chest and tree trunk arms filled the doorway. In stereotypical elite security fashion, his eyes were hidden behind a pair of dark wraparound glasses which looked vaguely ridiculous given the late hour. The coil of an earpiece dangled down one side of his jacket, and every few minutes he'd reach up and press on it, whispering furtively for a moment. Reporting in with the boss, probably.

And all of a sudden, a plan began to take shape in my head.

"Probably not, but maybe I can do one better," I replied. Without giving my brain time to object, I scooped up my drink and stood. I knew it was foolish, but my curiosity was almost overpowering now. I had to know what was going on back there. "Either of you coming?"

Louisa stared up at me like I'd lost my mind, but Ruth merely looked amused. "I think I'd rather just watch," she said, clearly certain that I was about to make a massive fool of myself. I wasn't entirely sure she was wrong. My plan was thin at best. But with a more than healthy dose of Dutch courage circulating inside me, I didn't really care. I was going through that door or getting kicked out in the process.

"Alright then. Let me show you how it's done girls."

And with that, I turned and began marching across the room.

I was basically the perfect level of drunk. Blissful, carefree, a little giddy, but not so far gone that I was slurring or staggering. But the guard didn't know that. The closer I got to him, the more I played it up. As his head turned my way, I threw up a vapid smile and began to stumble a little, gazing around the room in inebriated wonder.

The drunken flirt had gotten me past more than one lengthy club queue in my youth. Don't get me wrong, I don't consider myself to be a knockout or anything – I'd kill for a few more inches of leg, and skin that tanned instead of cooked – but I have certain assets that when emphasised, draw men's eyes nonetheless. The right kind of skirt, a few strategically unfastened buttons, and the rest is usually easy. Unfortunately, Louisa was right; it was going to take more than a smile and a little cleavage to make it through Mr Serious. But I had a special twist in mind for him.

As I arrived in front of the guard, I rocked backwards on my heels, blinking rapidly, as though spotting him for the first time. "Well hello handsome," I said in my best drunken drawl.

The man's lips tightened. "Miss, I'm sorry but this is a

private area."

I giggled and batted my eyelashes. "Oh come on now, I just want to talk. Doesn't it get lonely just standing here by yourself all night?"

"I'm fine, but Miss please, I need to keep the doorway clear."

I pondered this for a few seconds. "Well then, I have an idea. How about you come and join me for a drink over there. You can watch your little door sitting down, and I won't be in the way anymore!"

He stared down at me, unblinking and stony faced. "Miss, I'm sorry, but I'm on duty. Please return to your table."

My stomach tightened. I'd been planning on playing it more slowly, but he obviously wasn't in the mood to chat. It was now or never. "Surely you get a break?" I said, leaning in closer to brush his arm. "Even a man like you needs a—oh god I'm so sorry!"

He uttered something sharp and flinched backwards, a red stain already blossoming on his chest. I gaped up at him.

"I've ruined your shirt." Setting my now empty wine glass on a nearby table, I reached for some napkins. "I've always been so clumsy. I can't seem to go a day without spilling something. Here, let me clean you up."

As I talked, my eyes flicked to the small plastic receiver that was clipped to his breast pocket. I knew enough about security equipment to know that most earpieces had one. It sent and received signals from the main hub. The question was, had I hit it? In the dim light of the bar it was hard to tell.

I stepped closer to dab his shirt, hoping to get a better look, but he caught my arms in one strong hand. "You've done enough," he said, all politeness gone from his voice. "It's time for you to leave."

He raised his hands to his ear. "Command, this is Jones.

I've got a situation here." Seconds passed and nothing happened. He began to look worried. "Command? Hello?" A few more seconds. "Fuck!"

Jackpot.

Now came the real test. He glared down at me, seemingly unsure what to do. As far as I could see, he had two choices. He could wait there until someone came to find out why he'd dropped off the grid, or he could duck inside quickly to let them know there was a problem. Both options had their risks. I was banking on him choosing the latter.

But first, I had to convince him to let me throw myself out. I tried my best to look harmless and afraid, which wasn't difficult. He was an incredibly intimidating man, and his grip felt like a vice around my wrists. *What if I've already gone too far? What if I've bitten off more than I can chew?* I closed my eyes briefly and tried not to panic.

"Okay, okay, I'm sorry. I'll go," I said, keeping my voice meek.

He weighed this up momentarily. "I don't want to see you here again," he said, nodding to the bar.

"No sir."

"I'm going to go clean up, and when I come back, I expect to see you gone."

"No problem."

"Good." He released me.

Giving him one last apologetic smile, I turned and tottered off across the room, breathing a sigh of relief. So far so good.

The front door itself couldn't be seen from his vantage. The bar hooked around ninety degrees at one end, with the exit around the corner. Assuming he stayed put, I could hide there without actually leaving.

It was difficult to resist the urge to look back. I could feel his eyes following me as I walked.

Rounding the corner, I finally let the act drop. Throwing my elbow on the bar, I closed my eyes and sucked in several deep breaths. Even though everything had gone to plan, the whole experience had been decidedly more nerve wracking than I'd expected. Blood was roaring in my ears and I could still feel the buzz of adrenaline coursing through my veins. I briefly debated giving up. People that hired security like that typically did it for a reason; they didn't want to be disturbed. But most of the hard work was already done, and besides, the thought of trudging back to the table and seeing Louisa's snide smile was a little too much to bear at that moment.

Hiding as best I could behind a rack of glasses, I leaned back around the corner and peeked up over the bar. The guard was still at his post, looking conflicted. He cast his eyes around the room, weighing his options. If his employers were looking for privacy, they'd chosen a great location. Even when we'd arrived, the bar had contained less than twenty people, and now in the wee hours of the morning, that number had dwindled considerably. The few remaining patrons were huddled in bleary eyed groups, engrossed in soft conversation. None seemed to be paying much attention to what was going on up the back. It wasn't exactly a high risk situation.

Still, he took his time. *Go on you bastard. Do it.* And after an agonising few seconds, he did. Giving the room one final scan, he spun and marched through the doorway.

I had to restrain myself from cheering. *Not there yet. Now you actually have to get in.* I counted to three slowly in my head, and began walking casually back the way I'd come. Nobody in the room paid me any mind. Catching the girls' eyes, I flashed a triumphant smile. Ruth laughed and stuck up her thumb.

Pausing at the doorway, I took one last look around the

room, sucked in a deep breath, and walked through.

Chapter 2

Rather than opening directly into another room, the doorway led to a long passage that ran for sixty feet or so and then hooked off to the right. I reflexively pressed myself against the wall as I caught sight of the guard disappearing around the far corner. Thankfully, he didn't look back.

There was a low buzz emanating from the other end of the corridor. It grew steadily louder the closer I got. Since the door had opened, we'd witnessed maybe two dozen people let through. It was a decent sized group, but not nearly enough to make that sort of noise. I had no idea what it meant.

For the last hour, I'd been trying to picture what lay hidden back there. I'd conjured images of exclusive restaurants and secret board rooms. But nothing prepared me for the reality of what was around the bend.

I turned the corner, and stopped dead in my tracks, my eyes darting left and right, madly trying to take in everything that lay before me. The entire place reeked of decadence. If you took away all the trappings, it *was* basically just a function room, but it was the most lavish function I'd ever seen. The space was far longer than I'd expected; over two hundred feet of polished wood, lush curtains and decorative brass. To one side lay a long redwood bar, laden with more varieties of liquor than I could count. To the other sat circles of high-backed lounges, most of which were filled with suited men, laughing and chatting and swilling drinks. The whole room smelled of malt and cologne and the sharp, earthy scent of leather. There was enough testosterone in the air to corrupt a nunnery.

What really took me by surprise however, was the pool that wove its way up the centre of the room. It was a beautiful sight. Elegantly curved and bathed in colour, it shimmered under a dizzying array of shifting lights that shone down from the roof above.

As I'd suspected, there were far more people present than we'd seen enter. At least a hundred. But where the hell had they all come from? Obviously there had to be other entrances, but why not just come in the front? The whole situation was getting stranger by the minute.

It seemed that whatever the men were discussing, the girls weren't welcome. Most were making good use of the pool, either swimming or lazing on sun chairs to the side, chatting in little groups. A few of them cast eyes my way, like hopefuls at a casting call sizing up their competition. *Relax girls, I'm just visiting.*

As I scanned the room, I spotted several more security personnel posted along the walls. With their dark glasses, it was impossible to tell what they were looking at. At least one was talking into his earpiece, but nobody appeared to be moving towards me. Still, I knew I had to blend in fast.

Unfortunately, the whole place was so overwhelming that I had no idea what to do next. I couldn't see Chase anywhere, and even if I had, I wasn't sure what help that would be. It wasn't like I could just wander up and say hi. I was in over my head. To be honest, I don't think I'd really expected to make it that far. In the heat of the moment, the only plan that sprang to mind was, 'don't get caught.'

So, operating purely on instinct, I headed for the bar. I knew more drink was probably not the wisest move, but it was the most inconspicuous action I could think of, and it would buy me a little time.

"Champagne please," I said to one of the girls behind the counter, doing my best to look at ease.

"Of course. Would you like to see the full list? Otherwise I can recommend a few things. The Dom Perignon ninety-five, the Bollinger ninety-eight and the Krug eighty-eight are all drinking wonderfully at the moment."

I paused, before breaking into a laugh. *What did you expect girl, a ten dollar Prosecco?*

I opened my mouth to respond, but a voice cut in from a little way up the bar. "She'll have a glass of the Krug thanks Amber. And I'll take another Laphroaig. Neat." The man turned his attention to me. "The Krug is lovely. Dry, fruity, but with a hint of sweetness too. And the smell is to die for. I think you'll like it."

As he spoke, he rose and casually moved over to sit next to me. It wasn't my first rodeo. I knew when a man was making a move. And as much as his presumptuousness would normally have annoyed me, I found it difficult to muster much anger. He was gorgeous; a tall, lithe body wrapped in a crisp, charcoal three-piece suit. There's something so god damn sexy about a man who's confident enough to wear a three-piece. It's sophisticated, but with just the right amount of old school charm.

I cast my eyes over him unashamedly, taking in the breadth of his shoulders, the strength of his hands, the way his jacket pulled tight over the powerful curves of his chest. He looked like he'd walked in directly from the set of a Hugo Boss advertisement. My pulse quickened once more.

As I studied him, he stared back, an odd smile playing on his lips. He was older than me, but not old, maybe early thirties, and he had the kind of dark complexion that always set my stomach tingling. That perfect, tantalising combination of olive skin, rugged stubble, and black, unruly hair. However, it was his eyes that really took me down for the count. Sharp and forest-green, they managed to be playful yet incredibly intense. I felt strangely powerless beneath that gaze, like he wasn't just looking at me, but into me. It wasn't fair for a man to have eyes like that.

Eventually, he glanced away, breaking the spell. As my brain kicked back into gear, I was annoyed to find myself adjusting my top. *Come on Sophia, get a grip. He's hardly the first attractive guy who's ever hit on you.* I placed my hands purposefully back on the bar, trying my best not to blush.

"And how would you know what I like?" I asked, adding a little venom to my voice. I hated being taken off balance like that.

"Oh, I don't know. Call it...men's intuition."

I rolled my eyes. "In my experience, men's intuition is rarely as good as they think it is."

He laughed, a look of mock offence appearing on his face. "You'll just have to wait and see won't you?"

His voice was deep and melodic, with hints of an accent; a faint European lilt that I couldn't quite place. It sent a shiver up my spine. I really wanted to be annoyed — that sort of aggressive approach was usually a major turn off for me — but he was making it very difficult.

"I'm Sebastian," he said, offering his hand.

"Sophia," I replied, returning the gesture. His grip was firm, his hand surprisingly rough, and it lingered a little longer than I'd expected.

"What a lovely name."

"It does the job," I said slowly.

He nodded, but said nothing else, seemingly happy to simply sit and study me. "Well Sebastian," I said eventually, feeling strangely self-conscious in the silence, "do you normally approach random girls in bars and select their drinks for them?"

His smile widened. "Quite often, yes."

"And how does that work out for you?"

"It usually has the desired effect."

I laughed. "Oh, and what might that be?"

"A gentleman doesn't kiss and tell," he replied, in a way that did just that. I felt a brief flash of desire at the suggestion, but quickly smothered it. Sure he was attractive, but I wasn't there to become some CEO's trophy lay for the night.

I knew that this was a golden opportunity to find out who these people were, but slightly impaired as I was, I was struggling to find an opening. It didn't help that Sebastian had me completely on the back foot. At first glance he seemed confident and charming, the sort of guy I saw every day around the office. But behind that roguish charisma lay something dangerously alluring; a potent strength that seemed to beckon to my very core. It was intimidating, arousing, and more than a little distracting.

At that moment the waitress arrived, Champagne and scotch in hand.

"Allow me," Sebastian said, taking the bottle and popping the cork with one easy twist of his wrist. He somehow managed to make even that simple gesture look sensual.

As he leaned in to pour, I couldn't help but breathe in the scent of him; scotch and sweat and something much more carnal. He smelled like pure sex, like raw, distilled masculinity. It sucked the breath from my lungs and turned my insides to jelly.

The Champagne fizzed and bubbled as it hit the glass, bringing me back to my senses.

"To men's intuition," he said, handing me the flute and raising his glass. I lifted my own, but refused to acknowledge his toast or the smug smile behind it.

Irritatingly, he was right. The Champagne was amazing. I tried my best to look unimpressed, although I didn't waste much time before taking another sip.

"How is it?" he asked.

I raised my hand and wobbled it from side to side. "It's okay."

His grin said he wasn't fooled, but he played along. "That's a shame. Hopefully next time I can do a better job of pleasing you."

Something about the way he said it made me think he wasn't talking about drinks anymore.

"So Sebastian," I said, desperate to distract myself from the growing warmth between my legs, "when you're not accosting women at parties, what is it you do?"

"I work for Fraiser Capital. We're a venture capital firm. This is actually our gathering here. We throw these every now and again; little meet and greets for some of our clients."

"Ah of course," I said, trying to act like I recognised the name. We were in dangerous territory now. I still wasn't sure how much I was expected to know, or what kind of cover story I needed. I had to tread carefully.

I glanced around the room. "I didn't realise venture capitalists had this kind of money."

"Good ones do."

It seemed a little farfetched to me. The sort of excess on display seemed beyond any sort of corporate gathering. And that didn't explain what the hell Chase Adams was doing there. But pushing any more seemed like a good way to give myself away. "I see. And what makes a good venture capitalist?"

"The ability to know something special when you see it," he replied, staring directly into my eyes.

I couldn't help but smile at that. I had to hand it to him; he was incredibly smooth. But as much as it was pushing my buttons, I didn't want to give him the satisfaction. I knew how men like him worked. The Partners at my office were no different. It was like a sport to them; dangle a platinum AmEx in the air and watch the ladies flock. I'd even fallen for it a few times in my younger years; it's surprisingly easy to confuse other emotions for love when you don't know any better. Several horrible experiences later, I'd promised myself I'd never be one of those women again.

As if on cue, at that moment, a bikini clad girl appeared at his side.

"There you are, sir," she said, laying a hand on his arm. "I've been looking for you everywhere."

The look she shot me suggested she wasn't pleased about where she'd found him. A girlfriend perhaps? That certainly cast things in a new light.

She was pretty, albeit in a strange, childlike way. Thin, almost frail looking, she had straw blond hair and huge doe eyes that made her seem younger than she probably was.

Sebastian's smile wavered. "Hannah," he said, a hint of displeasure in his voice. "What have I told you about interrupting me?"

She balked at his tone, but decided to press on. "Oh, I'm sorry, sir. I just thought you might want to come for a swim with me. The water is lovely."

It didn't take her long to realise she'd made a mistake. In the steely silence that followed, her enthusiasm quickly melted away. It wasn't that Sebastian looked angry — in fact his expression never wavered — but nonetheless I felt something shift in the air, some dangerous charge that hadn't been there before. I knew without it being said that a line had been crossed. Judging by the way Hannah began shrinking into herself, she knew as well.

"It would be rather rude of me to abandon my new friend here in the middle of our conversation, don't you think?" He didn't raise his voice, but there was an edge to it now that said he expected to be agreed with.

It seemed to have the desired effect. Hannah visibly wilted. "Of course sir. You're right. I'm sorry I bothered you."

He nodded in acceptance. There was something strange about the exchange. I'd revised my earlier guess. The way he scolded her didn't make them feel like a couple. But what then? Colleagues? A younger sister maybe? I wasn't sure.

Now that he'd made himself clear, Hannah seemed eager to be anywhere else. Turning quickly without another word, she began heading back towards the pool. For a second I thought that would be the end of it, but just before she disappeared into the crowd, Sebastian called out to her. "And Hannah." She turned, a look of dread on her face. "We'll talk about this later." Hannah nodded slowly.

Watching the defeated girl trudge away, I couldn't help but feel a little sorry for her. I hoped I hadn't gotten her in any real trouble. His reaction seemed a little extreme, given the circumstances.

"I'm sorry about that," he said. "My secretary."

Secretary? Wow, that must be some work environment.

"It's fine. Really, I don't mind," I replied. "Go and have a swim if you want. I'm a big girl; I can take care of myself."

"I'm sure you can, but don't worry. Hannah and I will find time to have a paddle later." His eyes twinkled as he said that, like he'd just told a joke nobody else would understand.

"In any case, we're not done talking," he continued. "I'm afraid you have me at a disadvantage. You know a little about me, but I know nothing about you. When you're not being accosted by gentlemen at parties," I grinned at the joke, "what is it you do with yourself Sophia?"

"I'm a lawyer."

"Oh I'm so sorry," he said, his voice totally deadpan.

I just laughed. In my profession you rarely go more than a week or two without some kind of lawyer joke. It comes with the territory, and you learn not to take it seriously. "I know, right? If you want to turn and run I won't hold it against you."

"I'll keep that in mind. There are a few other lawyers here tonight actually. You didn't happen to come with any of them did you?"

My stomach clenched. There it was; a question I couldn't answer. My gut told me there were no unaccompanied women in the room, so I'd have to have a partner, and while he might not know everyone, I doubted I could bluff my way through it.

"A lady doesn't kiss and tell," I replied, trying my best to look coy. Inside, I was panicking. If he pressed the issue, that would be it. The jig would be up.

For a few seconds I was certain it was over, but eventually he broke into a laugh. "I'm sorry Sophia, I didn't mean to pry. I was just curious if there were any gentlemen lurking nearby who might be preparing to leap in and defend your honour."

I raised my eyebrows. "I didn't realise my honour was under threat."

His eyes seemed to flicker ever so briefly. "Give me a chance. We've only been talking a few minutes."

His directness was both offensive and exciting. I found

20

myself wondering what it might be like to succumb to his advances. Even now, just sitting and talking, there was something fiercely attractive about him. I knew he'd be mindblowing in bed. He exuded that sort of dominant authority that sent logic and self-restraint tumbling to the wayside.

Get a grip Sophia. This cannot happen.

"You seem rather sure of yourself," I said, trying my hardest to act unperturbed.

He gave a little laugh. "I prefer to think of myself as optimistic."

In truth, I doubted his confidence was misplaced. I struggled to see many women rejecting him, however blunt he was.

I realised then that I had to get away. The attraction I felt for him was verging on dangerous, and the longer we talked, the more likely it was that I'd do something stupid.

...okay, something *else* stupid.

"Well, unfortunately I'm going to have to leave your hopes dashed this time," I said. "I am actually here with someone, and it's about time I got back to him. I just left to get a refill, and that was ten minutes ago."

He studied me for several seconds. I expected him to look at least a little disappointed, but instead he seemed vaguely amused. "That's a pity," he said eventually. "But perhaps we'll run into one another again?"

"Perhaps." *No fucking way.*

"Excellent. Well, have a good evening Sophia." And with that, he turned and walked off into the crowd.

I blinked a few times and followed his receding form with my eyes, trying to work out what had just happened. It was like someone had climbed inside me and turned my hormones up to eleven. My heart was still thundering in my chest. *Fantastic Sophia. Ten minutes with tall, dark, and charming and you're hyperventilating like a twelve year old at a Justin Bieber*

21

concert. What the hell is wrong with you?

I took a deep breath and downed the rest of my drink in a single large gulp, hoping to jar my mind into action. As attractive as he was, pursuing him was not an option. All my reservations aside, I'd barely escaped our conversation without being exposed, and somehow I doubted he'd be so friendly if he knew the truth.

Besides, there was something almost terrifying about the way my body responded to him. Even now, I couldn't shake the image of those piercing eyes from my mind.

Glancing around, I suddenly became aware of how exposed I was. Nobody else in the room was standing alone. None of the guests had taken notice yet, but some of the staff were giving me strange looks. I knew I should take the opportunity to get the hell out of dodge, but I wasn't quite ready to face the girls just yet. The alcohol, the adrenaline, the lingering arousal; it was a potent cocktail. My mind was reeling. I needed somewhere to regroup.

"Excuse me," I said, to a pretty brunette behind the bar who was busy shaking up a lurid cocktail the colour of toxic waste, "where are the bathrooms?"

She gestured vaguely to the back of the room. "Just over there."

"Great, thanks."

I walked briskly, doing my best not to make eye contact with anyone. The girl's directions hadn't been very clear, but eventually I found an open doorway stashed in the far corner of the room. On the other side lay a corridor that ran for thirty feet and then hooked off to the right. There were no signs of any bathrooms.

I debated doubling back, but I hadn't seen any other likely openings. I figured they were just deeper in. So I began to explore.

Chapter 3

For a moment after rounding the corner, I thought I'd found what I was looking for. The next hallway was lined with doors. But as I drew closer, I saw that rather than 'Gents' or 'Ladies', they were all marked with heavy brass name tags bearing identical logos. Not bathrooms. Personal offices.

My eyes darted back down the passage as I suddenly became aware of where I was. Sneaking into a party was one thing, but prowling through corporate property was quite another. It was a strange location to put offices, but I didn't have time to puzzle it out. If caught, I'd be in serious trouble.

I turned to go, but it was too late. Voices began to echo up the corridor from the direction I'd come. My heart leapt up into my throat. I was cut off.

Even as panic set in, my mind began hunting for an escape. Running was out of the question with all that security, and the deeper I went into the building, the more trouble I'd likely be in if found. I could try talking my way out, but I'd already had my share of close calls tonight and my lies wouldn't hold up under any real scrutiny. That left only one choice that I could see.

I dove for the nearest door. The voices were getting louder. They sounded like they were just around the bend. By some miracle, the door wasn't locked. I yanked it open, threw myself inside and pulled it shut as softly as my shaking hands would allow. It closed with a quiet but audible click.

I held my breath and pressed my ear against it. The conversation was muted through the thick timber, but it sounded as though the speakers had stopped moving. I could hear them talking — arguing it sounded like — somewhere to my left.

I exhaled slowly, taking the moment's respite to study my hiding place. Having seen the bar outside, the office was no surprise. Opulent, masculine, and sophisticated. The floor was polished wood, the furniture sparse but beautiful, and all of it looked almost too old for anyone to actually risk using. Everything the owner could want was within reach, from a well-stocked bar to an en-suite to a small built-in wardrobe filled with pressed suits. I could probably have lived there and been relatively comfortable.

After a minute had passed, the voices still hadn't moved. Maybe they'd gone into one of the other offices. With any luck that would be as close as they came. All I had to do was wait them out.

Seemingly in no immediate danger, I slipped off my shoes and moved to explore the room a little. It was unlikely they'd hear my footsteps, but I wasn't taking any chances.

There was a laptop open on the desk with a password prompt on the screen. The user name read 'S.Lock'. *Well Mr Lock, your office is a hell of a lot neater than mine.*

Next to the computer was a single stack of papers. Unable to stop myself, I thumbed through the top couple of sheets. At first, I thought it might have been some kind of joke, because the front page was stamped 'Top Secret' in bright red ink, but as I skimmed through it, I began to get the sense that there might be more to it. If it was a hoax, it was an incredibly

24

detailed one. It seemed to be some kind of internal US government document. The content was largely alien to me — most of it had to do with oil in the Middle East — but as I ran my eyes over it, I got the distinct sense that it was a dangerous thing to be reading.

I was so focused on those pages that I nearly missed the sound of voices echoing up the hallway once more. By the time I noticed, they were right outside the door.

Oh Jesus!

Reacting purely on instinct, I scooped up my shoes and bolted for the nearest hiding spot; the cupboard. It was close, but I narrowly made it. The latch clicked shut behind me moments before I heard the rattle of a handle being turned. My pulse was hammering in my ears.

"—don't care what you do, I just need you to take care of it. Losing those panels will put us months behind schedule."

My stomach sank even lower. I knew that elegant voice. S.Lock. I hadn't just stumbled through any door. This was Sebastian's office.

Shit shit shit.

How unlucky could I get?

I crouched down, putting my eyes level with a row of slats towards the bottom of the door, and the room sprung into view. Sebastian was pacing behind the desk, talking to another man who was leaning against the door frame.

"I'll do what I can, but it's not like they left a nice polite note or anything," said the visitor. "It's going to take a little time."

"Well, not getting them back is not an option."

The other man raised his hands defensively. "Okay, okay. I'll get some people on it."

"Good. And send Hannah in on your way out would you?"

"Sure."

He closed the door, leaving Sebastian staring contemplatively into the air. After about thirty seconds, there was a knock, and the girl from before peeked her head in. "You wanted to see me, sir."

"Hannah. Yes, come in."

She walked slowly into the room, a penitent look on her face.

"Well, do you have anything to say for yourself?" he asked.

"I'm sorry, sir."

"Sorry for what?" His voice was hard and unforgiving.

"I'm sorry that I interrupted you."

"We've worked on this before," he said, starting to pace once more. "It's not your position to decide who I can and can't talk to. That's not part of our deal."

She nodded quickly. "I know, sir. I'm sorry."

I shifted uncomfortably. I didn't understand. Hannah was a grown woman, and Sebastian's employee, but she was being chastised as though she was a child.

"Unfortunately Hannah, sorry isn't good enough. You know the rules. What do we do with girls that misbehave?"

Hannah stared at him, wide-eyed, clearly dreading answering the question. "We punish them," she squeaked eventually.

"Indeed."

Oh my god. No wonder their relationship had seemed strange. I wasn't so naive as to not be familiar with BDSM, but I'd always thought of it as a niche fetish, something relegated to kinky underground sex clubs and the odd upper middle class basement. Truthfully, the whole idea seemed vaguely ridiculous. What kind of self-respecting woman gave up control of herself to her partner? It defied all logic. But crouched in that cupboard, watching Sebastian display such visceral control, I felt a small tingle of excitement. Part of me wanted to know what happened next.

He gazed at Hannah for several seconds. "I think it will be the black paddle today." She whimpered. "Go on now," he continued, "you know what to do."

I watched, mesmerised, as Hannah headed slowly over to the wall, opened up a small and rather cleverly hidden cupboard, and withdrew a long leather paddle. My mouth went dry at the sight of it. It was a scary looking implement about two feet long, and coated length to tip in rough, black leather. It seemed out of place given the class and sophistication of our surroundings.

I suppressed a morbid laugh as Sebastian's comment from before finally clicked. *"We'll find time for a paddle later."*

With the object in hand, Hannah hesitated momentarily.

"Bring it to me," said Sebastian, who had removed his jacket and began to roll up his sleeves. His arms were long and lean, but layered with taut ropes of muscle, like those of a professional tennis player.

Hannah sucked in a deep breath. For a second, I thought she was going to resist, but after steeling herself, she marched dutifully back across the room and placed the paddle in Sebastian's fingers. He swished it through the air a few times, testing the weight of it. "Perfect. Now, present yourself for me."

Trembling, she bent over the side of the desk. I was shocked that she was being so compliant, but on some level, I understood. The authority radiating from Sebastian now was almost palpable; a singular force of relentless will. Everything about him spoke of man in utter control; from the weight of his voice to the certainty in his eyes to the measured purposefulness of his movements. There was no doubt in his mind that Hannah would give him what he wanted, and as much as I hated to admit it, I found that determination incredibly arousing.

Sebastian growled in appreciation as he peeled Hannah's skirt back, exposing her naked ass to the air. "It frustrates me that we have to keep doing this," he said, reaching out to cup one cheek, "but I suppose it does have its advantages."

Hannah shifted, drawing in sharp little breaths while he caressed her roughly. As I watched, I found myself wondering what his touch would feel like on my body. His hands looked so strong, and there was something so possessive about the way he stroked her.

"Are you ready for your punishment?" Sebastian asked.

"Yes sir."

"Good."

I wasn't sure what to expect next. It seemed like there should be some kind of preamble, but instead, Sebastian simply whipped the paddle back and brought it crashing down into Hannah's ass.

"One. Thank you, sir," Hannah said through gritted teeth. He spanked again. "Two. Thank you, sir."

God, she even has to thank him. That's one thing you'd never catch me doing.

...or any of this other stuff either.

Jesus Sophia.

Clearly Sebastian was an experienced practitioner. He truly looked in his element now. Every gesture was graceful and precise, and with every stroke, his body flexed and bulged. I hadn't thought it possible, but somehow the situation made him look even more attractive. I felt the unmistakable throb of desire pulsing between my legs.

A glance at Hannah told me I wasn't the only one enjoying myself. Sebastian was so powerful, and every blow looked

28

more excruciating than the last, but as he settled into his rhythm, the shock on her face gradually melted away, replaced with something I could only describe as a kind of pained ecstasy.

Watching her take pleasure in being punished was confronting, but also strangely exciting. The dynamic between them was so raw and so intense that I could practically taste it in the air. I shifted uncomfortably, desperately willing my arousal away, but all I succeeded in doing was knocking a suit off the bar behind me. I caught it with an outstretched hand, but the damage had already been done. In an instant the closet door was flung open and I was once again pinned in place by that penetrating gaze.

Sebastian stared at me for several seconds. I saw him reacting a hundred different ways in my head, but eventually he surprised me by breaking into a laugh. "Well, well, well. Sophia. We did say we might see each other again, but I hadn't expected it to be quite like this." Strangely, he didn't seem surprised, just amused.

I gazed up at him with gaping eyes, blushing furiously. I didn't know what I could possibly say. The whole situation had gotten way out of hand. I briefly debated trying to talk my way out, but judging by the twinkle in his eye, the time for that had passed.

So I did the only thing I could think of.

I ran.

I leapt out of the cupboard and bolted for the hallway. He probably could have stopped me if he'd wanted — the gap between his leg and the cupboard door wasn't very large — but he didn't move, he just watched me, a curious smile on his face.

Before I knew it, I was in the corridor, and then the main room. The guests all stared as I tore across the wooden floor, but I ignored them. All I cared about was getting somewhere safe. Every part of me felt frayed, confused, agitated.

At some point, it occurred to me that I'd left my shoes behind. *Just like Cinderella,* I thought. *Although I'm not sure if the story traditionally contains quite so much masochism.*

For some reason, that thought struck me as perversely funny. I began to laugh as I ran. By the time I broke through into the bar's main room, I was cackling like a street corner drunk.

I was certain someone would be chasing me, but there were no signs of pursuit. Even the door guard was mysteriously absent.

"Come on," I panted to my gaping friends as I charged over to them, "we've gotta bail."

"Wha—"

"Now!"

They didn't argue further.

Thirty seconds later we were half way up the street, giggling with the adrenaline of a successful escape. They didn't even know what we were running from, but the fact that we were running was enough.

"So," Louisa said, when we finally began slowing down, "what the hell was that? What happened back there?"

"You're not going to believe me."

"Try us," Ruth said, looking at me with a mixture of disbelief and curiosity.

And so I told my tale. I described everything as best I could, the grand room, meeting Sebastian, my accidental corporate espionage. The only thing I omitted was the spanking. Something about it made me feel decidedly uncomfortable.

"That's crazy," Louisa said, when I was done.

Ruth shook her head. "You see? She sneaks in there, and five minutes later she's bagged a mysterious millionaire. I told you we should have followed her!"

"I'd hardly use the word 'bagged'," I replied. "Last I checked, trespassing and breaking and entering weren't exactly the keys to a man's heart, although perhaps I'm just out of touch."

Ruth laughed. "You're such a glass half empty kind of girl."

"Hey, I'm just glad he didn't call the cops." I turned to Louisa. "Lou, next time I try to do something like that, do a better job of talking me out of it, would you?"

"I'll do my best," she replied with a grin.

It was just a few hours shy of sunrise at that point, and so we went our separate ways. I caught a cab home and collapsed into bed without even bothering to change. I was exhausted and expected to fall asleep quickly, but my mind was still restless. Whenever I closed my eyes, I saw Sebastian staring down at me with that breathtaking gaze. Whatever his bedroom predilections, there was something undeniably alluring about him. I couldn't remember the last man that had set my heart racing so easily.

Chapter 4

The following morning was far from pleasant. I woke feeling like I'd loaned my head to a marching band. I debated simply rolling over and going back to sleep, but there was too much to do at the office. "You can sleep when you're dead," was a popular catch phrase amongst the Partners, and as much as they grinned when they said it, you knew they were being perfectly serious. Don't get me wrong, Little Bell wasn't any worse than any other big firm — technically it was named Bell & Little, but nobody called it that, no matter how many stern memos went out — it was just the norm in big law to bleed your employees for every drop you could.

A long shower, a coffee, and the world's greasiest ham and cheese croissant later, I was sitting in the back of a cab feeling marginally more human. But apparently I still didn't look it. As I exited the lift on my floor of the building, I ran into my friend Elle. She took one look at me and burst out laughing. "Big night hey Soph?"

I glanced down at myself and grimaced. "That obvious hey?"

Elle nodded. "You look a little haggard, yeah."

There's a funny camaraderie within law firms. Because we all work such long hours, we naturally become friendly. A lot of lawyers have no social lives outside of work. But it's always felt a little fake to me. Behind the niceties, there's as much backstabbing and petty bullying as in any school playground. With most of my colleagues, I kept my distance, but Elle was the exception. Unlike almost everybody else, she didn't buy into all the office bullshit, which meant we'd quickly become friends.

"What can I say? The girls are a bad influence."

Elle flashed an indulgent grin. We'd been out enough times together that she knew who incited most of the drinking. "Well, I hope you've saved some energy for tonight. Drunk Partners, a huge group of self-important corporate types; it's practically your perfect evening."

Shit. I'd completely forgotten about that. A few times a year, our company threw a party for all of its long standing clients. A kind of thank-you-please-keep-giving-us-buckets-of-money type deal. It seemed to work because our profits just kept climbing, but I hated those evenings. There was only so much corporate asskissery I could stomach. Unfortunately, we were all expected to be there if we could make it. We didn't actually do anything; the puppet masters just liked showing us off. A flexing of the company's considerable legal muscle. I usually made it tolerable by taking abundant advantage of the open bar, but with the memory of the morning's hangover still fresh in my mind, I wasn't sure I'd even be doing that.

"I kind of wish you hadn't reminded me. I could have slept through it and not felt guilty."

Elle chuckled again. "Oh come on, it won't be that bad. Do your bit, brown nose a few CEOs. Who knows, you might impress someone."

"And you'll be doing the same?"

"Hell no. I'll be drinking in a corner."

"That sounds like a better plan," I agreed.

A tiny smile appeared on her face. "So did you hear?"

"About what?"

"The Wrights case is a go."

My eyes widened. "No way. That's awesome!"

"I know right? It's going to be kind of novel actually doing something worthwhile, instead of just helping companies shit on one another day after day."

I nodded. It was exactly the kind of case I'd always wanted to work on. A David and Goliath class action suit between a group of Average Joes and a pharmaceutical giant. It felt like our own little Erin Brockovich moment.

The situation was horrible. Wrights had hidden the side effects of one of their antidepressants from the general public. The drugs worked fine on most people, with one notable exception. Pregnant women. It was only after several years that someone began joining the dots between the drug in question and the spate of juvenile health problems that followed. Now there were thousands of affected children out there, suffering everything from physical abnormalities to heart conditions. More than a few had died from their complications. It made me angry just thinking about it.

Beyond the chance to do something good, the case was also great publicity for the company, which meant it had the attention of the suits upstairs. There had never been a better opportunity to prove myself.

"Anyway, I have to run these to Freidburg," Elle said, gesturing to the pages in her hand, "but I'll catch you later, okay? Don't even think about sneaking home. I'm not sure I can sit through this one alone."

I raised my hands in defeat. "Okay, okay."

The day chugged along at an agonising crawl. Law isn't nearly as glamorous as it appears on television. Behind every dramatic hour in court there are hundreds of hours of paper-work.

At six o'clock, an office wide email went out calling everyone to the upstairs boardroom. We always hosted our gatherings in-house. For a company the size of Little Bell, appearances were everything, and we'd spent a lot of money making sure we could entertain with the best of them. With the tables cleared away, the band in place, and the bar and canapés laid out, the whole place had the classy but vaguely sterile feel of an expensive wedding reception.

Most of my colleagues were already there when I arrived. Seeing everyone standing together in one place really emphasised the gender imbalance in the company. There were jackets and ties as far as the eye could see. We had a few women on every floor, and a couple had even made it to the lofty ranks of Partner, but the firm was still very much entrenched in the old way of doing things.

Despite my earlier reservations, I decided I couldn't get through the evening without a least one drink, so I snagged a glass of champagne on its way past and then set out in search of a friendly face.

"You made it!" Elle said, as I found her at the other end of the bar. She was chatting to one of the new junior associates, a friendly young guy named Miles.

"You sound surprised," I replied.

"Well, this morning you did look a little like you might keel over at your desk."

"What, and miss all this?" I asked, gesturing dramatically to the room.

"It does have a certain... unique charm," Miles said, wearing a bemused smile.

"First time?" I asked.

He nodded.

"You're working under Alan right?"

He nodded again.

Elle and I shared an eye roll. "Has he taken you to run the executive gauntlet yet?" she asked

"I don't think so," he replied.

"Well, don't worry, he will," I said. "He likes to start grooming his flock early."

He gave a nervous little laugh. "I'm not sure I like the idea of being groomed."

"Me either," I replied. "Certainly helps if you want an actual career though."

His brow furrowed. "What do you mean by that?"

I gazed at him for several seconds, my tongue poised on my lips, before shaking my head. I didn't have the energy for a rant right now. Besides, he'd see soon enough. "Never mind. Forget I said anything."

"No, hang on," he persisted, "you can't make a comment like that and then just let it go."

Elle had been watching the exchange with a mixture of amusement and resignation. She understood. She was in the same boat as me. "What she means is, this place is very cliquey. You get in with the right people early, you're set."

He filled in the obvious blank. "And if you don't?"

Elle shot me a glance and raised her eyebrows.

I sighed. "Then expect to be shovelling shit for quite a few years."

He chewed the inside of his cheek thoughtfully. "How long have you two been here?"

"Six years for me, five for Elle," I replied.

"And you're both still juniors?" he asked.

I nodded.

"Fuck. I take it that's not normal?"

I shrugged. "Depends on your definition of normal. If

you don't kiss the right asses then yeah, that's pretty much the way it goes."

"Speaking of ass kissing, have you met the office's resident brown nosing queen yet, Miles?" Elle asked, nodding to the woman who was approaching us from across the room.

"Can't say that I've had the pleasure," he replied.

I grimaced. "Well it looks like you're about to get your chance."

There was nobody in the office I disliked more than Jennifer Smart. The two of us had started at Little Bell around the same time, and from day one, we'd seemed destined to be rivals. Everything about her rubbed me the wrong way, and although she was as sweet as honey to my face, I knew the feeling was mutual. I'd assumed my eighty hour weeks and pristine work would trump her grovelling, but apparently I'd been mistaken. Two years ago she'd made Senior Associate, while I was still stuck shuffling paper. It was a victory she savoured to this day.

"Sophia!" she said, flashing me a perfect beauty pageant smile. She had her fake nice act down to a fine art, but truth be told, I still didn't understand why so many people were fooled. There was something inherently unpleasant behind those angular features, a callousness that no amount of phony warmth could hide.

"I was wondering if you'd be here," she continued. "I know you don't much care for these little gatherings."

"Wouldn't miss it for the world, Jennifer," I replied, forcing myself to sound vaguely polite.

"Well good. It's good to keep in touch with our clients, don't you think? Speaking of which," she nodded at the older gentleman standing next to her, "this is Mr Chardy. He's the head of development at Marvin Lemac. We've been handling their fraud case."

I gritted my teeth. She had the most frustrating habit of making out that nobody else knew what was going on around the office except her. "I know who you are," I said to him, holding out my hand. "I'm Sophia Pearce. It's a pleasure to meet you."

"Likewise."

The others introduced themselves.

"Sophia, Elle, and Miles here are all part of our junior associate team," Jennifer continued. "I know when you meet with us it might seem like it's just me or Alan handling your case, but we really couldn't do what we do without these guys. They're the ones doing all the grunt work."

"Well you've done an excellent job so far," Chardy said.

I nodded in thanks, not trusting myself to speak. Back-handed compliments were Jennifer's speciality.

She glanced around the room. "Well anyway, it's been lovely chatting to you, but I want to introduce Joseph here to a few more people. You know how it is; so many Partners, so little time. Have a good night."

Taking his arm she led him off into the crowd.

"Well, she didn't seem that bad," Miles said, when she was out of earshot.

"Are you kidding?" Elle replied. "That smile was so sweet I think I threw up a little in my mouth."

"Have either of you actually done any work on the Marvin Lemac case?" I asked. They both shook their heads. "Exactly. She didn't need to introduce him at all. It was just another excuse to gloat." I threw back the rest of my champagne in a single long sip. "Fucking 'grunt work' indeed. I could strangle that bitch."

"It sounded like a compliment to me," Miles said quietly.

Elle and I looked at one another before bursting out laughing. "You have a lot to learn about this place," I told him. "Anyway, after that, I think I could use another drink. Back in a sec."

I could see my plans for a dry night evaporating before my eyes, but if that meeting was a sign of things to come, I'd need all the help I could get. Little did I know things were about to get even worse.

"What can I get you?" said the guy behind the bar.

And for the second time in as many days, someone answered for me. "She'll have a Cosmo. And get me another beer."

I rolled my eyes. "Actually, I'll have a glass of Shiraz," I said, turning to frown at my new companion. Taylor had started on my floor a year earlier, and since day one, he'd been trying to lure me into bed. I might have taken it as a compliment, if he hadn't done the same thing to every woman in the office. Sadly, many of them fell for it.

Objectively, I guess he was good looking, in that blonde, bulky, frat boy kind of way, but he was such a gigantic ass that I found it impossible to see anything else. His daddy was some big hedge fund type who was friends with everybody, so Taylor spent his entire life coasting around on his enormous sense of entitlement. I think it annoyed him that I was so resistant to his 'charms', although he'd never say it.

"If you're going to order for a girl, at least pay attention to what she's drinking, genius."

He gave a little laugh. "Hey, I was just trying to be friendly. Do you always bite guys' heads off when they try to buy you drinks?"

"This is the company bar, so you're not buying me anything."

He flashed a smile that he probably thought was seductive. "Not here I'm not."

I exhaled sharply. "Not anywhere."

"Come on Sophia, at least hear me out. It's no secret you hate these things, so what say you and I get out of here? My dad owns this sweet little wine bar just a block from my apartment. We could drink whatever we want, on the house. No Cosmos there, I promise."

I had to give him points for persistence, but at that moment I really just wished he'd disappear.

I looked him straight in the eyes and grazed my teeth slowly across my bottom lip in that way that guys seem to love. "Close to your apartment, hey?"

His face lit up. "That's right."

"What about your dad? Does he live nearby too?"

He blinked several times in confusion. "My dad?"

"Yeah. I mean if we're drinking on the house, that would mean it's really him buying me drinks. It'd feel kind of rude going home with someone else after that."

His expression crumbled, and I gave myself a little internal high five.

"Well, we could go somewhere else if you like..." he said lamely.

And then someone else spoke from behind me. "I don't think she's going anywhere with you." My heart turned a cartwheel in my chest.

Even before I looked, I recognised the voice; low and strong and smooth as caramel. For a moment I was overcome by a powerful sense of deja vu, but it passed as the reality of the situation came crashing into me.

"Hello Sophia," Sebastian said, sliding in next to me. "It's lovely to see you again."

I stared at him with wide eyes, my tongue frozen in shock. He was the last person in the world I'd ever expected to see again. But there he was in front of me, smiling like he hadn't caught me huddled in his office cupboard just a day earlier.

40

Taylor wasn't so easily rattled. He rocked back on his heels, an incredulous smile blooming on his face. "Hey buddy, we're having a conversation here."

Sebastian's eyes flicked to him. There was no anger there. If anything, he looked vaguely amused. "No, you're harassing a girl who quite clearly wants to be left alone."

Taylor bristled. "And I suppose she'd rather be talking to you?"

"She'd rather be doing a lot of things."

It was my turn to bristle, but nobody was paying any attention to me anymore. It was like I'd disappeared. They loomed up from either side of me, staring at one another as though they could make their adversary's head explode through sheer force of will. It was almost comical really, but laughter was about as far out of reach for me as humanely possible at that moment.

"Is that right?" Taylor asked, his jaw tightening. "And just who might you be, friend?" He gave that last word a sharp accent.

"Just a man who would like a word with Sophia, if you don't mind." In spite of the phrasing, there was no question in his voice.

Taylor continued to stare. Pissing contests like this weren't exactly uncommon around the office. Give a bunch of overachieving jocks huge salaries and inflated senses of self-worth, and you're just asking for testosterone to fly. When push came to shove, Taylor usually came out on top, but this time I could tell he was losing. There was something so utterly indomitable about Sebastian. From the easy confidence of his smile to the raw intensity of his gaze and the dangerous grace of his movements, he was the epitome of a man who knew he'd get what he wanted. Taylor may have been his physical equal, but whatever primal hormonal reaction decided the outcome of those sorts of engagements was telling him to head for the hills.

After a few seconds, he looked away. "Fine," he spat, snatching up his beer. "I'll see you around, Sophia." Turning, he stalked off into the crowd.

I shook my head slowly. "What the fuck was that?" I spluttered, finally finding my voice.

"That was me saving you from an unpleasant conversation." Sebastian didn't look even slightly embarrassed.

"Saving me? I was talking to a colleague! What if I was enjoying myself?"

He gave a little laugh. "What, with that guy?"

I shook my head slowly, trying to gather my thoughts. His approach was nothing short of infuriating, but there were more important things to focus on.

"Whatever. That's beside the point. What the hell are you doing here, Sebastian?"

"I wanted to see you again," he said, like it was the most natural thing in the world.

I had no idea how to respond. As confusing as it all was, part of me was happy to see him too. Just being near him again set something thrumming inside me. He looked every bit as gorgeous as he had the previous night. He'd traded his charcoal three-piece for a simple navy business suit, but it still did little to disguise the exquisite musculature beneath. His hair tumbled in long curls around his perfectly hewn face, framing a smile that hit me like a punch to the chest.

"Surely there are easier ways to go about that. Like, maybe, a phone call?" I said.

He laughed. "And would you have agreed to see me if I'd just rung?"

"I guess not," I said slowly. "But I don't appreciate being taken by surprise, either. How did you even manage to find me? And how did you get in here? This is my office!"

"It wasn't as difficult as you may think. There are only so many striking young lawyers named Sophia in Sydney." He glanced around. "As for how I got in, well Laurence Bell is actually an old acquaintance of my company. Once I knew where you worked, it was easy enough to organise an invitation."

He knew Mr Bell? That was odd. Our boss was a notorious recluse. Yeah, his name was on the sign outside, but he rarely even came into the office anymore. He was like the good china that only got brought out for special occasions.

Sebastian continued to stare, those magnificent eyes once again boring deep inside me. It made me uncomfortable. Sure, he was hot, and we'd gotten along well, but the whole situation had my hairs standing on end. Judging by last night, there was no shortage of women in his life. He had no reason to track me down. No reason, unless he was angry about having his privacy invaded.

"Well, I don't think this is appropriate," I said, shaking my gaze free.

"You mean after the way we left things last night?"

My cheeks heated. "Look, about that, I can explain..."

"About what? Breaking into my office? Or sneaking into our gathering?" He smiled at my expression. "That's right, I know. In fact I knew the whole time. You're not the only one who can act, Sophia."

I closed my eyes briefly and drew a slow breath. "So why talk to me? Why not just have me thrown out?"

"Does a man need an excuse to chat to a beautiful girl now?"

I rolled my eyes. "Yeah, because pretty girls were in short supply last night."

He grinned, and I felt myself melt just a little more. "Well to be honest, security was ready to escort you out the moment you walked in. We always have more than one set of eyes on that door. But I stopped them."

"Why?"

He shrugged. "I was curious. I wanted to know what kind of girl you were. Plenty of people have tried talking their way through that doorway over the years, but very few actually succeed." His expression remained mild as he spoke. He certainly didn't seem angry, but it was hard to tell what lay behind that charming exterior.

"Well, thank you for not making a scene. I'm sorry I intruded. I was just messing around and it got out of hand. I never meant to go into your office at all."

"You could make it up to me by coming home with me tonight."

I did a double take, certain I must have misheard him. In light of everything that had happened, the request seemed completely absurd.

"Are you joking?"

"Why would I be joking?"

"Oh, I don't know, because the last time you saw me I was huddled in your office cupboard, watching you smack your secretary like a child?"

"You didn't enjoy the show?" he asked, not the least bit ashamed.

I snorted. "It was a little Dita Von Tease for my tastes."

That only widened his smile. "Is that so? People are always afraid of what they don't understand. Don't write it off so easily. You might be surprised by what you'd enjoy." The certainty in his voice was unsettling. It sounded less like a suggestion and more like a promise. I shuffled awkwardly on my feet, memories of last night's strange excitement echoing through my mind. I still didn't know why I'd reacted like that.

This is what happens when you let your dry spells last too long. Even a spanking starts to seem appealing. You need to get laid, girl.

"Well sorry to disappoint you, but that's not my style," I said, doing my best to keep my voice level, "so I'm sure my vanilla sensibilities will be incredibly boring for you."

He reached out and brushed my neck lightly, raking his eyes over my body. "I doubt I could ever find *this* boring, regardless of what we're doing."

I swallowed loudly. My mouth suddenly felt like it had been baking in the sun for hours. As much as I hated to admit it, his overt sexuality was a huge turn on. There was nothing sleazy about it. He was just a man who was utterly comfortable with himself and his desires. Once again, I found myself imaging what it might be like to give myself to him. There was no other way to describe it. With other men, I might have said 'sleep with' or 'fuck' or one of the hundred other euphemisms that springs to mind at such times, but with Sebastian, I got the sense none of those were quite right. Even with nothing kinky involved, sex with him would not merely be physical, it would be an act of sheer possession and power.

Focus, Sophia. Think unsexy thoughts. Paperwork. Schindler's List. Ernest in a skirt.

Urgh, too far.

"What makes you even sure I *want* to sleep with you?" I said, purposefully pulling away from him. I swear it was like he had his own personal gravity.

Annoyingly, this just made him laugh. "Is that really how you want to play this?"

"I'm not playing."

"Well neither am I. You can pretend if you want, but it doesn't change a thing." He leaned in close, as though whispering a secret. That intoxicating scent hit my nose once more, sending my hormones into overdrive. "Your body says more than any words ever could."

A shiver rolled through me, coming to rest firmly in the centre of my chest. I hated how easily he could read me. It made me feel strangely helpless. How do you fend off a man who already seems to know your secrets?

"You're right, my body is saying a lot of things," I said. "Like leave me the hell alone! I've been with men like you before, Sebastian. Hell, I work with them every day. Even if I was attracted to you, I wouldn't be interested in being another notch on the bed post."

"What makes you think that's all you'd be?"

I scoffed. "Because we just met yesterday — in rather extenuating circumstances, I might add — and now you're asking me to go to bed with you?"

He shrugged like it was par for the course. "I prefer to be up front in my relationships. That way there's no mixed messages. No one gets hurt."

"Well, that's very noble of you, but I get the impression we don't want the same things."

"And what is it you want, Sophia?"

"Well, call me old fashioned, but something more than, 'hey, want to fuck?' would be a good start."

"I didn't pick you for a flowers and chocolates kind of girl."

"I'm not. I'm too busy for that crap. Casual suits me just fine. But there's a difference between casual and meaningless."

"Good, then we're on the same page. Look, you're right, I'm not the sort of guy that dates. I don't have the time or the inclination to be tied down, and I make no apologies for that. But that doesn't automatically make me some asshole who just uses women and then throws them away. If there's no spark, I'm not interested. And this right here, this has got me very interested."

I laughed. "Ah, the playa with a heart of gold. How touching. But unfortunately, I'm not good at sharing. I have this weird thing about wanting the men I sleep with to only be sleeping with me."

He let out a long breath. "Well, I don't usually do exclusivity."

I recoiled in mock surprise. "I'm shocked!"

He studied me for a few seconds, his expression hovering somewhere between frustration and amusement. "This doesn't have to be complicated, Sophia. There are so many things I want to do to that body of yours, and I promise that you'll enjoy every exquisite minute of it. Why do you need anything more than that?"

Something in my lower belly clenched. Despite how crude his approach was, I believed him. And a rather loud voice in the back of my head was begging me to let him have his wish.

But somehow, I rallied one more time. "It's not complicated for me. It's incredibly simple. I'm. Not. Interested! Now if you'll excuse me, I'm going to go back to my friends. I'll extend you the same courtesy you extended me and let you walk yourself out, but if I see you here again, I'm calling security. I don't care who your friends are, if you're harassing an employee, you'll be out of here before you can blink. Goodbye, Sebastian. It's been... interesting." And with much more confidence than I felt inside, I spun and marched away.

I could hardly blame him for the way my body reacted to his, but it was still immensely satisfying to storm off like that. *That'll teach him to get into my head. Bastard.*

I expected maybe a parting shot, but no words followed me. I resisted the urge to turn and look back. I was proud of myself for not caving to him, although there were very specific parts of me that were emphatically venting their disappointment. I suspected I'd be delving into my underwear drawer later for a little relief.

"Jesus Christ," Elle said, as I returned. Miles was nowhere to be seen, but she was peering over my shoulder with an awestruck gaze, her lips hanging slightly open. *At least it's not just me.*

"Who the hell was that?" she asked.

I shrugged. "I'm not sure actually. Just some guy."

"Seriously? That's like calling Ryan Gosling 'just some guy'!"

I shrugged again, trying to feign disinterest. The sooner we stopped talking about him, the better.

"Well, whoever he was, he looked hella into you," she continued.

"You think?" I asked.

She stared at me like I'd gone mad. "He was practically eye fucking you from the moment you guys started talking. How could you not notice that? I even bet Miles ten bucks he'd get your number."

I winced. "Sorry, no dice."

She shook her head slowly. "Fuck. Well, I guess that means he's still fair game, then."

I laughed. "If we see him again, he's all yours."

Our conversation turned to other things. Despite my best efforts, I found myself glancing around every so often, checking that Sebastian wasn't still lurking nearby. It seemed like he'd taken my warning seriously, but I got the sense such threats may not really mean much to him. After all, he'd tracked me down and infiltrated my office as easily as walking through his own front door.

The effortlessness with which he'd done that frightened me a little. When he'd shown up, my mind had been reeling too much to really think it through; but now the reality of the situation was becoming apparent. In a way, it was vaguely flattering that he'd gone to such efforts, but it also made me suspicious. Between that and the bizarre events of the previous night, I got the sense that there was more to Sebastian Lock than he was telling me.

Chapter 5

I spent the next two days on autopilot. Soon, we'd be starting work on the Wrights case, but at that point, it was just business as usual. It felt a little like the calm before the storm. There was already a noticeable buzz around the office, like that frenetic pre-Christmas energy that fills the air as December rolls around. I was excited, but also a little intimidated. We had those people's futures in our hands. Winning wouldn't magically fix the damage, but it would mean hospital bills paid, carers hired, and a huge quality of life improvement for all those affected.

Even without Wrights, we were busy. I usually did my best to at least get out of the office for lunch — there was only so much monochrome decor and recycled air I could take in one day — but my workload meant I just didn't have the time.

So on Saturday, when my boss called asking me to go and meet a new prospective client, I jumped at the chance. I normally hated those schmoozing business lunches, but anything that dragged me away from my screen was a win at that moment.

The meet was at an upmarket steak restaurant in Martin Place named Cuts. It was one of those places that looked like it'd been pulled straight out of the fifties. Dimly lit and dominated by leather and sandstone, it gave off the impression of being expressly made to host boozy lunchtime business rendezvous. I half expected to find the cast of Mad Men hunched in one corner, smoothly wooing prospective clients and chortling over their scotch. I'd been told that the sophisticated aesthetic wasn't just a bluff. The steaks were apparently some of the best in town, although in all honesty, one cut of meat was much the same as any other to me.

I arrived a little early. The restaurant was quiet. There were just a handful of groups dining inside and a lone guy sitting at the bar. I made a beeline for the main room, longing to get a glass of red into me before my client arrived. We hadn't met before — all I had was a name; Mr Keys — but it seemed like a good idea to loosen up a little first.

But as I approached, the man at the bar spun to face me. I froze.

"Are you fucking serious?" I said.

"Not much for traditional greetings are you?" Sebastian asked, clearly enjoying having shocked me for a second time.

As usual, a pang of desire rushed through me at the sight of him. I had no idea how I hadn't noticed him immediately. Even in the simple act of sitting still, that masculine poise was unmistakable.

"Not when I'm talking to men who appear to be stalking me," I replied sharply.

He gave a little laugh. "You arrive after me, but I'm the one stalking you?"

He had a point. I shifted uncomfortably. "Well, whatever. I don't have time for your games today, Sebastian. I'm here for a meeting."

His smile grew. "Me too."

It took me a second. "Oh, you didn't?" I said. But the

smugness in his expression confirmed it. "You bastard."

I thought back over the phone call with my boss. It hadn't occurred to me to ask why I was being sent over anyone else. I just assumed it was a random decision. "You asked for me especially?"

"I did."

Mr Keys. Mr Lock. Fuck. I should have seen it coming. "You can't just waste my time like this, Sebastian. I have a job to do."

"And I respect that. I've already paid for an hour of your time, so we're not wasting anything."

My eyes widened. "You paid that ridiculous fee just to get me down here?"

He nodded.

"Well... fuck." I wish I could say I was surprised, but despite the way we'd left things the other night, I'd had a hunch he wasn't done. He struck me as the sort of man who wasn't used to losing. I guess now I had some idea just how far he was willing to go.

I didn't know what to do. Being near him was dangerous. Even my frustration at his tenacity couldn't blunt the attraction I felt for him. My chest tightened as my eyes roamed involuntarily over the hardness of his body. One elegant hand was resting on the bar, tapping out a slow rhythm against the wood, as if serenading me with a piano ballad. Even his fucking fingers were gorgeous. All I could think about was having them playing across my skin instead.

"Give me ten minutes, Sophia," he said. "After that, I promise I'll leave you alone, if you want."

It seemed like I didn't have much choice. He clearly wasn't giving up without a fight. If I didn't hear him out, he'd be back. Perhaps it was better to end things properly, once and for all.

52

"Fine. Ten minutes."

He nodded in thanks and led me inside.

"Drink?" he asked, as we slid into our booth.

I shook my head. "I think I'd rather keep my wits about me for now."

I was rewarded with a grin. "Fair enough." He gestured to the waiter to stay put for now.

"I don't really know what else there is to say," I said. "I've told you, we don't want the same things. If you think you can change my mind with tricks and perseverance you've got another thing coming."

"Ah, but what if I have a new proposal?"

I couldn't help but laugh. Everything was like a business deal to him. Approach from different angles until you find one that works.

"Go on then," I said, rolling my eyes. "Make your pitch. But remember, the clock is ticking."

"Dinner."

"Dinner? As in, the two of us?"

He nodded.

"That sounds dangerously close to a date," I replied. "Wouldn't that be breaking the rules?"

He smiled ruefully. "Maybe, but I don't believe you've given me much choice."

"Of course I have. You could just leave me alone instead."

"I don't consider that an option at all."

There was an intensity to those words that was almost frightening. I had no idea how to deal with that. "Well, a meal together is all well and good," I said slowly, "but it doesn't change the fact that I'm not interested in joining your little harem."

As usual, the more caustic my tongue grew, the more it seemed to entertain him. "I get the impression you think I'm more debauched than I really am, Sophia. Just because I like to keep my options open doesn't mean I automatically hit on anything in a skirt."

"Just the skirts you work with then?" I asked.

"Actually, that's the other thing I was going to mention. Hannah is no longer in the picture."

I rocked back in my seat. "What happened?"

"I ended it. To be honest that relationship was a mistake to begin with. I've always made an effort never to mix business and pleasure, but Hannah was rather... eager. In any case, shortly after you left on Tuesday, she blew up at me. It was the last straw. It had gotten too messy."

He made it sound like it had been coming for a while, but the fact that I'd been the catalyst made me feel a little guilty.

I licked my lips. "And there are no other girls?"

"Nope. If you agree, it will be just you and me."

Those words had a lovely ring to them.

"So why not just tell me that the other night at my office?" I asked.

His expression slipped a little. "I was hoping it wouldn't be necessary. Like I said, I'm not entirely comfortable with exclusivity. I find it often leads to people getting too attached too quickly. But I'm willing to make an exception in this case, as long as we understand each other."

I really wanted to believe him. A light, casual, but monogamous relationship was exactly the sort of thing I needed, and he'd gone to such great lengths that it seemed unlikely he was looking to screw me over. But I was still wary. I'd been fooled before by men like him. For some of them, the challenge was even more fun than the victory itself. This could all just be part of the game.

And even if he was being honest, how long would his promises last? How long would a man with his pick of the litter be content to stay in one place?

"Why are you going to all this effort, Sebastian?" I asked, no longer able to disguise the conflict in my voice. "Surely you can get what you need elsewhere."

He smiled a secretive little smile and shook his head slowly. "You don't give yourself enough credit, Sophia. You were the most beautiful girl in the room that first night we met. I bet there are a lot of men out there who would go to great lengths for an evening with you, if only you'd give them the chance."

I blushed and looked away. I didn't think of myself as someone who was easily swayed by flattery, but I had to admit, I loved hearing the desire in Sebastian's voice when he spoke like that. It made me feel sexier than I had in a long time.

"Come on, one meal," he continued. "No strings attached. If you have fun, we'll take it from there, if not, no problem. I'll drop you home and wish you good night and never bother you again."

I could feel my resolve weakening. He was just so gorgeous, and he didn't seem to want to take no for an answer. What was the worst that could happen? It wasn't like I was committing to anything beyond a meal and a chat. I could bail at any time if I felt uneasy.

I closed my eyes and sucked in a deep breath. "Okay fine. One meal. But I'm not promising anything else."

"I'll be a perfect gentleman, I promise," he said, with a laugh. "How's tomorrow night?"

"Fine."

"Okay, I'll pick you up at seven thirty."

"Alright."

He took my hand and kissed it. It was the sort of gesture that's hard to take seriously, but he somehow managed to pull it off. The brush of his lips sent a pulse of warmth shooting between my legs. "Until then, Sophia."

And then he left.

It was only a few minutes later, after I demolished a glass of Shiraz, that I realised I hadn't told him where I lived. But then again, he'd managed to find my office; why would my home address be a problem?

I had no idea how he did the things he did. I'd sat down one hundred percent certain that nothing was going to happen, and yet in just a few short minutes he'd changed my mind. It was like he'd cast a spell on me.

Agreeing to go out with him was probably a mistake. I'd been down that road before with heart breakers like him, and it always ended in tears. I tried to tell myself that nothing was set in stone. Things would only progress as far as I wanted them to. But part of me wasn't sure that was really true. His persistence seemed endless, his magnetism almost irresistible. If he made a move, I wasn't sure I'd be able to stop myself, no matter how much I wanted to.

Chapter 6

The next morning I decided to walk to work. One of the reasons I moved to Newtown is that it's so much fun to stroll through. The people can be a little intense at times, but there's always something interesting going on. Markets, protests, impromptu street performances; it's an eclectic mix of colour and culture. I often go wandering when I need to unwind. There's just something about the vibe that I find relaxing.

After arming myself with caffeine, I slipped onto auto pilot and let my feet guide me the rest of the way. It was mid-October, and the air was just beginning to carry a little of that summer bite. The walk was going to make me late, but at that moment I didn't care. I was just relishing the sunshine.

I'd been trying my best not to think about my impending date, but truth be told, I was nervous. There was something so enigmatic about Sebastian. For the first time in a long time, I had no idea what to expect from a man.

It must have been weighing on me more than I realised, because at some point I veered off my normal route. I didn't even notice, until my eyes fell upon a familiar red shop front, and then it suddenly clicked into place.

Really, Sophia?

My legs had carried me all the way back to the bar from

that first night. In the light of day, it was an even sorrier sight than I remembered. Paint peeled in great ribbons from the walls, and the sign was missing enough letters that I wasn't even sure what it was called. Nobody would ever have guessed the sort of events that were hosted behind that crumbling facade.

The smart thing to do was probably to turn around and keep moving. I'd caused enough trouble there for one week, and I doubted Sebastian would appreciate me prying any more than I already had. But seeing the place again piqued my curiosity. Perhaps it was my chance to learn a little more about the man I'd be spending the evening with.

I wasn't even sure that the bar would be open, but the door fell inward with a creak at my touch. It took my eyes a moment to adjust to the darkness. The room was largely deserted. The only customers were two men, sitting alone in opposite corners, staring glumly into their glasses. They couldn't even muster the energy to look up as I entered.

There was a girl behind the bar who hadn't been there the other night. She blinked in surprise when she saw me. "Can I help you?"

My gaze flicked to the back wall. The door was there, just like I remembered. I let out a long breath. I'm not sure why, but even after seeing Sebastian again, part of me had still been convinced I'd made the whole thing up.

As expected, the door was closed, which suited me just fine. Charging back in for a second time was a sure fire way to get myself caught. What I needed now was a more subtle approach.

"Maybe," I said, approaching the bar. "I was here on Tuesday night for a function with my friend, and I think I left something behind."

The girl looked confused. "Function?"

"Yea, back there," I said, nodding to the back wall.

Her expression grew wary. "Ah." Apparently whatever went on back there was a sore spot for her. "Sorry, I can't help you."

"Please," I said, trying my best to look desperate, "it was a brooch, a gift from my grandmother before she died. It's really important to me. Do you have a lost and found or something?"

Her expression softened. "I'm sorry, I didn't mean to sound rude, but I really can't help. Anything back there stays back there."

"But surely you've got the keys?" I asked.

She shook her head. "Only the owners have access to that door. Apparently we're not 'trustworthy' enough," she said, making air quotes. "To tell you the truth, I've never even been back there."

"But what if someone wants to use it?"

She shook her head. "According to my boss it's not for the public. It's just for them. And they only use it every few months. We're not really meant to ask questions, but it seems kind of weird if you ask me."

"Yeah it does." Why on earth would you have a room that lavish if you're only going to use it a few times a year? And why stash it at the back of a place like this? It made no sense.

The girl leaned in conspiratorially. "You want to hear something even weirder?" I nodded. "We're not even allowed to work when they're using it. That's why I've never been back there. They bring in an entirely new staff, all their own people. Who *does* that?"

I shook my head slowly. "I have no idea."

Her eyes suddenly narrowed. "Hey, shouldn't you know all this already if you were here with them?"

I shrugged. "I'd never been before the other night. Like I

said I was just keeping my friend company. I only stayed maybe half an hour."

"Ah, fair enough." A smile bloomed on her face. "So, what was it like back there? I've always wondered."

I felt bad shattering whatever wonderful images she'd conjured in her head, but telling the truth would only make her more inquisitive. She might even get herself into trouble. "Honestly? It was nothing special. A bar, some tables, pretty much like any other corporate function I've been to."

Her shoulders sunk. "Oh. Okay. Well, I'm sorry I could-n't help with your brooch. I could try and ask my boss to speak to the owners if you want..."

"That's okay. I'll see if my friend can talk to them. He's the one who brought me along."

"That might be better, yeah."

"Thanks for your time," I said, turning towards the exit.

"No problem. Bye."

I left the building even more confused than when I'd en-tered. Everything about the place was slightly off. I only knew one thing for sure; Sebastian and his friends valued their pri-vacy. Perhaps they were simply eccentric in that way that wealthy people sometimes are, but where did those papers on Sebastian's desk fit in?

I knew it was none of my business. Sebastian's secrets were his own, and he didn't owe me any explanations. But nonetheless, I couldn't help but wonder; what on earth had I gotten myself into?

Chapter 7

As the evening drew closer, I began to grow excited. As bizarre as the whole situation was, it had been a long time since I'd been on a date, and never with a man as gorgeous as Sebastian.

It wasn't until I finished showering and went to dress that I realised how unprepared I was for the occasion. I'm not normally the sort of girl who spends half the night getting ready, but the shimmering fabrics and exotic cuts on display at his party had left me feeling strangely self-conscious. Suddenly, nothing I owned seemed even remotely nice enough. I had plenty of jackets, blouses and knee length skirts, and a few cocktail dresses for special occasions, but expensive meals with mysterious millionaires were definitely out of my comfort zone.

Half an hour and more than a handful of failed outfits later, I gave up and headed to the lounge to wait. I was wearing a simple black pencil skirt with a white V-neck top I'd dug from some long forgotten corner of my wardrobe. I assumed it was going to be wildly inappropriate for whatever he had planned, but if he didn't like it, that was his problem. I wasn't about to rush out and go shopping for that perfect something just to please him.

At seven thirty sharp, my doorbell rang.

"I'll be right out," I called.

He was waiting for me on the landing outside, leaning against the wall and gazing out into the street. Despite only seeing him yesterday, somehow I seemed to have forgotten how gorgeous he was. Tonight he wore his dark dinner jacket open at the front, his black shirt unbuttoned at the top to reveal just a hint of the olive skin and cut chest beneath.

Seeing him standing there looking so effortlessly masculine was like having a bucket of water poured over my head. I froze in place, my tongue involuntarily grazing my lips as I drank in the sight of him. The casual look suited him. It made him look more human. A godlike human, but still.

He smiled when he noticed me, those blazing eyes caressing my body like a soft wind, sending a tingle up my spine.

"You look lovely," he said.

I gave a little spin. "Thank you. It's not Prada, but it does the job."

He laughed. "What makes you think I want Prada? You make too many assumptions, Sophia."

"So if I told you this outfit was thirty bucks at Myer, you wouldn't send me back to change?"

"No. I'd say that most girls would kill to look that good for thirty dollars."

"Well if it's value you're looking for, I might be able to get it down to twenty if you give me a few more minutes to change."

He let out a little growl. "I know I said this dinner was strictly no obligations, but if you keep giving me excuses as to why you should remove your clothes, I won't be held responsible for my actions."

I blushed. I hadn't meant it that way, but once again he'd managed to turn an innocent statement into something much hotter.

Looping his arm through mine, he turned and led me down the stairs to the black limousine that was waiting by the kerb.

He nodded to the man who was standing next to the door. "This is my driver, Joe."

"Evening ma'am." Joe was a friendly looking gentleman of about sixty. He had the weathered face of a once sturdy guy who had been through a lot, and as he moved to open the door for us, I noticed that he walked with a bad limp.

"War wound," he said, following my gaze. "Took a shot clean through the knee. Shattered part of the kneecap."

"That's horrible."

He shrugged. "Maybe. I've always thought it rather Lucky myself. A foot higher and I wouldn't be here at all."

I nodded, unsure how to reply.

"Joe's been with me nearly ten years," Sebastian said.

"Has it really been that long, sir? The time has simply flown by." The older man's voice was heavy with sarcasm, but Sebastian merely grinned. Clearly there was more than professional courtesy between the two of them.

"Come on, we'll be late," Sebastian said, guiding me to the open door and ushering me through with a gentle push to the small of my back. Even that somehow felt like an incredibly sensual gesture.

"So where are we headed?" I asked, as the limo pulled out into the street.

"Well, I was lucky enough to get last minute reservations at Quay."

My eyes widened. I wasn't much for fine dining, but I knew enough to know that Quay was as fancy as they came. Now I definitely was under-dressed. "Isn't the waiting list like a month long there?"

He shrugged. "They had a cancellation."

It seemed a little unbelievable, but I didn't push. "So, how you feeling?" I asked instead. "You nervous at all?"

His lips quirked upward. "And why would I be nervous?"

"Well I imagine this is your first date in a while. You know, being the non-dating sort and all."

"Possibly."

"So I thought you might be a little worried. It's okay, it's perfectly natural. Just be yourself, I'm not going to judge."

He looked at me for several seconds then shook his head ruefully. "You're not planning on making this easy are you?"

"I don't know what you mean." I tried to keep my face straight, but a hint of a smile crept through anyway. After feeling constantly off balance with him, it was nice to put him on the back foot for once.

We sat for a few minutes just looking out the window. He'd seemed upbeat initially, but in the silence that followed, that all leeched away. The longer we sat, the darker his expression grew.

"A penny for your thoughts?" I said eventually.

He blinked several times. "Sorry. I didn't mean to be rude. I've just got a lot on my mind."

"Trouble in venture capital paradise?"

He grimaced. "It's not a big deal. One of our projects has just had some setbacks recently. It's frustrating, that's all."

"What kind of project?"

He smiled apologetically. "I'm not really at liberty to talk about it. It's company policy not to discuss our work with other people. We deal with some sensitive stuff from time to time."

Yeah, like US Government documents. I'd been debating whether to raise any of the questions that had been running through my mind. Obviously he had secrets, and that was fine. Casual meant not having to share much of yourself if you

64

didn't want to. But I couldn't resist trying to fish for a little more information.

"Well, whatever you guys do, you throw a mean party, I'll say that much."

"I'm glad you enjoyed yourself. Honestly those don't happen that often. A few times a year when we want to entertain prospective clients. You got lucky enough to stumble in at just the right time."

"I guess I did. Truth be told, I couldn't really believe it. It was kind of surreal, finding that sort of party behind a shitty bar like that."

He nodded. "Yeah, we get that a lot. We've actually owned that building for nearly a century. It's where the company started. As we expanded, we decided to upgrade it and turn it into a space for entertaining. There's still a few of the old offices left, one of which I believe you are somewhat acquainted with."

My cheeks heated. I wondered if I'd ever live that down.

"So why keep the bar at the front?" I asked. "Why not knock it down and build something nicer? You can obviously afford to."

He shrugged. "Call it sentimentality I guess. That bar's been there since the building was built. It's nice to keep a small piece of the old place around."

There was nothing in his voice to hint at any deception. Perhaps there really was nothing more to it. It was certainly the simplest explanation. Of course there were still the things the girl had told me that morning, and the papers on his desk, but were they really as odd as they seemed? It was hardly strange to want a little privacy, and I hadn't really had more than a few furtive seconds with that document. It was verging on paranoid to make any assumptions based on that. I decided to give him the benefit of the doubt.

A minute later, we arrived at the restaurant. It was a glorious sight. The whole building was a giant glass cylinder, offering a full panoramic view of Circular Quay. A suited maître d' led us to a table on the upper floor, which was right next to the window facing out across the water to the Opera House. The sun had just finished setting and the whole bay was bathed in the soft glow of the city lights from the south. It was a spectacular location.

The two chairs at the table were opposite one another, but after helping me into my seat, he took his and lifted it around, sitting right next to me, his leg brushing softly against mine. My heart quickened. In the blink of an eye, he'd made the whole meal feel much more intimate.

"I can't imagine why anyone would cancel on this," I said, watching as one of the night ferries pulled out of the dock, sending great ripples rolling through the harbour. "It's beautiful."

"I like everything about this place," he said. "I try to come as often as possible. The only thing better than the food is the view." He gave me an exaggerated look up and down. "And I must say, the view is looking particularly spectacular tonight."

I grinned and returned the leer. "It's not so bad from over here either."

Our menus arrived. If it wasn't already obvious, the service quickly made it clear that this wasn't just any lazy Sunday meal. Our waitress was polite, articulate and immaculately groomed. She knew the menu back to front and answered every question Sebastian asked, quickly and in great detail. While they spoke, a second waiter arrived, filling our water glasses and leaving a small basket of steaming bread for us to nibble on.

Sebastian wanted to order the nine course tasting menu, but I'd had bad experiences with that sort of food in the past.

"It always seems a little too pretentious for its own good," I told him.

"Trust me."

And so I relented.

The first course arrived almost instantly, a plate containing two 'Sea Pearls'; delicate spheres about the size of ping pong balls. They didn't look like much, but had the most amazing silky texture and they just melted to nothing in my mouth.

"So, how long have you been with Little Bell?" he asked. Apparently even outsiders knew about our little nickname.

"Just over six years now."

"You like it?"

I shrugged. "It's a great company. They do some really fantastic work and there's lots of variation."

"I'm sensing there's a 'but' coming."

I sighed. I hadn't really planned on whining to him on our first date, but he seemed genuinely interested, and I was sick of bottling up all my frustration. "But I'm starting to feel like it's a dead end."

"Why?"

"It just seems like if something was going to happen for me there it already would have. There aren't many people there who work harder than me, but no matter how much I bust my ass for them, I can't seem to make any progress."

He took a sip of wine. "So why not move somewhere where they respect your talents?"

"I don't know. It would make the last few years feel like a waste, I guess. I hate giving up. Once I start something, I tend to stick to it until I get the job done. Besides, Little Bell is one of the best in the business. If I can make it there, that's a big deal."

"Well, it depends on why you became a lawyer doesn't it?

If what you're interested in is 'making it' — and there's no shame in having that as a goal — then yeah, I'd say you're in the right place. But if you're doing it because it's what you love to do, then you might find yourself wasted there."

"What if it's a little of both?"

"That's where it gets tricky," he said with a smile.

"Don't get me wrong, I enjoy what I do," I continued. "And it's not that I care about image or status. I just like a challenge, you know? I want to prove to myself I can do it."

"That's something I can relate to. Sometimes I think I go out of my way to make things difficult for myself, just so it's more fun when I finally get there."

"Exactly," I said. "I've thought about leaving, but it would just be such a big risk, starting over again from scratch."

"Nothing worth having comes risk free."

The second course arrived. Objectively, it was probably as good as the first, but I wasn't paying much attention. Instead, I was rolling Sebastian's words around in my mind. This sort of discussion wasn't what I'd expected from him. Maybe I'd just been blinded by his initial approach, but I'd assumed our table talk would be a little lighter; a flirtatious game of back and forth. Instead, we'd ventured into a real conversation, and Sebastian was proving to be an excellent sounding board. He was honest, intelligent and articulate. It was a strange feeling, realising the two dimensional cut out in my head was deeper than I thought.

"So what about you? You enjoy working at Fraiser?" I asked.

There was a small pause. "It's great," he said with a nod. "I honestly couldn't imagine being anywhere else."

"Well, with the way they seem to take care of their employees, I can't say I'm surprised."

He chuckled. "We work as hard as we play, but they're good to us, yeah."

"I get the sense that they can afford to be."

He shrugged. "We've backed some strong horses recently. It's paid off."

"So that's what it's about then? 'Backing horses'? Sorry, I don't know much about venture capitalism. For me, it's always fallen under the umbrella of 'miscellaneous financial jobs that all seem vaguely the same'."

His indulgent expression said that was a common perception. "Well, in a nutshell, we take people's money and invest it in projects we think might be profitable. Some work out, some don't. We split the profits and losses with our investors."

"Is that what you did for Chase Adams?" The words left my mouth before I could stop them. I hadn't realised it, but that connection was still bothering me.

He did a double take, looking startled for a brief second, but it was gone again in an instant. "Ah, I'd forgotten he was there the other night. Well, to put it simply, yes. He's been a long standing client of ours."

"And now he just comes by and parties with you guys?"

"When he's in town."

I wouldn't have picked a Hollywood A-Lister to spend his time hanging with a bunch of corporate types, no matter how much cash they'd made him, but perhaps I was underestimating them. "So, you guys deal with some pretty big names then. Anyone else I might have heard of?"

He shot me a little smile. "Probably, but all of them would be quite upset if I began talking about their investments in public."

I tried my best to hide my disappointment. Stonewalled again. "Well, it doesn't sound like such a bad deal really," I said. "Getting paid to party with clients and throw huge sums of money around to see what sticks."

He looked amused. "It's a little more complicated than that." But he didn't elaborate further. Apparently, he took his bosses' penchant for secrecy to heart. Learning anything about him was going to be a slow process.

I watched him as he ate. Even doing that, there was an economic grace to his movements that was a joy to behold. It set my mind wandering, imaging what he might look like doing other things.

He caught me staring and grinned, exposing a row of perfect teeth. "And what are you looking at?"

I blushed, somehow sure he knew exactly what I'd been thinking. "Nothing."

"My mistake then," he said.

The third course arrived. Some kind of creamy crab dish that tasted so fresh I wouldn't have been surprised to learn it had been pulled from the sea just minutes earlier.

"So are you enjoying dinner?" he asked me, after we'd both scraped our bowls clean.

I nodded. "I was a little sceptical, but this place definitely lives up to its reputation. My only problem is, I'm not sure what I'm going to do once it's over. You might have ruined me for homemade spag bol and cheap Chinese forever now."

His mouth quirked up ever so slightly. "I have a few ideas about what we could do once it's over."

Wow. Again. He never missed an opening. "I'm sure you do," I said, keeping my voice neutral, "but I don't remember agreeing to anything beyond dinner."

"No you didn't." *But you will*, his eyes finished. A strange sensation rolled through my chest, and I looked away. I didn't know how to fight that, that unrelenting certainty. I'd done everything in my power to resist, and I'd still wound up at dinner with him. What chance did I have of stopping him now?

"Nonetheless, I'm glad you came," he continued. "For a while I was sure I'd scared you off."

"Your approach was a little... unorthodox."

He laughed. "Perhaps. But nothing about this—" he gestured to the space between us "—is orthodox."

"You mean you don't routinely pick up girls you find hiding in your wardrobe?" I joked, trying to guide the conversation back to lighter territory. If things turned any more risqué, I knew I'd be in trouble.

But he wasn't having any of it. "Surprisingly, I think that's a first," he said, his voice growing huskier. He reached out and ran a finger softly along my arm, coming to rest on my hand. "But I can honestly say I've never been so pleased to have my privacy intruded upon before."

And just like that, the tension in the air was back. It settled over my skin like a fine mist. I knew I should find something to say, but as always, his touch left my mind flailing.

"You know, I wanted you from the moment you first walked in through that door the other night, Sophia."

"You did?" I asked, my voice reed thin.

He nodded. "All I could think about after our first discussion was what it would be like to take you home with me. To watch your body tremble as I made you come."

The way he brazenly ventured into such erotic territory was disarming, and quite frankly hot as hell. I knew I should probably have been offended, but all I could think about was letting him do exactly what he'd just described.

"To have you like that would have been enough," he continued. "But after finding you crouched in my office, watching me spank Hannah, I realised something." He reached out and brushed my chin, guiding my eyes to his. "You want more than that too."

"I don't... I mean, we're not—" a single finger pressed into my lips, silencing me, teasing my mouth with hints of salt and musk.

"When I found you kneeling on the floor that night, you were practically radiating excitement. I could smell your arousal. You want this Sophia, you want to do more than just watch, and I'm going to be the one that shows you."

His gaze bored into me with steely promise. I felt myself growing hot. It was unsettling, hearing him say those things, giving voice to the fears that had been simmering inside me. That night had been a flurry of confusion and alien sensations. I still couldn't wrap my head around the idea of giving yourself to someone so completely. It felt too much like being taken advantage of, like being used. But if that was the case, why was my body so flushed with desire?

"I'm sure it works for some people," I stammered, "but I just don't think that's me."

"Who are you trying to fool?" he asked, his eyes ablaze. "You wouldn't have come tonight unless you were curious. It was always going to come to this. We'll go slowly, as slowly as you like, but you're coming home with me, and I promise you that by the end, you'll be begging for more."

My heart was hammering in my chest. Something told me this decision was important. I could say no, and things would simply return to normal. But then I'd never know for sure. Did I really want to spend my life asking 'what if?'

"Okay," I said, my voice barely more than a whisper.

He let out a long breath, the sigh of a man who had just gotten everything he ever wanted. Instantly he signalled the waitress. "I can't wait until after dinner. I need to be inside you now."

I trembled, feeling myself grow wet at the mere suggestion. I nodded. Food was suddenly the last thing on my mind.

72

The cheque arrived and he paid for the full meal without blinking. It was an astronomical sum for what amounted to a few sips and bites, but he didn't seem to care.

We made our way outside, but as I turned to head back to the car, he grabbed me by the arm.

"What—" I started to say, but in an instant I was spinning back towards him and his lips were on mine. In that kiss, I saw a prelude of what was to come. It was as strong and intoxicating as the man himself. He crushed his face against mine, sandwiching my body between his chest and the glass behind. His tongue explored my mouth greedily, darting and teasing, while his fingers prowled along my shoulders, my back, and the nape of my neck. I kissed back as best I could, but I felt a little like a shell on the beach, struggling not to get swept out by the tide. He was so powerful, so determined, and my body seemed to turn boneless in his hands. All I could really do was stand there and *be* kissed. It wasn't just an expression of passion, but one of possession. And it felt sinfully good.

I could feel a throbbing hardness building against my stomach as he ground himself against me. An intense pang of desire rushed through me, pooling between my legs.

What felt like a lifetime later, he broke away. "Jesus," he said, his voice ragged. "I'm not sure I should have done that."

"Why not?"

"Now I don't know if I can last the car ride home."

"Well," I said, running my hand gently down his stomach and coming to rest on the tip of his impressive bulge. "You said we could take it slow. 'As slow as you like,' I believe were your words. And I'd like to wait." In truth, I was almost at breaking point myself. If he'd carried me into the bathroom and bent me over then and there I'm not sure I'd have been able to object, but I was enjoying that rare moment of power over him.

He drew a sharp, shuddering breath and closed his eyes briefly, before seizing my wrist and pulling my arm away. "Then that's what we'll do," he said, a strained smile on his face. "But you should know, I have ways of dealing with girls who like to tease."

"I'm sure you do," I replied, thinking back to Hannah's raw ass. Strangely, in my aroused state, I didn't find the image as intimidating as I once had.

Chapter 8

We walked briskly over to where the limo was parked. "Home," Sebastian said to Joe, before ushering me into the back. He wore the determined look of the man on a very important mission. I wondered if Joe understood what was about to take place. After ten years, he likely had a good grasp of his boss's habits, so the answer was probably yes. Normally, that might have bothered me, but at that moment I was too turned on to care.

The car ride to Sebastian's house only took ten minutes, but it felt much longer. He didn't speak. His silence seemed almost meditative, so I didn't interrupt. I just stared out the window and considered what I was getting myself into.

Eventually, we pulled up outside a sleek white apartment building that looked out over Woolloomooloo Bay. The harbour was quiet at night, but I could still hear the gentle crash of waves breaking against the hulls of the moored yachts that lined the docks.

We said farewell to Joe and then Sebastian took my hand and led me inside. I thought the car ride might have cooled his excitement a little, but as soon as the lift doors closed behind us, he was on me once more. He kissed me with a hunger that was almost strong enough to be frightening, pinning me against the metal wall and driving his mouth onto mine. Free from any wandering eyes, his hands lost whatever sense of propriety they'd once had, running up my sides before sliding down to caress the curves of my ass. I moaned, half in pleasure half in protest, but there was no one to see, and no way to stop the relentless onslaught that was Sebastian Lock.

Seizing me more firmly, he lifted me up until our mouths were at the same height. I took the opportunity to loop my arms and legs around him and run my fingers through the black tangle of his hair, pulling him closer still. My dress was beginning to ride up, and the change in height pushed the pulsing mass of his cock directly against my dripping panties. He let out a growl and began to rock back and forward, using the lift wall as leverage.

"God, you're so wet. I can feel it even through our clothes."

"This is what you do to me," I said, my voice trembling.

He brought one huge hand up and wrapped it around my chin, raising my eyes to his. "No, this is just a taste of what I can do to you. There is so much more. All I've been able to think about since we met was making you come. I'm going to do it in a thousand ways, ways you didn't even know existed."

"God yes," I breathed, already able to feel an orgasm beckoning in the distance. The pressure of his crotch against mine was amazing, and his mouth was now doing divine things to my neck, kissing and nibbling in slow circles. The coarse brush of his stubble against my skin sent waves of sensation rolling through me, like the gentle scrape of sand on the wind.

I assumed we'd have to walk down some kind of corridor, but the lift opened straight into Sebastian's apartment. Without even breaking our embrace, he spun and carried me through the doorway. Pressed against him like that I could feel the taut strength of his muscles flex and shift as we moved. He held me as easily as a child. I couldn't wait to see the body that lay beneath those clothes. I could already picture it, all hard slabs and trembling sinew.

Entwined as we were, I barely noticed my surroundings. Sebastian navigated us expertly to the bedroom, never breaking our kiss for more than a moment. There was something so primal about being carried off to be ravished. I felt claimed, taken, possessed. It was an intensely erotic experience.

Throwing me down onto the bed, he climbed on top of me. My hands now free, I reached up eagerly for his shirt buttons, but he caught both my wrists in one hand. "You said you wanted to wait," he said, his voice teasing.

I started to protest, but his expression silenced me. "Before we go any further," he continued, "I want to establish some ground rules. I told you that we could go slowly, and I meant it. But nonetheless, it's important to me that everything we do is consensual. So with that in mind, you need to pick a safe word. Something distinctive that will never come up under normal circumstances. If what we're doing ever gets too much, you just utter that word and I promise everything stops. No questions asked. Understand?"

I nodded. At that particular moment he could have been asking me for my bank account number and PIN and I'd probably have given them.

"So, pick a word."

Surprisingly, one came to me instantly. "Cinderella."

He looked at me curiously. "That's an... odd choice."

He was right. I had no idea why I'd picked that, although it did make me realise I still hadn't gotten my shoes back. *Some fairy tale this is.*

"I'll explain later," I told him impatiently.

"Fair enough. Cinderella it is." He leaned in, planting a

soft kiss just below my ear. "And now, Sophia, I want to taste you."

I squirmed against him, those words amping the fire inside me up to fever pitch. I felt like my body couldn't possibly maintain that state of arousal for much longer, like I was prepped to burst at any minute. "Please."

Releasing my hands, he slid down the bed and shoved my skirt up around my hips. There was no preamble. He didn't even take the time to undress me. He simply tugged my panties aside and then his tongue was on my pussy.

"Oh...fuck." That first touch was like electricity, sending a wave of pleasure sizzling through me. Another joined it, curling around the first, and then another. Soon, I could feel nothing else save the vortex roaring inside me.

It seemed he'd been serious when he said he wanted to taste me. Rather than focus on my clit straight away like I'd expected, he worked the length of me, caressing my dripping opening with long, soft strokes and occasionally slipping inside to fuck me with his tongue.

"My god, you're so sweet," he said. "You're just as delicious as I'd imagined."

I could only moan in reply, grinding myself against him. I felt like I was coming apart at the seams, like every stroke, every lick was peeling away just a little more of me.

I reached out to take his head in my hands, desperate to pull him even closer, but again he seized my wrists. "No hands. Your pleasure is mine to control. I was going to save the ties for another night, but if you can't learn to behave, I'll have to bind you now."

My stomach twisted at the thought of being restrained. I'd be utterly at his mercy.

"I'll be good," I said, my voice soft.

"Excellent." He released me.

His hands now free, he brought one down and slid a long finger inside of me, tenderly stroking my G-spot while his tongue began licking a delicate figure eight across my swollen bud.

"Fuck you're tight. And so soft. God, it's killing me that I'm not inside of you right now."

"So fuck me," I said, the words barely recognisable. I wanted him more than I could remember wanting anything before. I was nearly delirious with desire.

"Soon, but first I want to watch you come. I want to feel you tighten around my fingers. And I want you to think about the fact that this is just the first of many. This is but the tiniest scrap of the things we can do together."

I writhed against the sheet, certain it wouldn't be long before he got his wish. I could already feel my muscles tensing, preparing for that explosion that would tear through me.

"Oh god, oh fuck," I cried, crossing the point of no return. My body buckled and my vision shattered as I rocked against him. Wordless sounds spilt from my mouth, animal sounds, sounds I'd never heard myself make before. And the whole time he gazed into my eyes, primal satisfaction painted on his face.

As my senses finally returned, I heard the snicker of a zipper being unfastened. "Oh no, not yet, I'm too sensitive and it's been so long. Just a few minutes," I whispered.

"I have to have you, Sophia. Now. I can't wait any longer." His voice sounded pained. He produced a condom from somewhere. "Are you on birth control?"

"Yes."

He tore it open. "Good. Next time, I'll prove that I'm clean. You'll do the same. And then we'll be able to dispense with these. I don't want anything between us in the future."

I nodded slowly, still unsure I'd be able to take him yet,

but one look at his face told me there was no stopping him now. He didn't even pause to remove his shirt. I caught the barest flash of hot olive skin as his pants hit the floor, then he was pressing himself slowly inside me. "Oh Jesus, Sophia," he groaned.

Even without seeing it, I could tell his cock was huge. The stretching sensation in those first few moments was almost overpowering, and my tender skin burned in protest. But my body had taken on a life of its own at that point. My muscles began to flex and ripple, hungrily drawing him in. I felt myself growing wetter still, and gradually the discomfort faded, replaced by a divine sense of fullness.

Once again I found my hands wandering, dancing across his chest. His muscles were taut beneath the soft cotton of his shirt. Unable to restrain myself, I traced my fingers up toward the collar and slipped inside, savouring the warmth and slickness of his skin. He allowed this for a few seconds, but then his hands caught mine once more, pinning them to the pillow above. Before I could object, he leaned down, sealing his lips over mine, his tongue shooting in to claim another part of me.

With his weight on top of me and my arms held, I couldn't move. I could only lie there as he had his way with me. I felt a rush of excitement. That sense of powerlessness was strangely intoxicating.

"That's it, I want you to take all of me," he said, his cock now deep inside me.

"God yes. Keep going," I replied, rocking my hips back and forward, easing him deeper still.

As I finally adjusted to his size, he began to fuck me harder. His body crushed against mine, grinding my clit while his cock hammered my G-spot. The sensation was exquisite. As impossible as it seemed, I could feel another orgasm rearing up inside me.

He was clearly not far away either. His breath was coming in little spurts and there was a low growl emanating from his throat. I loved that sound. I could feel it vibrating all the way through his body and into mine; another declaration of his possessive intent.

His hips worked like an out of control piston, steadily gaining force. His thrusts became wilder and his fingers tightened, digging into my skin. Leaning down, he brought his face just inches from mine.

"I'm going to come, Sophia," he panted.

"Oh fuck, give it to me."

My words seemed to send him over the edge. With one final mighty pump, he exploded inside me. His back arched and his eyes flared as my pussy clenched around him, milking every drop.

That sudden rush of heat was too much, and with another cry I came too. I hadn't thought it possible, but this orgasm was even more intense. It tore through my body like a tidal wave, curling my toes and leaving me breathless and limp.

When we were both spent, we collapsed onto the bed together. I was pleased to see he looked as drained as I did; face flushed, body slick with sweat.

Lying there nestled against him was lovely. I'd forgotten what it felt like to have a pair of strong arms wrapped around me. It was a surprisingly tender gesture, like what we'd just shared had stripped away a little of that professional armour.

"Wow," I said, when I could finally speak again.

He gave a short laugh. "My thoughts exactly. God, that was intense." His brow crinkled. "It wasn't too much was it? I wanted to take it slow, really. I didn't mean to grab you, but once I had you underneath me like that, I lost control."

I thought back to that rush of adrenaline when he'd seized my hands. It scared me to admit, but perhaps he was right.

Perhaps there were a few things I didn't know about myself. "No. In fact, when you pinned me down, I kind of liked that. It felt so... animal."

A huge smile split his face. "I was hoping you'd say that." He ran a hand gently down my naked ass, that emerald gaze searing into me. "Because now that I've had a taste of you, I don't think I can stop. There are so many things I want to show you."

I drew a deep breath. I didn't know exactly what I was committing to, but I wasn't sure I had a choice anymore. The strange hunger Sebastian had awakened inside me wasn't going away. It had started that first night crouched in the wardrobe, and tonight had been like pouring fuel on a fire. "Well, I think I want to be shown," I said, my voice shaking. "Slowly," I added, having sudden visions of him carrying me off, wrapping me in leather and chaining me in the basement.

"With you, I have absolutely no objections to taking my time." It sounded like both a threat and a promise. I suspected that whatever pace we moved at, the experience would be something special.

I licked my lips. I wasn't sure exactly what the typical rules of such arrangements were, but certain things still bothered me. "I have a condition though."

He looked amused. "Oh?"

"What we do stays strictly in the bedroom. Hannah may have let you control other parts of her life, but that's not me. Everywhere but in here, I'm my own person."

His smile grew. "Honestly, I wouldn't have expected anything else. Submission is different for everyone. It's an intensely personal thing. For Hannah, discipline was important, so I gave her what she needed." He ran a hand gently up my side. "But I'm perfectly happy just having your body in here."

"That sounds about perfect to me," I replied, savouring

the sensation of his touch. "Oh and one other thing. There will be none of that 'Sir' stuff. Like, ever. That seriously weirds me out."

He laughed. "Alright. Noted."

We lay for a few moments in silence.

"This was a lovely night," I said eventually. "It's been a long time since I went on a date; especially one that escalated this quickly."

His expression fell ever so slightly. "I'm glad you enjoyed yourself." He paused, as if choosing his words carefully. "But you know it won't be like this all the time, right? This—" he gestured to the bed "—I can give you, but I can't promise much more than that."

I nodded slowly. I had no illusions about the sort of man he was, and what he was proposing should have been exactly what I wanted; all the fun of a relationship and none of the fuss. But nonetheless, his candour made me a little uneasy. It was still difficult to wrap my head around the idea that I wasn't being taken advantage of.

"I know," I replied, trying to act nonplussed. "It was just nice to spend a night doing things the old fashioned way, you know? Most days I barely have time to scoff down a bowl of two minute noodles."

He relaxed a little. "That makes two of us."

We lay for a few minutes in silence. In an attempt to distract myself, I began to explore his body. He was still clothed from the waist up, but this time he didn't stop me as I slipped my hand beneath his shirt. I ran my fingers gently over his skin, admiring the smooth, hard curves beneath. And then I noticed something I hadn't seen before.

"Wow. You didn't strike me as a tattoo kind of guy," I said, hopping onto my elbows to get a closer look. Neatly inscribed on the right side of his chest, was an ornate letter A.

Something about the image looked vaguely familiar, but I couldn't place it. "What's it stand for?"

He hesitated. "Nothing really. Call it a relic from my younger and stupider days." He rolled slightly onto his side and reached up my skirt to cup my ass. "You know, if you keep touching me like that, you're just asking for trouble."

With his body pressed up against me, I could feel a throbbing presence begin to jut into my thigh. He was growing hard again. All other thoughts fled my mind.

I peeled back the sheet and his cock sprang into view. It was the first time I'd really gotten a good look at it. Long and almost as thick as my wrist, it had two large veins wrapped around it like decorations. Warmth gushed through me once more. I couldn't believe I'd had that inside me. It seemed impossibly big.

I'd always been a once-and-done kind of girl. I'd assumed I simply wasn't built for multiple orgasms. But Sebastian had already managed to shatter that illusion tonight, and now, against all odds, I found my body stirring once more. He had that look in his eye again; that raw, carnal need that I couldn't help but respond to.

I reached out to stroke the length of him. "Is that so?" I said. "Well, I think there's only one way I'm going to learn."

Chapter 9

My second time with Sebastian was even more tiring than the first, and when he finally dropped me home, I fell asleep almost instantly. I had no idea how he managed such virility. He seemed to have the stamina of ten men. Not that I was complaining.

I woke feeling refreshed, a pleasant ache between my legs. I assumed I'd get used to marathon sex sessions eventually, but for now, my body was not accustomed to such vigour. Thinking back to the four toe curling orgasms I'd had, I decided a little soreness was a fair price to pay.

My day at the office started with a floor wide strategy meeting. Normally our work was delegated across a mixture of small meetings, phone calls and emails, but whenever we began a big case like Wrights, we needed a little more coordination. I was excited to finally have something important to sink my teeth into.

After a less than rousing speech from Alan, the senior Partner who ran our floor, about the importance of "obtaining justice for those that might otherwise slip through the cracks," we got down to business.

Work was gradually parcelled out, with everyone heading off to begin their assigned tasks. Soon, there were only a few people left in the room.

"As for the rest of you," Alan said, "we need you to hold down the fort with the rest of our case load for now. Wrights is important, but it's not the only thing on our books."

Those words were like a punch in the stomach. Again I was being relegated to the bench.

It wasn't considered proper to object about your duties, but I was sick of playing second fiddle to people with less dedication and experience than me.

"Excuse me, sir," I said to Alan, as the others were filing out. I didn't know him well, but he had a reputation for being difficult to deal with, so I wanted to tread carefully.

"Yes Sophia, what is it?"

"I just wanted to talk to you about my assignment. To be honest I'm kind of disappointed not to be working on the Wrights case."

He shot me a sympathetic smile, but it lacked any real warmth. "I know it's not ideal, but we need people on our other cases too."

"I know. It's just there are plenty of less experienced associates working on the case. I think I can be more useful there than here."

His lips tightened. "Nobody doubts your talents, Sophia. They're the reason we've got you doing this. We need someone with your kind of experience keeping things on track elsewhere. You'll get your chance on the Wrights case soon enough, don't worry."

It was a classic Partner trick; act like the shitty job you've just doled out is more important than it actually is. But there wasn't anything I else I could really do. The only person who might consider helping was my direct boss Ernest, and Alan outranked him.

I thanked him and headed back to my desk.

With the majority of the floor now occupied with the new case, my morning quickly grew hectic. Phone calls and emails streamed in, never giving me time to catch my breath. I was so set in my rhythm, that when a call arrived around one o'clock, I didn't even notice that it was from a familiar number.

"Sophia Pearce," I said, doing nothing to hide the strain in my voice.

"Well hello to you too." I recognised Ruth's voice instantly.

"Shit, sorry. Kind of busy here. Thought you were another fucking client who didn't know his ass from his elbow. What's up?"

"What's up is that I'm downstairs."

"Why wou—ah shit."

She exhaled loudly. "I take it that means you forgot?"

"Possibly."

"This was your idea, for Christ's sake. 'Come have lunch on Monday,' you said. 'We'll catch up, just the two of us.'"

"I know. I'm sorry. I'm just really busy today and it slipped my mind."

"Well, I can wait a few. Finish up what you're doing and come down."

"I don't know, Ruth. I've got a mountain of stuff to do here—"

"Even mountaineers need to eat. Come on, I came all the way across town. The least you can do is give me half an hour. We'll go to Pablo's."

It was my turn to sigh. Ruth wasn't going to give up. And as much as I knew I should power on, the thought of escaping, even for a little while, was very appealing. "Okay fine. Give me five."

"Atta girl. I'll be out front."

Fifteen minutes later we were climbing down a narrow staircase and into a dimly lit basement. Pablo's was one of my favourite restaurants. It had the perfect combination of up-market panache and homely comfort food. The tables around us were piled high with steaming olive rolls and mounds of bolognese, while waistcoated waiters darted nimbly between them like insects, ensuring the glasses of wine and sparkling water never quite reached empty.

More than a few men's eyes followed us as we walked. I sometimes liked to pretend that those stares were for me, but the truth was, whenever Ruth was in a room, it was all eyes on her. There was just something about her that men couldn't resist. She wasn't stunningly beautiful — she had a little too much of her mother's sharp nose for that — but she had a way of moving that just exuded sexuality. Men seemed to melt in her presence; a fact she took ample advantage of.

"So, how are the unhappy couples of Sydney treating you?" I asked, once we'd ordered. Ruth was a family law attorney, specialising in messy divorce.

"No complaints. Things are a little quiet, but that's just the calm before the post-Christmas storm."

"Post-Christmas storm?"

"Yea. Haven't you noticed I'm always super busy come January?"

I thought about it. "Sure, I guess. But why?"

"Two words. Christmas parties. Unlimited booze, no spouses, lots of mistletoe; it's like divorce lawyer heaven."

I laughed. "Good to see you're still bringing that notorious professional sensitivity to the table."

She raised her hands defensively. "Hey, ninety percent of the time the divorcee is getting what they deserve. I've got a couple of doozeys right now." She leaned in close. "This one poor guy just found out that his wife was cheating on him...

with his dad."

"No shit?"

Ruth shook her head. "But it gets worse. They have a kid, about four years old. Paternity tests just came back."

"Not his?"

She shook her head.

"Fuck."

"Exactly. The guy has been raising his own brother. You couldn't make this shit up if you tried. It's like an episode of Jerry Springer. But anyway, enough about my sordid little life. I've already said too much. How are things on your end?"

"Fine, fine, just busy."

She gazed at me for a second. "You look tired, Soph. Busy doesn't mean you can't get a proper night's sleep every once in a while."

I rolled my eyes. "Yes mum."

"I'm serious! You can't keep working yourself into the ground."

"It's not like it's intentional. Sometimes there's just too much to do. We just landed a really big case, so I doubt things will let up any time soon."

"Is that Wrights? The one you were telling me about?"

"Yep."

"Well, that's awesome!" She noticed my resigned expression. "Right?"

"It would be if I was actually working on it."

She blew out a long puff of air. If anybody knew about my frustrations at work, it was Ruth. "They're seriously not using you at all?"

I shrugged. "Not so far. It's early days yet, and Alan said I'd be rotated in, so maybe I'm just being bitter. I'm just so sick of sitting on the sidelines."

"I know. They're idiots for wasting you like that." She

reached out and squeezed my hand. "But eventually someone there is going to recognise how fucking great you are at your job, and when that happens, the sky's the limit."

That drew a smile from me. Ruth was always wonderful at cheering me up. "Thanks."

"No problem." Her expression turned cheeky. "You know if you want, we could go out tonight. Lou is away at her mum's, so it would just be us two single gals. Maybe we could find ourselves a couple of willing young gentlemen to take our minds off our troubles?"

I sucked in a sharp breath. I'd really been hoping the conversation wouldn't go down that path, but I should have known better with Ruth. I wasn't sure how to respond. I hated the idea of lying to my friend, but I didn't feel comfortable talking about Sebastian just yet. I barely had a handle on the way he made me feel. I didn't need the challenge of trying to describe it to someone else.

I opened my mouth to brush her off, but I must have waited a beat too long, because suddenly her eyes lit up. "You sneaky little hussy! You're already getting some right now, aren't you?" I turned red. "Yeah, busy with work indeed. You're busy getting banged all night long. No wonder you look so tired."

There wasn't much point in lying now. The jig was up. "I wouldn't describe us as busy exactly. We only just met." A small grin slipped onto my face. "It did last most of the night though."

Ruth laughed. "That's a promising start. Well, don't keep me in suspense. Who is this mystery Casanova?"

"Well, remember the other night when I snuck into that party..." I trailed off, waiting for Ruth to fill in the blanks.

It didn't take long. "Oh, you didn't? You did!" She laughed. "That guy you were telling us about? How? When?"

And so I told the story. In typical Ruth fashion, she did her best to extract the more pornographic details, but I managed to keep Sebastian's kinkiness largely under wraps.

"Sounds like quite a guy," she said when I was done.

I nodded slowly. "That he is. Honestly, it's a little intimidating. Every time I'm around him I seem to lose my head completely."

She flashed a knowing smile. "They're dangerous when they're that gorgeous."

"It's not just his looks." I shook my head. "I don't know if I can really explain it. There's just something about him that pushes all my buttons."

"Is it the accent? Fuck, I love a good accent." She leaned back in her chair and gazed up at the ceiling, a dreamy grin blooming on her face. "Remember that Spanish guy I was seeing a year or so back? God damn. He could read out the shopping list and I'd still get off."

"You did mention he had a talented tongue, but I didn't think that's what you meant."

She laughed. "That man had a variety of skills, most of which cannot be discussed in polite company. Anyway, it sounds like you're living the dream. Exclusive, casual sex with a gorgeous, mysterious millionaire. I dare say I'm a little envious."

"Yea it's pretty awesome." I tried my best to sound enthusiastic, but some part of my uncertainty must have leaked through, because her expression fell.

"So why don't you sound happy?" she asked.

"I am!" I sighed. It was frustrating how little I could hide from her. Who said best friends were a good idea anyway? "It's just, I'm kind of waiting for the other shoe to drop, you know?"

"Jesus. You really know how to look a gift horse in the

mouth, don't you?"

"I'm not trying to. I just want to keep things in perspective. After what happened with Connor, I want to be a little more careful, that's all."

She grimaced and leaned in close, taking my hands in her. "Soph, listen to me. Connor was a one of a kind psychopath. He was a serial cheater who seemed to get off on lying to you. I've told you before, men might be assholes sometimes, but he was a special piece of work. They aren't all like that. You can't let that one experience cause you to shut up shop forever."

I nodded slowly. "I know."

"You need something to do besides work and drink, and if you ask me, this sounds perfect. A casual fling with a guy who is as busy as you are. Just take it slow and enjoy it for what it is."

"That's the plan."

"Good." She took a drink and then shook her head. "I swear, you don't know how lucky you are. This sort of thing doesn't come along all that often."

I thought back to our bizarre courtship. In the rational light of day, it barely seemed plausible at all. "I think I agree with you there."

Chapter 10

The next few days were uneventful. A little of the Wrights case work trickled down to me, but nothing significant. I debated confronting Alan again, but I got the sense I'd already made a mistake complaining the first time. Pushing any more was likely to just make the situation worse. So instead, I swallowed my pride and focused on the tasks that were given to me.

I didn't hear anything from Sebastian. When we'd parted, we'd made no concrete plans to see each other again and that was fine with me. After all, what was the point of a casual fling if it filled your diary with obligations?

But as the days became a week, I began to grow uneasy. I wasn't expecting daily phone calls, but it felt like there should be some kind of communication. To make matters worse, I realised that I had no way of contacting him. I might have been able to find his building again if I really wanted to, but he'd never given me his phone number or even an email address. Our relationship effectively existed entirely on his whim.

"It's partially my fault I guess," I said to Ruth on the phone one night. "I should have asked for his number. But that doesn't make the situation any better. It's like I'm just lying around waiting until he feels like fucking me again."

"Isn't that what a casual relationship is?" she asked.

"I guess," I replied slowly, "but it's not supposed to be this one sided. What if *I* decide I'm in the mood?"

She laughed. "Feeling a little hot under the collar are we?"

As much as I hated to admit it, I was. My sex drive had never been much more than a low buzz in the background before, but my one night with Sebastian seemed to have kick started my libido something fierce. I found my eyes wandering much more than they used to, and my dreams had taken a notably erotic turn. It was quite inconvenient really.

"Maybe a little."

"Well," she continued, "I'm sure he didn't keep his number hidden on purpose. Just ask for it next time."

Knowing the sort of man Sebastian was, it wouldn't have surprised me if it had been intentional, but I didn't argue.

"What really bothers me is... what if there isn't a next time?" I said. "What if my gut was right and he was just looking for an easy lay?"

"A few days of silence is hardly a big deal. This is what you signed up for, remember? No fuss."

"I guess," I said again.

"And if it turns out he did take advantage of you, then yea he's an asshole, but worrying isn't going to change anything. Think of it this way; there are far worse things than one night stands with handsome foreign gentlemen who are great in bed."

I laughed. Ruth certainly knew how to put things in perspective.

I tried my best to take her advice to heart, but as more time passed, my restlessness grew. What was the threshold for when that sort of behaviour became unacceptable? Two weeks? A month? I had no idea. It felt like he'd gone to a lot of trouble just to sleep with me once and then drop me, but the evidence was growing increasingly hard to ignore.

Then one day nearly three weeks later, when I'd basically given up hope of ever seeing him again, I returned from a lunch meeting to find my office door open. Sebastian was leaning casually against my desk, suited, chiselled, and looking as dapper as ever.

"Seriously?" I hissed. Under other circumstances I might have reacted more calmly, but the way he stood there, smiling like his presence was totally normal, made my blood run hot.

"Still haven't got those greetings down pat yet, have you?" he replied, looking bemused at my dark expression.

"That's really the best you can do?"

"I'm not sure what else you were hoping for."

I strode into the room, slamming the door behind me. "I don't hear anything from you for three weeks, then you think it's okay to just show up at my office when the mood finally strikes you?"

His jaw tightened. "I didn't realise I owed you minute by minute updates of everything I did."

"You don't. You don't owe me anything. I guess I just hoped you might *want* to check in on me. A text message every once in a while isn't a big ask."

"It's not that I don't want to. I've just been busy." He began pacing. "I thought we understood one another, Sophia."

"So did I, but apparently I didn't make myself clear. That one dinner doesn't give you license to just ignore me until you feel like getting laid again."

"That's not how it is."

"Well that's how it seems to me."

He exhaled slowly. "I thought you were okay with keeping things simple."

"Simple is fine. Simple is great. I don't need romantic dates or bloody hand crafted mix tapes, but I do need to feel like I'm more than just a walking vagina that operates at your beck and call."

He studied me for several seconds, his expression growing concerned. "I'm sorry. I never meant to make you feel that way," he said in a soft voice.

I felt some of my rage draining away. He looked genuinely distressed at having hurt me, although that didn't change the fact that he had. Part of me wanted to just end it then and there. For a casual relationship, it was already proving to be more emotionally taxing than I was prepared for, and with work ramping up, I couldn't afford any distractions.

But then I heard Ruth's words playing through my head. *"This sort of thing doesn't come along all that often."* That statement was truer than she'd realised. The chemistry between Sebastian and I was unlike anything I'd experienced before. It was practically nuclear. And he'd promised that there was so much more to learn.

I closed my eyes for a moment, collecting my thoughts. "Look Sebastian, I'm going to go out on a limb and guess most women you sleep with don't have a problem with this sort of arrangement. I bet they're pretty happy to take whatever you give them. But I'm not like that. I can't just be another pretty ornament."

"I never considered you to be," he replied, his expression earnest.

"Then start showing it. I'm happy to keep this relationship simple, but simple doesn't mean totally one dimensional. If we're going to continue, I need to feel like you're putting in at least a little effort. It doesn't have to be much, a quick bite to eat once every few weeks, a phone call or message now and then. If that's too much to ask, well, I'm sure you can find what you're looking for elsewhere."

He contemplated this. It didn't seem like I was asking much, but apparently it wasn't an easy decision.

"If that's what you need to feel comfortable, I'll do my best," he said eventually. "But in return, you have to understand that there are times I might not be able to contact you. I seek these sorts of relationships for a reason. It's true, I tend to keep my distance out of habit, even when I don't need to, but the fact remains that my schedule is incredibly unpredictable. I could be called to fly overseas tonight, and even when I am here, I'm often so busy I barely have time to eat or sleep."

I nodded. "I can sympathise with that." His words seemed fair. I knew the toll work could take on a person's personal relationships. Suddenly, I felt embarrassed at the way I'd reacted. He was just like me in a lot of ways; career driven and focused, almost to a fault. I could hardly hold that against him.

"I'm sorry too," I continued. "Maybe I overreacted. I'm not good at this stuff. I'm willing to compromise if you are."

"Sounds good to me," he said.

"Excellent." I still felt a little uneasy, but I'd said my piece and he seemed to have taken it to heart. I couldn't ask for more than that. "So why did you decide to pop in anyway? I assume it wasn't to get told off."

He smiled. "Actually I brought you something."

"Oh? Trying to bribe your way out of trouble then?"

"Not really. It's more of a return than a gift." He reached into his bag and pulled out the shoes I'd left on his office floor that first night we'd met. "I believe you were a little too pre-occupied to take them with you the other week."

I couldn't help but laugh. *So now he brings them.*

"Am I missing something?" he asked.

"Oh it's nothing," I said, suddenly aware of how childish

the story seemed.

"No, go on."

I sighed. "It's stupid really. Remember when I said I'd explain my safe word?" He nodded. "Well, when I was running away that first night, it occurred to me that the situation bore some passing similarity to Cinderella. You know, shoes left behind at the ball and all that."

He seemed to find this incredibly amusing. "I'm a little rusty with my fairy tales, but I don't remember Cinderella being quite as sordid as that particular evening."

"You mustn't have been reading the right version."

"Apparently not." He grinned. "Well, that does explain why you were in such a hurry to leave. And here I was thinking you were embarrassed."

I shook my head. "Nope. I just had to escape before pumpkin o'clock."

Sliding closer, he wrapped his arms around my hips, locking my body against his. "So if you're Cinderella, that makes me Prince Charming then?"

Whatever lingering frustration I'd felt instantly melted away. "I guess so," I said, my voice suddenly fluttering. *How the hell does he keep doing that to me?*

"Well then, I believe that means that since I've returned your lost slippers, we're meant to kiss now."

I knew I should probably stop him. Someone could walk in at any moment. But as usual, I seemed to have no willpower where he was concerned. Craning his neck, he brought his mouth down to meet mine. The kiss was somehow firm and hungry, yet impossibly soft, and the warmth of it flowed through me. As our bodies rocked back against my desk, he reached up and ran one hand roughly through my hair, driving us together, as though someone might steal me away at any moment.

Some indeterminable time later, he broke away. "I do believe I should bring you things more often," he said with a smile.

"I'm not sure I'd ever get much done if you did." Glancing and the clock I winced. "Speaking of getting things done, you should probably go. As much as I don't want to go back to this stuff, it'll just be there tomorrow if I don't do it today."

I slipped out from under his arms and reached to open the door, but he followed behind me, catching my wrist in his hand and sliding up against me until my body was pressed into the wood. Trapped again.

"I'm sorry we don't have more time," he said, drawing his free hand softly down my hip. "I do like the idea of fucking you right here."

I could feel his excitement jutting into my lower back like hot metal. *Just a few inches lower and... Jesus Sophia, you're at work for fuck's sake.*

"This is my office, Sebastian," I said, trying to sound disapproving. I didn't do a very good job.

Dropping his head down he brushed his lips gently across the curve of my neck. "Well, I guess that wouldn't be proper," he whispered. "We'll just have to wait. Are you free tomorrow night?"

"I think so."

"Good. Then come to the Royal Bay hotel, room four hundred, at eight o'clock."

"Why?"

"You said you wanted to start learning more about what it is to submit, so tomorrow I'm going to show you. I think you'll find the experience... eye opening." Releasing me, he took a step back and opened the door himself. "Until then, Sophia." And before I could muster a reply, he was gone.

I stood for a few moments trying to collect myself, his

final words still ringing in my ears. Last time we'd been to-gether, in the heat of the moment, I'd said that maybe I wanted to be shown something more, but now he'd called me on it. *Well what the hell did you think he'd do, missionary with the lights off forever?*

In spite of what his dominance did to me, I still had my doubts. There was a big difference between a bit of playful restraint and the sorts of things he enjoyed. Was I really one of those girls?

Apparently I was about to find out.

Chapter 11

The next morning I took a long shower and then ventured outside to find breakfast, looking forward to doing not much of anything. At the start of the year, I promised myself I'd take one Sunday a month off from work entirely. When you work for a big law firm, it's easy to lose all sense of balance. One day a month doesn't sound like much, but it's enough to feel like you've still got some semblance of control over your life.

I brought a book along with me. I used to love to read in high school, but with free time an ever shrinking commodity, my 'to read' pile kept growing faster than I could get through it. Those Sundays were about the only time I ever made any progress.

I leafed through a few pages, trying my best to concentrate, but my mind kept wandering back to Sebastian. It annoyed me. I wasn't the sort of girl who pined after men. For me, sex had always been just another fun way to pass the time. Except with Sebastian, it was something more.

I wasn't sure whether to be afraid or excited about the coming evening. He'd given me almost no clues about what to expect.

Almost.

That morning, I'd received a text message.

I want you to bring something with you tonight. A length of red ribbon, about three feet long.

I didn't know why he couldn't simply bring it himself, but at least I had some vague idea of what lay in store. As far as I could see, a ribbon could only be to bind me, so I knew I'd likely be restrained, but beyond that I was still in the dark. I suspected that was part of the experience. On the plus side, I now had his number.

I finished my breakfast, stubbornly forcing my way through a few chapters, before throwing in the towel. It was time to go shopping.

There was a fabric store just a few blocks from my place. It was a little strange to be hunting for something so kinky in such a mundane location. Sebastian had turned a simple act of shopping into something decidedly more sordid. As I walked the aisles, I found myself staring at the ground, trying my best not to meet the eyes of the other customers. It didn't help that the store seemed to be entirely populated by little old ladies. There was no way they could know why I was really there, but nonetheless, after I paid, I hustled out of the store as quickly as possible, burying the ribbon in the bottom of my bag.

The rest of the day passed at a snail's pace. I tried to enjoy my time off by catching up on some television I'd DVR'd, but I found it difficult to concentrate. I was nervous and buzzing with energy.

Seven thirty rolled around, and after finding nothing that screamed 'kinky hotel rendezvous' in my wardrobe, I threw on the closest thing I had — a bright red cocktail dress that flared at the bottom — and headed for Circular Quay once more. I was probably going to be early, but I got the impression that tardiness would not go down well tonight.

The hotel was only a minute's walk from the restaurant we'd been at a few weeks back. *A girl could get used to this kind of living*, I thought, as I walked along the wharf.

There was a storm rolling in from the south. The sky looked angry, bruised purple and swollen with rain; sea spray rode on the whipping wind. People seemed to have wisely taken the hint and stayed inside. Aside from a few gallant restaurant patrons, the area was largely empty.

The Royal Bay was a deceptively simple looking building. Unlike most city hotels, it was only a few stories tall, and the warm glow that trickled from the windows lent it a homely feel. But sitting on the docks, just meters from the water, it was definitely a step up from the Holiday Inn.

"Hi," I said to the elegant middle aged woman behind the reception desk, "I'm here to meet a friend of mine. He said to come to room 400."

Her smile wavered for the briefest instant before returning to full strength. *Shit*. It hadn't occurred to me before, but sexed up like I was and visiting an unnamed male guest in his room alone, I realised what I looked like. *Yep, lawyer by day, high class hooker by night. That's me.* I could have laughed if I wasn't so mortified.

"Of course, just take the lift over there up to the fourth floor. It's the first door on your right."

"Great, thanks," I said, doing my best to keep my expression neutral. Trying to correct her seemed like more trouble than it was worth.

As the lift gradually ticked its way upwards, my nerves continued to build. In the past, my sexual encounters had always been vaguely predictable. Even when the relationship was new, I had some idea what to expect. It was still exciting, but there was a comfort in that familiarity. With Sebastian, however, I was going in blind. The whole thing was a mystery.

With my heart thumping, I made my way slowly down the corridor until I found the room. Taking a deep breath, I knocked twice. There was no response. I tried again with the same result. Had I gotten mixed up somehow? I was fairly sure I had the details right, but Sebastian didn't strike me as the flaky sort. Not knowing what else to do, I reached out tentatively and tugged on the heavy brass handle. The door fell open without a sound.

At first I thought I was in the wrong place. The lights were dim and the room appeared to be empty. I made my way inside, glancing around nervously like a girl in a horror film, but Sebastian was nowhere in sight.

The room was stunning. Decked in soft creams and whites, it offered the kind of open space most hotel guests could only dream of. In front of the giant king sized bed was a rolling window that opened directly on to a balcony, offering me a perfect panoramic view of the harbour. I gazed out for several seconds, watching a lightning bolt sear the sky a blinding white. The storm was drawing closer.

It wasn't until I spotted the envelope that I realised I hadn't messed up. It was resting on a chair in the middle of the room. *Oh so that's how we're playing is it?* A thrill surged through me as I approached.

There was something else sitting beside it; a strip of dark silk about as long as my arm. I picked it up, running its softness through my fingers and trying to imagine what it was for. More restraints? Or something more sensual?

The whole situation had a clandestine flavour to it. The dark room, the mysterious props, the secret instructions, they all made me feel incredibly naughty; like I was doing something much more illicit than simply having sex.

Written on the front of the envelope was a single word. 'Sophia'. There was something about the way he said my name that carried more weight than normal. I found myself hearing the word in his voice as I read it.

Inside was a simple set of instructions:

Sophia.

I'm happy you could join me. I think you will find tonight's activities most enlightening. To prepare, I want you to strip down to your panties. I trust you've discovered the blindfold I left for you. Once you're undressed, stand in the middle of the room. Place the ribbon I asked for on the bed next to you and then cover your eyes with the scarf. Wait like that until I come for you.

-S

I picked up the silk gingerly and held it up to the light. It was completely opaque. Once it was secured in place, I'd be utterly blind. He'd be able to do whatever he wanted and I wouldn't even see it coming. The thought made me tremble.

For the hundredth time I considered calling it off. He'd promised to leave me alone if that was what I wanted. All I had to do was turn around and walk out of the door and everything would return to normal.

Except I knew that wasn't really true.

The fire that had been lit inside me wouldn't just disappear. As frightening as the thought of presenting myself for him - exposed, blind and helpless - was, the alternative was even more so. For better or for worse, I had to know.

I began to strip off, folding my clothes neatly on the bed, before pulling the ribbon from my purse. Just looking at it again made me blush. Mindful of my skin, I'd bought the softest, lightest weave I could find. I played with it for a few seconds, winding it around my wrists, trying to imagine what it would feel like to be bound with it, before placing it on the bed too.

I fidgeted for a few more moments, ensuring everything was in order, but eventually I knew I was just making excuses. *Christ, here goes nothing.* Picking up the blindfold, I gazed at the room one final time, before slipping it over my head and knotting it at the back. Everything went black.

My pulse instantly quickened. Stripping off my clothes was something I did every day. It hadn't felt unusual. But the second I covered my eyes, I'd crossed a line into the unknown. Anything could happen now.

We'd begun.

I wasn't sure how long I stood there. Unable to see, time seemed to slow down. Every tiny hotel noise made me jump, and my mind was racing at a million miles a minute. Was he even coming at all? Maybe this was a test of some sort, to see how long I'd stay put. And if he did show, could I ask him to remove the blindfold? It really was terrifying, but that might be against the rules. I didn't even know what the rules were. Was I allowed to object? Oh Christ, what the hell was I doing?

"Hello Sophia," said a voice from behind me.

I squealed in surprise. He'd made no noise, nothing to give himself away. He must have been hiding in the bathroom the whole time, simply watching and letting me stew.

"Hello," I managed.

"I'm very happy you didn't have a change of heart. I think we're both going to have a lot of fun."

"That's easy for you to say, you're not naked and blind."

He laughed. "Believe me, that's just the beginning."

Being unable to see made me incredibly tense. I had no idea what was going on around me. He could have filled the room with a live studio audience and I wouldn't have known. My muscles were tight with anticipation, my body primed, although for what I wasn't certain.

His voice moved around me in a slow orbit. "I didn't really get to look at you the other night. Things were a little... rushed." I flinched as a hand trailed across my stomach, moving tantalisingly close to my breasts. "God, you're gorgeous. You look every bit as ravishing as I expected."

There was something vaguely dirty about being ogled so openly by a virtual stranger, but part of me was enjoying the attention.

"Are you afraid?"

I hesitated, before nodding slowly.

"That's okay. But don't worry; I'll take care of you." His voice was soft now, and it hovered just inches from my ear, the heat of his breath tickling my neck. "We both know you want this as much as I do. You need this."

And despite all of my apprehensions, I knew he was right. I couldn't help but think back to the previous night when he'd pinned me down. The surge of adrenaline, the primal need that had seized me in that moment, was unlike anything I'd experienced before. I had to have that again.

"I know," I said, my voice barely more than a whisper.

His hands continued to traverse my body, gently teasing my back, my arms, the slope of my neck. He never stayed in one spot for very long, pulling away before surprising me from another angle. Every stroke left my skin tingling. In the darkness, the tension inside me grew. On some level I knew this was part of the game, drawing things out until I was at breaking point, but it was hard to be rational in such a position.

Eventually I felt him slide in behind me. "Are you ready to begin?"

I swallowed loudly. *Last chance, Sophia.* But there was no

going back now.

"Yes."

"Good. Then put your hands behind your back, arms together."

Shaking, I did as I was told. I stood there, waiting to feel the soft touch of the ribbon, but instead something slick and fibrous wrapped around my wrists.

"What about the ribbon?" I blurted out.

"What about it?" he replied, looping and tying off the rope. "I never told you what it was for. Don't worry; we'll make good use of it later."

I took a deep breath and tried to rein in my pounding heartbeat. "This just isn't what I expected."

He gave a little laugh. "The game's no fun if it's predictable Sophia. And on that note..."

Before I knew what had happened, another length of rope was passed around my ankles. I cried out in alarm.

He worked quickly, and in a matter of seconds my legs were pinned as tightly as my arms. "Perfect," he said.

Instinctively I tried to wriggle free and nearly fell over in the process. A wave of panic washed over me. Trying to remain calm, I tested my bonds more carefully, but it quickly became obvious that there was no way out. The knots were firm, the pressure high enough to restrict mobility while not being painful or dangerous. He was clearly a master of his craft. I was held as thoroughly as any prisoner.

I came incredibly close to just ending it there. My safe word sat on the tip of my tongue. But I managed to subdue my fear. *Harden up, Sophia. This is what you signed up for, remember?*

I'd been expecting him to bind me. That was BDSM 101. I just hadn't realised how thorough he'd be. I'd had this image in my mind of being playfully tied down, able to escape but choosing not to. The reality was far more intense. I couldn't move. I might have been able to hop to the door given time, but I wasn't even sure what direction it was in, anymore. He could now do anything he wanted to me. I was totally at his mercy. It was as exhilarating as it was terrifying. Like the helplessness of the previous night, but a hundred times stronger.

The rope also surprised me. If the ribbon wasn't to hold me, then what was it for? What other surprises did he have planned? The only certainty I had left was that I was completely in his hands.

A low rumble resonated from his throat. "I haven't been able to stop thinking about this all day. Our night together was amazing, but it wasn't enough. I need to have you all. For tonight, Sophia, you're mine."

I nodded, not trusting myself to speak.

Hands encircled my body. "I want to hear you say it."

"I'm yours," I said, my voice quaking. There was a sense of finality about that statement that echoed within me long after the words were gone.

"Louder."

"I'm yours," I said more steadily.

He purred softly against my neck. "And I plan to take full advantage."

I suppressed a squeal as his powerful arms wrapped around me and scooped me into the air. For the second time in as many days he carried me across the room and lay me gently on the bed.

"God you look sexy, all tied up for me."

The mattress shifted under his weight as he straddled me, and then his lips were on mine. The kiss was strong and urgent, and my body turned to liquid beneath it. His tongue slipped into my mouth, exploring, teasing, exciting, while his hands found their way to my chest.

"I've been waiting to play with these since the first time I saw you," he said, squeezing my breasts gently. Wrapping his lips around one nipple, he flicked his tongue over the hardened peak before circling the areola lazily. I arched beneath him, stretching against my bonds, powerless to the pleasure that was coursing through me.

Unlike our last encounter, he took his time. He worked his way down slowly, stroking and kissing every part of me as if claiming uncharted territory. Places that had never seemed sexy to me lit up under his touch, leaving me a trembling, panting mess.

By the time he reached the top of my panties, I was soaking wet. Every touch of his tongue seemed like a promise.

"Fuck, you smell so good," he said, his lips softly caressing my thighs. "But tonight you have to earn that kind of pleasure. From now on, you aren't allowed to come until I say so. Understand? Your orgasms are mine."

I moaned in protest.

"Good things come to those who wait," he chided. "Right now I want to see your ass."

He climbed off me, slid his hands underneath my body and turned me over. With my wrists bound behind me, I had nothing to rest on at the front, which left me kneeling at an angle, my head resting on a pillow and my bottom jutting out into the air.

He made an appreciative sound. "Fuck, it's perfect," he said, stroking me roughly. There was something in the way he touched me there that made my stomach tighten. It conjured memories of Hannah bent over the desk awaiting her punishment. I had an uneasy feeling I knew what came next.

"You know, we still haven't dealt with your little penchant for teasing," he said, as if on cue, punctuating the statement with a single gentle smack.

I tried to recoil, but there was nowhere to go. "I'm not sure... I mean..." but I couldn't get the words out. The conservative part of my mind was screaming at the indecency of what was about to happen, but the deeper I went down the rabbit hole, the more muffled that voice got. The whole thing felt unavoidable. There I was, bound, bent and blindfolded in front of a man I barely knew, my skin hot, my body flushed with hormones. He'd told me he'd stop if I gave the word, but at that point I wasn't really sure if that was true. What was scarier was that I didn't know if I wanted him to.

"Shh, shh," he said. "It's your first time. I'll be gentle."

Before I could complain, he swept me up in his arms again and spun me around until I came to rest over his knee. The ease with which he could manipulate me was a huge turn on. Even if I wasn't bound, I couldn't have stopped him.

He tugged my panties together in the middle, exposing more of my skin to the air. "Now this will sting at first. Give it a chance. Try to embrace it. Pain and pleasure are closer than most people realise." He rubbed my ass tenderly. "Are you ready?"

I quivered. I didn't know if I'd ever be ready. But nonetheless I found myself nodding.

With my eyes covered, I couldn't even see it coming. One second his hand was resting lightly against me, the next it was crashing into my left cheek. The pain was hot and sharp and instant, like a tiny explosion against my skin. I grunted through gritted teeth.

The blows began to fall in a steady rhythm. There was no conversation, just the meaty crack of flesh on flesh. At first, I felt nothing but pain. My skin burned under the onslaught, and every slap seemed to sting a little more than the last.

But as my body adjusted, a strange sense of peace began to settle over me. Each smack was as inevitable as the last, so rather than shy away, I did as he'd suggested. I began to embrace them. They still stung on a physical level, but gradually I began to realise that there was more to the experience than just pain.

My skin had grown more sensitive than I'd ever thought possible, and every touch sent waves of sensation rolling through me. Pain and pleasure wound themselves together, until it was difficult to see where one ended and the other began. It was an exhilarating combination.

There was also something incredibly erotic about being turned over Sebastian's knee, having him do those things to me. With the ropes, I'd given control over to him, and now he was exercising it. The intense display of dominance I'd witnessed while crouched in the wardrobe was now directed at me. And it felt fantastic. The simple satisfaction of complete submission.

Again, Sebastian showed an uncanny ability to read me. "You see? It feels good doesn't it?"

"Yes," I replied. And I meant it.

Feeling more confident, I began to experiment. I shifted against him, lining my crotch up with the curve of his thigh. The next blow caused them to grind together, chasing the pain with a tremor of ecstasy. My cries began to dissolve into moans as the line blurred even further.

With the last of my resistance bleeding away, everything began to take on a new dimension. The ropes that I'd struggled so hard against became exciting in their strength. My blindness, once terrifying, now amplified every sensation. I was no longer afraid to discover what wicked secrets Sebastian had planned; I was excited.

He paused and ran his hands lightly over my burning flesh, soothing it in small circles. "Mmm, cherry red. I love a good spanking. I'm not really much of a sadist as far as doms go — whips and chemicals are a bit beyond me — but the sight of a girl bent over my knee, red ass in the air, just drives me wild."

His fingers slid down and slipped inside my panties, parting them to one side, causing me to moan in anticipation. "It looks like I'm not the only one who enjoyed that," he said, running his fingers slowly up my slit. "It's a pity you can't feel how wet you are for yourself. But I think I can do one better."

There was a pulling sensation against my legs and a loud rip. He'd torn my panties free! I opened my mouth to object, but before I got out so much as a word, he crammed them between my lips.

"You were wondering what the ribbon was for," he said, as I felt something soft loop around my head. "Well now you know. I want you to taste yourself, to taste how wet I made you. I want you to understand how much you enjoyed getting bound and spanked."

The scent of my arousal was almost overpowering. It filled my nostrils and rolled down my throat. He was right; I'd never been so turned on before.

He tied the ribbon off behind my head. "Perfect."

With the gag in place, my helplessness grew. One by one, my freedoms were being stolen away. I couldn't move, I couldn't see, and now I couldn't even talk properly. He'd reduced me to little more than a life-sized doll that he could pose and play with however he wished.

"Seeing as your mouth is currently occupied, if you want me to stop at any point, clap your hands. Understand?"

It hadn't occurred to me that my safe word would be useless, but once again his experience shone through. I nodded.

"Excellent. You know, you're doing so well, I think you've earned a reward."

I nodded again eagerly. My whole body ached for him,

begging to be satisfied.

For a few agonising seconds nothing happened. I began to think maybe he had another surprise in store, but then his finger was pushing into me. I moaned into the gag.

"Fuck, you're so wet for me," he said, slipping past my folds with liquid smoothness. "I love that I can do this to you. You have no idea how hard it makes me, seeing you like this."

I made a noise, something between a cry and a plea. His finger felt amazing, but it wasn't enough. I needed more. I bucked against him, pushing him deeper, and he responded, siding in to the lowest knuckle and crooking his finger in a 'come hither' gesture that made my insides melt.

"God, you're greedy tonight aren't you? Well, I've never been one to turn down an invitation." A second finger joined the first, stretching me wider, while the rough pad of his thumb found my clit and began to work it in slow circles.

I knew I wouldn't last long. The night's intricate, sensuous torture had my body humming just millimetres below the edge. I braced myself against his legs, preparing for that sweet release to come tearing through me.

But right as I was on the brink, he pulled away.

"Now, now," he said over my wordless protests, "remember what I said earlier? You can't come without permission. Your orgasms are mine."

He set me down on my knees on the bed. There was a rustling of material, but I barely noticed, too focused on the pleasure inside me that was slowly ebbing away. I'd been so close!

"You know with a lot of practice, I may be able to teach you to come for me on command," he said, stroking my back soothingly. "I gave one girl a screaming orgasm in a crowded mall with just simple instructions. It's amazing what people are capable of when they truly surrender themselves."

It sounded ridiculous. Orgasms were hard enough to achieve the regular way. I doubted any level of submission would change that.

"I know you probably don't believe me. It's true, you're a long way from being able to do that, but you might be closer than you think."

His fingers wrapped tightly around my hips as he leaned in close. "Now I want you to come for me," he growled, and with a single violent thrust he rammed his cock inside me.

The effect was instantaneous. My orgasm roared back to life, exploding through my body in a surge of muscle curling warmth. The breath drained from my lungs as my pussy clenched tight around his hardness, until I was sure I must be hurting him. It was the most intense orgasm of my life.

"You see, you might be capable of more than you think."

As my body convulsed one final time, I couldn't help but agree. I had a lot to learn about myself.

"I'm not done with you yet," he said. "Christ, you feel good. You're wet enough to take all of me already." To prove his point he thrust himself deep, burying his shaft all the way to the root. I moaned with the size of him.

With no need to ease into it, the animal took over. He drove himself into me with a bestial urgency. One hand fell onto my back, pushing me into the bed, while the other seized my shoulder, grinding me against him in time with his thrusts.

I had never felt so utterly possessed before. In that moment, bound and held, I was his, every part of me, to tease and touch and fuck as he wished. I wasn't sure I'd ever get enough of that feeling.

His pace slowed and I felt his hand slide up to the back of my head.

"I think it's time to remove these," he said, fingering the

blindfold and ribbon. "I want you to see how you look trussed up for me. I want you to watch me as I fuck you."

He gave a tug and they both fell to the floor. The room sprang into view. It was strange being able to see again. For a second I merely blinked, struggling to get my bearings. Then my eyes fell on the mirror that occupied the far wall.

"You see now what you've let me do to you?" he asked. "And this is just the beginning. I can show you a whole world of pleasure just like this."

The image of my bound body being mounted from behind was almost too much. Sebastian had shed his clothes. He stood behind me naked, taut, and glistening with sweat. A pure, primal picture of masculinity. It was the first time I'd seen him fully undressed. There was barely an ounce of fat on him. From his perfectly toned biceps to his powerful chest to the magnificent V of muscle that hugged his pelvis, the sight of him took my breath away.

I watched with wild eyes as that magnificent cock disappeared inside me, his body quivering with barely restrained ferocity. My ass glowed red in the lamplight, still raw from our earlier games, and every thrust sent a little sting coursing through me, as his stomach brushed that tender skin.

"Yes," I moaned, "I want you to show me."

Shifting angles, he brought his hand up to my ass, his fingers playing gently across the delicate, rosy ring at the centre. Under other circumstances I'd probably have been shocked by that alien sensation, but as excited as I was, I took it in stride.

"Have you ever let a man fuck you here?" he asked, lubing himself with my juices and pushing just the tiniest way inside me. I felt an unexpected thread of pleasure shoot through me.

"No," I replied. "I've done a little anal play, but it was a long time ago."

"Then we'll go slow," he said. "But I want to have you there eventually. I want to have you everywhere, Sophia. Every part of you is mine." There was no question in his voice, and I didn't object. I knew it was true. Besides, of all the things I'd let him do, this seemed almost tame by comparison.

His breathing began to quicken. I could hear it in his sounds, those raw, animal grunts; he was getting close.

"I want you to come with me, Sophia. I want to feel you tighten around me as I blow inside you."

"Oh god, oh fuck," I cried, already well past the point of no return.

"Now Sophia, I'm coming!"

I'd always thought simultaneous orgasms were a phenomenon reserved for porn and cheap romance novels, but Sebastian seemed to be making it a mission to show me how much I didn't know. We rocked together, our bodies writhing in ecstatic unison as our climaxes took hold. There was an incredible sense of connection in that moment, like we were sharing one orgasm that burst outward into both of us. He buried himself inside me almost to the point of pain, and I pushed back, my whole body clenching and tingling.

When it was over, we both fell boneless and breathless to the bed. For a while we just dozed in silence, content to bask in the glow of what had just happened. It seemed like I should say something, but I wasn't sure I could put into words what I was feeling at that moment.

My arms and legs were still bound, but I didn't mind. Lying there with one of his powerful arms wrapped around me, I felt completely safe.

"That was wonderful," he said, sometime later.

I nodded and let out a little sigh.

He reached up and began to unbind me. "You're a natural submissive, you know that? I know you were afraid, but once

117

we began, you were perfect."

"I didn't know being tied up was considered a skill."

He laughed. It was a big, boisterous sound that shook the bed beneath me. "Don't think of it as a skill. Think of it as a mindset. It takes a lot of courage to give yourself to someone like that. Not everyone can do it."

"I guess so." A shiver rolled down my spine as I thought back on all the things I'd just let him do. "To be honest, it wasn't really what I was expecting," I continued. "Even after the other night, part of me still thought it would feel... wrong somehow. Like I was being exploited."

He nodded slowly. "Society has a lot of misconceptions about what we do. That's one of the big ones. Don't get me wrong, there are plenty of guys out there who use it as an excuse to abuse women, but that's not what submission is really about. A true dom only has as much control as their partner allows. It's a gift given from one person to another, and don't think for one second I'm not thankful for that."

"Well, you're welcome," I replied, feeling a little bewildered by his words. "I hadn't really thought of it that way before, but it makes me feel better knowing you're not just waiting for the right moment to chain me to the bed and never let me leave."

"Only if you give me permission," he said with a grin.

"I'll keep that in mind."

A few minutes later, he drifted off. I tried to join him, but sleep wouldn't come. My mind was spinning, still trying to process all the new sensations and emotions that were swirling inside me.

I no longer had any doubt that Sebastian was right. I was a submissive. The way my body turned to hot clay in his hands was proof enough of that. But I had to be careful. I couldn't let myself get in too deep. It was hard not to feel some kind of connection when you gave yourself to somebody so completely like that, but the fact was that this was just business as usual for him. Something fun to pass the time. Letting myself believe it was anything else was dangerous. All I could do was enjoy it for what it was.

After another twenty minutes of tossing and turning, I decided that maybe I needed a little help shutting down. Slipping out from under the covers I headed over to the mini bar. The tiny bottle of champagne was thirty dollars, but given the rate for the room was almost certainly more than my monthly rent, I figured Sebastian wouldn't mind.

I'd been so drained by what we'd done, I'd had no time to look at the aftermath, but standing there in the moonlight, gazing at the scattered clothing, underwear, and kinky paraphernalia that littered the floor, I couldn't help but smile. If anyone were to burst in at that moment they'd have no trouble guessing what we'd been up to.

Surveying the room really highlighted how impressive it was. I made pretty good money, and was no stranger to splurging on the occasional fancy hotel when I felt like a treat, but this was unlike anything I'd ever seen. It made me wonder again about the man I'd tangled myself up with. I knew that kind of wanton disregard for money was common amongst the super-rich, and although I'd had my suspicions, he'd had answers to all of my questions. It should have been enough, but I still couldn't shake the feeling that there was something more to him than that.

Then again, perhaps I was just being paranoid. I had no illusions about my trust issues, and I didn't put it past my subconscious to try and sabotage a good thing before it could hurt me.

My reverie was interrupted by a buzzing sound behind me. Turning, I discovered that Sebastian had left his phone on the counter above the bar. The screen was lit up with a text message that had just arrived. My eyes ran over it before I could stop them. It took me a few seconds to process what I saw.

His wallpaper was a picture of a girl. Slim and blonde with a stunningly beautiful face, she wore one of those serene smiles that screams 'young and in love.' I felt a pang of jealousy gazing at those perfect features.

But it was the text message that had just arrived which really caught my eye.

Still thinking of you. Call me.

The number was not a listed contact, but there was an accompanying attachment. With shaking fingers I scooped it up and tapped the screen to open it, and a naked female body appeared before me. Her head wasn't visible, but her open legs and seductive pose left little doubt as to her intentions.

Nausea twisted my stomach, and the phone fell from my hand. I couldn't believe it. I'd just let Sebastian tie me up and do unspeakable things to me, and he'd been lying all along. My first instinct had been right. He wasn't any different, just another guy who would say and do whatever it took to get a girl into bed, and I'd fallen for it hook line and sinker. Who knew how many other women there were right now.

I suddenly felt dirty. Used. Nothing more than another water cooler story for the office next week.

Before I knew it, I was out the door, and then stumbling through the lobby. There was a different woman behind the counter now, younger and kinder looking. She gave me a sympathetic smile as I stormed past. It didn't surprise me. I was probably quite a sight. With my hair a mess, my makeup smeared, and my dress unfastened, I probably looked the epitome of a jilted lover.

Outside the storm had passed, leaving the ground slick and the air sharp. I wrapped my arms around myself to try and ward off the chill. It was late and I was a long way from my house, but I stubbornly ignored the taxis driving past. I couldn't stomach the idea of being around anyone at that moment.

The entire way home one thought just kept playing through my mind. *How could I have been so stupid?*

Book Two: Lockout

Chapter 1

The morning after fleeing the hotel I woke, bleary eyed and exhausted, to the sound of my phone buzzing in my purse. When I'd finally found my way home it had been well after midnight and in spite of everything that had happened, I'd passed out almost instantly. A quick look at the clock told me I'd overslept.

I slipped my phone from my bag just as the ringing stopped.

12 missed calls.

I didn't even have to look at the caller ID. There was only one person who had any reason to ring that many times. I was vaguely surprised that Sebastian was so frantic. I'd figured that since the game was up, he'd admit defeat and take the opportunity to slink away quietly, but for some reason he seemed intent on fighting it out.

A night's sleep had done little to temper my anger. I hate being lied to. A tiny part of me thought that perhaps I'd over-reacted, that I should have given him a chance to explain, but my past mistakes were constantly looming in my mind. I'd seen signs before and I'd turned a blind eye. I wouldn't fall into that trap again.

The phone started ringing again before I even made it to

the shower. Flicking it to silent, I shoved it into my purse. I figured if I ignored him for long enough he'd eventually get the message. But I was wrong. As I was trotting out the door, I felt it vibrating against my side. And again, three minutes later, in the taxi. Twelve calls became twenty.

There was only so much I could take.

"What?" I said, answering gruffly.

"Sophia, thank god. I've been calling all morning."

"Really? I hadn't noticed."

"I didn't know what else to do. What the hell happened to you? Why did you run off?" He sounded breathless and there was a faint crack running through his voice that I'd never heard before.

"What do you care? You got what you wanted. And judging by that text message, you don't need me anymore."

"Text messa... oh Christ. Why were you looking through my phone?"

"I wasn't. I got up to get a drink and it went off behind me. Bad luck for you, hey? You nearly got away with it."

"Listen, it's not what you think—"

"Save it. Look, Sebastian, this whole thing was a mistake. I should have trusted my gut to begin with. I need you to stop calling. This is my work number and I can't have you tying up the line all day." It was a lie, but a believable one.

"Please, if you just let me come and see you for five minutes I can explain." If I didn't know better I'd have said he almost sounded desperate. It was nearly enough. Even through the phone I could feel him pulling at me like gravity. The desire to see him again was almost overpowering. But I closed my eyes and steeled myself.

"So you can sweet talk me again? No thanks. I'm done listening to your lies. Say hi to her for me."

"But, Sophia—"

"Goodbye."

I mashed the end call button with more vehemence than necessary. I half expected him to ring back again, but the phone remained silent.

I should have felt happy, or at least relieved, but instead I just found myself second guessing my decision. It didn't make any sense. I barely knew Sebastian. I should have been able to cut him free without breaking a sweat. But try as I might, I couldn't ignore the strange sense of loss that was forming like a grey puddle in my stomach.

As the cab pulled up to my office, I did my best to compose myself. I couldn't afford to be distracted today. After my day off, I knew my inbox would be dangerously full, and it was going to take at least an hour just to sort through.

The rest of the morning was a blur of meetings, telephone calls, and emails. Immersed in work, Sebastian gradually slipped to the back of my mind. He was still there, like a niggling splinter, but I managed to ignore him and focus on the task at hand.

It was the sort of day that seems like it will never quite end. Calls streamed in one after the other, partners who wanted information tracked down or clients needing documents drafted. My original day's work fell to the wayside as I madly attempted to juggle the new requests that were flowing in faster than I could deal with them.

It was hectic, but I have to admit there's a certain thrill to be had when you're under the gun like that. The higher the pressure, the more I enjoy my job. It's an art balancing so many tasks at once, and it's an art I excel at.

By the time the dust began to settle, it was ten o'clock. Somehow, I'd finished everything that needed doing. My stomach rumbled as I stepped out onto the street, reminding me exactly how long ago my last meal had been. There hadn't been time for such trivial things as dinner.

After wolfing down a Pad Thai from a nearby restaurant, I flopped into a cab and headed home. As the afternoon's adrenaline began to fade, I realised how wiped out I was. My fitful night's sleep and twelve hour day were catching up with me, and I still ached in several places from Sebastian's games.

Sebastian.

He hadn't called again. I didn't know if I was pleased or frustrated by that. Knowing the effect he had on me, it was probably for the best. Who knew what other lies he might have spun if given the chance. This way I could put him out of my mind and focus on what was important.

However, when the car pulled up outside my house, that plan promptly went to shit. Standing on the front porch, looking as breathtaking as ever, was the man himself.

I cursed under my breath. He couldn't have chosen a worse time. My hormones put me at enough of a disadvantage when talking to him without adding tiredness to the equation. But there was no way to avoid him now.

"Sophia," he said, as I stepped out onto the footpath. His usual look of serene confidence was gone, replaced by something darker and more drawn.

"What are you doing here, Sebastian? It's ten thirty at night."

"You said not to call, and I didn't want to upset you any more."

"So, what, you've just been waiting for me to get home?"

He nodded.

"How long have you been standing there?"

He shrugged. "I'm not sure. A few hours. It's not important. I wanted to speak to you."

It was a strangely touching gesture. But my resolve held. "Well, I don't want to speak to you."

I took a step towards my door, but he slid in front of me, blocking my path. "Five minutes, Sophia. That's all I ask. Hear me out, and if you don't believe me, I'll leave you alone forever."

I knew from past experience how persistent he was. He wouldn't give up until I did as he wanted. I sighed. "Fine. Get on with it."

He nodded. "Thank you. Look, I'm sorry you saw what you saw, and I completely understand why you reacted the way you did. But I promise I haven't told any lies."

I raised my eyebrows and gestured for him to continue.

"That picture; it was from Hannah." I started to object, but he cut me off. "I ended things with her just like I said I had. I swear it. I had her transferred to someone else in the company, to avoid any professional conflict. I even blocked her old phone number. I did everything in my power to cut her off."

I snorted. "And so her revenge is to send you erotic photos of herself?"

He licked his lips. "She didn't take the news very well. To be honest, I've got several of those messages over the last few weeks. Judging by some of the things she's written, she thinks she can win me back, but I promise you that won't happen."

I stared at him, unsure what to think. It did make sense. I'd seen the way she looked at him. And at me, for that matter. But the best lies were always based on the truth.

"What about the girl on your wallpaper?" I asked.

He froze. For a brief moment, a look of pain crossed his face. It was gone almost as soon as it arrived, but there was no doubt I'd touched a nerve. "I didn't realise you'd seen that." He gave a small shake of his head. "She's an old flame. I'd rather not go into detail, but she's not in the picture anymore, I promise. The photo is just something to remember her by."

So he hadn't always been the uncompromising player he was now. Someone had gotten through those walls once. Interesting.

I weighed his defence. It sounded genuine, but that was no guarantee. I'd been lied to in the past, lied to by men with sincere eyes and silver tongues. "I'm not sure if I believe you."

He began pacing. "Why would I lie? You think I'm so hard up I need to trick girls into coming to bed with me? You think I stand on porches for hours on end on the off chance it might get me laid?"

He had a point. If he was trying to deceive me, he was going to an inordinate amount of effort. "I don't know what I think anymore." I closed my eyes and shook my head. "Why me? I mean, why go to all this effort for me? You just said it yourself, you're not exactly lacking feminine attention. Hell, if what you're saying is true, Hannah would basically do anything you asked."

He exhaled heavily. "I don't know. There's something about you Sophia. I can't explain it, but the moment I saw you at our party I knew I had to have you. And after last night..." He paused, as if gathering his thoughts. "The way you taste, the way you smell, the feeling of your body underneath mine; I'm not ready to give that up."

Swallowing suddenly became difficult. In spite of all my emotional turmoil, once again he'd managed to flick that switch inside me. I swear I felt the space between us crackle to life.

"I just don't kno—" I began, but the words died on my tongue as he took two big strides towards me and seized my hands in his. With our chests just inches from each other, I was once again reminded of how big he was. His towering frame dwarfed mine, that potent magnetism washing over me like a warm breeze.

"Sophia, listen to me. Last night, the things we did, the ropes, the blindfold; that takes an immense level of trust. You put yourself totally in my hands. Why can't you extend me the same trust now?"

And although I hadn't thought of it that way at the time, I realised he was right. I couldn't have done those things if I didn't trust him. Sure, I'd been afraid, but it was fear of pain, fear of the unknown, and in spite of that fear, I'd given myself to him anyway, trusting that he'd take care of me.

I realised then that I was afraid of something else too. I was afraid that Sebastian would get in his car and drive off and I'd never see him again. I didn't know why, but that fear was worse than anything I'd felt last night.

"Okay," I said quietly.

"You believe me?" The relief on his face was almost palpable.

I nodded slowly. I felt like an idiot. "I'm sorry. I should have given you a chance to explain. I don't have the best history when it comes to judging men. These days I tend to err on the side of caution... or possibly paranoia."

He looked like he wanted more details, but thankfully he didn't ask. I didn't want to have that conversation now. Later maybe, but not now. I'd already exposed him to enough of my crazy for one week. "There's nothing wrong with a little paranoia," he said instead, shooting me a smile. "It'll help keep me on my toes."

"Thanks, but I still feel stupid."

He took my hand. "Don't. I understand I'm not the easiest man to trust. I can't promise you much, Sophia, but I promise I'll never lie to you."

"That's all I can ask."

For a few seconds, I simply stood staring up into his eyes. I still didn't really understand what had transpired between us. For someone so intent on keeping his distance, the lengths he'd gone to seemed excessive. He was a puzzle, and despite my best efforts, it looked like I'd get a little more time to solve him after all.

"You want to come in for a drink?" I asked, flashing my best provocative smile. I could feel the makings of a killer makeup sex session brewing inside me. "Maybe I can find a way to make it up to you."

He grimaced. "I wish I could, but I actually have a trip to take. Something unfortunate has happened with one of our projects, and I'm being sent down to Melbourne to sort it out."

"You can't even spare twenty minutes?" I asked, running my hand slowly down his chest.

He closed his eyes and drew a slow breath. I could almost feel the battle that was being waged inside him. "Sorry, but the plane is sitting waiting on the tarmac right now."

I rocked back in disbelief. "You held up a plane to come and talk to me?"

He shrugged. "It's our company plane, and it was only for a few hours. I didn't like the thought of leaving knowing you were upset with me."

"Well, you sure know how to make a girl feel special," I said with a laugh. "When will you be back?"

"I'm not sure. Could be a few days, could be a few weeks."

I tried my best to hide my disappointment. "Okay. Stay safe."

"I'll try." He turned and began to make his way down to the waiting car. "And Sophia, don't worry. I have a few ideas about how you can make it up to me. I'll be in touch."

There was something wicked in his smile that made the muscles between my legs clench. I had the sneaking suspicion

that even from across the country, the sexy games would continue.

Chapter 2

The rest of the week passed in a familiar rhythm. It turned out that Monday's flurry of work was a sign of things to come. The phone just wouldn't stop ringing. I tried my best to get my other jobs done quickly, hoping some Wrights work would come my way, but the deluge of menial tasks simply wouldn't let up. It was frustrating. Other associates were across the hall doing something really meaningful, and I was stuck drafting settlement agreements for petty insurance claims and cleaning up my colleagues' contracts.

In spite of my busyness, Sebastian was never far from my mind. It was strange. I felt like we'd known each other a lot longer than a few weeks. It irked me to admit, but I realised that I missed him.

His text messages certainly didn't help. They started innocently enough.

Sebastian: I'm sorry I had to leave the other night. I wanted to stay, but my hands were tied.

Sophia: That's alright. I know how it is. Is everything okay down there?

Sebastian: Not really. We've had some major setbacks. Hopefully I can get things back on track soon though. I'm already sick of being stuck down here.

I liked that he was thinking of me even when he was busy. It seemed like our argument in my office had done some good.

But as usual with Sebastian, things quickly grew hotter. I started one morning with this exchange.

Sebastian: You know, I haven't been able to get our last night together out of my head.

Sophia: Oh? =)

Sebastian: I can't wait to do that to you again. I can't wait to tie you up and fuck you until you can't even speak anymore.

Sophia: So hurry up and get back here!

Sebastian: Haha. Patience. Sometimes a little wait does a lot of good. I'm enjoying thinking of all the things I'm still yet to do to you. You have no idea how hard I'm going to make you come.

Yeah. How the hell is a girl meant to function with messages like that in her inbox?

They didn't come too often, but they were just frequent enough to leave my libido on constant simmer. To make matters worse, no matter how hot I got, I wasn't allowed to relieve myself. He'd made it very clear that was against the rules. Several nights when I was nearly at breaking point, I considered doing it anyway, but something stopped me. *He'd know. Somehow, he'd know.* And so I powered on and did my best to ignore it.

Because of the sheer volume of work coming in, I spent the entire weekend at the office. There were a few less people around then, and so some more meaty jobs trickled down my way, but by Monday they'd all dried up again. Finally I decided I'd had enough of sitting on the bench.

"Ernest, have you got a minute?" I said, knocking on my boss's door.

"Sophia, sure. Come in."

I shut the door behind me and took a seat in front of the desk. I never quite knew what to make of my boss. A slim, balding man of about fifty, he constantly wore a harried look, as though he were just an instant from being overwhelmed by it all. He was the law firm equivalent of middle management; reasonably competent, but totally unambitious. He'd been a partner at the firm for the last twenty years, but never seemed to care about moving any higher than that.

He'd always seemed to like me, which is why I felt comfortable going to him. His relatively lowly position meant he couldn't intervene directly to change Alan's orders, but he still held more sway than I did. If he pushed hard enough, he might be able to make something happen. Besides, I was desperate.

"I just wanted to talk to you about the Wrights case."

His eyes brightened. "It's fascinating isn't it? A real coup for us."

"I wouldn't know. I've basically done nothing but pick up the slack for the last week."

He looked a little uncomfortable. "Oh now, I'm sure that's not true."

"It is true. You know what I spent the morning doing? Cross referencing Nick and Will's notes for that fraud case."

He licked his lips. "Well, that kind of thing needs to be

done too. You know how it is, you don't always get to pick and choose what you do. Work gets given to the people best suited to the task."

"Sorry, but that's bullshit, Ernest. I'm one of the best associates on this floor and you know it. So why aren't I being allowed to help?"

His mouth curled into a sympathetic smile. "I'm not coordinating this case, Sophia. Believe me, if I were you'd be at the top of the list."

I slumped deeper into my chair. That was pretty much the response I'd been expecting. "Okay, let me ask you a different question then. Do you have any idea why Alan dislikes me so much?"

"Alan doesn't dislike you. He's just very... particular about how he does things." It was an incredibly diplomatic way of saying that he played favourites.

"Well I wish he'd be particular in my direction occasionally. Seriously, I bust my ass for this company, Ernest, and lately I get nothing in return."

He gazed at me for several seconds. "Look, how about this. I'll make some calls and see if I can't call in a few favours. But in the meantime I need you to ride this one out. If you kick up too much of a fuss you might piss off the wrong people. You know how this place is."

I felt a glimmer of hope. "That would be great, Ernest. Thanks." It probably wouldn't do much good, but it was better than nothing. "Now if you'll excuse me, I better get back to it. I think there's a child in my office who needs his school absence note drafted."

He chuckled. "Good luck with that."

Well, I'd played my hand. All I could do now was wait.

"It's something," said Ruth, when I called her a few hours later.

"Yeah. I don't think it'll amount to much though." I let out a heavy sigh. "Maybe it's just the girl factor. Maybe I need to suck it up and find a nice boutique firm somewhere where a cock isn't considered mandatory equipment for success."

"Hey, there's always a job for you here. Helping unhappy couples tear each other apart financially is rewarding in its own way."

"I'll keep that in mind," I said with a laugh, although I knew that wasn't really me. I could never do what Ruth did. It was a little too daytime chat-show for me.

"So how are things with your mystery man?" she asked. I swear I could hear her grin travelling down the phone line.

"Okay. Actually to be honest, I had a bit of a freak out, but it turned out I was just being an idiot. We talked it through, and things are good now... I think."

"You think?"

"Well, he had to fly to Melbourne for work the day we made up. We've texted a little, but I haven't actually seen him since then."

"Ah bummer. Oh well, absence makes the heart grow fonder and all that crap."

"It's not his heart I'm interested in."

She laughed. "Ah, well it can make that grow fonder too. Trust me."

I didn't sleep well that night, and the next morning I arrived at work in a foul mood. However, it didn't last long. Resting in the centre of my desk when I walked into my office was a neatly wrapped box. There was no postage stamp or delivery address. Instead, on the face, in elegant, flowing script, was a single word. *Sophia*. My heart leapt. I'd only seen that handwriting once before, in the Royal Bay, but everything about that night was etched permanently into my brain.

I walked over and picked it up, weighing it in my hands.

It wasn't particularly heavy, but there was something solid within. Shutting the door to protect from wandering eyes, I sat down at my desk and slowly peeled away the ribbon.

Rather than containing the object itself, inside the first box was another box. On top rested a note. I found myself grinning. Games within games. That was so like him.

Dear Sophia.

I'm sorry I've been gone so long. Things here are still messy and I have to stay until we can sort them out. Please forgive me.

I know I promised you a way to make up for the other day, and as much as I would like that to involve me being inside you, it will still be a few days until I return. Fortunately, I've come up with an alternative that I think you're going to enjoy.

Today I have a task for you. After you finish reading this note, I want you to sneak off into the bathroom, lock yourself in one of the cubicles, and masturbate through your panties. Play as long as you want, but our rules still stand: you're forbidden to come. Take the second box with you. When you're done, open it. There will be further instructions within. Have fun.

-S

A tingle rolled through me as I read. The request was both exciting and risky. Aside from Sebastian's kiss the other week, I'd never so much as fooled around in the office before. My job was just too important to me, and I didn't want to do anything that could come back to bite me. But the fact that Sebastian had commanded me to do it made it much more alluring. I could hear the words in his voice as I read, that strong, implacable tone that seemed impossible to resist. It was as though he was right behind me, leaning over my shoulder, strong hands lightly caressing my body as he whispered in my ear. And I felt compelled to do as I was told.

Glancing out into the corridor I saw that the building was still largely empty. Most days I tried to arrive before the bulk of my colleagues; I found that first hour of silence before the daily office buzz began was my most productive. And at that moment, it provided the perfect cover. Picking up the smaller box, I slipped casually out the door and headed for the ladies' room.

I passed a few other early-birds as I went, nodding greetings and trying to look calm. Were their smiles just friendly, or was there something smug behind them? It seemed impossible, but I couldn't shake the feeling that they knew what I was up to. It was like the fabric store all over again. I knew it was all part of Sebastian's game, but that didn't make it any easier. I clutched the box to my chest and began to walk faster, my cheeks burning with embarrassment, or excitement, or some baffling combination of the two. I'd never thought of the threat of being exposed as appealing before, but I was quickly learning that there was something strangely thrilling in that fear.

I made it to the bathroom without anyone crying foul and slipped into a cubicle with a sigh. Giving my heart a moment to settle, I sat on the toilet seat and inspected the smaller box. It was made from the same dark cardboard as the larger one, and as I tilted it from side to side, I could feel the object inside sliding around through the thin walls. Like a child on Christmas day, I began to try and guess what lay within. Judging by his request, it was probably something sexy, maybe a vibrator? Or something I might have to wear? I was incredibly curious. It took a lot of restraint not to simply tear the lid off then and there. But he'd asked me to wait, and so I did.

Instead, I reached down and hiked up my skirt, exposing my intricate pair of black lace panties. Like most girls, my underwear collection ranged from stuff I didn't wear out of the house to a few Victoria's Secret pieces I saved for special occasions. Normally for work I wore something in between, but since meeting Sebastian, my sexier pieces had been getting all the attention. As much as I hated the idea of grooming to please a guy, with his spontaneous appearances and unconventional approach, I never knew when I might need to look my best.

Masturbate through your panties. It seemed like an odd request, but I'd already learned that with Sebastian, the specifics were often important.

After listening once more to make sure there was nobody else hidden away in another cubicle, I reached out and ran a hand tentatively across my shrouded sex. Even through my underwear, I could feel how turned on I was. My juices had already begun seeping through the sheer cloth. I had no idea how he could do that to me with a simple letter, but I wasn't about to waste time considering it any further.

I began to stroke myself in a slow, steady rhythm. I was no stranger to a little fun for one. When you work the kind of hours I do, you just don't have time to seek out the real thing as often as you'd like. But this was a totally new experience. Being in a public place gave it a frenetic edge that seemed to heighten every sensation. At any moment, one of my workmates could burst in and catch me in the act. After just a minute, my heart was thundering in my chest and I could taste something sharp on my tongue.

It felt a little like I was putting on a performance. Sebastian wasn't there to see of course, but nonetheless he knew what I was doing. He knew that sometime that morning I'd be in the office bathroom, just thirty feet from my colleagues, pleasuring myself at his command. I imagined him doing the same thing, stroking that magnificent cock and picturing me. That thought drove me wild.

A moan escaped my lips as I shortened my motions, strumming my trigger with increasing urgency. The lace of the panties was rough against my skin, and the faster I rubbed the more it bit into me. Perhaps Sebastian intended it that way, perhaps he knew the kind of underwear I'd be wearing. Such precise planning wouldn't have surprised me — he'd long since proven how easily he could read me — but in truth the sensation didn't bother me. It was nothing more than a tickle compared to the delights he'd already shown me.

My breath began coming in short, sharp bursts, and a trickle of sweat lined my brow. I could feel an orgasm swelling up inside me, beckoning to me with unrestrained promise.

You're forbidden to come.

The words echoed in my head. I wanted to obey him. I knew there was a purpose behind everything he asked, a purpose that would undoubtedly lead to more pleasure later, but I was already so close. Every part of my body burned with desire. That week of waiting while my imagination ran wild seemed to have built up inside me, and now it was all bubbling to the surface. Another few seconds and I knew I'd be past the point of no return.

The tiny, logical part of my mind that wasn't flushed with hormones began to make peace with the fact that I was going to fail. He'd probably have a punishment prepared, and I doubted he'd be as gentle as last time. I might even be forced to meet the paddle. But there was nothing I could do, the pressure was too great.

Then, moments before my climax took hold, I heard the bathroom door fly open.

It was like somebody had pulled the plug out from inside

me. All the passion and arousal instantly drained away as I let out a mortified gasp. How much had they heard? I had no idea how loud I'd been. As excited as I was, it wouldn't have surprised me if the entire floor knew what I was up to. It was one thing to savour the threat of getting caught, but it was quite another for it to actually happen.

There was a pause, as though the person was deciding whether to speak.

"Are you okay in there?" she said eventually. The sing-song voice instantly sent a slinking sensation down my spine, like a wayward insect. Jennifer. I cursed silently. Of all the colleagues that I'd want to walk in on me, she was at the bottom of the list. Hell, if you threw my mother, grandmother and all my ex-boyfriends on there, Jennifer was still at the bottom.

"Hello?" she continued. "Do you need any help?"

I winced. "I'm fine. Just ate some bad prawns last night I think."

I could almost picture her face twisting into that supercilious smile as she recognised me. "Ah, Sophia, I didn't realise it was you. I hope it's not serious." Did she sound smug because she knew about my little date for one in here? Or was it just general pleasure at my discomfort? It was impossible to tell. Jennifer always sounded so damn self-satisfied.

"It's alright. I'll be fine in a couple of minutes."

"Good, good. The Wrights case is really ramping up and we need as many hands on deck as we can get. I'd hate for you to miss out because of a weak stomach." The woman's tone was saccharine sweet. I growled quietly to myself. Why wouldn't she just leave?

"I know. I wouldn't miss it for the world."

"I know you wouldn't." I heard the tap begin running, followed by the tear of paper towel. "I just came in here to freshen up. Big meeting this morning. Mister Bell himself is going to be there. Anyway, I have to run. I do hope you feel better. If you need anything, just sing out. Ta ta."

The door opened, and then the room fell silent once more. *I'd go to hell and back before I went to you for help.*

I took a deep breath and tried to calm myself. It seemed like I'd gotten away with it, although it was hard to tell with her. She'd be just as likely to keep it to herself for a few months and pull it out at an opportune moment as to rub it in my face then and there.

On the plus side, I technically hadn't disobeyed Sebastian, although it was through no strength of my own. I wondered if that counted.

Regardless, I wasn't finished yet. My eyes flicked down to where the box lay on the floor.

Take the second box with you. When you're done, open it.

I was still shaken from my near miss with Jennifer, but I scooped it up anyway. A trace of my earlier fire flared between my legs as I gazed at it. Sebastian was nothing if not inventive, and I was rapidly discovering just how much I liked his games. It was a simple gesture, classic really, an unexplained package left quietly on a desk, but he always knew how to give things just enough of a twist to set my blood pumping. Sexy commands, boxes within boxes; it was like some kind of kinky Russian doll.

Unable to wait any longer, I tugged gently at the ribbon and the box fell open. "Oh god, he didn't," I said, to no one in particular.

It had been years since I'd seen a butt plug. One past boyfriend had been more than a little fixated on my ass, so I'd consented to a little anal play. We never actually progressed to sealing the deal — it turned out my ass wasn't the only one he was fixated on — but we made it as far as a little toy play.

I didn't have the fondest memories of those times.

I exhaled sharply. In the throes of my last passionate encounter with Sebastian, I'd expressed a willingness to consider anal play, but in the cold, hard, fluorescent light of reality, the idea lost most of its charm.

I picked the plug up slowly, turning it in my hand. It wasn't particularly big — three inches long and about the thickness of a large index finger, with one end that tapered to a round point — but in the context of where it was supposed to go, it looked positively daunting.

There was another note in this box, lying next to a small white tube that I assumed was lubricant. I picked up the note gingerly.

Dear Sophia.

I trust you enjoyed that. I must admit, the thought of you pleasuring yourself kept me awake most of last night. I will definitely require a more intimate show when I return.

But the game is not quite over yet. You've obviously discovered my little gift. In my opinion, it's something every girl should own. I know you're probably a little uncertain about such things, but I think you'll come to take pleasure in them eventually. Besides, it would make me extremely happy.

I originally bought it to use on you myself, but since I've been delayed, I figured maybe you could get started without me. There's no time like the present.

With that in mind, I want you to remove your panties and place them in the box. Give the plug a healthy dose of lube and then insert it as far into your ass as you can. Don't be shy; the deeper the better. Then, I want you to return to your desk and continue working as normal.

I have no doubt it will be uncomfortable to begin with, but that will pass. I love the idea of you going about your day exposed and penetrated for me. Even though I'm not there, you'll have a little piece of me inside you, a constant reminder of my presence.

You don't have to leave it in all day; it's best to start slowly. An hour or two should do it, and if you enjoy the sensation, we can go from there.

Now, if you followed my instructions properly, your panties should be in quite a state. I wish I were there to do something about that myself—I can practically taste you on my tongue right now — but seeing as I'm not, I'd like you to save them for me. You're forbidden to wear them for the rest of the day. Just keep them there in the box. And to make things a little more interesting, I'd like you to keep it on your desk until you leave. I do hope you don't get too many visitors.

I will be in touch later in the day to see that my orders have been followed. Have a lovely day.

-S

My mouth fell open as I read. The plug wasn't just a gift. He expected me to wear it right now.

My eyes darted to the lube, then back to the toy, and I swallowed loudly. Theoretically, nobody would notice — it was small, and I wasn't exactly in the habit of flashing my work mates — but still, the very idea was crazy. Walking around the office all day wearing a sex toy was about the most inappropriate thing I could think of. Except perhaps leaving a pair of sex-wet panties out on my desk. I got the sense it was more about the risk than the panties themselves, and while it was true they'd be hidden inside something, it wouldn't take much for someone to start asking questions.

But even as my rational self madly tried to dissuade me, the new Sophia, the one that had only recently awakened, was buzzing with excitement. Being commanded to do such risqué things was a huge turn on. It made me feel like the naughty little minx I'd never known I wanted to be. And beyond that, it would make Sebastian happy, which was a reward all of its own. His pleasure became my pleasure; he'd made that very clear.

I began preparing. Breaking the seal on the lube, I squeezed a healthy dollop out onto my hand and smeared it all over the plug. *You're not basting a damn turkey,* I thought, admiring my handiwork. *That thing is going* inside your ass, *don't be stingy now.* So I took a second squeeze and did it again. Soon, I could barely keep a firm grip on the thing.

Not giving myself a chance to change my mind, I hiked up my skirt once more, slipped my underwear free, bent over, and brought the small rubber tip up to my delicate ring. The lube was cold against my skin, but the light pressure was not unpleasant. I thought back to our last night together, to the gentle probing of Sebastian's finger. In the heat of the moment, I'd kind of enjoyed that. Perhaps it wouldn't be so bad.

With a deep breath I began to apply pressure. The first inch was surprisingly easy, slipping in with little resistance, but as the shaft gradually grew wider, it began to hurt. My sphincter started to spasm and tighten, rebelling against the foreign sensation. I gritted my teeth and tried to relax, but it was impossible. My body seemed to have a mind of its own. I growled in frustration.

Closing my eyes for a moment, I tried to regroup. *Think of that night in the hotel. Think of the wonderful things Sebastian still has to show you, the things he'll do to you if you please him.*

And somehow, it worked. Slowly but surely, my muscles loosened and the plug began to slide deeper. It was a lengthy process, and I stopped twice to apply more lube, but eventually I buried the entire thing inside me, right down to the handle.

I let out a deep sigh, followed by a wince. The toy was as painful as I'd feared. My ass burned with the fullness of it. I experimented, shaking my hips back and forth and applying gentle pressure to the plug with my hand. Every motion sent a sting coursing through me as my muscles stretched far beyond what had been asked of them recently. It was an invasive sensation, and far from comfortable, but it was done now. Stubbornness meant I would see it through, at least for a while.

After checking that the room was empty, I slipped out of the cubicle and inspected myself in the mirror. I looked a little flustered, and somehow I'd given myself a perfect sex hair makeover despite the fact that I'd been playing solo. *Also, you're walking like you've got a stick up your ass, which I guess in a manner of speaking, you do. On the plus side, that should make you a shoe-in for partner.*

I spent a minute washing the heat from my cheeks and collecting myself, before taking another deep breath and marching out through the door. I half expected Jennifer to have gathered the entire building to witness my walk of shame, so I was pleasantly surprised to find the corridor outside empty. Perhaps I really had gotten away with it.

The walk to my desk seemed to last an eternity. Every few steps I found myself reaching out to smooth the back of my skirt, certain there was a large, plug shaped knob visible under the material. At one point, one of my colleagues decided to pop out of his office for a chat. It was one of the most excruciating conversations of my life. I could barely string two words together, and with every stumble I felt more certain I had given myself away. After a minute or so, I mumbled something about needing to go, and took off before he could stop me.

I'd never been happier to arrive at my office. Slipping inside and shutting the door, I pressed myself against it and closed my eyes. Safety.

A nervous laugh escaped my lips as I considered the lunacy of what I'd just done. Little Bell was one of the oldest and most eminent law firms in Australia. It was a company steeped in tradition, yet there I was marching the hallways with a pair of sodden panties in a box in my hands and a sex toy between my legs. It was crazy. For the hundredth time, I asked myself why I was giving Sebastian so much control, but of course I knew the answer. Because I enjoyed it as much as he did.

The next few minutes were extremely uncomfortable. Having something buried in my ass was such an alien feeling that I could barely concentrate. Several times I came close to giving up. But gradually, as my muscles began to adjust, the discomfort ebbed away. That unwavering pressure was still there, but the longer I worked, the less it bothered me.

At some point, I realised that I was actually beginning to enjoy it. It wasn't pleasurable in a direct way, but the sense of fullness was extremely satisfying. And beyond that, there was the psychological effect. Sebastian was right, the plug acted as a constant reminder of his presence. I'd be working through a dense case file, my mind utterly focused on the task at hand, when a sudden shift in position would send a wave of sensation curling through me. It was distracting, but also immensely erotic; as though he was stimulating me from across the country. The message was clear: even when we were apart, I was still his.

It was difficult to work at my normal pace. I tried my best to focus, but I couldn't slip into my normal steady rhythm. The morning's activities had left me buzzing with energy. My latent orgasm still simmered somewhere inside me, and whenever I looked up from my work, I found my eyes wandering to the box that sat just a few inches from my keyboard. It was closed of course, and looked fairly innocuous, but nonetheless it was nerve-wracking knowing that such a thing was out in the open, just waiting to be discovered. It seemed so damned obvious. I swore I could smell hints of my earlier excitement hanging in the air.

For a while it seemed like I might escape the day without any visitors, but around lunch time, I heard the dreaded sound of a knock at my door.

It was Elle. "Feel like ducking out for a bite, Soph?"

My cheeks instantly turned red. *Just chill. She probably won't even notice it.*

"I better not," I replied. "I've got a ton of stuff to do here."

She grimaced. "Bah. I guess it's me and the boys again then. I have to say, I'm getting a little tired of pretending like I give a shit about football."

"Next time," I said, smiling sympathetically.

She nodded. "Sure thing."

I thought I'd gotten away with it, but as she began to turn away, her eyes suddenly lit up. "And what have we here?" she said with a grin. "A secret admirer perhaps?"

Even though she hadn't moved, I found my hand darting out to clutch the box anyway. *Good work, Sophia. Could you be any more obvious?*

I tried to remain composed. "I wish. It's just my sister trying to make up for forgetting my birthday."

She frowned. "That was two months ago."

"What can I say? She's a crappy sister."

She studied me for several seconds, but eventually gave a short nod. "Fair enough. Get anything good?"

I breathed a silent sigh of relief. "Movie vouchers and chocolate. Original hey?"

Elle laughed. "Not really, but I wouldn't be complaining. Anyway, the others are waiting, so I better bail. I'll catch you later."

"Sure. Seeya."

Even after she'd gone, it took a few minutes for my muscles to unclench. That had been a lot closer than I'd hoped. I had to admit though, again, part of me had enjoyed the perverse thrill of coming so close to exposure. It was such a simple thing, but so naughtily creative at the same time. I had no idea where Sebastian's mind came up with such ideas.

The afternoon passed slowly. As my excitement wore off, I began to find my groove again. At about two o'clock, my desk phone rang. The caller ID showed an unfamiliar number.

"Hello," I said tentatively.

"Hello, Sophia. I hope you enjoyed your present."

I let out a little sigh. It was nice just to hear his voice again. "I did. I'm wearing it right now in fact."

"How's the fit?" he asked, his voice playful.

I laughed. "It was a little tight to begin with, but I think you got my size just right."

"Excellent. How about my other requests?"

"All done."

"I'm impressed. Had any close calls?"

"One, but I dealt with it."

He chuckled. "I'm glad to hear it."

I hesitated, choosing my words carefully, not wanting to sound too needy. "So how's the trip? Are you nearly done there?"

"A few more days probably. There's still one or two things to take care of."

"Good, because after this morning, I'm thoroughly in need of a good seeing to."

He laughed. "I know the feeling. Christ, I'm hard just thinking about you sitting there with no panties on. But in any case, good behaviour deserves a reward. Since you did such a wonderful job this morning, I'm going to lift the rules. You're free to come as many times as you want until I return."

I blew out a slow breath. Part of me wanted to run back to the bathroom that very moment and finish what I'd started. But I restrained myself. "Are you sure?"

"Yes. You've earned it. But save a little something for me. I've got plans for you when I get back."

"I'll do my best. And you should know, I'll be thinking of you the whole time."

"I would expect nothing else," he said. "On another note, I saw on the news yesterday that your firm has picked up that big pharmaceutical class action suit. I bet that's pretty exciting."

I sighed. What a way to kill the mood. "It is, for the people working on it."

"And I take it by your tone that you're not one of them?"

"Not at the moment."

"I'm sorry, Sophia."

"Hey, it's okay, I'm used to it," I replied. "Anyway, I should go. I may not be working on Wrights, but I have a pile of other stuff to do."

"No problem. I'll be in touch when I get back. Have a good night."

"I most certainly will. Bye."

Knowing I had Sebastian's blessing to relieve the pressure made the rest of the day a little easier. I got through everything I had to do by six o'clock.

I think I was beginning to appreciate the new side of me

that Sebastian was gradually teasing out, because I found the walk out with no underwear on immensely enjoyable. It was my little secret that nobody else knew, and it made even the simple act of saying goodbye to people sexy. Plus I knew that somewhere, a thousand kilometres away, it was driving Sebastian crazy, which made it hotter still.

A few people tried to stop me on my way out to chat, but I politely excused myself. I had more important things on my agenda. Like a long overdue date with a battery operated friend.

Chapter 3

The next night, I gave myself an early mark and headed home from the office at five on the dot. If they weren't going to assign me the work I wanted, I sure as hell wasn't giving them maximum effort. I decided a little me-time was in order.

After taking a long, luxurious bath, I settled on the couch with a bowl of bolognese and a glass of wine, and flicked on the television. I couldn't remember the last time I'd gone full couch potato. Even those rare moments when I did find a little spare time, I usually felt like I shouldn't waste it on the likes of commercial television, but there's something to be said for just sitting down and zoning out occasionally.

I channel surfed for a while, flicking from one terrible reality show to the next. Even by my vegging out standards, most of the stuff was truly appalling.

At some point in my wandering I skipped to BBC News.

"—been nearly a week and police still don't know the motive behind the killing, but a source inside British parliament says it could have been politically motivated."

I froze. There was a picture of a shirtless man on the screen. He looked to be in his sixties, but was still fit, with a broad chest and thick arms that belied the wrinkles on his face. I'd never seen him before, but nonetheless there was one very familiar thing about him. Tattooed on his right bicep was a stylised letter A. The image was grainy and indistinct — it looked like a hasty camera phone holiday snap — but the mark appeared almost identical to the one Sebastian wore.

The shot cut to a police man. "Our initial findings indicate that Mister Reynolds was tortured, possibly for several days, before eventually dying of his injuries. We're working closely with the government in our investigation."

The program moved on to another story, but I was no longer paying attention. I'd never seen that symbol before meeting Sebastian. If the two of them had shared a different tattoo, a dragon or skull and crossbones or some other generic ink, I wouldn't have thought much of it, but this was a very specific image with very specific typography. It looked to be a different size, and was in a different place on his body, but still, it was a little eerie.

Firing up my laptop, I began looking for more information. The man's name was Christian Reynolds and he'd been the environment secretary of state for the British Government. He'd been a British citizen his whole life and a government employee for thirty years. No one knew for sure why he'd been killed, but based on the extensive torture he'd suffered, it was suspected to have been about information. I couldn't find a better picture of him, but after taking a closer look at the one shot that was circulating, I was fairly convinced that the marking was the same.

It had to be a coincidence. He and Sebastian were worlds apart. Different countries, different careers, different generations. Perhaps it was just a more common symbol than I realised.

I knew the smart thing to do was just forget about it. I'd caused enough trouble already by letting my paranoia get the better of me. What was I going to do? Wander up to Sebastian and say, "Excuse me, but do you happen know this random dead guy from the other side of the world?" It sounded absurd.

But as I flicked the television to another station and tried to focus on My Kitchen Rules, my mind continued to wander. Something about that ornate little symbol bothered me. I just couldn't put my finger on it.

Chapter 4

A few nights later I was once again out having drinks with the girls. My week had gone steadily downhill since Sebastian's call, and when Lou had suggested we hit the town, I'd jumped at the opportunity.

"Nothing says 'Friday Night' like a tray of Mojitos," I said, setting our drinks on the table.

"Hear hear," replied Ruth, raising her glass. She took a long sip and sighed appreciatively.

"So now that it's had a few weeks to sink in, how's it feel to be the future Mrs Steven Page, Lou?" I asked.

"No complaints. To be honest it's pretty much the same, but it makes Steve more comfortable. We want to start trying for kids soon, and his parents just wouldn't be able to stomach it if we didn't tie the knot first."

"Bah, kids, weddings, I don't like all this growing up," said Ruth. "Pretty soon I'll be sculling cheap vodka alone in Jackson's on a Friday night, while you two host dinner parties and play charades, or whatever the fuck it is responsible people do in their downtime. It's selfish, is what it is."

"Hey don't lump me in with that crowd," I said. "There are no nappies or white dresses in my future."

Lou grinned at me. "That's not what I hear. I hear you

might have a mystery gentleman of your own, now."

I shot Ruth a look.

"Hey, she dragged it out of me!"

I glared at her for a few seconds, but eventually broke into a laugh. I'm not sure what else I expected. Once you told Ruth something it was as good as front page news.

"It's not like that. It's strictly a casual thing," I told Lou.

"So? These things always start out casual. That's what the first few dates are. Doesn't mean it can't go somewhere eventually."

"With this guy, I think it does. He's not exactly the settling down type. I struggle to picture any woman keeping hold of him for very long. Besides, he's made his intentions perfectly clear, and I'm fine with that."

At that moment, my phone started buzzing in my bag with Sebastian's name flashing across the screen. "Speak of the devil," I said.

"He's back in town?" Ruth asked.

I shrugged. "Let's find out." I answered the call. "Hey."

"Sophia." The word sounded impossibly sweet off his tongue. He claimed he'd trained girls to come with a simple command, and the longer I knew him, the more I believed that might be true.

"Back in sunny Sydney?" I asked.

"Yes, I arrived this afternoon."

"Good flight?"

He laughed. "Flights are never good. Let's go with the word tolerable."

"Fair enough."

"I'd like to see you, Sophia. Tonight, if possible."

"Aww, did you miss me?"

"You don't know the half of it. I couldn't get the image of you playing with yourself out of my mind. I haven't been able to concentrate for days. I intend to make you do that again and this time I'm going to lick your pussy clean myself."

I blushed. There was something so hot about discussing such intimate things with my friends just a few feet away.

"I think I can arrange that," I said coyly.

"Excellent. There's a little company gathering I need to go to now. Nothing like the other week, a small group, but there are some people there I have to talk to. Why don't you come with me? We can have a drink, and after we can see about that show."

"I'm out with the girls at the moment," I said, although both of them were waving me on. "Also, I'm not dressed for a fancy party."

"How many times do I have to tell you that I don't care what you're wearing? You look gorgeous no matter what. Besides, if I have my way, you won't be wearing much of anything for very long. Will your friends mind if I steal you away?"

I glanced at their eager faces. "I think they'll cope," I said.

"Wonderful. Where are you?"

"Zeta bar, in the Hilton Hotel."

"I know it. I'll be there in half an hour."

"See you then."

Ruth snorted as I stashed my phone back in my purse. "Yeah, casual indeed."

"What?" I replied.

"Look at you, you can't wipe the dopey smile off your face."

"I can too!" I said, making a conscious effort to twist my mouth into a scowl. It was surprisingly difficult.

"Lou?" Ruth said, turning to the other woman.

She grinned at me. "If you'd been any more gooey-eyed, Soph, you'd have been melting onto the table."

159

I shifted uncomfortably in my seat. Sure, I was excited to see Sebastian, but that was purely my raging libido talking. "You can shut up, both of you. It's just fun because it's new, you know? That's all."

"If you say so," said Lou, although her expression said she didn't buy it.

"Anyway, he'll be here soon, so I'd appreciate if you two could do your best not to embarrass me."

I was secretly looking forward to them meeting Sebastian. I'm not ashamed to admit that I wanted to show him off a little. I'd been with attractive guys in the past, but none had nearly the same visceral impact that he did. His sheer presence and overt sexuality were a sight to behold. I couldn't wait to see the effect he'd have on the girls.

He didn't disappoint. A little while later, I spotted him sauntering through the crowd.

"So somehow she thinks it's my responsibility because..." Lou was saying to Ruth, however she trailed off as Sebastian appeared behind me.

"Sophia," he said, laying a hand gently on my shoulder.

"Right on time," I replied. "Sebastian, these are my friends, Ruth and Louisa."

"A pleasure to meet you," he said, shaking each of their hands. They returned the gesture dumbly, their mouths hanging slightly open like they'd forgotten how to speak. It was incredibly satisfying seeing them stilled like that, although I couldn't say that I blamed them. He looked good enough to eat. Somehow he'd managed to maintain that perfect level of rough stubble he'd worn the first night we met. That, combined with his wild black curls and roguish smile, gave him an exotic, devil may care look that practically screamed, "mind blowing orgasms!" I didn't think there was a woman in the room who would be immune to that.

160

"You too," said Ruth eventually. "Would you like to sit down? We could get another round."

"As much as I hate to turn down the company of three beautiful women, we should go. The party has already started. You two don't mind if I take her away do you? I'd be in your debt."

They both shook their heads slowly.

"Wonderful. I'm just going to get a glass of water and then we'll go, okay?"

"Sure," I replied.

I could only grin as their eyes followed him across the room.

"Jesus, Soph," said Lou, when he was out of earshot, "I take back what I said before. I think you'd be hard pressed not to go a little gooey with him on the other end of the line."

Ruth exhaled slowly. "Yeah, I've gotta hand it to you hon', that is one fine specimen of a man. I don't suppose he has any eligible friends?"

I laughed. "I'll let you know after I meet some of them tonight."

She turned to Lou. "Think you could find your way back to that bar? Maybe there's another function we can slip our way into. Something with firemen, hopefully."

"Give me another few drinks and I might just be on board," Lou replied. She grinned at Ruth's surprised expression. "What? I'm engaged, not dead. I can look!"

At that moment Sebastian returned. "Ready?"

I nodded. "Yep."

"You have a good night, girls," he said.

"You too," replied Lou.

Joe was waiting by the curb outside. "Hi Joe."

"Good evening, Sophia."

"What did you get up to while Sebastian was gone? Did

you go out and paint the town red?"

"Oh, nothing as exciting as that I'm afraid. It was a lot of staring at the phone and waiting for him to call, looking back wistfully on old pictures of me driving him around, that sort of thing."

Sebastian grinned. "That's what I like about you, Joe, that unwavering respect."

"I try, sir."

Joe opened the door and Sebastian ushered me through, easing in behind me. In a few moments the engine growled and we pulled out into the Sydney traffic. It was peak hour and the streets were thronging with cars. I never tire of that busyness. The first chance I got I moved from the suburbs to the city and never looked back. There's a living vibration to it, a sense of constant fluctuation that's a thrill to be a part of.

The back seats of the limo were spacious, with room for five or six to sit comfortably, but nonetheless Sebastian had guided me to one corner and then slid in next to me until our thighs were touching. I couldn't have moved even if I'd wanted to. Not that I did. I'd fantasised all week about being close to him, and now that I was, my body was kicking into overdrive. His raw presence radiated over me. There was an amazing sense of banked power to him. Even in the simple act of sitting in a car, he somehow looked primed, like a lion at rest between meals.

He looked over at me, something carnal flaring in his eyes. "Sophia," he said, and then taking my head in one hand and my shoulder in the other, he pulled me in, capturing my lips in his. Instantly, the heat simmering in my stomach began to boil over. This was what I'd been waiting for.

His kiss was hungry and fierce, an act of raw desire. He ran his hands through my hair, desperately pulling me closer, as though trying to fold the two of us into one. I loved that I stoked such passion in him. In that one simple gesture I could feel the weight of the week we'd been apart. He hadn't been lying. He'd been longing for me as much as I had him.

Our tongues darted together, exploring each other's mouths. I don't know why, but he tasted sweet, like strawberries and wood smoke. I quivered and sucked in a sharp breath as his fingers began to work their way up the soft flesh of my thighs, gradually peeling back my skirt. Meanwhile his other hand had slid down my neck and looped inside the shoulder strap of my dress.

"My god, you don't know how much I've been thinking about you," he said, breaking the kiss. "I don't think I can wait until after the party. I need to have you right now."

I cleared my throat. "Here?" I asked, nodding quickly out the window. The glass was shaded, but I was still incredibly aware of the shifting crowd and other cars visible all around us. Not to mention Joe. We were separated by the privacy window, but nonetheless he'd have to be a fool not to realise what was going on.

"Here," said Sebastian, his voice leaving no room for argument. And before I had time to protest, he wrapped both hands around my hips and spun me around on top of him.

As my legs slid into place around his, my sex came to rest on the bulge in his pants, and whatever resistance I'd felt instantly melted away. He was firm as stone, and he pressed against me with an urgency that was impossible to ignore. I could feel the heat of him radiating through our clothes, making me acutely aware of how little material separated him from being inside me. At that moment I no longer cared about Joe, or the masses of weary commuters just a few arm's lengths away. I wanted him to take me. I needed it.

And he responded. He gripped me roughly, grinding his cock against me while pulling me in for another kiss. The pressure was so intense, the stimulation so overwhelming, that I felt like I might come then and there. I let out a low moan, misting the window next to me with the warmth of my breath.

"You know, it was very generous of you to change the rules for me the other day," I said, "but I've got a secret to tell you." I ran my hands over him, playfully caressing his chest before pulling him in to whisper in his ear. "I never finished the job."

"You didn't?"

I shook my head. "I came close. My vibrator was out and ready to go. But at the last second I realised it just wouldn't be the same. I wanted to save it. I wanted it to be you."

He closed his eyes, a low rumble emanating from his throat. "That is so insanely hot. How is it you can be such a perfect sub with so little training?"

"I'm just that talented, I guess," I said with a grin.

He laughed. "Well then, I'd better not make you wait any longer."

Slipping the dress from my shoulders he pulled it down, allowing my breasts to fall out into the open. "My god you're beautiful."

And then he dove on me. Suddenly, his mouth seemed to be everywhere. I let out a gasp as his tongue began playing out an exquisite velvet pattern across my chest. He kissed and licked his way in slow circles, greedily sucking on my nipples and teasing with the barest brush of teeth. His stubble felt coarse against my skin, contrasting deliciously with the softness of his lips.

As he ravished me, his hands began to traverse further, weaving behind me to ruck up my skirt. He didn't waste any time. A moan of anticipation fell from my lips as he yanked aside my panties.

164

"Are you nice and wet for me?" he asked, that low silky voice ratcheting my excitement up even higher.

I nodded furiously. "I've been wet for you for weeks."

He let out a long breath. "I love it when you talk like that." With agonising slowness he slipped his hand underneath me and drew a single finger along my slickened opening. I shuddered in pleasure.

He brought his finger forward, the tip glistening with my juices. "You weren't kidding." He gave it a long, slow, tantalising lick. "And you're just as sweet as I remember. Later I'll have a proper taste, but I can't wait anymore. I need to fuck you."

I let out an affirmative grunt, not wanting to delay him one second more. I could feel the weeks of excitement burning wildly inside me.

Taking me by the hips once more, he hoisted me up, placing me on my knees next to him with my ass in the air. With panther grace he rose into a crouch and unfastened his belt, letting his pants fall to the floor. Seeing his cock in the flesh sent a bolt of desire rolling through me. I'd never wanted anything inside me so badly before.

Seizing me in a powerful grip, he dragged me across to him and plunged his shaft straight into my pussy, burying it all the way to the base in a single explosive thrust. He let out an animal cry.

The strength of that motion stung as my body madly adjusted to accommodate his girth, but I didn't care. The longing in his movements dwarfed everything else. That I inspired such lust in him set me soaring.

"God Sophia, you're so tight. You feel amazing."

"I'm tight because you're big," I said, my voice broken and quavering. His cock stretched me out like nothing I'd ever felt before. I moaned with the fullness of it, every muscle cinching tight around him, savouring that exquisite pressure. He responded in kind, wrapping both powerful hands around my shoulders and yanking me closer, giving him more leverage to grind himself against me. He fucked me with the desperation and ferocity of a man with one day to live.

With other men I'd been with, sex had always been an act of giving; give your partner pleasure and receive it in return. With Sebastian, there was no give, only take. He wasn't giving me an orgasm, he was taking it from me, claiming it for himself, and he did it with a fervour that bordered on frightening. That intensity ignited something inside me, a kind of deep-seated passion I'd never known I was capable of.

I wasn't going to last long. The glow of my orgasm was already rising up inside me. My muscles clenched tighter still as my body began to stretch and tremble in anticipation.

"No, not yet," he said, his voice hoarse. Even as aroused as he was, he knew I was close. His awareness of my body was almost inhuman. "You were saving it for me, so I want to watch you as it happens."

With a grunt, he pulled free of me, leaving an aching emptiness between my legs. Seizing me by the thighs, he flipped me easily onto my back.

I gazed up at him, breathless and quivering. He'd shed his jacket, and sometime in the commotion several of his shirt buttons had come undone. Crouching there, half dressed and coated in sweat, he looked wild and impossibly beautiful. His cock jutted out from his body, slick and shining with my juices. It pulsed and twitched in the sex-heavy air.

He slid in close, pressing the swollen head gently against my cleft.

"Please," I moaned. "Please."

Leaning in close, he gazed at me with those spectacular eyes. "You've earned this." He pushed himself back into me

166

and began rocking back and forward, reaching out with one hand to stroke my clit. "This is what you've been waiting for."

"Sebastian!" I cried, my body heaving as my climax took hold. I thought the phrase 'seeing stars' was just an expression, but as a week's worth of pent up desire exploded inside me, that's exactly what happened. The whole world seemed to shatter before my eyes. The strength of it was so overwhelming I was sure I was going to black out.

As my pleasure began to subside, his movements grew faster. What little control had been evident on his face fell away as he finally gave in to his own desires. The noises from his throat became more guttural, his thrusts longer and harder.

I was still sensitive from the intensity of what had just happened, but the promise of having him burst inside me was so enticing it barely registered. My body wanted more of him, as much as he could give.

After a few more seconds he shuddered and went rigid. Watching him come in such an intimate position was the most erotic thing I'd ever seen. The ferocious ecstasy on his face, the way his body flexed and corded, it was almost enough to send me over the top again.

"God, Sophia," he said, when it was over. "I don't know how you keep doing that to me."

"Doing what?"

"Making me lose control. I was planning on waiting, drawing it out, but the second I saw you, I got hard."

"You're still hard now," I said with a giggle.

"And you're still wet. Believe me, it's taking most of my control not to take you again right now."

I reached out and ran my hand softly up the length of his erection. "Why don't you?"

He closed his eyes and drew a deep breath. "I want you

to save some energy for later. I have plans for you, plans that won't be much good if I've already tired you out."

"I'm not sure I could ever get tired of having this inside me."

"If you don't stop being such a tease I'm going to be forced to turn you over my knee," he said, stroking my ass delicately.

I trembled, remembering the last time he'd spanked me. "Is that a promise?" I asked.

He stared at me for a second, then shook his head and chuckled.

We stayed in a dishevelled, half naked embrace for several minutes while the streets blurred past around us. I loved the feeling of his arms around me. It was protective, comfortable, safe.

Chapter 5

A few minutes later, the car pulled up outside a towering apartment building. It looked like a new development; all sleek curves and stark colours.

"Take those off," Sebastian said, nodding at my panties as we were making ourselves presentable. "I loved thinking about you walking around naked under your skirt for me the other day. I want to spend tonight knowing there's nothing between me and that beautiful pussy."

I loved the way his mind worked. Everything was a naughty adventure with him.

Smiling seductively, I slid them down my legs, letting them dangle from my toes. "Why don't you hang on to them for me?"

"I believe you already owe me one pair of your underwear," he replied.

"Think of this as a down payment then."

He laughed. "How can I argue with that?"

They disappeared into his pocket. He ran his eyes over my now naked sex. "God, this is going to drive me crazy."

I knew the feeling. Now I'd be conscious of the fact that I was naked for him all evening.

As he began fastening his buttons, my eyes fell upon his

tattoo once more. Despite my best efforts, I hadn't been able to stop thinking about the man on the news. I knew it was stupid, but I couldn't shake the feeling that there was something more to it. I couldn't ask Sebastian about it directly of course. That would be opening a whole other can of crazy. But that didn't mean I couldn't fish for a little info.

"You know, I've been thinking recently about getting a tattoo," I said.

"Oh yeah?"

"Yeah. I've been planning to for a few years. I mean, I like the idea of it, but I keep putting it off because I can't pick a design. It's going to be on my body forever, so I want it to be something I love."

"That's fair enough."

I glanced casually at his chest. "How'd you pick yours?"

He laughed and looked a little sheepish. "Honestly? It was just one of the pre-made ones they have in-store."

"Really? That doesn't seem like you."

"What can I say? I wasn't always the pinnacle of sound judgement that I am now. In retrospect, I wish I'd had your foresight, but at the time it just seemed like something fun to do."

His regret sounded genuine. *See, Sophia, just a coincidence. Now can you stop trying to ruin this for yourself and forget about it?*

We hopped out of the car. "Go and get some dinner, Joe," Sebastian said. "I'll call you when we're done."

"Of course, sir." He didn't display any hint of embarrassment at what had happened, but perhaps he was simply used to that kind of behaviour. *Business as usual.* That thought brought me back down to earth a bit.

With that same gentle pressure as before, Sebastian guided me into the lobby. A girl buzzed us through and we took the lift up.

Much like Sebastian's apartment, this one was spacious, elegant, and masculine. The entire far wall was sheet glass from floor to ceiling, offering a stunning view out over Hyde Park, and it opened on hinges to one side, leading to a softly lit balcony, complete with its own outdoor bar. There were people milling everywhere, all dressed like they'd just committed a group robbery of the Harrods designer section. "Low key, hey?" I asked.

He grinned. "Do you *remember* the last party of ours you were at? It's all relative."

"Fair point." This certainly wasn't as overwhelming as that first night. More casual richness than unbridled decadence.

Several pairs of eyes turned to us as we entered.

"There he is," said an energetic looking man who broke off from a group near the door. Like most of the men in the room he was handsome and well groomed, with closely cropped golden hair and a strong jaw. In many other circumstances, I'd probably have found him attractive, but watching he and Sebastian shake hands just emphasised how gorgeous my date was. With him in the room, every other man was relegated to second fiddle.

"Thomas, sorry we're late. We had a little car trouble."

I blushed, suddenly very aware that less than ten minutes earlier I'd been having wild, rough, explosive sex in the middle of a crowded road. I ran a hand through my hair, making sure everything was in place. Could Thomas tell? Sebastian had fucked me so thoroughly it felt like it should be obvious.

"This is my friend, Sophia," Sebastian continued.

"Lovely to meet you," Thomas said, extending a hand.

"You too," I replied.

He clapped. "So, what are you two drinking?"

"I'll get something in a minute," said Sebastian, scanning the room. "I want to have a word with Gabriel. Do you mind?" He gave me an apologetic smile.

"It's fine, go play businessman." He nodded thanks, turned and disappeared into the crowd.

"Well, what about you, Sophia?" Thomas asked. "Drink?"

"I wouldn't say no to a glass of red."

"I have just the thing. Come with me."

I attracted more than a few appraising glances as we headed for the balcony. Although everyone appeared to be having a good time, there was a certain cattiness in the air that the men seemed largely oblivious to. I could see it in the girls' postures and smiles and the way they sized each other up when they thought nobody was looking. It was the same vibe I had felt that first night in the bar, that this was all a competition and they were fighting tooth and nail for the best position. Anyone new was a threat. It made me feel decidedly uncomfortable.

"So, you and Sebastian work together?" I asked, trying my best to distract myself.

He nodded. "Locky and I started at Fraiser around the same time."

I snorted. "Locky?" I couldn't imagine anyone addressing Sebastian like that. He didn't seem like the sort of man who people made nicknames for.

Thomas grinned. "Yeah, an old joke from way back when. He hates it, so I save it for special occasions. Use it well."

I laughed. "I'll do that."

I strolled over to the balcony edge while he poured the wine. "You have a beautiful place here. The view is amazing."

He came over to join me, two glasses in hand. "Thanks.

I've been lucky. Fraiser Capital has been good to me."

"It seems like it's been good to all of its staff," I replied, gazing around. "No offence, it's just all a bit surreal."

Thomas laughed. "Believe me, I know what you mean. You kind of just get numb to it after a while. To be honest I barely come out here anymore. I know it makes me look like an asshole, but at some point you just start taking it all for granted."

I decided that I liked him. His self-deprecating humour was refreshingly different from the sort of stuffy, self-important conversation I'd been expecting. He felt like the sort of guy who'd be more at home in a local bar than a ritzy penthouse apartment.

"I don't think you're an asshole," I replied. "It's just hard to get your head around, you know?"

He nodded. "I know. When I first started actually making real money, it took me a solid year to adjust. I spent the first six months living off spaghetti and toasted sandwiches like I always had. I couldn't believe that people lived like this. Sometimes I actually think it might all be too much. Then again," he held up his glass, "it does have its perks.

I took a sip of my own wine and swished it lightly in my mouth. It was delicious, a cavalcade of flavours I didn't have the vocabulary or palate to identify. I had to agree; I wouldn't be complaining.

"So you weren't born into all this?" I asked.

He laughed. "Hell no. I grew up in a shitty little two bedroom fibro house down on the outskirts of Melbourne. I never had more than a few hundred bucks to my name until I started at Fraiser."

"Sorry. I just kind of assumed this was an old money sort of crowd."

"Oh it is, for the most part. But a few of us worked our

way in from the ground up. Sebastian is one of them actually."

My eyes widened. "No way. Really?" Thomas nodded. "But he seems so... comfortable here. So in control."

"He's always been like that. But yeah, he comes from some little town in Europe somewhere."

"So how did he wind up here?"

Thomas shrugged. "Not sure exactly. Fraiser Capital is multinational. We've got branches all over the place, so I assume he got recruited by one of them, but beyond that I don't know. He doesn't talk much about his past. He's kind of a private guy."

I laughed. "I'd noticed. He's got the dark and mysterious thing down to a T."

Thomas studied me for a few seconds, his expression growing sober. "You haven't been with Sebastian long, have you?"

I shook my head. "We only met a little over a month ago."

"Right. Well, can I offer you a piece of advice?"

"Sure, I guess."

"Try not to get in too deep."

I shifted uncomfortably. "What do you mean by that?"

He sighed. "Look, I don't know what sort of relationship you have with him and I don't want to know. It's none of my business. I'm just saying, be careful. He's a great guy, but he's also not the sort who stays put for very long, if you catch my drift. You seem like a nice girl and I'd hate to see you get hurt."

He was the third person tonight who'd seemed to think that maybe my feelings for Sebastian ran a little stronger than a casual fling. It made me uneasy. I'd thought I had a fairly good grasp on what our relationship was, but now I was starting to question that.

"I can take care of myself," I replied, a little more force-fully than I'd intended.

He raised his hands defensively. "Hey, I don't doubt it."

At that moment, we were approached by another man. "Hiding all the beautiful women outside again, Thomas?" he said, with a friendly grin. He was incredibly young looking, with a smooth round face that barely seemed like it should be out of high school.

"How else am I meant to protect them from the likes of you?" replied Thomas.

The stranger gave a little laugh. "Hi, I'm Trey," he said, extending his hand.

"Sophia," I said.

"Lovely to meet you. Please don't tell me you're here with this lout."

"Actually," replied Thomas, "she came with Sebastian."

"Ah," said the other man. "Well that makes more sense."

"Trey here is another of our illustrious colleagues," con-tinued Thomas. "He's what you might call the baby of the group."

Trey sighed good-naturedly and rolled his eyes. "I'm twenty six," he said to me. "Thomas here is just threatened by my youthful exuberance. He knows it's only a matter of time before he's the one answering to me."

"Yeah, that's definitely it," said Thomas.

"Does that mean you're his boss?" I asked, spotting a chance to learn a little about the company.

The two men shared a glance. "In a manner of speaking," said Thomas. "Fraiser has a pretty loose hierarchy. Most of the time everyone is working on their own projects and can pretty much do what they want, but when push comes to shove there's a certain order to how we operate. It helps keep the ship on course."

"Makes sense," I said with a nod. "Although it's funny, I can't really see Sebastian taking orders from anyone."

Thomas smiled wryly. "Most of the time he ends up giving the orders, even if he perhaps shouldn't"

"Now *that* I can see."

I felt a set of hands slide around my waist. "My ears were burning," said Sebastian. "And it's a good thing, too. I leave you alone for ten minutes and the vultures start circling." Again, there was something so personal, so possessive about the gesture. No wonder people suspected something more serious between us. It was easy to forget the nature of our relationship when he behaved like that.

Tilting my head to the side, he leaned in for a lingering kiss. I could almost feel the testosterone radiating from him. The message was clear: *mine*. These were his friends, but still he couldn't help laying claim to what was his. I don't know why, but I liked that masculine jealousy.

Trey cleared his throat. "Lovely to see you too, Sebastian."

"They're both being perfect gentlemen," I told him. "Are you done already?"

"No, not yet. There's one more person I need to talk with, but he's not here yet, so I came to see how you were doing."

"I'm fine. Just learning a little more about you, Locky," I said, not quite able to contain my grin.

Sebastian's lips tightened, before curling up ever so slightly. "I should have known better than to leave her with you, Thomas."

He raised his hands defensively. "Hey, it just came up okay?"

A man approached from inside. "Gentlemen. Any of you feel like losing a little cash? A seat just opened up in the game."

I shot Sebastian a questioning look.

"Most Fridays we run a small poker game," he said.

"I know a little about poker," I replied. "Can I watch you play?"

As a child I'd spent more than a few Friday nights watching my father and his buddies play cards. Games have always fascinated me. I love the challenge of working out how to beat an opponent within the confines of a specific set of rules. I think that's why I became a lawyer. When my dad realised how interested I was by it all, he took me aside and taught me how to play. Most of the time it was just the two of us, but occasionally he let me sit in with his friends. "The big game," he called it. Over time I learned to hold my own, although I hadn't played for years now.

Sebastian pondered for a second. "Sure, why not. Excuse us."

"Sure. Good luck," replied Thomas.

I leaned in to Sebastian's ear as we were led inside. "Your friends seem like fun. Perhaps I actually might be able to land Ruth a sexy venture capitalist of her own."

He chuckled. "You might be barking up the wrong trees there. Thomas works even harder than I do. He's a company man through and through. Relationships just get in the way, according to him. And Trey has been off the market for the last year or so."

"Pity. Oh well, the night is young. Plenty of time for me to play cupid."

He could only smile and shake his head.

We followed the other man across the lounge and through to an adjacent room. Inside was a group of men, chatting and laughing loudly around a large felt covered card table. The surface was littered with stacks of chips in varying size and colours.

"I should probably fold but... fuck it, I call," said one of the players, as we entered. He was an older man, and his strong features and heavy Scottish accent made me think of Sean Connery. "What have you got?"

The man he was speaking to stared for a few seconds before breaking into a rueful smile. "You've got me." He threw his cards towards the centre of the table.

"I knew it!" roared the Scot. "Don't try and cheat a cheater, Jack, you'll never get away with it!"

A few of the players noticed our presence. "Ah, Sebastian," said the one sitting nearest them, "come to try your luck? Someone needs to break Ewan's hot streak or we'll never hear the end of it." He nodded at the older man, who was now grinning and scooping in the pile of chips from the centre of the table.

"The more the merrier," replied Ewan. "His money's as good as anyone's." He spotted me for the first time. "Is this your secret weapon, Sebastian? Your own personal cheer squad?"

I opened my mouth to defend myself, but Sebastian got in first. "Settle down, Ewan. She just wants to watch." He turned to me. "Sorry, just try to ignore him," he whispered. "He gets like this when he's had a few."

I still felt like I should say something, but I didn't want to cause a scene, so I let it go. Taking my hand, Sebastian led me around the table to the spare seat. I pulled up a bar stool and sat behind him, my hands resting lightly on his shoulder.

"So, how much you in for, Sebastian?" asked the man who had greeted us.

Sebastian glanced around the table, sizing up the other player's stacks. "Five hundred I guess."

Several towers of chips were cut out and placed in front of him. It wasn't really what I was expecting. I'd had visions of bricks of hundred dollar bills being tossed around like dollar coins, but things seemed to be much more relaxed than that. It wasn't a small game by any stretch of the imagination — by my count some of them had several thousand dollars in front of them — but compared to the sort of wealth I knew they commanded, they were playing what amounted to penny stakes.

"Five hundred it is," said the dealer. "Shall we play?"

The game resumed. It took me all of two hands to work out that this wasn't an ordinary poker game. The action was fast and reckless; exactly what I'd expected from men playing stakes far below what they could afford. Almost every other hand ended with a huge pot. Often, that's the sign of a weak player, but as the game progressed, I began to see that they weren't playing badly at all. They had a kind of raw cunning to their style that made up for their lack of restraint.

Even during the lulls, I was enjoying being a fly on the wall. It was fascinating watching Sebastian with his colleagues. Seeing him laugh and joke along with the rest of the guys made him seem more human, somehow. He still had that steely intensity, but the camaraderie tempered it a little. It was a side of him I hadn't seen before.

Every so often he glanced back at me and smiled, making sure I wasn't bored. It was nice that just because he was with his friends he hadn't forgotten about me.

Ewan continued to drink and get more raucous, drawing more than a few uncomfortable looks from the other players.

"Why don't you guys just kick him out?" I asked Sebastian quietly.

He sighed. "You know that annoying uncle you don't really like, but are obligated to keep inviting? That's Ewan."

"My mum kicked *my* uncle out at Christmas last year for making a scene."

He laughed. "Somehow that doesn't surprise me. But be that as it may, we don't do things that way here. Our office is like a big family, and people don't get excluded."

A few hands later Sebastian got involved in a pot with a quiet, dark skinned man that everyone called Jav.

"Two fifty," Jav said, throwing some chips into the middle. It was a big bet. Big enough to be scary.

Sebastian sighed and checked his cards once more. His hand was weak. He'd been going for a flush and had missed, so he effectively had nothing at all.

I could tell he was about to throw his cards away, but I reached out and tapped his arm. "He's full of shit," I whispered. While the others had been chatting, I'd been paying close attention to the game, and had a pretty good feel for how everyone was playing.

"What?" Sebastian said.

I hesitated. I realised Sebastian might not appreciate me giving him advice. Also there was a chance I was wrong and would cost him a bunch of money. But my gut told me he was making a mistake, so I decided to bite the bullet. "Jav, he's full of shit. Remember a few hands ago when he bet small at the end with the straight? He likes to sucker you into a call when he's strong. He wouldn't bet this big if he had it. His hand missed as well. You should raise. He'll fold and you'll win the pot."

Sebastian studied me for a few seconds, a curious smile playing on his lips. "You're sure?"

I nodded slowly.

"Okay." He reached for a stack of chips. "Raise to five hundred," he announced.

Jav instantly threw his hand away. "All yours," he said.

"You know 'a little about poker' hey?" Sebastian said to me, as he raked in his winnings.

I grinned. "A little." It felt good to know I wasn't out-classed by these world-conquering men.

"I'll keep that in mind."

The game continued, and Sebastian gradually increased his stack. Soon, it was almost as big as Ewan's, with two towers of the green chips I'd worked out were fifties. It was an intimidating sum of money to be gambling with. Several more times during big hands Sebastian turned to me, seeking my advice about a particular decision. I don't know if he was just indulging me, or genuinely wanted my help, but it was nice to be included.

A few minutes later, one of the players left and was re-placed by Trey.

"Gentlemen," he said.

"Well well well, if it isn't my favourite ATM," said one of the other men. "Time for your weekly donation, is it?"

"Not tonight my friend," replied Trey, "tonight is going to be my night. I can feel it."

The amused expressions that sprung up around the table said nobody really believed that.

"What's all that about?" I whispered to Sebastian.

He gave a little shake of his head. "Trey is just terrible at poker, that's all. And everybody knows it but him. At this point it's become a matter of pride more than logic, I think."

It only took a couple of hands for me to see that Sebastian was right. Trey was nothing short of awful, bluffing when he had no business bluffing and calling when presented with a clear fold. Mostly due to good luck he managed to win a little, but luck inevitably runs out in the end.

As one hand ended, a man who had been lingering by the door approached. "Sebastian, I hear you've been looking for me."

Sebastian nodded a greeting. "Will. About time you

showed up. Can we go and talk for a few minutes?"

"Sure."

He turned to me. "Want to hold down the fort while I'm gone?" he asked, gesturing to the table.

The huge wall of chips loomed up at me. "Oh I can't play with that kind of money."

"Sure you can. You've been doing just fine from back there. Why not take a turn in the hot seat?"

I waved him off. "Really, I wouldn't want to ruin all your hard work."

"If I thought you were likely to do that, I wouldn't ask. Look, either you play, or we lose our spot. It'll just be a few minutes, I promise."

I eyed the men around the table. As intimidating as the prospect of playing with them directly was, it was also kind of exciting. You don't get into law unless you have a healthy competitive streak. "Well, if it's just for a few hands..."

"Excellent." He got to his feet. "Everyone, Sophia here will take my place until I get back. Play nice with her." He winked at me. "Back in a few."

I slid into his seat.

"Not sure we've ever had a girl at this table," said Ewan, clearly not happy about the fact.

"It's kind of nice," said one of the other men. "Gives us something prettier to look at than your ugly mug." Laughter rippled through the room and Ewan scowled at me, although he kept silent.

Play resumed, and soon enough Trey found himself in a tight spot. All the cards had been dealt, and he was facing a massive final bet. I knew straight away his opponent had something strong. He had shown no propensity to bluff in spots like that. But Trey appeared oblivious. Rather than folding as he should, he seemed to be considering making a heroic call. Sure it would look amazing if he was right, but the chances of that seemed impossibly low.

Sure enough, after about thirty seconds, he pushed his chips into the middle. "Call." He wore a rather triumphant look, but it quickly dissipated as his opponent flipped over his cards.

"Full house," he said with a smirk.

Trey stared for a few seconds, before smashing a fist down on the table and throwing his hand away.

"Have you ever considered taking up knitting, Trey?" Jav asked. "Or maybe stamp collecting? There's not a lot of profit there, true, but at least you wouldn't be actively losing money."

Trey just stared down at his few remaining chips and shook his head. I felt bad for him, but there wasn't much I could do.

The game continued. I still hadn't played a hand. Part of me wanted to jump in and throw my chips around as recklessly as the rest of them, but I was afraid of putting Sebastian's stack at risk.

"Is that your plan then?" asked Ewan, after a few minutes of this. "Just play scared and fold until Sebastian gets back?"

Despite the fact that he was right, I was sick of his banter by that point. "I'm not scared. I'm just waiting for the right hand to take your money, that's all," I replied, as sweetly as possible.

There were several chuckles. "That sounds like a challenge to me, Ewan," said Jav.

"That it does," the other man replied, staring straight into my eyes. I knew that from that moment it was game on between us. The second I played a hand, he'd be all over me.

And a few minutes later, I was dealt something I couldn't

ignore. A pair of Queens. One of the best starting combinations possible. My pulse quickened. This was it.

I raised, and several people came along for the ride, including my new friend. The first three cards dealt into the centre looked harmless, so I bet again. Everyone folded until it got around to Ewan.

"Finally found some stones, hey?" he asked. "Alright then, let's play." He threw in enough chips to match my bet. Everyone else folded.

The next card didn't change much, but nonetheless I began to feel nervous. The first few bets in any given hand are relatively small, but as the money in the middle grows, so do the size of the wagers. There was already a large sum in the centre of the table. This hand had the potential to get out of control very quickly.

I considered just cutting my losses and giving up, but I couldn't stomach the thought of giving Ewan that satisfaction. I'd sat down to compete, and so compete I would. With shaking hands, I bet again.

He thought for about thirty seconds, staring me right in the eyes. "Okay," he said, then called once again.

The final card was an Ace. It wasn't very likely that it helped Ewan at all, but it was still a scary card. One of the only ones higher than my pair. I didn't think I could bet again.

"Check," I said, passing the action over to him.

Instantly he pushed a tall stack of greens into the centre. "Nine hundred."

I exhaled slowly. It was a huge bet; all of my remaining chips. My first instinct was to fold. I couldn't imagine calling such a bet and being wrong, and Ewan had made a habit out of betting big when he had the goods. For all his recklessness, he hadn't shown much of a propensity to bluff.

184

But as I thought it through, I couldn't shake the feeling that I was just being bullied. My presence clearly offended him, and this was the perfect opportunity for him to show me who was boss.

As if on cue, he spoke. "Just let it go, girl," he said. "You've still got most of your lad's money. There's no shame in admitting you're outgunned here."

I'm not sure if it was his tone or the smug look on his face that did it, but I suddenly knew I couldn't fold. If I was wrong, I was wrong, but I wasn't going to let him intimidate me.

With my heartbeat thundering in my ears, I silently pushed my money forwards and flipped up my hand.

He gazed at me for what felt like a lifetime, his mouth slowly twisting into a snarl, before shooting wordlessly to his feet and storming from the room. The table erupted into applause.

"I guess he folds," said Sebastian from behind me. I hadn't even realised he was back. "God, that was the most satisfying thing I've seen in a while."

I grinned. "It felt pretty damn satisfying too."

"You should bring her along more often, Sebastian," said Jav. "I can't remember the last time I enjoyed a show as much as that."

Sebastian grinned. "I told you you could handle it," he said to me.

"Oh I knew I could too, I just didn't want to embarrass your friends here."

He laughed. "That's very gracious of you."

I smiled. "After that hand though, I think it's time to call it a night. Not sure my heart can take much more." I started gathering up the chips. "Still, over a thousand bucks profit for a couple of hours work. Not a bad night."

"It was a little more than that."

I paused and did a quick count in my head. "Well, I guess it might be closer to one point five, if you add up all the change."

He stared at me for several seconds. "Sophia, that hand you just won was worth a little over two point two million dollars."

I did a double take. "Excuse me?"

"You didn't know?"

Something hot surged through me. "Know? How could I know?" I said, my voice getting progressively louder. "You said you were buying in for five hundred."

"Yes, five hundred thousand."

I looked down at the stack of chips once more, my eyes wide. There was more money in front of me than both my parents had made in their entire lives. I was no stranger to extravagance — the partners at work were notorious for their heinous disregard for money — but this took it to a whole new level. It seemed almost impossible to comprehend. "Holy shit. How the hell could you let me play with that kind of money? I could have lost it all!"

"But you didn't."

I shook my head slowly. "I know but still...fuck."

"Relax. You showed me you knew how to play. I had faith things would work out. And if they didn't, then c'est la vie. It's only money."

Several of the other players were watching this exchange with amusement. "He's lost more than that in a night before, Sophia," said Trey, who seemed to have recovered from his own loss. "And I dare say I'd take you over him if it were my money," he said with a wink.

Sebastian tried to look offended, but he couldn't quite hide his smile. He really did seem completely at ease with the situation. Perhaps he really would have been okay if I'd lost.

"Still," I said to him, "the next time you put me in charge of a million dollars, do me a favour and let me know, okay?"

"Of course. Sorry, I really thought you were aware. Anyway, look on the bright side. Since you're responsible for a large chunk of the winnings, you're entitled to a cut of the profits. How's fifty fifty sound?"

I gaped up at him. "I can't do that."

"Of course you can. You earned it."

"No, I didn't. I won it by accident, using your money, playing for stakes that I was totally unaware of."

"But you deserve some kind of reward. I want you to have it."

"Well I don't want it. It feels too much like a handout."

"Sophia—"

"—I'm not taking it, Sebastian! End of discussion."

Something in my tone must have got through to him, because his expression softened. "Okay. I'm sorry. I didn't mean to push."

I took a deep breath. "It's alright. I just don't do well with charity, you know? I like to earn my success."

He nodded slowly, a strange smile appearing on his face. "I completely respect that. Like I said, I'm sorry. Can we not let this ruin our night?" He leaned in so only I could hear his words. "I still have plans for you and I'd hate for them to go unfulfilled." As he spoke, he reached out and ran a hand tantalisingly down my hip.

I could already feel my tension ebbing away. It was difficult to be too angry at a man whose only crime was offering you half a million dollars. Especially if that man was a smoking hot sex god who wanted to take you home and do unspeakable things to you.

I sighed dramatically. "Fine. You know you're lucky

you're so damn sexy."

"Am I now?" he said with a laugh.

I tutted and shook my head. "Fake modesty doesn't suit you. Shall we go?"

"Sure." He signalled for someone to tally up his chips, explaining that the money would be wired to him later. We said our goodbyes and headed for the car.

He must have called Joe at some point, because the older man was waiting for us when we got downstairs.

"Good night, sir?" he asked, as he opened the door.

Sebastian nodded. "Yes, although I do believe it's about to get better."

I blushed, although I'm not sure why. Given that less than two hours ago we'd been having incredibly obvious sex not five feet away from Joe, it felt like the time for embarrassment had passed. We slid into the back cabin and the car took off.

Our lack of restraint on the earlier trip had left me sated, but that melted away almost as soon as the door closed behind us. Trapped with Sebastian in the privacy of the car, the air instantly seemed to grow warmer. It was like we couldn't be alone together without there being some kind of sexual charge.

He must have felt it too. Sliding closer, he leaned in and planted a soft kiss on the nape of my neck. "I can't wait to get you home," he whispered in my ear. "I believe I was promised a show."

"And I intend to give you one," I replied.

I reached for him, trying to pull him in for a kiss, but he caught my hands in his. "Uh uh. I lost control once tonight. I'm not going to do it again. I want to wait until I've got you exactly the way I want you."

The way he said that made my sex clench with anticipation.

We sat quietly for a minute, Sebastian staring thoughtfully out the window.

"Most girls would have taken the money," he said eventually.

"What?"

"Inside earlier, most girls I've dated would have taken the money."

"Well, I'm not like most girls."

I thought perhaps we were going to go round two over my refusal, but instead he just smiled ever so slightly. "No, you aren't." A few seconds passed. "You know, I think you left quite the impression on my friends."

"Oh yeah?"

"Ewan was right, I don't think there have been many women at that table. Not because they weren't wanted, it just doesn't really happen. But still, you handled yourself wonderfully. You didn't let them intimidate you."

I looked sheepish. "Would it shatter your impression of me if I said I was actually scared shitless?"

He laughed. "No. You might have been scared, but you went with your gut anyway and that's what matters. Fearless in the face of pressure. I can see now why you make a great lawyer."

I blushed and looked away. I didn't know why his praise meant so much to me, but it did. "Well, thanks. The pressure in law is usually a little different though. Mostly it's just pressure not to fall asleep in the middle of a document." I cleared my throat, hoping to change the subject. "Speaking of work, tell me about your trip."

He hesitated. I could almost feel that shield begin going up inside him. "Nothing to tell, really. I spent most of it in meetings."

"Come on, you can do better than that," I replied. I'd decided earlier in the day that I was going to try and get something out of him. I was still vaguely uncomfortable with how little I knew about his day to day life. It was like dating a secret agent. "Just give me generalities. You know a little about what I'm going through at work, I'd like to know the same."

He considered this, before eventually nodding. "I guess I can do generalities. In a nutshell, I'm working on a project. It's going to be a pretty big deal if it gets off the ground. A real revolution. But as with any progress, there are people who would rather it didn't happen."

"What, like competitors?" I asked.

"Exactly. Anyway, it's making things rather difficult for our clients."

"But surely that's their problem? Don't you just provide funding?"

"Yes and no. We've built up quite a few connections over the years, so if we can help clients in other ways, we do our best. Their success is our success."

"Right. So, I'm picturing a lot of secret lunch meetings and nondescript briefcases changing hands."

He laughed. "Sadly, it's not nearly that cool. Mostly it's just paperwork and boardrooms."

"Well, now it just sounds like my job."

Even though it was fairly mundane, I liked the fact that he'd given me something. I wasn't under any illusions that it meant much, but it was nice to feel like he trusted me, even if it was just a little.

Chapter 6

Soon we pulled up in front of his building. We said farewell to Joe and headed inside. As the lift rose to his apartment, Sebastian stepped around behind me, encasing me in his arms. His mouth found my ear, nibbling delicately. "Fuck, you don't know how difficult it was for me to get through those discussions earlier."

"Oh?" I asked, trying to sound innocent.

"All I could think about was that I had your panties in my pocket." His hand slid down my stomach, coming to rest provocatively close to my crotch. "You're naked under here for me right now."

"Naked and wet," I replied.

He growled softly. "We'll have to take care of that, won't we?"

The doors opened into his apartment. Without a word he took my hand and led me toward the bedroom, his movements radiating primal intent.

As we entered, he spun me lightly onto my back and then climbed on top of me. His mouth locked over mine, so sweet and so strong, and my body yielded beneath him. I'd never met a man whose kiss could break me so. Every stroke of his tongue seemed to echo through me all the way to my toes.

I felt his hands snaking across my skin and I responded in kind, enjoying the little moans and sharp breaths that I coaxed out of him as I explored his most intimate places. Under his shirt, his chest was warm and firm, and he still smelled lightly of sweat from our earlier exertions. I don't know why, but I liked that scent. It was so perfectly *him*.

We writhed together like that for some time, his fingers wandering, but never making any effort to remove my clothes. Eventually they found their way to my thighs and peeled up my skirt, my legs falling open without the slightest resistance. Every nerve in my body seemed to be standing on end. And this was just the beginning.

"I don't know why you were worried about your outfit," he said, pausing to study me. "You look hot as hell all corporate and sexed up."

"I'm glad you like it," I replied.

"I do. In fact, I don't want you to remove a thing. I want to watch you play with yourself right now."

I smiled seductively. "I think I can manage that."

He slid off the bed and sat on a nearby chair, his eyes never leaving my body. "Touch yourself for me, Sophia."

And I did as I was told. I was already impossibly excited. My finger glided with silken ease across my aching slit. I was tentative at first. Even given all that we'd shared, it was strangely invasive having someone else in the room while I pleasured myself. But as my passion mounted, my hesitance gradually fell away. I found the exhibitionism of performing intensely exciting. It was a different kind of intimacy. I was showing him something I'd never shown anyone before, something usually reserved just for me.

"Go slow," he said, barely able to drag his eyes away from my dancing fingers. "I want tonight to last."

I eased up, rubbing myself in gentle circles, savouring the

look of desire that burned on his face. There was a wonderful sense of power, seeing what my show was doing to him. The bulge in his pants was growing with every passing second.

I let out a soft moan as I brought my second hand down to play too, slipping it inside me while my first continued to focus on my clit.

"God, you look so fucking sexy like that," he said.

"I promised you a show didn't I?"

"You certainly did. I just have one suggestion."

"Oh?"

He reached out and opened a nearby chest of drawers, withdrawing a long, pale blue vibrator. It was thick and elegantly curved, with a smooth, rounded head and a small secondary arm about three quarters of the way down. "I bought it especially for you."

I took it from him, weighing it in my hand. It was larger than the one I had at home, almost as large as Sebastian's cock. A few weeks earlier I'd probably have said it was too big, but recent experience had taught me that I didn't know my limits as well as I thought.

"It's lovely." I said.

"It will look even more lovely inside you."

Taking the hint I flicked the switch to the lowest setting and the toy buzzed to life. My pussy was already wonderfully slick and the smooth rubber slid in easily. "Oh god," I groaned, as the head found my G-spot, sending a steady stream of pleasure rolling through me.

"That's it," he said. "Feels good, doesn't it?"

"God yes," I breathed.

With a little experimentation, I found the right angle to let the smaller arm work my clitoris at the same time. The simultaneous stimulation was exquisite.

"Now imagine how good it's going to feel when it's my

cock inside you instead."

"So get over here and fuck me!"

"Patience. Like I said, I want to draw it out. I will, however, give you a preview."

Reaching down, he unfastened his zipper, freeing his shaft from his pants. The sight of it made my whole body throb. Although I hadn't laid a finger on him, he was stiff as iron.

With tantalising slowness, he began to stroke himself, gripping the base firmly in his fist and working up and down. I'd never watched a man masturbate before. It had never seemed particularly appealing when we could be doing other things, but just a few moments with Sebastian showed me how wrong I'd been. This was off-the-charts hot, and made hotter by the fact that it was my body he was staring at. With every flick of his wrist, his cock seemed to swell just a little more.

"Don't stop," he said, and I realised that I had. The sight was so captivating that I'd forgotten my own pleasure. "But remember, you have to restrain yourself. If you come before I say so, there will be repercussions."

I resumed, now acutely aware of how close I was to the edge. I was doing my best to restrain myself, but the whole experience was so sensual that I didn't know if I could hold back. Our passions seemed to feed off one another, and as his pleasure mounted, so did my own. I loved staring into his eyes, watching him react as I performed for him, knowing that I was having the same effect on him. We weren't touching at all, but nonetheless there was a sense of connection to the situation that rivalled anything else I'd shared with him.

Our rhythms synchronised. As he stroked up, I thrust in. With every passing moment, my longing to have the real thing inside me grew. I burned for it. Despite the distance between us, in my head he was already buried eight inches deep, unravelling me with that tender ferocity as only he could.

Soon, I couldn't take any more. The charge pulsing between my legs threatened to overwhelm me. "I'm close."

His eyes narrowed. "Did I say you could come?"

"Please," I moaned, shifting the vibrator restlessly. I tried to move it to a less direct angle, but every part of me was humming by now, begging for release. "Please."

"Take out the vibrator, Sophia." The sudden sharpness in his voice caused me to slow. It was the same deep tone he'd used with Hannah the first night we'd met, that heavy command that seemed to echo right through me. Impossible to resist.

Mustering a mammoth amount of self-control, I withdrew the toy, my pussy clenching in protest.

"Better." He got to his feet and slid onto the bed and pinned my arms behind my head, capturing me beneath him. Leaning down, he planted several soft kisses along my neck. "Thank you for the show," he murmured into my ear. "It was wonderful, but now I think I want to take over."

"I think I'd like that," I replied.

Leaving one hand gripping my wrists, he brought the other down and wrapped it around his cock once more, guiding it between my legs until it was just an inch from entering me. "Is this what you want?"

"Yes." It took all my restraint not to take matters into my own hands and push myself onto him.

"You'll have to do better than that," he replied, easing his length closer still until the crown was resting softly against my lips. "Ask for it," he continued.

"Please, I want your cock. I want you to fuck me." The words came without the slightest hesitation. He had rendered me utterly shameless with desire.

He began to rub himself up and down, dipping towards my opening, before climbing again to tease my swollen trigger. The sensation was exquisite, almost to the point of pain; perfectly measured to tease, but never summon my release. I let out a strangled cry, a kind of desperate plea that came from deep down inside me where there were no words.

"I'll give you what you want, Sophia. I'll fuck you until you don't remember your own name." He brought his hand up to brush my cheek, staring down into my eyes. "But not just yet."

Before I realised what was happening, his hands slipped under the pillow, and something cold and metallic clicked into place around my wrists. I let out a surprised squeak. I'd known handcuffs were probably going to be part of the deal at some point, but nonetheless the sensation was a little frightening. These weren't your stereotypical fluffy, pink, 'I'm a kinky housewife' restraints. These were the real deal. There was no give, no softness or sensuality, just the implacable strength of steel.

Rather than simply pinning my arms in place, this time my bonds were linked to the bed frame. Not only was I restricted from using my hands, I couldn't escape, even if left alone. He had me at his mercy for as long as he desired.

To my credit, I managed to keep my mouth shut. I'd come to realise that surprises were just part of the experience with Sebastian. I simply had to trust that he'd never take me too far too fast.

"Perfect," he said, leaning backwards to admire his handiwork. "Now you're completely mine." His hands began to unfasten my buttons, chased by his mouth, licking and teasing the freshly exposed skin. Shock had temporarily sent my arousal scurrying to the back of my head, but the moment his lips touched me, it began pushing its way to the front again.

"This is mine," he said, planting a soft kiss across the centre of my belly. "And this," he continued, brushing his lips along the curve of my hips.

My shirt fell open, and he paused, savouring the sight of my lingerie. Thanks to my newfound obsession with sexy underwear, the bra I was wearing was rather low cut, and while the handcuffs prevented him from unfastening it completely, it didn't take more than a soft tug to pull the cups down slightly, exposing my hardened nipples. "And these are definitely mine," he said, taking one into his mouth and teasing the peak with his tongue.

I desperately wanted to reach out and push his head between my legs, but of course I couldn't. He could take as much time as he wanted. And he took ample advantage.

With agonising slowness he continued to work his way around my body, seemingly intent on leaving no stone untouched. He was a master of his craft, steadily stoking the fire inside me, but never letting it flare too much. I writhed against him, pleading for the climax that lay just out of reach, but he simply smiled. "This is what it is to submit, Sophia," he said. "To put your pleasure in the hands of another and trust that they'll take care of you." I had no answer for that. As maddening as it was, I knew he was right.

The exquisite foreplay continued. I lost all track of time. Soon, every inch of my skin was flushed and tingling. He was clearly enjoying watching me come undone. I started to think maybe he was never going to let me come, that he'd leave me chained there all night, a squirming, flustered wreck. But finally his kisses began to hone in on the soft flesh of my inner thighs.

"Please," I cried again, sensing that this was the time.

"Please what?" he asked.

"Please eat my pussy. Please make me come."

"Do you think you've earned it?"

I nodded vigorously. "I have."

He paused, and for a few dreadful seconds I thought I'd been mistaken. "I think so too," he said at last, and with a soft growl, he planted a long, slow kiss on my sex. I gasped. His tongue parted my aching folds, caressing me with strokes that managed to be strong and demanding, yet soft as a cloud. I rocked against him, the metal rim of the cuffs biting into my skin, yet the pain went all but unnoticed.

"Yes, yes," I moaned. "Keep going."

Most of the work had already been done. My body felt ready to burst. My hips began bucking, gyrating wildly as the pleasure cascading through me reached its crescendo. "Sebastian, I'm coming!"

With expert dexterity he guided me over the edge, milking every ounce of pleasure from my body, until I sunk, panting, into the bed.

He gazed at me for several seconds, radiating satisfaction. "That's the first of many tonight. I'm not done with you yet."

"I suspected that might be the case," I said weakly.

His cock flexed invitingly. As I stared at it, I knew what I wanted to do next. I needed to taste him like he'd tasted me. "But first, there's something I'd like to do to you," I continued, giving my lips a slow lick.

He let out a short laugh. "Oh? And what might that be?"

"Take off your clothes and I'll show you."

Smiling in amusement at the role reversal, he did as he was told, stripping away his suit until he stood naked before me. The sight of that lithe form caused my body to stir once more.

"Much better. Now come here and uncuff me. I want to suck your cock." Two months ago, I'd have laughed if anyone told me I'd be saying something so bold to a partner, but with

Sebastian, the old Sophia was nowhere in sight.

In moments he was just inches from my face, but he didn't reach for my restraints. "I'll let you give the orders this once," he said, "but we're still playing by my rules. The cuffs stay."

Well, that would be a new experience. But I'd never been one to shy away from a challenge. Shifting my position, I leaned forward and wrapped my lips around his swollen crown.

He exhaled slowly. "Oh Christ, that feels wonderful."

He tasted fantastic; warm, musky, and slightly salty. The width of him filled my mouth. I worked my lips slowly up and down, paying special attention to the soft track of skin just below the head, while my tongue swirled an intricate pattern across the underside of his shaft. It was an incredibly submissive position to be in, splayed below him, gazing up at his body while I pleasured him. He'd spent so long focused on me, I loved that I could give him the same in return.

"Lick it," he said, sliding free, and I did as ordered, lavishing him with slow strokes all the way to the root, then darting up to engulf him once more. Being bound changed the experience dramatically. I longed to reach out and seize the base in my fist, to pump it while I sucked him, but that wasn't an option. Instead, I focused on swallowing as much of him as I could.

"Yes, that's it, take it deeper," he said, seizing my head in his hands and guiding his length further down my throat. I drew a sharp breath through my nose, certain I was about to gag, but again he proved he was perfectly in tune with my body, never taking me over my limits. Gradually, he took over. I'd enjoyed being in control of his pleasure, but there was something erotic about having him fuck my mouth too. It was base, it was possessive, and it was hot as hell watching his self-control unravel before my eyes.

His fingers clenched tight around my hair as his strokes grew wilder. Our mutual masturbation had clearly taken a toll. He was close. I could feel each individual vein shift and pulse against my tongue. "Oh fuck, I'm going to come so hard," he groaned, and with several more mighty drives his body stiffened, and warmth exploded down my throat. His semen was sweet and salty and oh so good, and I swallowed every drop.

As he pulled free, I stared up at him, licking my lips once more for effect.

He shook his head and smiled. "God you're sexy." Leaning down, he locked his mouth over mine. "And extremely talented, if you don't mind me saying."

I grinned. "Not at all."

"I'm going to uncuff you now," he said, seizing my restraints. "I want you on all fours for what comes next."

"Next?" I asked.

He looked at me like I'd forgotten something incredibly obvious. "I still want to fuck you, Sophia."

"Don't you want a break or something?"

"Do I look like I need a break?" he asked, nodding to his cock. It was still rock hard and glistening with my saliva.

"Well, that's enough to offend a girl."

He laughed. "Don't be. It's a compliment. You drive me crazy. I seem to be hard all the time, since I met you."

His words stoked my arousal. "Well, it would be a shame not to take advantage of that."

"My thoughts exactly."

With barely concealed urgency, he flipped me onto my knees and slammed into me. I let out a long moan and rocked against him, revelling in the sensation of finally having him inside me.

"Fuck, I love how ready you are for me," he said.

I couldn't muster a reply. His body was thrumming, his strokes slow and purposeful, and they echoed through me in great waves. Wrapping his hands around my hips he yanked my body against his, burying himself in me as deeply as he could. The air was soon thick with our grunts and cries.

I'd been expecting my pleasure to build slowly, but it wasn't long before I could feel myself cresting again, helpless against that exquisite rhythm.

"Have you been wearing your butt plug like I asked?" Sebastian said, his fingers firmly squeezing my ass.

"Yes," I whispered, although the implication was lost on me. All I could focus on was the swelling inside me. A few more moments and I would be past the point of no return.

He slipped one hand underneath me, stroking my moistened lips with his thumb, coating it with my juices. "Then you might want to hold on."

That got my attention. But before I could voice a question, I felt a firm pressure against my rosette as he pushed his way in, and then all capacity for speech instantly fled.

I'd had no idea a finger there could feel so good. It magnified everything else he was doing to me a hundred times over. Something broke inside me, and my knuckles curled white around the bed sheets. I'd never come like that before. Not even with him. It felt like every individual cell in my body was rupturing all at once.

It was the kind of orgasm that should have left me in a crumpled heap, but Sebastian didn't stop, he didn't even slow, he just kept thrusting as my body clenched and buckled beneath him.

"More, Sophia. I need more. I'd make you come all night if I could."

And somehow, my body responded. With him, I felt like

201

perhaps I *could* go all night. The raw physical connection between us drowned out everything else.

Seizing my hips he flipped me around onto my back and lifted my legs to rest on his shoulder, squeezing my pussy even tighter around his hardness. With great drives he began fucking me once more, the new angle striking some long forgotten spot deep inside me. I could feel every inch of him, hot and rigid, as he urged my body towards another climax.

This one was different, less intense, but longer, and I yelled wordlessly as he brought me over the cusp.

"One more," he said, letting my legs drop back to the bed. The fire in his eyes made him look like a man possessed.

I winced. "Sebastian I can't. I can't."

"One more," he repeated.

With my legs free he altered positions again, leaning down and wrapping one arm behind my neck, locking us in a lover's embrace. His mouth found mine, grazing softly across my lips, before moving down my neck to flit gently across my nipples. His thrusts became soft, almost delicate, as he gradually coaxed my spent body back to life.

The intimacy of it all threatened to unravel me. We'd gone from kinky domination to tender lovemaking in just a few short minutes. I didn't understand. It was the kind of sex I expected to have with a lover of several years, not a self-professed anti-romantic playboy like Sebastian.

Christ Sophia, don't read too much into it. Can't you just enjoy a good thing for what it is?

But as we climaxed one final time together, clawing desperately at each other's bodies and choking out each other's names, I felt a wave of contentment unlike anything I'd experienced before.

Yeah, you might be in trouble here, girl.

Chapter 7

The whole next day, my conversation with Thomas played through my mind. In light of the things I'd felt last night, it was getting harder and harder to convince myself it was just sex with Sebastian. Our previous times together had been eye-opening, but this had been something more, something intimate. It filled a space inside me that I hadn't even known existed.

But there was no future there. Thomas had said it, as had Sebastian himself. Whatever I felt from him had to be my imagination. Letting myself think otherwise was a recipe for more heartbreak. And so I knuckled down and tried to concentrate on work.

A few mornings later, I received what appeared to be good news. In amongst the usual drudgery of my inbox was a request from Ernest to do some work on the Wrights case.

Hope this is more like what you were looking for. Enjoy!

I grinned. He'd come through after all! It was an important task too; hunting through client testimony and trying to distil it down to its core points. It was this sort of stuff that our case was built on. *High five, Sophia!*

Working as fast as I could, I ploughed through my other tasks. I figured I'd have them all done by midday, then I could spend the afternoon on the meaningful stuff. I should have realised that it was too good to be true.

At eleven thirty, I received an email from Jennifer.

Hey Soph.

Hope you're feeling better. Those prawns can be nasty things.

Need you to take care of something. This came down from Mr Bell himself and Alan asked that I get our best people on it, so naturally I thought of you. It needs to be taken care of ASAP. Have fun.

Attached was a series of case files for some tiny corporate litigation we were handling, with a note telling me to sift through and check for errors. It was lengthy, painstaking work, the kind most lawyers dread. To make matters worse, it took me all of a few seconds to see that the case wouldn't even make it to trial. There was barely enough evidence to make an accusation, let alone get a favourable judgement. She couldn't have crafted a more colossal waste of my time if she'd tried.

Although Ernest technically outranked her, Jennifer had invoked both Mr Bell's and Alan's names, which should have pushed it to the top of my pile. I doubted either of them had really laid eyes on it, but proving that would be annoying, time consuming, and probably fruitless.

I closed my eyes and attempted to contain my rage. It was impossible that it was mere coincidence. I finally received some real work, and out of the blue Jennifer miraculously conjured some mindless task for me. Not to mention her sickening faux chummy tone. She might as well have written "hahahaha" at the end of the email.

Before I knew what I was doing, I'd left my office and was storming across the floor to hers. Telling off a superior wasn't the smartest career move, but at that moment I didn't really care.

"Really?" I said, striding into her office unannounced.

"Sophia," she replied, smiling up at me like that was the most normal greeting in the world. "What a pleasure. Is everything okay?"

"What do you think? I've just been assigned work for the most pointless case on our books."

Somehow she managed to look perfectly innocent. "Oh?"

I glared at her. "The Phaidan File?"

"Oh that. Come on, you're being a bit dramatic don't you think? If anything it's a compliment. We needed someone with a good eye for detail, so I assigned you."

I felt my hands contract involuntarily into fists. I was a hair's breadth away from leaping over the desk and rearranging the details of her face. "It's bullshit, is what it is. That case is never going to see the inside of a court room and you know it."

"Oh I don't know about that. In any case, I'm just doing what I'm told."

"Oh yeah?" I said. "Well I'm not. I'm not wasting my afternoon on that crap when there's real work to be done."

She stared at me for several seconds, a calculating glint in her eyes. Eventually she shrugged. "Well, suit yourself. Obviously I can't force you." Her voice turned sweet. "I just hope nobody upstairs hears that you're rejecting assigned work. You know how this place is; it's a slippery slope to the bottom."

At that point I knew I'd played right into her hands. This was exactly the sort of reaction she'd been hoping for. It probably wasn't enough to land me in serious trouble, but causing me any kind of grief seemed to be a win in her books. She loved watching me squirm.

"Why, Jennifer?" I asked, hating myself for sounding so defeated.

For a moment a look of unrestrained glee spread over her face, but it was gone again in an instant. She was too smart to give up the game so easily. "Why what, Sophia?" she replied, her tone perfectly neutral.

Unable to stand another second in her presence, I spun and fled back to my office. Slamming the door behind me, I sat down and let out a long breath. *Calm blue ocean, Sophia.*

As much as Jennifer's antics angered me, I didn't know what I could do about them. The hierarchy was everything in our office, and despite how little she deserved it, she outranked me. That made her basically untouchable. Sure, I could try going to the higher ups, but it was career suicide to go behind a superior's back unless the problem was really serious. Once you had a reputation as a backstabber, nobody wanted to work with you. All I could really do was hunker down and try to roll with the punches.

I considered just giving in and doing the work she'd assigned, but try as I might, I couldn't make myself start it. Either way she was going to win. At least by refusing I kept some shred of dignity. I doubted she'd actually be petty enough to take it up the ladder, and if she did, well, it would probably only be a slap on the wrist.

So, gritting my teeth, I opened the Wrights files and began to work.

Chapter 8

Despite my best efforts to stay positive, Jennifer's meddling sent my mood plummeting. Even though she hadn't actually stopped me from working on Wrights, she'd soured the experience for me. Suddenly it felt like the wrong thing to do. I hated her for that.

To make matters worse, I kept running into her around the office. At first I thought it was just chance, but soon I realised she was doing it on purpose. She never said anything about our altercation, but the smarmy little smiles she shot me told me all I needed to know. She'd enjoyed her little prank immensely.

After two days of feeling like shit, I found myself reaching for the phone. I wasn't sure if emotional support fell under the terms of my relationship with Sebastian, but he was the first person I thought to call. There was something about his presence that made me feel comfortable and protected, and right now that was exactly what I needed.

He answered after five or six rings. "Sophia."

"Hey," I replied, trying my best to sound less morose than I felt. It didn't work.

"Is everything okay?" he asked.

I sighed. "Not really. Having a pretty rough few days actually."

"Oh, I'm sorry. Work stuff?"

"Yeah. Any chance you're free tonight? I could use some cheering up."

He hesitated. "I don't know, I've got a lot to do here."

"Just for a little while? I'd really like to see you. I'll even come to you."

There was another pause. "I guess I can spare an hour or two. Is ten okay?"

"Totally fine. I'll see you then."

Knowing I was seeing him later made the day a little more bearable.

He greeted me at the door when I arrived, looking as fresh as if he'd just woken up. Despite the late hour, he was still wearing a suit, although the tie was missing. Perhaps that was as far as 'casual' went for him.

"Hey," he said softly, pulling me in for a hug.

I stood there for a few moments enjoying the feel of his arms. "Hey," I replied eventually.

He led me inside.

"Thanks for making time," I said, once we were seated in the lounge room. "I know you're busy. I just really needed a friendly face."

He gave a dismissive wave. "Don't worry about it. I didn't like the way you sounded on the phone. So what's wrong?"

I sighed. Now that I actually had to explain it, it all felt a little petty, but there was no backing out now. I told him about what had happened.

He listened patiently, compassion evident on his face. He seemed genuinely troubled that I was upset.

"You think Jennifer is the reason you've been having so much trouble lately?" he asked, when I was done.

I shrugged. "I don't know. I doubt it. I mean, she's just a senior associate, not a partner. She doesn't have that kind of authority. Don't get me wrong, I'm sure it doesn't help and she probably takes every opportunity to talk me down when she can — in the sweetest way possible of course — but at the moment she seems content to just fuck with me instead."

"And you can't take it up the ladder at all? Surely that's office harassment or something."

"It wouldn't do any good. She's kissed the ass of every bigger paycheck in the company. All I'd do is make more trouble for myself."

He frowned. "So what are you going to do?"

I exhaled sharply. "I don't know. Either way I lose. I basically have to make a choice; the work I want to do, or the work I should do. It's so unfair." Those last words came out as a kind of high pitched squeal, and I suddenly realised how I was coming across. "God, I've turned into a whiny high-school girl. I'm sorry."

He smiled and reached out to stroke my knee. "It's okay. Seems to me it might be justified. Why does this woman dislike you so much?"

"I don't know. She seems to dislike most other women around the office. You'd think she'd want to stick together, but I get the sense she'd be happier if she were the only one. Plus, I think it pissed her off the way tasks got distributed when we both first started. Despite her position, she's just not really that good at her job, and it showed in her work. She got stuck doing the things I'm doing now, while I was working on the good stuff. It was only once she got her claws into the higher ups that she managed to drag herself out."

"Well, she sounds like a petty bitch."

Those words brought a smile to my face. I hadn't expected to hear Sebastian say something so catty. "That's a fairly accurate assessment." I shook my head. "I don't know, maybe I'm making too big of a deal out of it. Sometimes it just kind of feels like the whole place is conspiring against me, you know? I have no idea how long this Wrights work from Ernest is going to last. I suspect he had to fight pretty hard to get me assigned."

"Well, at least you've got someone on your side."

"That's true."

"You deserve better than this, Sophia."

"Thanks."

He slid closer on the couch and looped his arm around me. "I just wish there was something I could do."

"You've done plenty by just listening. I wasn't expecting any solutions, just someone to vent to."

He nodded but didn't reply.

We sat like that for a few minutes. It felt good to be snuggled against him. I hadn't been sure what to expect from this encounter, but he'd been incredibly kind and understanding. He'd even joined me in a little therapeutic spitefulness.

I leaned up and kissed him. It was meant to be just a short tender gesture, a thank you for being there for me, but whatever explosive chemistry our bodies shared seemed oblivious to any sort of context. In a matter of moments, our kiss deepened, his tongue entwining with mine while his hands found my neck. I felt something stirring inside my stomach, the first pleasant thing I'd felt since my encounter with Jennifer.

I broke away. "You know, I believe I was promised cheering up. I'm certainly feeling a little better, but I wouldn't describe myself as cheerful yet."

His expression turned sly. "Is that so? Well then, I still have work to do." Wrapping his hands around my thighs he lifted me on top of him.

As his lips began to trace their way down my shoulder, I

threw back my head, closed my eyes, and gave myself over to him. My body bowed and shuddered as he teased the spark inside me into a raging fire, one exquisite kiss at a time. His fingers wound towards to my buttons and began to work their way down, unwrapping me with torturous slowness.

The intimacy of the position filled me with warmth and security. The trust I had in moments like those made me feel so safe, so protected. In his hands, I could simply lose myself in the moment, utterly confident that whatever we were doing, he'd take care of me.

Slipping my blouse to one side and snapping my bra free with one deft flick of his wrist, he freed my breasts. He leaned backwards momentarily, gazing at my body with a heat so intense I was surprise I didn't burst into flames. "Has anyone ever told you how fucking perfect you are?"

I couldn't help but smile. "Not in those exact words."

"Then all the men you've ever met are idiots."

He resumed his maddening exploration. My nipples were hard peaks, begging for his mouth, and he obliged, grazing them softly with his tongue in a way that made my whole body contort. I curled my fingers through his hair, savouring the silky texture of it as he roved across my chest.

"Stand up, Sophia," he said.

I did as I was told. His eyes heavy with purpose, he reached around and unfastened the zipper of my skirt. With slow reverence he pulled it down, his breath stalling as my legs slowly came into view. Nobody had ever made me feel that way before; so utterly worshipped.

My panties came down next, and his pants followed, and then I was straddling him once more. I could feel the rigid heat of him radiating between my legs even before he entered me. His eyes widened as he gradually pushed his way past my folds, my body welcoming that sweet invasion with trembling hunger.

Reaching out, he wrapped one hand around my waist and the other around my shoulder, and began to guide me up and down. His grip was firm, but his motions remained slow and measured. I had no idea how a man could be so strong, so powerful, and yet so tender. I knew the animal was still locked away inside him somewhere, but this was exactly what I wanted right now, to make love, not to fuck, and so that's what he gave me.

I'd never been on top with him before. I liked the sensation of riding him, the way I could subtly shift my hips to change the angle of our motion. But even with me in such a position of strength, he was definitely still running the show. With firm pressure, he rocked my body against his, sheathing himself completely and grinding my clit against his pubic bone with a rhythm that set my whole body cresting.

"Oh Christ, don't stop," I moaned.

He reached up with one hand to caress my breasts, while leaning in and planting a string of hungry kisses along my collar bone. "I won't. I've got you, Sophia."

As I pressed my face into his hair, the scent of him washed over me, that perfect masculine potency. Nothing else had ever smelled that good.

"Are you going to come for me?" he asked, his voice full of warmth.

"Yes," I breathed, the pressure inside me swelling and rippling, following his command. Maintaining the same tantalising pace, he guided me over the edge, pulling me in close and sealing his mouth over mine as my release took hold. It wasn't the most powerful orgasm he'd given me, but it was the most affectionate, which at that moment made it utterly perfect.

He came wordlessly about twenty seconds later, his body

quivering beneath me. The whole time, he never broke that kiss.

"Well, consider me cheerful," I said, as we lay there afterwards.

He pulled me close. "I aim to please."

There was a wonderful sense of protection being encased between those arms. My troubles were still lurking in the back of my head somewhere, but I'd turned down the volume as best I could. I'd come to Sebastian to make me feel better, and he'd done an amazing job. Now I just wanted to enjoy that sensation for as long as possible.

Chapter 9

The following morning I woke to an empty bed, but it was not my own. It was the first time Sebastian and I had spent a full night together. Joe had always driven me home in the past. I didn't know if my staying over was intentional or not, but I chose to believe it was.

When I finally managed to drag myself from Sebastian's impossibly soft sheets, I found a folded white robe waiting for me on the dresser. It was accompanied by a note.

Your clothes were positively filthy, so I had them put in the wash. Your underwear too. They're drying at the moment, so you'll have to make do with something else for now.

I held it up in front of the mirror. Sheer and short, with a hem that barely covered the middle of my thighs, it hardly deserved the name 'robe' at all. I had no idea where he'd gotten it from.

My clothes may have had a day's wear, but "positively filthy" was definitely a stretch. It didn't take a rocket scientist to see that this was another of his little games. And as much as I enjoyed playing them, I felt a sudden desire to turn the tables on him.

A few minutes of exploring his extensive wardrobe turned up an over-sized tie-dyed tee shirt that fell all the way to my knees. It wasn't the sort of thing I could ever see Sebastian wearing, but it suited my needs just fine.

I found him in the kitchen. "Morning," I said nonchalantly, as I strolled in.

"Good morning." He did a double take. "Where on earth did you find that?"

I shrugged. "In your cupboard somewhere."

"Was the robe not to your tastes?"

"Oh it was fine. I just figured if you were going to hold my clothes hostage I'd do the same to you."

He laughed loudly. "Fair enough. Although I have to say, if commandeering your clothes causes you to dress like this every day, I'm not sure I'll be giving them back any time soon. Are you naked under there?"

I grazed my teeth over my bottom lip and tried to look innocent. "Maybe."

He made an appreciative noise. "Well I have to say, you look fucking sexy wearing my clothes."

"So it is yours?" I asked, grinning widely.

He sighed. "Regrettably, yes. Let's just say I was going through a phase."

I laughed. It was impossible to picture Sebastian looking anything other than perfectly dapper — even now, naked, save for a pair of loose fitting slacks, he looked stunning — but it was nice to know he was human too.

My stomach rumbled as my brain finally registered the smell of oil and eggs. Looking around, I realised that breakfast was already well on the way. There was coffee brewing in a rather elaborate drip filter pot, and several fry pans were sizzling on the stove. Sebastian was busy flitting between them, spatula in hand. There was something about the image that made me giggle.

"What's so funny?" he asked.

"Nothing, I just didn't take you for much of a cook."

A look of mock offence crossed his face. "And why would you think that?"

"I don't know. I just assumed you'd have somebody to do it for you."

"Because money means you never do anything for yourself?"

"I didn't say that! It's just an amusing image. The millionaire dom who liked to cook. It's like a bad erotic book title."

He grinned. "Even us steely sadists have to eat."

"Well it smells great." I slipped closer to survey what was on offer. "Mmm, Chorizo for breakfast? You're living dangerously."

"I do everything dangerously, Sophia," he deadpanned. We both laughed.

"You know, I honestly can't remember the last time a guy cooked me breakfast," I said, taking a seat as he slid a plate in front of me. "I have to say, I kind of like it so far."

He joined me at the bar. "Sounds to me like you've been dating the wrong guys."

"You can say that again." As much as I willed it to stay put, the smile fell from my face. I hated that two years later, Connor still had the power to hurt me, but he did. Just thinking about him made my stomach knot with shame.

Sebastian gazed at me for several seconds, his expression mirroring my own. "He must been one hell of a bastard."

I nodded. "He wasn't exactly boyfriend of the year."

"I'm sorry, I didn't mean to bring him up."

I sighed. As much as it hurt to discuss, I still felt a little like I owed Sebastian an explanation for my past behaviour.

"It's fine. I should be able to talk about this stuff by now."

He hesitated, but took the hint. "What happened between you two exactly?"

"Nothing worth talking about. He was rich and charming, I was young and naive. It was a match made in heaven... for him at least."

"Were you together long?"

"A few years. Long enough to make me feel like an idiot for ever trusting him." It came out more bitter than I'd intended.

"Hey," he said, reaching out to stroke my arm, "everybody's allowed a mistake, here or there. God knows I've got my share."

"There's a difference between a mistake and outright stupidity. All the signs were there — unexplained nights away from home, mysterious texts — but he always had an excuse ready, and I ate them up. Looking back on it now it seems so fucking obvious."

"People don't behave rationally when they're in love. You can't hold that against yourself. Besides, from where I'm sitting, you're not the one that really fucked up."

"Oh?"

He smiled. "You're a strong, beautiful, amazing woman, Sophia. He may have had you for a year or two, but he gave you up. One day, someone is going to have you forever, and then they're going to be the ones making *him* look stupid."

I stared at him for several seconds, a rush of some foreign emotion blazing in my belly. Talking about Connor always left me feeling angry and embarrassed, but somehow Sebastian had washed all that away with just a few lovely words.

"Well, it's hard to argue with that," I said.

"Then don't."

We moved on to lighter topics. Sebastian had several less

than flattering stories about Thomas. I think he was just trying to get revenge for 'Locky'. The whole experience was a bit
of a revelation. Every time I was with him, he revealed a new
side to himself, and I had to admit, lazy Tuesday morning
Sebastian was quickly becoming my favourite. As fantastic as
the sex was, it was nice just sitting around and chatting with
him too. Away from prying eyes he seemed more relaxed; the
professional superman persona was stashed away in the wardrobe alongside his racks of designer suits. Here he was just
Sebastian, a man who wore old clothes and cooked scrambled
eggs and delivered sweet words over coffee. What's more, he
seemed at ease doing those things with me.

In spite of what Thomas had said and the initial discussions between Sebastian and I, it was hard not to feel like
things were changing. Our last two nights together had been
anything but casual, and it seemed impossible he didn't feel it
too. The word 'forever' lingered in my mind. I didn't know
how to take that comment. Was there more to it than simple
comfort? Part of me wanted to think so.

After breakfast, we found our way back to the bedroom.
He told me to leave his shirt on while he fucked me, pinning
my arms behind my back and whispering dirty things about
how hot I looked in his clothes. There were no cuffs or pad-
dles or lengths of rope, just the unbreakable strength of his
hands and the exquisite pressure of his cock. It was more than
enough.

Afterwards, we lay snuggled in bed, flushed and glowing
and blissfully satisfied. I desperately didn't want the morning
to end, although I knew I couldn't delay much longer.

"Has anyone ever told you you tend to go above and beyond the call of duty?" I asked, dozing against his chest.

He began stroking my shoulder. "In what way?"

"Well, I tasked you with cheering me up, but apparently

you weren't satisfied with that. Right now, I've left cheerful way behind. Seriously, you can't even see that shit anymore. I'd say I'm well into blissful territory. You deserve a commendation, sir."

His hand froze. "I'm glad you're feeling better."

"Next time, I'm totally going to call in sick and see how far we can push this."

There was a pause. "Next time?"

"Next time we do this. I'll tell you; a girl could get used to sleepovers and homemade breakfasts."

The silence that followed should probably have set alarm bells ringing in my head, but I was too content to really notice. All I could think about was how for the first time, it felt like things were really coming together for us.

How wrong I was.

Chapter 10

It turned out that I needn't have worried about being relegated to the bench again. The Wrights case had hit the front page once more after a new batch of victims came forward, so we were ramping up our efforts. For now, it was all hands on deck.

It was fascinating, and a little horrifying, to be a part of. A perfect illustration of the power mega companies can bring to bear when profits are under threat. I was no stranger to the greed of big business, but there was a callousness about their approach that made even me balk. They were like a truck, calmly driving along, ignoring every traffic signal. Most people managed to dive out of their way, but those that didn't weren't even worth a second glance. They were just squashed underneath like bugs. In spite of the pain and hassle a proper trial would involve, part of me hoped they refused to settle. The more I read, the more I wanted Little Bell to crush them in the court room.

Nothing came of the situation with Jennifer, so I figured she'd just been messing with me for her own enjoyment. I felt a little stupid for overreacting. It wasn't a big deal in the grand scheme of things.

I should have been happy that I was finally working on

my dream project, but I couldn't really enjoy it. Something had changed with Sebastian. There was no doubt in my mind anymore that my feelings for him had grown, but ever since our morning together, his seemed to have moved in the opposite direction.

It wasn't that he was ignoring me. He still messaged every day or two, but they were short and monosyllabic and lacked any of the warmth I'd come to expect. In person he was no better. Aloof, almost to the point of being cold, we rarely had a discussion that lasted more than a few minutes. That amazing man from just a few nights ago was nowhere in sight.

I clung on, hoping it was just stress. Over the next two weeks, our encounters took on a fairly predictable rhythm. A spontaneous text message, a frenetic sexual rendezvous, and then a hasty departure. On the surface, it was great. I was working overtime, even by my standards, and it was the sort of comfortable arrangement that fit perfectly around that. The problem was that wasn't the kind of comfort I was looking for anymore. I often found my mind wandering back to that morning chatting over coffee, and to the night before, to the overpowering rightness I'd felt as I drifted off to sleep cocooned in his arms. And the more I thought, the more I longed for that closeness again.

"You could stay, you know," I said to him one night, as he stood up and began to gather his things.

"I really should get home." He even looked different now. There was a permanently harried cast to his eyes that I'd never seen before.

"Is everything okay?" I'd tried several times to pry something out of him, even the tiniest hint of what had gone wrong, but it was useless.

He nodded. "Yeah. I just have a lot to do, that's all." He tried shooting me a reassuring smile, but it didn't quite cut through the hardness on his face.

I didn't understand. Our connection had felt so real and so powerful to me, and I'd been so sure he felt it too. But now I was starting to doubt myself.

Maybe I really had just imagined everything. Maybe I had no idea how to read men at all. My past relationships certainly said as much. But if that was the case, could I keep going the way things were, knowing there was nothing more to it? It felt wrong to throw away something that was so theoretically perfect, but every night that we said goodbye, I felt my heart break just a little more.

Still, I wasn't quite ready to give up just yet. People always said the way to a man's heart was through his stomach, and that was one approach I had yet to try. So when the weekend rolled around, I sent him a text.

Sophia: Hey. Hope they're not working you to the bone over there. I thought maybe you could come around for dinner tonight night if you're free. I'm not much of a chef, but I do make a mean carbonara. Thought I could pay you back for breakfast the other week. Let me know.

He replied a few minutes later.

Sebastian: Not sure I should. But maybe I can swing by later on?

I'd expected it, but I still felt a pang of disappointment.

Sophia: Okay, sure.

But as the day progressed, my frustration grew. I kept turning his message over in my mind. It was the phrasing that bothered me. There was that word *"should"* again. *"Not sure I should."* That wasn't the same as *"Not sure I can."* It could mean that he was too busy or had something else on, but it could also mean that he simply didn't want to. If that was the case, then I was wasting my time. I tried to convince myself to stop overthinking it, but by the time the evening rolled around, I still felt uneasy.

Mostly out of stubbornness, I made a pot of carbonara anyway, and ate a bowl of it while reading on the couch. There wasn't much to do but wait. He hadn't given an exact time.

At about eleven o'clock, there was a knock at the door.

"Sophia," he said by way of greeting.

"Hey." Even with the turmoil I felt, I found myself smiling. It was good to see him. There was something addictive about the way I felt when we were together, some beautiful nexus of hormones and emotions that made everything seem a little brighter, a little more real. I desperately wanted to keep feeling that as often as possible.

Not even waiting until we'd made it inside, he moved in to kiss me, and for a few seconds, my body began to yield to his. But as he pressed me up against the hallway wall, his hand already teasing the curve of my ass, I felt something crack inside me.

"Sebastian... wait..." I said, forcing myself to pull back.

"What? Is something wrong?"

I closed my eyes for a second and cupped my face in my hands. "Just once in a while could we maybe wait more than a few minutes before you start feeling me up?"

His smile slipped. "I'm sorry. I just missed you, that's all. You know what your body does to me."

"It sounds like you missed my body a lot more than the rest of me," I replied, a little more harshly than intended.

He didn't seem to know how to reply to that.

Suddenly feeling uncomfortable in such an intimate position, I ducked under his arm and moved into the lounge room. He followed me in silence.

"I'm not sure I understand," he said, after about twenty seconds.

"Well that makes two of us." I hadn't planned to go on the offensive tonight, but the churning feeling in my stomach couldn't be ignored any longer.

"Did I do something wrong?" he asked.

I laughed bitterly and shook my head. "Nope. You've done basically everything just the way you promised."

"So what's the problem?" I didn't respond. "Is it about dinner?"

I threw up my hands. "Yes... no... I don't know. I thought it would be nice, that's all. Spend a little time together. You've been distant, lately."

"We've seen each other three times this week."

I shot him a pointed look. "Distant and physically present aren't mutually exclusive."

He ran a hand through his hair and began pacing. He always seemed to do that when things didn't go to plan, as though enough steps would simply carry him away from the problem all together. "I don't understand what you want from me, Sophia."

"I want some bloody consistency. Why is it okay for you to cook me breakfast, but I can't make you dinner? Why is it okay for me to stay over at your place, but you won't ever stay here?"

There was a pause. "I don't know. I didn't plan any of that, it just sort of happened."

"So? That's how these things are supposed to go. They

progress gradually. What I want to know is, why are you trying so hard to make sure it doesn't 'just happen' again?"

He shifted awkwardly and looked away. "Like I said, I've been extremely busy lately. I just don't have that much time—"

"It's not just about the time! It's everything; the way you act, the way you talk to me. It's like there are two different Sebastians. Some days I get the kind, sweet, intensely passionate man who makes me feel wonderful, and other days it's his evil twin who barely wants to do anything but fuck, and who ignores me for weeks on end. How the hell am I meant to deal with that?"

He pursed his lips. "I'm the same man I always was."

"That's what I'm worried about."

His face was a mask of intensity now. "So what are you saying, Sophia?"

I shook my head slowly. There was no going back now. "You want me to spell it out? Okay, fine. You were right to be worried at the beginning; apparently your 'charms' are just too strong. I'm no longer happy just to write this thing off as a casual fling. Don't get me wrong, the sex is great, but it's more than that to me now. I like being with you, Sebastian, naked or not, and I can't go on doing whatever the hell it is we're doing anymore without admitting that. I thought maybe you felt the same way, but apparently I was wrong."

I must have watched one too many sappy romantic comedies, because I was actually disappointed that my declaration didn't cause him to break into a glorious smile and sweep me up in his arms. Instead, he stared at me with an unreadable expression, his jaw working wordlessly.

That silence was almost crushing. A car horn blared somewhere in the distance, punctuating his lack of response. "Say something for god's sake," I said, after a few seconds.

"I'm thinking," he replied.

White hot rage filled me. "*Thinking*? This isn't a moment for thinking Sebastian. This isn't a game anymore. There are no smooth lines to deliver, no different angles to approach from. If you have to think, then this whole thing is a lost cause!"

He continued to sit, utterly motionless, his expression hard as stone.

It was too much. I shot to my feet, suddenly desperate to be anywhere but in his presence. I couldn't even meet his eyes anymore. I should have known better than to expect something more from him. "I need you to leave," I said. "Consider our 'arrangement' over. I'm sure that will give you plenty to think about."

I began moving towards the staircase, but as I passed him, his hand snaked out and caught my wrist. "Sophia, wait. Look at me." His voice was a dry rasp. Barely human.

Reluctantly I turned. The look on his face was frightening enough to stop me in my tracks. It was like his expression so far had just been a mask, and now the entire thing had just broken right up the middle. His cheeks were pinched and flushed, his mouth drawn tripwire tight, and there was something new in his eyes, something I could only describe as terror. It was so intense that I could practically feel it rippling in the air around me. There was no way I was misinterpreting that. Ending this frightened him as much as it did me.

"It's not just me, is it?" I asked, my voice surprisingly soft.

He gave a tiny shake of his head. "Of course it's not just you."

I sank heavily back into my seat. That admission didn't make me feel as good as I'd expected. It lifted one weight while replacing it with another.

"So what is it, Sebastian?" I asked. "If we both want the

same thing, why run away?"

He drew a deep breath. "It's complicated. I'm complicated."

"*Relationships* are complicated," I replied. "There's no avoiding it. We made a good effort at minimising all that and just sticking to the fun stuff, but I for one can't go on that way anymore. As inconvenient as it might be for both of us, this thing means something to me now, and I want everything that comes with that, including your complications."

He gazed into my eyes, a ghost of a smile touching his lips. "It means something to me, too."

"Then stop pushing me away!"

He hung his head. "I want to. I really do. But you don't know what you're asking. You terrify me, Sophia. I've never felt so consumed by another person before. And every time we see each other, it's like I lose another piece of myself in you. You criticise me for thinking too much, but the truth is, around you I don't think. I just do. I have no control. I'm sorry if I freaked out, but I don't know how to deal with that."

They were the most bittersweet words I'd ever heard. His feelings were as strong as mine, but apparently that was only half the battle.

"Why are you so afraid, Sebastian?"

He studied me for what felt like an eternity. I knew this was the moment that would make or break us. He could throw his armour back on, pull down his mask, and march out the door, and there would be nothing I could do to stop him.

"Have you ever lost someone?" he asked eventually. "Someone important?"

I felt a sinking feeling in my stomach. "Two grandparents, although I was too young to remember one very well."

He nodded. "I've lost more than my fair share, but one

cut a little closer to the bone than the rest."

I knew instantly who he was talking about. "The girl in your phone background?"

He swallowed loudly, then nodded.

I thought about her every now and again. That night outside my house was one of the rare moments I'd seen cracks in Sebastian's impeccable facade. They were the same cracks I could see now, only this time, they were a hundred times worse. What the hell had I just started?

"What happened?" I asked, as gently as I could.

His lips compressed and he gazed down at the table. "Some men broke into her house," he said, his voice completely hollow. "The police said they were probably high, looking for money or something to sell." He gave a sad little laugh. "She was always a fighter. Never backed down from anything. That's one of the things I loved about her." He paused again. "There was a struggle. They beat her senseless. She died before the ambulance even arrived."

My hand flew up to my mouth. "Oh god." I reached out to take his fingers in mine. "I'm so sorry, Sebastian. I didn't mean to make you dredge that up."

"It's okay," he replied, although his expression said otherwise. He looked close to tears. It was jarring seeing him like that. He was always so strong, so in control.

"It was serious?" I asked tentatively.

He smiled the most gut-wrenching smile I'd ever seen. "You could say that. We were engaged."

"Oh god," I said again. I had no idea what to say. It was the kind of grief I knew no words would soothe. Even though I'd wanted to know, part of me felt awful for putting him through this. It kind of put my commitment issues into perspective. All I'd done was make a few terribly naive choices; he'd lost the person he loved most in the world. I had no idea how I'd recover from something like that. I suspected I wouldn't.

He closed his eyes and drew several long breaths. "I nearly told you that night outside your house, you know. Nobody besides my closest friends know about Liv, but even then, part of me felt compelled to explain it to you." He brought his eyes up to meet mine, seizing my free hand in his. "There are lots of things I want to share with you, but sharing isn't easy for me. You deserve someone who can give you everything, and I'm afraid if we go any further, I'm going to disappoint you."

For the short period I'd known him, Sebastian had always been a mystery to me. It was like watching a magician perform. I knew there was a trick there somewhere, but I was too dazzled to spot it. But in that moment, I felt like I finally understood him just a little. Behind all those walls, behind that radiant charm and those perfect features, lay a scared and lonely man. I hated seeing him like that, but at the same time, his candour filled me with hope. I knew how much of a gift he'd given me.

"One step at a time, hey?" I said. "I don't need to know all of your deepest, darkest secrets right away. All I need to know is that this is real, because if we go any further and I find out that it's not, I think it will break me."

He studied me for several seconds, a small smile managing to puncture through his otherwise grim expression. "This is the realest thing I know, Sophia."

And then before I could even finish processing what he'd said, he was kissing me. This time I didn't try to stop him. I couldn't. I was certain if anything were going to break that moment, the very planet would have to collapse off its axis. In that kiss, I saw a vision of everything I'd ever wanted. And it was wonderful.

Chapter 11

It's amazing the difference one night can make. Weeks' worth of tension and uncertainty, all dissipated with a single conversation. I woke with my body pressed against his, feeling more content than I had in a long time. The smile on his face when he opened his eyes said that he felt the same.

After a leisurely love making session that involved several creative uses for a dressing gown tie, we headed for the kitchen to squeeze in a quick breakfast before work. Now that we'd acknowledged our feelings, it was more difficult than ever to say goodbye. I really just wanted to spend the whole day together, but that was the peril of a relationship between two dedicated professionals. Time was a limited commodity.

Thankfully we had phones. I used to mock those couples who seemed to require constant contact. I had a friend at university who spent every day glued to her phone, eagerly waiting for the next inevitable text from her boyfriend. It wasn't like they were long distance or anything. She'd see him every night after class. I never understood why she couldn't just wait a few hours to say what she had to say. But now I finally got it. There was something comforting about those little connections. It wasn't so much the words themselves as what they symbolised; that someone out there was thinking of you. And

Sebastian and I made sure to let each other know that as often as possible.

Two days later, I woke up to find a message from him.

Sebastian: You're coming out with me tonight.

I couldn't help but smile. No request. Just an order.

Sophia: And what if I have plans?

Sebastian: I won't be stood up for a stack of subpoenas and a glass of red.

Sophia: Haha. You know me too well. Fine. Where should I meet you?

Sebastian: I'll come to you. I want it to be a surprise. Be home and ready by 6.30. And wear comfortable shoes.

Of course. Why tell me what we were doing when he could just keep it shrouded in mystery instead? I had to hand it to him, he knew how to keep a girl guessing. The comfortable shoes tidbit was interesting. It seemed to imply that we'd be walking somewhere, but I'd long since learned that his hints could rarely be taken at face value.

As usual, my excitement made the day go by at a crawl. This would be our first full night together with everything laid out on the table. For the first time, I could be completely unashamed of the way he made me feel. That was a truly glorious prospect.

When five thirty rolled around, there was still a mountain of work needing to be done. The Wrights case had everyone with their noses to the grindstone. In times past, I'd blown off dates under such circumstances, but the thought didn't even enter my head tonight. I tidied up what I could, sent a few quick apologetic emails, and headed home. Little Bell had been my top priority for six long years; it could spare me the odd night here and there.

Sebastian was perfectly on time as usual. As I stepped out of the front door, he cast his eyes over me and made a little throaty sound. "You're a sight for sore eyes."

I grinned. "We saw each other two days ago."

"And every minute of those was agony," he replied with a dramatic flourish. He did a double take when he spotted my shoes. "The princess is wearing her slippers out again I see."

I'd wondered if he'd notice they were the same pair from that first night. In my experience, men didn't pay much attention to shoes, but Sebastian didn't seem to miss anything. "Well, after the prince so graciously returned them to her, she figured she should make good use of them. Besides, they're the most comfortable shoes she owns."

"Fair enough."

I curled my hands through his hair and pulled his mouth towards mine. God, I'd missed him. In that moment, I was certain I would have been quite happy just standing on my front step with our lips locked together for the rest of the night.

As if reading my thoughts, he pulled away. "Easy now. Let's not get ahead of ourselves. There will be plenty of time for that."

I made a show of pouting, but let him lead me to the car anyway.

The trip was longer than I'd expected. Rather than dropping us somewhere in the city, Joe continued to drive out over the Harbour Bridge.

"Where are you taking me?" I asked, more than a little

curious by now.

But he merely smiled. "If I told you, it wouldn't be a surprise."

Once we crossed the Spit Bridge, I had a better idea, and my suspicions were proven right when we pulled up outside the Manly boardwalk. Manly is one of the suburbs that sprawls along the north side of Sydney Harbour. It's a lovely area; a dynamic mix of beach culture and nightlife. I'd had several messy nights there in my youth, although not for a few years. Old age had made me cynical and territorial, and I tended to stick closer to home now.

"Ah, so another waterfront meal is it?" I asked, feigning disinterest.

He gazed down at me in amusement. "Would it be a problem if it was?"

"Oh, I guess not," I said, trying to hide my smile. "You may want to consider some new material, that's all."

"You underestimate me, Sophia. I've got a few more tricks up my sleeve yet."

Linking arms with me, he led me along the pier. I'd expected him to take me into one of the softly lit, glass panelled restaurants that looked out over the bay, but instead he guided me into the back streets. After just a few minutes of walking, we were essentially in suburbia. I kept my mouth shut now, content to just wait and see.

Eventually we ducked into an alley which appeared to be lined with houses. Sebastian stopped and exchanged a few words with a man who was standing outside a fairly unremarkable doorway. After a few moments, we were led inside and down a narrow staircase. The whole thing had a clandestine feel to it, much like that first night we met, and much like that night, I was not disappointed by what I found.

"Wow," I said, as we reached the bottom. "This is awesome."

I had been half right. It was a restaurant, but it was one of the liveliest restaurants I'd ever seen. The room was packed full of people, all sitting at long tables laughing and chatting and passing around colourful plates laden with food. The air was heavy with a million fragrances, garlic and paprika and the sweet bite of fresh chili. The whole place had an amazing vibe, like everyone had a tacit agreement to shed their troubles for one night and just enjoy themselves. I would have been surprised to spot a single unsmiling face.

"Welcome to Mi Casa," Sebastian said.

"My house?" I asked, vaguely conjuring the translation from some long forgotten primary school Spanish class.

He nodded.

"A bit of a strange name for a restaurant."

His smile widened. "It's not just a restaurant. Come on, they're holding a table for us." Taking my hand, he led me up to the front counter. The man there recognised him instantly, and after a few emphatic words, he guided us towards the back of the room.

"This is my favourite place in the whole of Sydney for a night out," Sebastian said, once we were seated. "I don't get to come here very often anymore, but every time I do, I enjoy myself."

"I can see why," I said.

Without us even having ordered, a waiter appeared at our table bearing two glasses and a tall jug of sangria.

"Standard issue," said Sebastian, with a wink. I wasn't complaining. It was delicious, sweet and rich, but with a hint of spice.

After studying the rather intimidating menu, I gave Sebastian leave to just order for the both of us. There were so many dishes that I had no idea where to start.

It was certainly a far cry from the last restaurant he'd taken me to. Quay had been quiet and sophisticated; the epitome of fine dining. This felt more like a well-kept family secret. From the plastic table cloths to the gregarious patrons, to the giant, warming plates of food, it was the kind of place that instantly made you feel at home. At one point, while Sebastian was ordering, he actually had to start yelling because a group behind us spontaneously broke into song.

"Sorry," he said to me, when the waiter had gone. "This place can get a little rowdy."

"Don't apologise. I love it. Who doesn't want a little show with their meal?"

"Well, the meal will be even better than the show. The food here is out of this world. One of the only places that does paella as good as back home."

"I'm looking forward to it." I took a sip of wine. "So you're originally from Spain then? I have to admit, that accent has always confused me."

He nodded. "I get that a lot. I was born there, and my father was Spanish, but my mother was Australian. Growing up, I didn't really watch television or anything, so with just the two of them teaching me to speak, I kind of wound up with a mix of both accents."

"Spanish and Australian, hey? Well, I must say, that's one hell of a hot combination." I thought back to my discussion with Thomas. I longed to know more about Sebastian's past, but I didn't want to push him. He'd already opened up about Liv, I figured the rest would follow when he was ready.

Instead, we played catch up. Finally free to get to know one another, we covered every topic usually reserved for first and second dates; movies, books, music, TV shows. Neither of us had much time for that stuff anymore, but we fit it in where we could. It turned out he was a big horror movie fan, and he loved Jack Reacher books as much as I did.

"He's the kind of practical hero I can get behind," he said.

These were just tiny pieces, almost inconsequential when taken alone, but each one added just a little bit more to the jigsaw puzzle of him that I was slowly assembling in my head.

The food was as good as he'd promised. He'd ordered far too much — enough for a family of five or six — but he waved away my complaints, insisting that I try everything.

"Are you having a good time?" he asked, when we'd about eaten our fill.

"I'm having an amazing time. Although I'm still a little confused as to why I needed comfortable shoes. Are we going to run off our meal later on?"

He smiled like a man who had a secret he was bursting to share. "You'll see soon enough."

About ten minutes later, there was a commotion in the centre of the room. Looking over, I frowned as I spotted the bulk of the floor staff beginning to gather up tables and chairs and stack them to one side. It seemed a little early to be cleaning up, although nobody else appeared to mind. Most of the diners had vacated their seats and were standing to one side watching.

"Kicking us out already?" I asked.

Sebastian laughed. "Hardly. Watch."

The waiters worked with a well-oiled precision, and in a few minutes, all but our corner of the floor was devoid of furniture. I'd had a few drinks by that point, so it still hadn't quite clicked, but a few moments later, the music that had been meandering in the background suddenly grew louder, and the tune went from sedate to bombastic.

"Oh, no way," I said, watching in wonder as the crowd began to drift towards the centre of the room once more, their bodies now weaving in time with the rhythm. The energy in the room instantly spiked through the roof.

"Like I said, not just a restaurant," he replied.

"Apparently not." At that moment, the last piece of the puzzle fell into place. "Oh shit. Are you expecting us to dance?" If I'd been going out with anyone else, that thought might have occurred to me earlier, but Sebastian wasn't the sort of guy I ever pictured going out dancing. The freedom of it seemed so at odds with his iron sense of self-control. I figured it would just make him uncomfortable.

"You look surprised," he said, hopping to his feet.

"I just thought you were more of a scotch and poker kind of guy."

"Can't I be both?"

I shook my head slowly in disbelief. "Just when I think I'm starting to get you pegged down just a little..."

He laughed. "There's a lot about me you don't know, Sophia."

"Does all of it have the capacity to embarrass me as much as this?"

"Oh come on, don't tell me you've never gone out dancing with your friends after a few too many."

"Of course I have," I replied, "but replace 'a few' with 'a lot'. I'm certainly not that drunk yet. Besides, that was always at a club. If you can stumble in a circle with your arms over your head, you fit right in in those places. This is different. This looks like an audition for So You Think You Can Dance."

I wasn't exaggerating. I didn't have the knowledge or vocabulary to describe everything that was going on in front of me, but it felt like everyone in the room had at least some kind of dance training. Couples writhed together in perfect unison, their movements wild, yet graceful and assured. No two routines were quite the same. Some pairs clung to one another like lovers on a bed, swaying and rocking in a permanent embrace. Others moved with more swagger, an ever shifting whirlwind of bare legs and muscular arms. There was something incredibly sensual about it all. I felt almost voyeuristic just sitting on the sidelines watching.

"You're overthinking it Sophia. Remember what you said to me the other night? 'If you have to think then this whole thing is a lost cause.'" He pulled me to my feet. "You probably don't pay attention to the way you move, but I certainly do, and that body is made to dance."

I looked on helplessly as waiters swept in to clear our table away too. "I thought dancers were meant to be tall and thin."

He smiled a wicked smile and ran a hand gently down my hip. "Ballet dancers perhaps, but that's not really what I have in mind." He nodded once more towards the throng. "Come on, all you have to do is follow my lead."

Maybe it was the pull of the music, or the seductive energy of the dancers, I'm not sure, but I found myself nodding. He led me into the fray.

Instantly, I felt the adrenaline of the crowd wash over me. It was a tangible thing that filled the air, seeping through my skin and setting my body thrumming. The speakers were blasting out a driving rhythm, something modern, but with a distinctly Latin bent, and Sebastian was quick to find his stride. I don't know how I'd ever thought he'd look awkward. One glance at that lithe body and anyone could see how at home he was on the dance floor. His innate sexuality translated savagely well to such expression. Every gesture, every subtle shift of his hips, made him look even more alluring.

Pressing one hand to the small of my back and seizing my fingers with the other, he began to lead me across the room, his feet a rhythmic blur, his body undulating like a flag in the breeze. I didn't want to make him look like a fool, so I tried my best to match him, but my muscles felt stiff in his hands. The show going on around us was elaborate, chaotic, beautiful, and I had no idea how I could possibly match it. I felt impossibly out of my depth.

"You're still thinking," said Sebastian, sensing my discomfort. "Stop focusing so hard. This is meant to be fun, not a competition. The room doesn't exist. They don't exist. It's just you, me, and the music."

I liked that idea. Closing my eyes, I leaned in against him and tried to relax. It was easier with everything out of sight. All I had to go by was the churning beat of the speakers and the touch of Sebastian's hands. Gradually, I let my muscles go soft, trusting that he would guide me. The throbbing bass was like a beacon, and I let my body follow as it desired.

"Much better," Sebastian said.

I had no name for what we were doing. Maybe I still looked stupid, I didn't know, but I no longer cared either way. It just felt right. I loved the sensation of being pressed up against him, letting him steer my limbs as though they were an extension of his own. In that moment, we were one entity moving in perfect harmony. It felt more than a little like when we made love — his hands manipulating me as my body bent to his, yielding to his control — and it was no less exciting for us being fully clothed.

But beyond the physical element, there was something deeper. I knew it was a side of him that he rarely shared, which made it all the more special that he was doing so with me. One by one, his walls were tumbling down.

As the first song ended, the music changed. The new tune was slower, more sultry, and Sebastian was quick to adapt. A delicate twist of his wrist and I was spinning away, then suddenly snapping backwards to rest against him once more, this time with my back against his chest. With torturous softness, his hands began to trace their way across my sides and down my thighs, flirting with the hem of my dress. Such intimacy in a public place should have made me balk, but the sensuality in the air was infectious. I was utterly lost in the moment. I could feel his breath hot on my skin as his lips teased the air just above my neck, tantalising but never touching. With every vacillation of our hips my ass grazed against his pants, letting me know that I wasn't the only one finding this to be a powerfully erotic experience.

Other couples were throwing propriety to the wind too. Several men swept passed us with open shirts, their chests glistening with sweat, their partners slicing the air with their skirts like fans. One woman had shed her top all together and was twisting from side to side in just her bra like a belly dancer. All around the room, people were laughing and clapping and cheering in time with the beat. I'd never been part of such an unrestrained expression of joy before.

"You look stunning," Sebastian breathed into my ear.

"Do I now?" I replied.

"You do. Although it might have something to do with the fact that everything you're doing right now, I'm imaging you doing it naked."

I laughed. "Is that so? Well then, I probably shouldn't do this." Slipping free of his grip, I turned once more and began to glide around him in a slow circle, swaying my hips provocatively and dragging my hands slowly up and down my body.

A low, masculine sound escaped his throat. "God, I can only restrain myself so much, Sophia."

I grinned, but didn't stop. It was thrilling putting on that kind of show for him in the middle of a crowded room. I could see the outline of his excitement pressing urgently against his pants. The truth was, with all the electricity that was coursing through my veins, I wasn't sure I wanted him to restrain himself. I'd had the elaborate foreplay, now I wanted what that promised.

He didn't disappoint. At the end of my second orbit, he seized me once more and pulled me in for a kiss. The intensity in that gesture was almost overpowering, and for a few moments, I lost all sense of where we were or what we were doing. All that existed was the two of us, our tongues dancing together like our bodies just had.

When he finally backed away, snatched my hand, and began leading me from the dance floor, I didn't say a word. It was a ludicrous thing to be considering with a roomful of people around us, but the longing I felt dwarfed all sense of logic.

Somehow, he found a little privacy; a small function room hidden behind a curtain at the back of the room. It didn't provide much protection — there were no locks, nor even a real door — but I don't think there was an obstacle in the world that would have stopped us at that moment. Taking a second to unzip his fly and pull himself free, he looped his hands under my thighs and lifted me up, bracing me against the wall. I wrapped my legs around him, and then with a flick of his wrist, he nudged my panties aside and rammed his shaft inside me.

Heat instantly tore through me.

"You see how you make me lose control Sophia?" he rasped, his face contorted in pleasure. "I'm addicted to you. It's not enough. It's never enough." Every statement was punctuated by a powerful pivot of his hips.

I moaned and buried my face against his shoulder, content to let him take from me as much as he wanted. Every nerve in my body already felt like it was vibrating, but with each forceful stroke Sebastian strummed my arousal just a little more. My legs tightened around his hips like a vice, pushing him deeper still, spurring him on.

"Harder." My voice sounded strained.

"Ask properly," he purred, nibbling my earlobe.

"Fuck me harder, Sebastian. Please."

For a moment he slowed. Then, angling my legs slightly, he slammed back into me. I cried out, nearly biting down on his flesh in the process. His plunges became punishing, almost to the point of pain, but my body swallowed each one as hungrily as a breath of air. I loved that desire, that raw, unrestrained need. Every stroke was a reiteration of a promise. *"You are mine, every inch of you."*

My back arched, my hips trying to add their own motion to the equation, but there was no space for me to move, nowhere for me to go. I was pinned helplessly against the wall, being fucked less than twenty feet from a cheering, surging crowd. And it felt amazing.

I could still hear that trembling beat pumping in the next room. The bass of it echoed in my chest. It made our lovemaking feel like just an extension of the dance, our rhythm shifting and slowing in time with the music. It was beautiful; the perfect culmination of the perfect night.

Nudging my head backwards, Sebastian engulfed my mouth with his, the softness of his tongue contrasting deliciously with the firmness of his cock. My hands ran wild across the hard expanse of his back, revelling in the vibration of his muscles as he drove himself into me.

I felt a pressure building in my core, signalling that my body couldn't hold out much longer.

"I'm close," I said breathlessly.

"Then look at me." I brought my forehead up to meet his, placing our eyes just inches apart. "Don't close your eyes.

242

Don't even blink. I want you to watch me as I make you come, Sophia, every moment of it."

And with a powerful rocking motion, he pushed me over the edge. The rawness, the affection, the risk of getting caught, it was an intensely powerful combination. I clawed at his skin, my whole body quivering with the ecstasy of my release. I'm fairly sure I screamed, but with the noise in the next room, nobody seemed to notice.

His turn came soon after. With several final bestial pumps his fingers dug deep into my legs, his body stiffening to iron as he burst inside me.

As his pleasure faded, he shook his head slowly. "You know, one of these days you're going to get us into trouble, Sophia."

"Me?" I asked, trying to look innocent. It was difficult. He still held me pinned in the air, his semi-erect penis still buried inside me. "I believe you were the one that dragged me in here and ravished me without so much as asking."

He raised an eyebrow. "I do seem to remember warning you of the consequences of your actions. And if you're going to pretend you didn't enjoy yourself, I may be forced to prove you wrong." His mouth dipped down to my neck. "I bet I could make you come again right here against this wall. I bet I could make you scream so loud the entire room out there would hear."

I closed my eyes for a moment, enjoying the soft teasing of his lips. "As wonderful as that sounds, I'm not sure I'm quite ready for a live audience."

"That's okay, neither am I. Now that I've got you, all of this," he nodded towards my body, "is mine and mine alone. I don't want to share even the sight of you."

"Well, if this evening is any indication of the way you take care of your possessions, then I believe that arrangement will work just fine."

After cleaning up and doing our best to make ourselves presentable, we slipped back out into the crowd. Nobody paid us any mind. The room still bore a frenetic energy, and part of me wanted to rejoin the party, but coming that hard had left me feeling a little weak at the knees, so we headed for the door.

I expected Joe to magically appear the way he always seemed to do, but the street outside was empty.

"I think we've been abandoned," I said.

He laughed. "I wouldn't put it past Joe, but that's not the case right now. I thought we could take a walk before leaving."

My arm broke out in goosebumps as a gust of sea breeze swept through the alley. Despite the time of year, the night was unseasonably cold. "I don't know, I'm kind of chilly. Maybe another night?"

"Come on, I want to show you something. It's not far." Removing his jacket, he slipped it over my shoulders. "Better?" he asked.

I smiled. "Ever the gentleman." It certainly was warmer, although I didn't know how he wasn't freezing now. On the plus side, that left him in just a shirt, which showed off the hard curves of his chest considerably better. "Fine, let's go." He wrapped his arm around my shoulder and began to lead me towards the main street. "But I have to say," I continued, "I'm a little uncomfortable with all this romance. Late night walks along the water might send the wrong message. We have boundaries, remember?"

He laughed loudly. "After seeing you shake it like that in there, there's no more boundaries, Sophia. You've officially ruined me for anyone else." He gave my ass a playful slap to illustrate the point.

"Oh, so that's what I have to do to earn a spanking is it?"

I asked, shaking my hips a little.

"Aww, feeling neglected are you?"

I grinned. "Just curious, really. It's been a while since you brought out the heavy artillery in the bedroom. It's enough to make a girl think you've gone soft."

He returned my smile. "I believe I showed you exactly how hard I can be just a few minutes ago."

That made me laugh. "That you did."

"But seriously," he continued, "not every dominant is the same. I have to be in control in the bedroom, that will never change, but we're not all leather wearing, paddle wielding machines. Don't get me wrong, I love a little kink when the mood is right, but truth be told, I think I often used that really hardcore persona as a kind of shield. It was always much easier to keep distance between my partners and I when I was playing a role. But with you, I just want to get as close as possible."

It was still novel hearing him express his feelings for me so openly. It made me tingle all the way down to my toes. "So no more tie up then?" I asked cheekily.

He slipped in behind me and pinned my arms to my side, stopping me in my tracks. "Oh I wouldn't say that." I closed my eyes as I felt him brush his lips gently against my ear before nipping softly at my neck. "There are still plenty of things I want to do to that body of yours. I'm just waiting for the right moment."

"Then I guess I'll just have to be patient," I replied, my voice suddenly breathy.

"Exactly."

We walked in silence for a while. I'd been expecting him to lead me to the beach, but instead he veered off down another side street. My confusion mounted when he turned again, this time off the road all together, onto a narrow dirt path that wove between two houses. Canopied and devoid of street lights, I could barely see more than three feet ahead.

I paused at the opening. "You said you liked horror movies, well this is exactly how most of them start."

He smiled. "Trust me."

We walked for about a hundred feet, the incline growing steeper with every step, until eventually we broke through the other side.

"Wow," I said for the second time that night. The view in front of me was nothing short of spectacular. The hidden track had opened out onto a wide expanse of headland that looked out over Manly Cove. We could see everything; the moonlit shoreline, the forest of yacht masts in the bay, even the electric outline of the city in the distance.

"How did you even find this place?" I asked.

"Luck." He looked sheepish. "Or perhaps stupidity. I'd spent a night at Mi Casa with some friends and we indulged a little too much. I went for a walk, got turned around finding my way back, and somehow wound up here." He gazed out over the churning waves. "I'm kind of glad I did though. I love this view."

"It's beautiful," I agreed.

He led me over to an open space a few feet from the lip of the cliff and we sat down. Leaning in, I laid my head on his shoulder and snuggled close. Although the breeze was even more intense up here, with my body pressed against his, I no longer felt cold.

He nodded towards the docks where several sleek white boats were slowly swallowing and disgorging passengers. "The thing I like most is the ferries. I've always loved ships, even since I was a kid. There's something about the beginning of a journey that fills me with hope."

I couldn't help myself. "You know they're just going to the city, right? Half of them are probably going to wind up throwing up in a gutter in a few hours."

He laughed. "Come on, where's your sense of wonder?" His expression shifted from amusement to something more reflective. "The truth is, I actually got away on a ship."

I hesitated. I could tell straight away that we were venturing into darker territory. It had been such an amazing night, and part of me didn't want to do anything to ruin that perfect vibe, but he'd brought me up here for a reason. I'd said I wanted more openness. I couldn't deny him now. "Got away?"

He licked his lips. "Like I said earlier, I didn't have the easiest time growing up. The place I lived... well, it wasn't exactly fit for kids. Or anyone, for that matter. There were no trains, no buses, not even any real roads. But there was the sea. I used to sit on a point a lot like this and stare at the boats that pulled in and out of the docks on the other side of the bay. I always loved the thought that they were going away. I didn't even care where. Just, away. Eventually, when I was old enough and strong enough, I swam out and stowed away on one and never looked back."

I spent a few seconds processing this. It was a lot to take in. "I thought you said you were from Spain."

He gave a sad little smile. "A lot of people don't realise how much poverty there is in big European countries. My parents and I lived in a little shanty town about an hour outside Barcelona. There's more of them than you'd think. France has hundreds. Portugal too. Entire groups of people who have just slipped through every support network available, until they land in the only place that will take them."

"A shanty-town?" I asked uncertainly.

He nodded, then grimaced. "Our house was made mostly from old plywood doors held together by nails. The roof was a single sheet of corrugated iron. I remember that whenever it rained, it used to make the most awful noise, like a clap of thunder that lasted the entire night."

"Fuck," I said, shaking my head in disbelief. "I can't even imagine living like that. Why didn't your parents do anything? I know if I had a child, I'd do everything in my power to get them away from a place like that."

He nodded. "I used to hate them for that, but I don't anymore. They were good people, I know that now. That sort of life just has a way of sapping your willpower. Everyone there had been defeated so many times they'd almost given up. Besides, when you fall in with those sort of people, even if you do want to leave, it's not as easy as just packing up and hitting the road."

I understood the implication, but the strain in his voice told me not to delve any further. Whatever his parents had or hadn't done, it didn't change the sort of man Sebastian was.

"Well, you got out," I said, smiling and squeezing his hand. It awed me knowing that he'd been through so much and still managed to turn into the magnificent, confident man sitting next to me.

"That I did."

"And you've done rather well for yourself since then. How does one go from shanty town urchin to professional jet-setting millionaire anyway?"

He smiled. "That's a story for another time, I think. Can we just enjoy the view for a while?"

"Okay, sure." A few moments passed. "And Sebastian. Thanks."

He answered by pulling me closer and kissing my hair softly.

I'm not sure how long we sat there. We stayed until long after the last ferry had pulled away from the dock. To tell you the truth, I would have been perfectly content to spend the whole night there, cradled in his arms, his fingers gently stroking my cheek. I'd never felt happier in my entire life.

Chapter 12

Sebastian stayed the night at my place, and the next morning we went out for breakfast. It was a little unprofessional to be late to the office again, especially after ducking out early yesterday, but the truth was that I didn't care. Last night had shown me how perfect our relationship could be, and all I wanted to do was keep feeling that same euphoria for as long as possible.

"What's your schedule like for the next few days?" I asked him, as we were finishing up our coffees.

He grimaced. "Busy, unfortunately. I suspect I'll be eating all my meals at my desk for the foreseeable future. You may have to entertain yourself for a few days."

I felt a pang of disappointment, but I brushed it aside. "Fair enough. We're getting pretty stuck into the Wrights case now anyway, so I won't exactly be bored." I picked up my coffee spoon and drew it in and out of my mouth slowly, dragging my tongue along the underside. "Of course, I may require entertaining once more before you disappear."

He grinned. "You know, it just so happens that I have a block of free time that has just opened up right... now."

Suffice it to say that I was even later to work than I initially planned.

In truth, I wasn't as upset about Sebastian's busyness as I should have been, because he'd given me an idea. His surprises were becoming a regular fixture in our relationship, and I wanted to even the score a little. So I decided that if he was too busy to go out, I'd bring myself to him.

When lunch time rolled around the next day, I picked up a couple of sandwiches from a nearby deli and headed for his building. A little subtle questioning over breakfast had told me that while he did have that office stashed behind the bar, that was only used during functions. He actually spent most of his time at the main Fraiser Capital building, which turned out to be only a ten minute walk from mine.

The building was as impressive as I'd been expecting. A sparkling cylinder of dark glass that shot up into the sky like a raised fist. It was somewhat intimidating being at Sebastian's office. There was nothing overtly strange about it, but the secrecy with which his company approached their work made me feel a little like a soldier venturing behind enemy lines.

I marched up to the front desk, trying my best to look like I belonged.

"Can I help you?" asked the receptionist, smiling a little too widely. She was a pretty young girl, albeit in an overly made up, magazine cover sort of way.

"Yes, I'm here to see Sebastian Lock."

She glanced at the screen in front of her. "Do you have an appointment?"

"Not really. I was hoping to surprise him." I held up the paper bag containing our lunch.

"Oh, I'm sorry, but nobody goes upstairs without an appointment. Company policy."

"I appreciate that, but it's not like I'm a stranger. I'm his girlfriend." It felt a little funny to say that out loud. We'd never used terms like that before. But still, it was true, wasn't it?

The woman behind the counter smiled in that slightly patronising way that people usually reserve for small children. "I'm sorry, but I can't make exceptions. I can call him if you like, maybe get him to come down?"

I exhaled sharply. I had hoped to surprise him in his actual office, but if this was my only option I guess I had no choice. "Okay sure. Thanks."

She tapped a few buttons on the phone and sat patiently, but nothing happened.

"I'm sorry, but he doesn't seem to be in. I could take a message for you if you like."

I closed my eyes and took a deep breath. Perhaps it was a stupid plan. He was a busy man. I should have just organised to see him over the phone like a normal person.

"Sophia?" said a voice behind me.

I turned and came face to face with Sebastian's friend Thomas.

"It is you. I thought so," he said. He managed a small smile, although he didn't look quite as pleased to see me as he had the other night. Apparently Sebastian wasn't the only one under a lot of stress.

I nodded. "Hi, Thomas."

"You here to see Sebastian?"

I felt a glimmer of hope. "Well I was hoping to, but they won't let me up."

He winced. "Yeah, we're not really meant to have guests upstairs. It's a bit draconian I know, but it's the rules."

"But if I went up with you, it'd be okay, right?" I said, flashing him a smile.

He chewed on his lip. "Technically you have to be a client..."

"Please! I was really hoping to surprise him. I only need a

few minutes."

I thought my feminine charms had done the trick, but eventually he shook his head "Sorry. If anyone found out I'd be in a crazy amount of trouble. Hell, Sebastian himself would chew me out. But since you came all the way here, I can go and find him for you if you like. He's in a meeting, but shouldn't be much longer."

I deflated a little, although I don't know why I was surprised. Sebastian had described Thomas as "a company man through and through." Expecting him to break the rules was probably unrealistic.

Still, his offer was better than nothing. "Okay, sure, that'd be great."

He gestured for me to follow. As we walked towards the lift, he glanced down at the bag I held. "A hand delivered lunch? Sebastian's a lucky man."

"It's more out of necessity than romance I fear. We're both so busy we barely get to see one another. I figured fifteen minutes over a sandwich is better than nothing."

"For sure." He was silent for a few seconds. "So things must be going pretty well between you two then."

My strong, independent side hated the goofy smile that bloomed on my face. *Fuck, Sophia, you're practically swooning.* But try as I might, I couldn't get rid of it. "Yeah, I think so."

"That's good. That's good." But something in his tone said he didn't necessarily believe that. I didn't know what to make of it. Did he still worry about Sebastian's ability to commit? I had to admit, I still had the occasional doubts, but our night at Mi Casa had gone a long way to settling those.

After a few more seconds, the lift arrived. "We'll probably be a few minutes," he said, stepping inside. "Feel free to make yourself comfortable." He pointed to a long sofa that rested against the far wall.

"No worries. Thanks, Thomas."

"My pleasure."

I sometimes wonder what would have happened if I'd just done as he asked. It was one of those seemingly inconsequential decisions that turns out to have massive ramifications.

Instead of sitting and waiting, I couldn't resist the urge to have a little wander. It was becoming clear that I may never get the chance to see Sebastian's actual office, but that didn't mean I couldn't check out the building a little. I was still incredibly curious about the sorts of things they did.

The bottom story appeared to be mostly admin staff; young women in blouses and dark pencil skirts bustling back and forward down long corridors. A few of them shot me strange looks, but nobody stopped me, so I figured I wasn't in breach of any major rules.

I didn't intend to wander very far, just enough to get a glimpse of what went on back there, but the place was a maze, and at some point I managed to get turned around. Before I knew it, I found myself standing in a narrow corridor that was devoid of doors or people. It felt like I'd gradually been moving in a loop, so I headed to the end and turned the corner, expecting to be taken back to the main access point.

Instead, I found something that caused my mouth to drop open.

This hallway was shorter, and it had a door. Just one. The access keypad off to one side said that I wasn't going any further in that direction. Not that I needed to. The door itself told me everything I needed to know. There was no signage, nothing to indicate what lay beyond. That is, except for the small golden letter A that was inscribed on the surface.

There was a grinding sensation in my head, the feeling of a host of gears all suddenly clicking into place. I knew now why that symbol had looked so familiar. This wasn't the first door I'd seen it on. I thought back to the night Sebastian and I had met, to the hidden offices I'd inadvertently prowled through. The name tags had thrown me off, but now I remembered; they were all marked the same way.

Something heavy and dark began to claw at my stomach. I'd asked Sebastian outright about the tattoo, and he'd lied. There was clearly a lot more to it than a drunken generic design. All the strange occurrences and eccentricities that he'd talked his way out of raced through my head. The hidden offices, the secret parties, the strange documents, they were all tied to this. They had to be. Each one taken by itself was fairly innocuous, but throw in the dead man on the news, and this one tiny symbol suddenly pulled it all together into something much more sinister.

Who the fuck were these people?

Somehow, I found my way back to the lifts and threw myself down heavily on the sofa. I had no idea what to do. It wasn't fair. Things between Sebastian and I had finally felt like they were making sense. I'd been happy dammit. But now I could feel that slowly bleeding out of me, replaced by an overwhelming sense of fear.

I'd known there were things about his job he had to keep quiet. I'd accepted that. But I'd assumed that meant client names and project details and other random minutia. This was something else entirely. Part of me wanted to just ignore it, to shove it under the rug in the back of my mind and let things continue the way they had been, but I knew that wasn't possible. I had to know what on earth I was dealing with.

A few moments later, the lift doors split open and Thomas and Sebastian strode out. "Well, isn't this a pleasant surprise," Sebastian said, grinning at me, although the smile fell rapidly when he caught sight of my face. "Sophia, what's wrong?"

Thomas seemed to sense my mood had changed. "I've got something to take care of," he said, shooting me a curious look before heading in the direction of the main foyer. I was thankful for the privacy.

I stared at Sebastian for a few seconds, uncertain where to even begin. "Why can't I come upstairs?" I asked eventually.

That seemed to catch him off guard. "Sorry. I know it's a bit strange. It's just company policy."

"So you're not hiding anything up there?"

Something flickered across his face ever so briefly. "What would I be hiding?"

"That's what I'm trying to figure out."

He looked puzzled by that. Slipping onto the seat next to me, he placed one hand gently on my knee. "I don't understand. What's this about?"

I didn't answer directly. "Do you remember what you told me that night outside my house," I said instead, "the night before you went away? 'I promise I'll never lie to you.'"

He nodded slowly. "I remember."

"So why did you?"

There was a pause. "I'm not sure what you mean."

I sighed. I hadn't really expected him to just spill everything of his own accord, but it had been worth a try. "Let me be more direct then. Why is there a door back there," I nodded towards the centre of the building, "that has the same mark on it as the one on your chest?"

His eyes widened. There were a few seconds of stunned silence. "I think you must be mistaken," he said shakily, but even he didn't sound convinced.

I felt a small flash of anger, but I smothered it. I'd already overreacted once with him. I wanted to give him a chance to explain. "Please, at least do me the courtesy of dropping the act now. I'm not stupid, Sebastian. I know what I saw. I saw it that first night we met as well, I just didn't remember until now."

He had a panicked look in his eyes now, his pupils madly darting left and right. "I'm sorry," he said eventually.

"I don't want apologies, Sebastian. I want explanations!"

He ran a hand through his hair and stared down at the floor. "You don't know what you're asking."

"I'm asking for you to be honest with me. That's all. It's pretty clear you're not who you say you are, and between the secret offices, the strange symbols, and the dead foreign dignitaries, this has me confused and to be honest, a little frightened."

His eyes shot up to meet mine, and any lingering doubts I'd had about the connection vanished. "Dead foreign dignitaries?"

I nodded. "I saw a dead man on the news a few weeks ago. A British politician. He had the same tattoo as you, only on his arm. At the time I thought it was just a coincidence, but your reaction basically confirms that it's not."

He gazed at me, his face utterly distraught. It was the look of a man with an impossible choice to make, and it sent a fresh wave of dread rolling through me. After all we'd shared since that night at my house, I'd honestly been expecting us to get past this. It had felt like he finally trusted me, and that it was only a matter of time before the rest of his walls came down too. But now I wasn't so sure. Whatever he was still hiding was apparently bigger than everything else. Was it bigger than what he felt for me?

"This isn't fair, Sophia," he replied eventually. "You knew we had secrets. I never hid that."

This time the surge of anger was bigger. "It isn't fair? Are you kidding me? Look, I understand some jobs deal with sensitive information, and I totally respect that. I'm in the same boat myself with case details. But this is something else entirely. Do you understand how this looks to me? You have a bloody tattoo of some secret company logo on your chest! I can't even begin to imagine what that means."

His fingers clenched and unclenched rapidly, his head shaking back and forward in a steady rhythm, as if he could send everything into rewind through sheer force of will. "Please don't make me do this," he pleaded.

"What choice do I have?" I asked. "How am I meant to be with a man who keeps things like this from me? How can I trust anything you say? I thought I was starting to get to know the man behind the mask, but now I feel like I'm looking at a stranger." Saying it out loud just made the pain worse. I felt heat welling behind my eyes, but I blinked it away. I was *not* going to cry in the middle of his office.

He drew a heavy breath. "Everything you saw was real, Sophia. I'm a lot of things, things that might not be easy to understand, but I'm also the same man I was a few days ago. The man who danced with you and held you and felt so impossibly lucky to wake up next to you. The man who thinks he's falling in love with you."

I recoiled as if struck. Of all the things he could have said to shock me, that was at the top of the list. How could I possibly deal with that?

"Love?" I said, barely able to wrap my mouth around the word. "Seriously? That's how you're going to wriggle out of this one?" I thought I'd been confused before, but that one little word had set off a bomb inside me. My emotions now lay scattered in a thousand tiny pieces.

He looked almost as surprised as me. "I'm not wriggling out of anything. Look, I've kept things from you, that's true, and I'm sorry beyond words for that, but they were only the things I had no choice but to hide. I have never lied to you about the way I feel. *Never*." There was fire in his voice when he said that, an earnestness that was almost impossible to ignore.

I shook my head. No matter what I said or did, it felt like it would be the wrong decision. I didn't understand this man. This man that could make me feel so treasured one minute, then so alone the next.

"Even if that's true, it's not enough," I replied slowly. *Of course it's enough*, a tiny part of me was screaming, but it was drowned out by the chorus of other voices, all yelling with equal fervour. "I'm not going to pretend like I have any idea what the hell is going on here, but I can't deal with the constant questions anymore, Sebastian. I can't keep finding new secrets behind the curtains."

"I know," he said wearily.

"So can you promise an end to all that?"

There was a long pause, perhaps the longest of my life. It felt like that moment in my house all over again, that agonising wait, the whole relationship teetering on the next words out of his mouth. Only this time, I didn't get the response I'd hoped for.

Eventually, he closed his eyes. "I don't know."

Every muscle in my body tightened. I let out a long breath. "Then there's nothing more to talk about."

I was surprised by how calmly I got to my feet. I expected him to object. He'd proven his tenacity time and time again. But he didn't. He just stared mournfully at the floor and let me walk away.

I caught sight of Thomas on my way out. He was sitting in an armchair a little way around the corner, sorting through some papers, although he gave me a sympathetic nod as I walked passed. Apparently he hadn't gone far after all. So much for privacy.

259

I made it into the back of a cab before I began to cry. The driver shot me several uncomfortable glances, but my mind didn't have space to focus on him right now. There was too much pain. Too much confusion. I had no idea how I was meant to have reacted to what just happened. The scope of Sebastian's lies still hadn't sunk in. I didn't know what it could possibly all mean.

And then there was that word.

If he'd meant what he said, how could he just let me leave? Love was supposed to be a connection that triumphed over everything else. I tried to convince myself that it was just a ploy, a desperate, last ditch attempt to save what we had. But the pain in his eyes had been so real, the conviction in his voice so strong. It didn't make any sense.

None of it made any sense.

Chapter 13

The next couple of days were rough. I wandered around the office like a zombie. I think that was my body's way of trying to get through work — just shut down completely. It seemed to do the trick. I wouldn't have called myself a model employee, but I made it through most of my tasks with at least some level of competency.

But at night, I couldn't help but turn the situation over and over in my head. The whole thing had left me utterly dumbstruck. Our relationship had gone from perfect to catastrophic in the blink of an eye. What on earth went on behind the doors of Fraiser Capital? I'd run the gamut of possibilities through my head a thousand times. Was Sebastian a secret agent? A gang member? Part of some kind of bizarre corporate fraternity? Each possibility was as ridiculous as the last, but no plausible option seemed to fit.

I wanted to be angry, and a lot of the time I was, but try as I might, I also couldn't push the things he'd said out of my mind. I hated him for making it so difficult. If he'd just kept his mouth shut, I think it would have been easier to let go, to dismiss what we'd had as lust taken too far. But that one word changed everything. It forced me to confront my feelings for him head on.

My history with love was chequered at best. I'd thought I loved Connor, but obviously that hadn't worked out so well. And I'd been going down the same path again with Sebastian — blind adoration for a man who wasn't honest with me. On the other hand, Connor had never made me feel that divine sense of bliss I experienced when Sebastian and I were together. Even now, with everything that had happened, I often found myself longing to just lose myself in his arms. That had to mean something, didn't it?

It made me feel like the biggest fool on the planet, but part of me kept hoping he'd call and explain himself. I didn't know if I could deal with the truth, or if I'd even believe whatever he had to say, but I hated that he didn't try. It was a coward's move to invoke that word and then not fight.

The weekend passed quietly. I was starting to feel a little better. The initial feeling of panic had ebbed away, replace by a kind of grim acceptance. He wasn't going to call, and that was okay. It seemed devastating now, but the world would keep spinning. *One day at a time*, I told myself. *It can only get better from here.*

I was wrong.

On Monday morning, I got a call from Ernest.

"Sophia, could I see you in my office for a moment?"

Ernest wasn't much of a face to face manager. He preferred the buffer offered by phones and email. To be called in to see him was either very good or very bad, but the sinking feeling in my belly told me it was probably the latter.

"Okay, I'll be right over," I said, a small tremor evident in my voice.

As soon as I opened his door and saw Alan sitting calmly at the desk, that fake smile spread across his face like lumpy butter, my fears were confirmed.

"Sophia," he said, "please, sit down."

Ernest looked almost sheepish, like he felt guilty about leading me into an ambush. I tried to muster a little token anger but, truth be told, it didn't make much difference. If Alan himself had called, I would have had to go just the same.

I did as I was told, sliding into one of the guest chairs that faced the two of them. I suddenly felt cold, the kind of chill that seems to seep right into your bones. I was fairly sure I knew what was coming.

"I'm going to get straight to the point, Sophia," Alan said. He'd do most of the talking. Ernest was just here as a courtesy, most likely. "We need to have a talk about your performance recently."

I stayed silent. I figured I may as well make the conversation as difficult as possible for them.

"To be frank, it hasn't been up to par," he continued.

"In what way?" I asked. My voice was strangely quiet, almost dangerous. It seemed to catch him off guard.

"Well look, you must understand, we respect that work/life balance is important—"

"I'm not in the mood for your bloody jargon, Alan," I interrupted. "Just spit it out."

He rocked back a little in his chair, reflexively tugging at his suit jacket. At least I had him off balance. "Well, you've been arriving late, leaving early, taking long lunches, that kind of thing. Like I said, our goal isn't to work you to the bone, but this firm expects a certain level of commitment which at the moment you're not reaching."

In a way he was right. I had been lax lately, but the injustice of it ran like fire through my veins nonetheless. "I bet if you went back and looked at the last few years," I said, "you'd find I've billed more hours overall than any other associate on this floor. Probably more than you yourself."

He bristled. "I don't know about that. In any case, we all

appreciate your dedication to the company. But you can't just rest on your laurels in this business. And the fact remains that your recent work has not be up to standard."

I hated how he kept using the word 'we', like he and Ernest were somehow cohorts in this little game. Ernest couldn't have looked more uncomfortable if he'd tried.

"So what is this? Am I being fired?"

Alan gave a little laugh, one that was as fake as his smile. "Now, let's not be hasty. We know as well as anyone that this job can get overwhelming at times. No, we just feel that your poor attendance, coupled with recent events, mean that—"

"Recent events?" I said, my tone somehow growing colder still.

He hesitated once more, but I didn't need him to fill in the blanks. I'd done so the moment I walked through the door.

"You mean with Jennifer?" I finished.

The dip in his expression confirmed it. I'd underestimated her. That little weasel really did want me gone, and between my recent lapses in attendance and my reaction to her prank, I'd handed her all the ammunition she needed to make it happen.

"She mentioned that you'd ignored some of her instructions, yes."

"Did you actually read what those instructions were?" I hissed.

Something in my voice must have jarred him to his senses, because he sat up straight in his chair, seeming to realise exactly who outranked who. "That's not really relevant," he said, his voice growing stern. "I trust Jennifer to do the right thing. What this comes down to, Sophia, is attitude. It's about showing you're a team player. Work is distributed the way it is for a reason. When people start going off on their own, things begin to break down. Jobs slip through the cracks. Everyone has their role to play. If you can't understand that, then maybe you *don't* belong at Bell and Little."

Ernest still hadn't said a word.

"And what do you think about all this, Ernest?" I said. I didn't really expect him to leap to my defence, but it was worth a shot.

He shifted in his chair. "I think that this isn't you, Sophia." He looked almost sad when he said it.

Alan cleared his throat. "What I was trying to say before is, we think maybe you should take a little time off. You've got a significant amount of leave built up. Why not use it to get your head right? There's no shame in saying you need a little R and R."

It was phrased as a suggestion, but that was just an illusion. I was being exiled. It might not have sounded like a big deal — a little holiday, then back to the grind — but I knew better. It was really a dismissal in disguise. That's how Alan liked to operate; ease someone out of the office quietly, and then let the axe fall. Much less messy that way. I could see it in Ernest's eyes. He knew I wasn't coming back.

Strangely, I wasn't really upset. I figured maybe that would come later. Instead, the numbness coating my insides just seemed to thicken. Truth be told, I'd expected it — or something similar — the moment I walked through the door.

I stood up. There was no point in arguing. "Okay."

"Okay?" Alan asked.

"Okay, I'll take some time."

And without another word I turned and left.

I snatched my bag from my office and then made straight for the lift. I desperately wanted to avoid talking to anyone. The wafer thin barricade was holding my emotions in check was ready to burst at any moment.

But of course, she couldn't resist her chance at a parting shot.

Leaning against an office doorway near the lifts, was Jennifer. She was chatting idly with the person inside, but there was no doubting her true purpose. She caught sight of me from across the room as I approached. There were no words, no taunts or mockery, just the smallest upturn of her lips and a victorious flash in her eyes. She'd won and she knew it.

I fled. I didn't even bother waiting for the lift, I just bolted down the fire escape as fast as I could. Everything was unravelling before my eyes.

I had to get away from that place.

Chapter 14

I'm not certain exactly how I got home. I think I took a taxi, although I can't be sure. All I remember was being overcome by a great wave of tiredness. The moment I walked through the door, I threw myself into bed, pulled the covers over my head, and slept.

When I woke it was dark. The power was out. There was no storm that I could hear, just a horrendous wind that was screeching up and down the narrow alleys that surround my house.

Glancing at my phone, I discovered it was ten o'clock. I also saw that I had several missed calls from Elle. No doubt word had gotten around. Gossip spread faster than the plague in our office. She was probably worried, but I couldn't deal with talking to her yet.

I really wished I could just go back to sleep. The enormity of everything that had happened was absolutely staggering. I didn't know how to begin dealing with it all. It made the prospect of simple unconsciousness incredibly appealing. But I could tell I wouldn't drift back off again.

Not knowing what else to do, I lit some candles and went to the kitchen to pour a bowl of cereal. I wasn't particularly hungry, but I figured I probably needed to eat. It tasted like shredded cardboard, but I barely noticed.

Halfway through my meal, everything finally caught up with me. One minute I was staring blankly down at my food, the next I was bawling my eyes out. I'd never felt so utterly lost before. My life had always felt like it had been on rails, with the next stop visible just a little way up the track. School, a law degree, internships, a job; everything had unfolded as planned. But now suddenly, the track had collapsed underneath me, leaving me wobbling at the edge of a precipice. I had no idea where to go from here.

It was soul destroying to watch six years of hard work crumble to dust before my eyes. The prospect of starting again from scratch was impossibly daunting. I lay my arms on the breakfast bar and buried my head between them, sobbing until I felt like my eyes were just empty husks.

The worst part was, I had no way to distract myself. I was going to wake up tomorrow with nothing to do. And the day after that. And the day after that. That was a terrifying prospect. I thrived on hard work, on meeting deadlines and tackling problems. That was my drug. Without that, I had nothing. Just endless time to consider where I'd gone wrong.

The urge to call Sebastian was incredibly strong. I didn't even know if he'd answer, or what I'd say if he did. Nothing had changed between us. But I was desperate to hear that soothing voice, to wrap my arms around him and hold on for dear life before the weight of it all pulled me under.

But I restrained myself. I couldn't deal with any more heartbreak at the moment. Instead I popped a couple of Valium I had left over from my last international trip, and curled up on the couch.

For now, oblivion would do.

* * * * *

The letter arrived two days later.

For a while I just stared, unsure whether I should even open it. Seeing Sebastian's flowing script used to fill me with excitement, but now there was only trepidation. I wasn't sure I was ready to deal with whatever he had to say, not on top of everything else. This wasn't a reconciliation. You didn't fix our sorts of problems by post.

But in the end I knew I couldn't ignore it. Too much had passed between us for that. With trembling hands, I tore open the seal.

Sophia.

I'm sorry to do this in writing. I wanted to come to you — I nearly did several times — but I'm afraid of what will happen if I do. I always thought I was a strong man, but you have this way of making me feel utterly powerless. I'm worried I'll break yet again.

I'm so sorry that things have to end this way. It sounds hollow and empty, but I never meant to hurt you. I really thought that maybe I could do this again, that things would be different this time. But now I see how impossible that is. I can never have a normal life. The risks are just too great.

You have questions, but the answers I owe you aren't mine to give. It's not fair, but I need you to know that it's for the best. There is more at stake here than you can possibly imagine.

I know you probably don't believe me, but I want to tell you again: I never lied about my feelings for you. Every word was true. I never thought I'd care about anyone again the way I care about you. I thought Liv had burned that right out of me. But I was wrong. You're the most amazing woman I've ever met. I feel more in a day with you than I have in a lifetime with anyone

269

else. You deserve someone to share everything with, but that's not something I can give you, no matter how badly I want to. Perhaps it would have been better for both of us if I'd just stayed away to begin with. I knew you were dangerous from the moment I laid eyes on you. But I can't apologise. I don't regret a single moment we spent together.

I won't be in contact again. I ask that you please do the same. Like I said, it's for the best.

Yours forever.
-S

The room around me blurred into nothingness. All I could see were his words, blinking up at me like a neon sign. My organs felt like they'd been twisted into a thousand ragged knots inside me.

I no longer doubted that he'd been telling the truth about his feelings. I felt his passion right through to my bones. But that didn't matter anymore. Whatever his secrets were, they were apparently bigger than us, and they left no room in his life for anything more.

Despite the fact that I'd been expecting it, the finality of that last line ripped through me. Even after his office, with the weight of a thousand lies bearing down on us, some tiny part of me had still held hope that we'd get through it. There was a chance, however slim. But now that chance was over.

We were over.

Chapter 15

Time passed. I slept and ate and did my best to occupy myself, but it was all done with the kind of blank obligation that leaves next to no real impression. I felt so utterly disconnected, like I was watching a video of something that was happening to someone else.

I hated myself for being so weak. I'd never been one to wallow in self-pity before. Problems weren't things to dwell on, they were obstacles to be overcome on the way to better things. But in this situation, I didn't even know where to start.

I must have read Sebastian's note a hundred times over the next few days. It consumed me. I had no idea how one single piece of paper could make my heart soar so high yet still shatter into a million pieces. I wanted to hate him for not choosing me, but the way the letter was phrased made me question if he even had a choice at all. That scared me a little. The things he alluded to were every bit as unbelievable as those my imagination had conjured. Perhaps he really had been doing me a favour.

Eventually, after several days of ignoring my phone, I woke up one afternoon to find Ruth banging on my door.

"Holy shit," she said, when I finally answered. "You look like you've just returned from a week long bender."

"That good, huh?" I replied, managing a small smile. I'd thought I couldn't stomach company, but now that she was there in front of me, I realised how much I appreciated seeing a familiar face.

She stared at me, her brow furrowed in concern.

"So, word got around then I take it?" I asked.

She nodded. "Elle called me saying you weren't answering your phone. Explained what had happened. I came as soon as I could." She stepped towards me and pulled me into a hug. "I'm sorry, Soph."

I didn't know what to say, so I just hugged her back.

"Can I come in?" she asked. I nodded and lead her into the lounge.

"Now, tell me about it," she said.

And so I did, being careful to avoid mentioning Sebastian. She obviously had no idea about that, and it was still too raw for me to talk about.

When I was done, she let out a long breath and shook her head slowly. "I'll never understand how the people in that place are so blind. It's like it's all just a popularity contest. And if I ever meet that bitch Jennifer, she's going to need more than some weaselly little partner to hide behind."

I found myself grinning. Now *that* was what best friends were for. Making you feel like you weren't totally alone.

"So, there's no chance this will all just blow over?" she asked.

I shook my head slowly. "This is 'firing people 101'. Get them out of the building quietly, and then finish the job. And even if it wasn't, you can't work in a place like that when someone so senior has it out for you. Not unless you want to eat shit for the rest of your natural life."

Ruth nodded slowly, her mouth pulled tight. "Okay, so then we start out trying to find you something new. It sounds like Ernest wasn't on board with all this, right? So he'll write you an awesome reference. That plus a resume like yours and I bet you can stroll into any of the other big law firms in town." She looked thoughtful for a moment. "Maybe your mystery man could help out as well? If he knows one of the equity partners at Little Bell, he probably has other connections too."

I gazed at her, desperately willing my face to stay composed, but I couldn't hold it all back.

"Oh shit, not him too?" she asked.

I nodded.

She reached out and squeezed my shoulder. "Damn, the universe really knows how to kick a girl when she's down. I'm sorry, hon'. So he turned out to be an asshole after all?"

I blinked a few times. "I don't know. I don't think so. I'm still not really sure what happened." I sniffed sharply, realising that a few hot tears had begun to trace their way down my face. "Could we not talk about him? It won't make any difference. It's over. Maybe in a few months I'll be ready to laugh and dissect it with you and Lou over mojitos or something, but for now I think I just need to deal with it in my own way, okay?"

She hesitated. "Okay, sure. But just remember; I'm here if you change your mind."

"I know. Thanks."

She studied me for a few more seconds before clapping her hands. "You have, however, given me an idea. If there was ever a better excuse for midday mojitos, I haven't heard it."

I groaned. "I don't think going out and getting tanked at three o'clock on a Wednesday is the best way to start rebuilding my life."

"Who said anything about getting tanked? I'm just trying to get you out of the house. Have you even been outside since it happened?"

I sighed, then shook my head.

"Exactly. So come out for one drink and some food that doesn't come out of a plastic packet. You'll never make any progress if you just hide out in here forever."

"I don't know, Ruth, I—"

"I'm not taking no for an answer," she interrupted. I knew there was no point in arguing. She was as stubborn as me when she wanted to be.

"Fine. One drink."

"Attagirl."

After taking a few minutes to shower and change into something half respectable, we headed for King Street. It felt surprisingly good to be out of the house. We found a little Tapas joint and settled in for lunch.

The longer we talked, the better I found myself feeling. It was inane conversation, mostly about Lou turning into a frumpy housewife, but that's exactly what the doctor ordered. I even laughed a few times, which I hadn't thought I'd be capable of anymore. It wasn't much more than a distraction, but it was a start.

* * * * *

Determined to begin regaining some semblance of control over my life, I made myself get up at nine the next morning. It was a tiny gesture, but at that moment every deliberate action felt like an achievement. Some bacon and eggs, a shower, and a lengthy grooming session later, I actually felt vaguely human.

I'd promised Ruth I wouldn't stay cooped up all day, so with nothing else on my schedule for the morning, I decided to take a walk. It was a lovely spring day outside, and I figured the sun might do me some good.

I wandered around Newtown for an hour or so, nabbing a coffee and a Danish in the process. It was nice just being outside among the hustle and bustle. It served as a reminder that despite how awful I felt, the world hadn't stopped turning. Things changed, and new opportunities were out there. I just had to find them.

Eventually, I headed home. The sooner I began hunting, the sooner I'd be able to start rebuilding my life. Snagging my mail from the letterbox, I strolled in through the front door, dumped it down on the sideboard, and headed for my laptop. It wasn't until I fired it up and sat down that I noticed anything was amiss. There was a breeze blowing into the room from the back door. The back door that now lay in a splintered mess on the kitchen floor.

It was one of those slow realisations that happens a fraction too late. An unexpected sight, a dumbfounded stare, and in the blink of an eye it's over. I sensed movement to my left, but before I could spin, something dark was slipped over my head and I felt a sharp jab on one side of my neck. I tried to yell for help, but whatever drug they'd injected me with worked fast. All I managed was a strangled squeal that cut off sharply as everything began to fade out.

Book Three:
Unlocked

A Note from the Author

I just wanted to give you all a little advanced warning that, while the first two books were purely from Sophia's perspective, Unlocked moves between both Sophia and Sebastian. It was something I wanted to do earlier, but I couldn't make it work without giving away too much. I hope you enjoy being in Sebastian's head as much as I did!

Chapter 1

Sophia

The first thing that I remembered was that I was cold. Everything was still black and my body wouldn't respond, but I shivered nonetheless. Then, gradually, things began to swim into focus, as though I were floating upwards from the darkest depths of the sea.

I coughed. Then again. And then sucked in several great breaths. One by one, I could feel muscles spark back to life. They were like dead weights, attached to my body, but at least I could move.

It took a few minutes for my mind to drag itself out of neutral. My first thought was that my lunch with Ruth must have turned into the bender to end all benders. It had happened before, and the cotton wool sensation in my head was at least a little reminiscent of my nastier hangovers. But then I remembered the following morning. My walk through Newtown. My newfound resolve to start getting things back on track.

The broken back door.

The stabbing pain in my neck.

The strong hands catching me as I fell towards the floor.

Oh Jesus. Oh fuck. What the fuck had happened? Where was I? And how long had I been out?

I flung myself into a sitting position, a move I instantly regretted as it sent a powerful coil of nausea twisting through my stomach. *Right, then. No fast movements.*

Drawing a few calming breaths, I steadied myself and surveyed my surroundings. At first glance, the room around me appeared fairly ordinary. Sparsely furnished, with just a bed, table, and bookshelf, the cream coloured walls and smooth wooden floor boards made it feel a lot like the guest bedroom in my parents' house. However it didn't take long for the differences to become apparent. Firstly, there were no windows, just a small space above the bed that looked to have been painted more recently than the rest. Similarly, the door looked somehow out of place; a giant slab of thick timber with a heavy iron lock.

Battling a bout of vertigo, I dragged myself to my feet and stumbled over to it. I knew what I'd find, but my chest still tightened when the handle refused to budge. The room may not have looked like a traditional prison cell, but it would hold me just as effectively.

This time, the nausea came on more strongly. It clawed at my insides like a wild animal. I tasted bile, sharp and hot, at the back of my throat. Somehow I managed to stagger to the corner of the room before my stomach emptied itself on the floor.

When it was over, I dragged myself back to the bed and curled into a ball. I knew I should try and approach the situation logically, but all I could focus on was the terror that was running like ice water through my veins. How could I possibly react rationally in the face of something like this? I'd been kidnapped from my house by unknown assailants, shot full of God knows what, and was now being held prisoner, for reasons I didn't understand. It was straight out of a horror movie.

Even through the haze in my mind, I knew that this had something to do with Sebastian. It was the only explanation that made sense. The fear I'd seen in that final letter told me all I needed to know. Whatever he was involved in was extremely dangerous, and now I was in the thick of it. And I had no idea why.

Take a deep breath, Sophia. Crying isn't going to do you any good.

I started with what I knew. They hadn't killed me outright. As horrifying as it was to consider, they could easily have done so. That meant they wanted something. Was someone trying to extort Sebastian? He certainly had the wealth for it. If that were the case, they'd probably already told him they had me. The ball was in his court. Would he do what they asked? It pained me to admit, but I didn't know. I had no doubt that he loved me, but the stakes were obviously much higher than I'd imagined. Perhaps they were too high.

Of course, extortion was probably the best case scenario. There were much darker possibilities. If Sebastian's secrets were as large as they seemed, it made sense that he'd have enemies, enemies who may be under the impression I knew something important. I suspected that if that were the case, they wouldn't be gentle about extracting the truth. My mind filled with terrifying visions; knives and saws and long iron pokers, heated to a glowing red.

Deep down I knew there was a third possibility too. Maybe my kidnappers weren't strangers at all. No matter how I approached it, I couldn't see Sebastian having anything to do with this, but I couldn't say the same for his colleagues. We hadn't exactly kept our discussion in his building private.

I knew Thomas had overheard and it certainly wasn't unreasonable to think that others might have as well. I had almost no idea what went on at Fraiser, a few scraps at best, but perhaps it was enough to make them feel threatened. And if that were the case, my gut told me that they wouldn't hesitate to do anything to rectify the problem.

I tried to convince myself that Sebastian was just moments away from tearing down the door and riding in on his white horse, but the truth was he had no way of knowing what had happened. He'd been very clear that all our ties were severed. Even if my captors had told him they had me, they wouldn't have been stupid enough to give away their location. For now, I was on my own.

Gradually, whatever they'd shot into me seemed to wear off and I began to feel more human. My mind ran in a constant circle, my body surging with some powerful combination of fear and anger. I paced the room, testing the lock over and over, searching for breaks in the plaster, anything that might hint at some chance of escape. I knew that it was all but impossible — this wasn't some hasty, spur of the moment snatch and grab — but I couldn't simply sit there and wait for what came next. It felt too much like admitting defeat.

I had no idea how much time passed. It's funny how quickly you lose sense of the hours in a room with no clocks or natural light. Eventually though, during one of my circuits of the far wall, there was a rattling at the door. Steeling myself, I took a few steps towards it and poised there. I wasn't sure what was coming, but I wanted to be ready, should an opportunity present itself.

The door flew open and a burly looking man in a suit walked through. He had dark olive skin, darker than Sebastian's, and heavy black curls that were cropped close to his head. He was carrying a tray with a sandwich and a glass of juice resting on it.

"Dinner," he said. He spoke with a sharp accent; Russian maybe, or Middle Eastern.

I had no doubt he wasn't the only one on guard duty, and judging by the easy confidence with which he moved, he wasn't particularly concerned about me escaping. But as he walked closer, I caught a glimpse of the open door behind him and all my survival instincts kicked in.

"Thank you," I replied, amazed by how little my voice was shaking. I reached calmly for the orange juice and began raising it to my lips, then with a flick of my wrist I tossed the liquid into his face and darted for the door.

In my head, it worked flawlessly. I saw him collapse to the floor as the citric acid set his eyes burning. I saw myself finding the guard outside sleeping on his chair and, after stealing his gun and handcuffing him in place, making a daring escape. Unfortunately we weren't in a movie. This was real life.

Instead of falling, my captor let out a short hiss, and one hand flew up to his eyes, but he was obviously well trained because despite his temporary blindness, he moved to block my path. In retrospect, it was a pretty stupid plan; there was only one place I could go and he knew it. But desperation is a powerful emotion and I only had two words running through my head at that moment. *Get away.*

I ploughed right into him. He must have weighed at least double what I did, but that didn't stop me from trying to fight. I let loose with everything I had, pounding his chest, his stomach, his neck. I landed a few good blows, but they barely seemed to register. It was like punching a mattress. The heavy muscle that coated his body absorbed everything. I shifted my focus, trying to strike him between the legs, but by that time his eyes were open once more and he blocked my attacks with ease, seizing my arms and pinning them together with one giant, meaty hand.

"Nice try," he said with a smirk. "Now, my turn." And then with almost derisive casualness, he flicked back his arm and struck my face with a colossal backhand. I spun through the air, my vision flaring white as I slammed into the floor. The impact knocked all the breath from my lungs.

"Eat," he said. "The boss wants to talk to you, but it may be a while." He glanced down at the now empty cup. "I guess you're going thirsty until then."

And with another smirk, he pulled the door closed behind him.

I crawled over to the wall and propped myself up against it. My whole head was ringing, and my cheek felt like it were on fire. It would be a lovely shade of purple in a few hours. *Great plan, Sophia. Just beat up Mr Universe over there and make a breezy escape. That'll work a treat.*

I knew I should probably eat, but just glancing at the sandwich made my stomach turn. How could I think about food at a time like this?

I desperately wanted to retain my composure, but that encounter had really driven home the hopelessness of the situation. I began to cry; fat, salty, desperate tears that flowed like a river down my face. I was utterly helpless. Escape was not an option. Whatever they wanted from me, they were going to take. The only question was how they would go about it.

* * * * *

Somehow, I managed to fall asleep. I don't know if it was the lingering effect of the drugs, or my body's way of trying to cope with the situation, but the next thing I remember is waking up to some sort of commotion in the hall outside.

I had no idea what it meant; the walls were thick and the sounds indistinct, but at this point, I assumed that any activity was probably bad. It signalled that we were progressing on to whatever happened next. I desperately wanted to hide, but there was nowhere to go. My chest felt impossibly heavy, and my heartbeat was like gunfire in my ears.

There was a brief lull, but after about thirty seconds of silence the lock jangled once more. I braced myself. The door flew open...

... and in stormed Sebastian, a sleek black pistol in his hand.

My stomach turned a cartwheel.

His face was a picture of desperation, fear etched into every line on his skin. Seeing him again made my whole body ache, the wound left by his letter tearing open inside me once more.

His eyes were wild, almost insane, but they lit up as they fell upon me. "Sophia," he cried, taking three quick strides and lifting me into the fiercest hug I'd ever experienced.

As he wrapped his body around mine, everything surged inside me. I finally let myself feel the full magnitude of the situation. I found that I was crying again. My chest shook with great heaving sobs, incoherent thanks spilling from my mouth. He was warm and strong and radiated control, and I buried myself deeper against him, as if his body could somehow shield me from everything I was feeling.

He took my reaction in his stride, holding me close and stroking my hair softly. "I know, I know. It's okay. I've got you."

His touch was soothing. His presence washed over me, filling me with that primal sense of security. I knew things were a long way from being okay, and I still had more questions than I knew what to do with, but at that moment, I'd never been more relieved to see another person in my life.

After some time, the flood finally began to ease and I found myself able to speak again. "Can we get out of here? I can't be here anymore."

"Of course."

As I pulled away, he caught sight of my face and his expression hardened. "Did they hurt you?"

"Well they did this," I said, gesturing to my cheek where I assumed a bruise was blossoming, "but that was mostly my own fault for trying to do a runner."

"None of this is your fault, Sophia," he said, sounding impossibly sad.

He led me out into the hallway. Somehow, I'd gotten into my head that Sebastian had done this alone, James Bond style; but, of course, that was ridiculous. Waiting for us outside were five hulking men, sporting earpieces and stubby black guns. Their crisp suits and grim expressions made them dead ringers for my visitor from before. If I hadn't known any better, I'd have guessed they were on the same side. *Maybe all the world's evil organisations shop at the same rental agency. Rent-A-Thug.*

But even my inner monologue's attempt at wit couldn't bring a smile to my face at that moment. Seeing them all standing there, alert and armed to the teeth, really drove home exactly what kind of shit I had embroiled myself in. They had guns, for Christ's sake. I'd never seen a drawn gun in real life before. Australian firearms laws are notoriously tough, so it's just not the kind of thing we are exposed to. But here were five men, carrying pistols as casually as if they were newspapers; and judging by the way they handled them, they were perfectly comfortable putting them to use. I couldn't see any sign of struggle in the hallway, but I doubted my captors had just invited Sebastian and company in for afternoon tea. Blood had been spilt here somewhere. Blood that, in a round-about way, was on my hands. I shook my head rapidly, trying to clear the image. That kind of thinking would do me no good.

Several men scouted ahead while the rest walked with Sebastian and I to the front door. It was dark outside, but judging by the suburban buzz in the air, it wasn't too late at night.

My prison turned out to be nothing more than a large, two-story house. Obviously some significant changes had been made, but to the casual observer, nothing would have stood out as strange.

There were several cars waiting for us. Sebastian guided me into one and followed me into the back seat, and in a matter of seconds we were turning the corner and pulling out into the night-time traffic.

Safety.

With every meter we put between us and the house, the tension in my muscles eased just a little more. I still felt like I might break down again at any moment, but at least the sense of sheer terror was subsiding. Now, I just felt exhausted, vulnerable, and utterly utterly confused.

Sebastian seemed to be almost ignoring me now. He was staring out the window, the initial relief on his face gone, replaced by a kind of heavy thoughtfulness. For my part, I didn't know what I was supposed to be doing. I was so ill-equipped to deal with the situation. Part of me just wanted to throw myself back into the comfort of his embrace, but now that we were making our escape, the questions began to come again, piling up in my head almost faster than I could process them.

"Where are we going?" I asked, figuring that was as good

a starting spot as any.

He looked over at me. "Somewhere safe."

"Safe from who?"

There was uncertainty in his eyes, that innate defensiveness he'd spent a lifetime fostering. "Can we not do this now, Sophia? You've just been through one hell of an ordeal."

"Exactly, and now I want to understand what happened. So who the hell were those guys?"

His jaw worked wordlessly for a few seconds, but eventually he let out a small sigh. "Honestly, I'm not sure."

"Seriously? No idea at all?"

He shook his head wearily. "We're working on it."

"Then how the hell did you find me?"

He hesitated. I could see what looked like guilt on his face. "After I sent you that letter... I know this looks bad, but I was worried about you. So," he drew a deep breath, "I left someone watching your place. It was just a precaution, but thank God I did. They saw the whole thing go down."

My eyes widened. "You mean you expected this?"

"No. No! Of course not." He ran a hand through his hair. He looked utterly distraught. "Like I said, it was a 'just in case' measure, that's all. Some of the people we deal with...well, there's not much they're not capable of, and things are a little unstable at the moment. I just wanted you to be safe."

"So why didn't your guy intervene?"

"There were three men that took you, and they were good - professional. He didn't think he could stop them by himself, so he called it in and followed, instead."

"I see." I couldn't say I wasn't thankful he'd had someone there, but it was a little like handing someone a fire extinguisher after you'd set their place alight. Also, it drew my mind to the elephant in the room. Last time I'd gotten too curious, Sebastian had offered me nothing but heartbreak, but this was different. I was no longer merely a spectator. My life had been put in jeopardy. That entitled me to know a few things.

"How about we cut to the chase then. You may not know who they were, but you sure as hell know who you are. What kind of man are you, Sebastian? And what the hell is all this?"

He gave a desperate little shake of his head, his eyes darting towards the unnamed guard sitting in the driver's seat. "You know I can't answer that."

"So, what, I have to go along with all this without any idea what's happening to me?"

His brow furrowed. "I'm sorry."

I felt a surge of anger and I latched onto it. I may not have been able to take out my frustration on my captors, but I sure as hell could lash out at Sebastian. "Sorry? You're sorry? Are you for real? I just got kidnapped! Do you understand that? Sorry doesn't really cut it. Maybe in whatever secret, corporate world you guys play in that's normal, but in regular person land, that's kind of a big fucking deal."

He hung his head. "I know."

"At least give me something. What about a motive? I mean, what would anyone want with me? I have no idea about whatever it is you're into. As you just illustrated, that knowledge is clearly not for the likes of me."

His lips tightened. "I don't know exactly. We're trying to work that out."

I rolled my eyes. "Awesome. You don't know who they are, or what they want. Is there anything you do know?"

His expression hardened. "I know that I'm not going to let it happen again."

I gave a sour little laugh. "Forgive me if that doesn't fill me with confidence."

"What else do you want, Sophia? I'm sorry beyond words

that this happened, and I'm going to do everything I can to make it right."

Tears stung the back of my eyes but I forced them away. "How? How can you possibly make this right? There are people after me, Sebastian, and I'm guessing they're not going to stop just because you foiled them once. My life is officially in tatters and I don't even know why."

His mouth opened and closed but no words came out.

"You know, I lost my job," I said, after a few seconds of silence. My voice sounded strangely wooden, now.

For a moment, confusion flooded his face. "What? When?"

"A few days after I went to your office. Jennifer finally made her move." Surprisingly, I couldn't even muster much anger at her. My being fired already felt hazy, like a distant memory. "When it happened, it felt like the end of the world. All I could think about was the fact that I had to start from scratch. Now, I don't even know if I'm going to get that opportunity."

He looked like he'd been struck. "I promise that you will, Sophia. I'm going to get you through this. You'll get your life back."

"When? When will I be able to go back home and start rebuilding? When can I see my family? My friends?"

He glanced away and gave a little shake of his head. "I don't know, yet."

"That's what I thought. God, it seems like being in a relationship with you should come with an advance warning: may involve significant peril." Realisation slammed into me, and I rocked back in my seat. "Oh my God. Sebastian. The thing with Liv... was that like this?" I didn't know how it hadn't occurred to me earlier. The coincidence was impossible to ignore.

292

He closed his eyes and drew several long breaths, his fingers clenching into a fist by his face. There was something in that gesture that was stronger than mere anger, a kind of deep seated mental agony. "I don't know, exactly," he said, after a few moments. He spoke slowly, his tone soft and hollow. "We never arrested anyone. As far as we know, there was no kidnapping. It all happened in the house. Not a day goes by where I don't wonder about it, whether it was because of me." His face twisted in pain. I could hear him sucking back tears. "But this here, what happened to you, this is definitely my fault, and I know it's probably little comfort to you, but I'll never forgive myself for putting you in harm's way."

I stared at him, a torrent of conflicting emotions raging through me. Part of me was still furious. He had every right to feel ashamed. After all, if I'd never met him, none of this would have happened. He'd pursued me, despite knowing that there may be risks, and I'd paid the price for that.

But I couldn't ignore the anguish in his voice, the guilt that was etched on his face. He meant what he said about never forgiving himself. He would carry this forever. It was a strange role reversal, but suddenly I felt the urge to comfort *him*. Regardless of everything that had happened, I still hated seeing him hurt. The connection between us still blazed like an inferno inside me. It was like his pain flowed out through his pores and into mine, seeping into me.

I spent the rest of the trip gazing out the window, watching the houses roll by. My fear may have eased, but my confusion was at an all-time high. I still had no idea what I was involved in, but I knew it had to be big.

Whatever came over the next few days, I suspected that my life would never be the same again.

Chapter 2

Sophia

After driving for another half an hour we wound up at a giant old manor house, somewhere in the depths of eastern Sydney. It looked like the sort of place that belonged in a nineteenth century British period drama. A long driveway, manicured gardens, ivy snaking over the ageing brickwork like a network of veins. It was shielded from the outside world by a tall, concrete wall, with a Gothic looking wrought-iron gate providing the only access point.

"It's a secure location," Sebastian told me as we pulled in, although it was a somewhat redundant comment. One look at the expressionless men with automatic weapons, who were posted around the grounds, said that this wasn't somewhere you stumbled into uninvited.

A voice inside me wanted to know who the hell had multi-million dollar safe-houses just lying around for situations like this, but when stacked next to everything else that had happened, it somehow seemed to make sense. I felt a guilty little rush of excitement. Whatever world Sebastian had tried to keep from me, I was now being taken into the heart of it.

I'd decided to save the rest of my questions until we had a little more privacy. It seemed unlikely his friends would kidnap me, only to break down the door and rescue me a few hours later, but I was going to be cautious nonetheless. I was swimming in unfamiliar waters now. I couldn't afford any mistakes.

Sebastian and I hadn't said another word for the rest of the trip. There was something strangely distant about him now. It didn't make sense, but it almost felt as though he were angry at me.

Surprisingly, there were about ten people waiting for us inside, including several faces I recognised. Thomas and Trey both approached as I entered.

"What's with the welcoming party, guys?" I joked, bemused by their presence.

Thomas flashed a quick grin. "Someone called ahead. Said they'd got you. I'm glad you're okay."

"Yeah, you gave us one hell of a scare," said Trey.

"Well, thanks," I replied.

The two men shuffled awkwardly in place, their eyes darting to the floor. There was a strange tension in the air, and it didn't take a genius to figure out why. Whatever Sebastian's secret, the whole room was clearly in on it, and at that point it had to be obvious to everyone that I knew more than I was supposed to. I'd seen too much to still be in the dark.

Thomas and Trey appeared to be taking it in their strides, but not everyone looked so happy to see us. Several more of Sebastian's colleagues, including Ewan, were standing in a nearby doorway, assessing him with dark expressions.

"What's the deal with them?" I asked.

Thomas glanced over and grimaced. "Eh, just office politics. Don't worry about it."

Before I could delve any deeper, Sebastian appeared next to me. "There's a room made up for you upstairs. There's also food, if you're hungry."

I knew I should probably eat, but my stomach was still churning from the enormity of everything that had happened. What I really needed was a chance to process everything.

I shook my head. "I think I'll just hit the hay, if that's okay."

"Whatever you want," he replied.

I nodded farewells to the guys, who flashed tight little smiles before drifting back towards their colleagues. I wondered if they were going to get chewed out for talking to me. I got the sense that I wasn't exactly a guest of honour.

Sebastian led me upstairs and round the corner to a plainly made up bedroom. "There's a bathroom if you want a shower, and something to change into."

"Thanks," I said. That strange sense of hesitation was still there in his demeanour, like he was dealing with a distant cousin he only saw at family get-togethers. The desperation, the burning need I'd felt when he first burst into my prison, was nowhere in sight.

"Is there something else going on?" I asked.

"What do you mean?"

I nodded towards the foyer. "I'm not stupid enough to think they're all here for me."

He paused. "Things have been a bit crazy around here. Your disappearance... well, it wasn't an isolated event."

I wanted to ask more, but the way his brow furrowed and his voice shook when he spoke told me that perhaps the other situations hadn't turned out so well. There would be time to discuss it later.

He moved to leave, but paused in the doorway. "Like I said, this place is as secure as possible. You saw the guards as we came in, and nobody outside of us even knows it exists. You're safe here, Sophia."

I nodded, although it felt like a lie. In spite of the virtual fortress around me, I wasn't sure I'd ever really feel safe again.

* * * * *

In the past, I'd always considered sleep a sanctuary. A lot of people in high powered jobs struggle to get enough rest, but no matter how stressed or strung out I was, it had always come easily for me. I love that sense of complete escape, of just shutting down and blocking it all out for a few hours.

But tonight was different. Every time I closed my eyes, it was like being plunged into biting water. I kept remembering the way it had felt that morning, in my house, fading out as the drugs took hold. The brief explosion of dread like a hand closing around my heart as I realised, too late, what was coming. Suddenly the darkness of sleep wasn't soothing, it was terrifying.

And every time I did manage to drift a little, I always woke in a cold sweat, just minutes later, a montage of terrifying images playing through my head. I hated that sense of powerlessness. I was the one in charge of my mind, dammit. The experience had been horrifying, but now it was over. There was no reason to let it affect me anymore. But logic didn't seem to be relevant. This was beyond rationality. Something had broken inside me.

The third or fourth time I woke, it was with a sob. Moonlight cast the room as a series of jagged silhouettes, and despite knowing I was somewhere safe, the unfamiliarity of my surroundings sent something sharp skittering through my chest.

Suddenly, it felt like everything was closing in around me. I let out another cry and burrowed deeper under the covers, feeling fresh tears welling in my eyes. I didn't want to be this person, this person who cried at shadows, but I didn't know how to deal with the emotions that were roaring up inside me.

I felt another bolt of fear as I heard the door open, but in a moment there was a familiar weight on the bed, and then Sebastian's arms were circling my body from behind.

"It's okay," he said, his voice soft. "Let it out."

I have no idea how he knew I was in distress, but in spite of everything that was still unresolved between us, I loved that he'd come. The sheer strength of his presence dwarfed everything else, dulling the fear. He was my rock and I clung on for dear life, lest I slip back below the surface again.

He didn't say anything else and so neither did I, but just the act of being together was enough. I lay there, listening to the sound of his breathing, enjoying the sensation of that solid chest rising and falling against my back. Gradually, my turmoil began to dissipate. I had no idea how he had such a calming effect on me. When we were together, nothing else seemed to matter.

He felt like home, and for just that night, I pretended like he still was.

Chapter 3

Sebastian

I hadn't expected Sophia to sleep at all, not after what she'd been through. Trauma like that can break a person. But somehow she'd drifted off. I had no idea where she found the strength to be that tough. She never ceased to amaze me.

For a while I lay there, trying to get some rest myself, but the events of the last two days had thrown my whole world into chaos. It was all happening again. The fact that I'd averted the worst didn't make the situation any better. I was an asshole. I should never have let it get to this point, but I was weak, and it had nearly cost the woman I love her life. How the hell could I sleep, knowing that?

To make matters worse, even now I couldn't stay away. She was as secure here as anywhere, but the moment she'd left my sight I began to feel agitated. I still hadn't managed to shed the mindless terror that had seized me when I first heard she'd been taken. The urge to go to her, to simply hold her and never let go, had been almost overpowering.

I'd tried to distract myself. There was certainly no short-age of work to be done — most of my colleagues were holed up together in the board room, planning well into the night — but I was useless there. My mind only wanted to focus on one thing, and soon I found myself sitting, propped up against the wall outside her room, nursing several fingers of scotch in a heavy crystal tumbler. I didn't know why, but just being close to her helped. I made myself vow not to enter. It had taken an immense level of control to cut her off the first time, and every moment in her presence stretched my will-power just a little more. I would keep her safe and solve all this, and then when it was all over, I'd let her go again. It was the only way.

But the moment I heard her sobbing through the door, all sense of self-control fled. Before I knew it, I was on my feet and in her bed. I expected her to fight, after all, I had to be the last person she wanted to see, but she didn't. Instead she just burrowed into me without a word. I hated how perfect that felt, the way her body fit like a missing puzzle piece against mine. I still didn't understand how such simple con-tact could make me so content, but it did.

And now she slept. I couldn't help but run my eyes over her again. Truth be told, I'd barely been able to stop staring since the moment I entered the room. She looked so fucking beautiful lying there, her face utterly peaceful, her curves per-fectly accentuated by the thin cotton sheet. She'd taken the T-shirt I left her, but not the pants, and now in the throes of sleep she'd managed to knock part of the cover free, exposing one delicate hip. It was a tiny thing, the barest hint of pale skin and black cloth, but the sight took my breath away none-theless. I felt impossibly low, ogling her after everything I'd put her through, but I was powerless to do anything else. Her body was like a drug, a burning rush through my system that was impossible to ignore. I knew how that hip would feel, if only I'd reach out and touch it. I had every inch of her body charted in my head; so perfectly soft, so perfectly feminine.

Fuck. I had to pull myself together.

Ripping my gaze free, I eased my arm out from under her. I'd done what I came to do. She was resting. There was no reason for me to stay.

She stirred briefly, and I came within a hair's breadth of pulling her back against me once more, but after a few moments she settled. Taking one last look, I moved quietly out into the corridor and resumed my watch. I'd be there if she needed me, but anything beyond that was too hard. There was no happy ending here, and letting myself think otherwise would only destroy me more.

* * * * *

I spent the entire night in that hallway. After a few hours my back was killing me, but I refused to move until the sun rose. It was stupid — there were many men much more dangerous than I, stationed around the complex — but I felt compelled to guard her personally, just that once, like that could somehow make up for my earlier failure.

At around seven, I heard her stirring. Not wanting her to know about my vigil, I slipped downstairs and headed for the kitchen. I'd sent enough mixed messages for one night.

I had no idea what the day would bring. Ever since I'd heard about her kidnapping, I'd been operating purely on instinct. A kind of base fury that blotted out everything else. But now that I had her, I had to face the reality of the situation. Now the fallout would begin.

She came downstairs while I was eating breakfast. She looked impossibly angelic; eyes bright, hair tussled. God, no wonder I was in trouble where she was concerned. Even first thing in the morning, frightened and bruised, she was utterly gorgeous, and every time I saw her, it was like seeing her again for the first time.

She shot me a small smile, but it was cautious, deflated. I didn't blame her. "Hey," she said.

"Hey," I replied. "Sleep okay?"

She nodded, apparently unsure if she should say anything about my visit. "Eventually, yeah. I'm starving now though."

"I expected you might be. There's toast or cereal. I'm sorry it's not scrambled eggs, but we're a little unprepared here."

She blinked a few times, her expression unreadable. I don't know why I made reference to that morning. It felt like a lifetime ago.

"That'll be fine," she said, and set about making herself something. A minute later, she joined me at the table.

We ate in silence for a while, but I knew that was temporary. She had that glint in her eye again, and the curious little curve of her mouth that I'd seen so many times before. It was the first thing I'd noticed, months ago, when she snuck into our party. I'd known that curiosity was dangerous, but somehow when I opened my mouth to send security after her, I found myself dismissing them instead. The worst part was that, even now, I couldn't make myself regret it.

"So," she said, after a few minutes. "What happens now?"

I grimaced. I didn't know what to tell her. All of this was unprecedented. Her very presence here went against every rule in the book. "Now, we try to find who did this."

She nodded slowly. "And what about me?"

"You'll stay here until it's safe for you to go home."

She stared for several seconds. "And that's it?"

I shrugged and nodded.

302

"You're still not going to give me any kind of explanation?"

I knew it was pointless, but I tried to fend her off nonetheless. "Like I told you before, Sophia, these secrets, this life, it isn't mine to share. Nothing about that has changed since I wrote that letter."

Her jaw tightened. "Nothing has changed? Are you kidding me? I just got kidnapped, Sebastian. Kidnapped! If that doesn't change things, I don't know what does."

I didn't know how to reply. She was right. Of course she was right. But that didn't give me license to break two millennia of tradition. "I'm sorry," I said, but even I knew it sounded weak.

"That's not good enough. It was one thing to keep me in the dark when it was just our relationship on the line, but it's more than that now. This is my life, for Christ's sake. I didn't ask for this, but like it or not, I'm here now. I deserve to know what the hell I'm involved in."

I stared into my coffee. There were no right choices. If I told her, I'd be betraying my brothers. But if I didn't, I'd be betraying her. She wasn't going to take that lying down either. If I didn't give her answers, she'd try to find them on her own. And who could blame her? If I were in her position, I'd want to know. But if she started digging, it would only make things worse.

"This isn't a secret like other secrets, Sophia," I said, feeling impossibly heavy in the chest. My heart and my brain continued to wage war inside me, but I think the battle was already decided. I wanted her to understand why I'd made the decisions I'd made, why I'd caused her such pain. "This isn't the kind of thing you promise to keep to yourself, then get drunk and spill to your friends."

She rolled her eyes. "I kind of figured that when it caused

a couple of men to break into my house and drug me. I get it, this is serious business."

I exhaled slowly and glanced towards the door, realising exactly how dangerous this was. Most people were still asleep, but all it would take would be one early riser to overhear, and both of Sophia and I would wind up in the firing line. The severity of everything else that was going on here had allowed me a little leniency with the rules, but that would only extend so far. Sharing our secrets was one of the most serious breaches possible.

I got up and checked the corridor, then shut the door. "You can't let the others know I told you. I mean that. They're not stupid. They must already realise you know more than you should, but there's a difference between suspicion and confirmation. If they even catch a hint of this discussion, they'll have grounds to take the matter further, and at that point I doubt I'll be able to protect us."

Her breathing quickened a little, and for a few seconds I could see her wrestling with herself, but eventually she gave a quick nod. "I understand." I couldn't help but smile. Told that this information could get her killed, she barely blinked.

I closed my eyes. I felt a little like I was about to jump out of a plane. "I'm... part of something," I said. "Something very old and very big. We're called the Alpha Group."

"That's what the 'A' stands for?"

"Yes."

She nodded to herself. "Okay. So what is it?"

"It's tough to describe. The best phrase would probably be a secret society, but thanks to Dan Brown, that now conjures up images of religious cults and portals to other worlds. The truth of it is a little subtler than that."

"A secret society?" she said, enunciating each word carefully. She didn't look surprised, in fact she seemed incredibly calm. "Like the Freemasons?"

"Kind of, but not really. These days, they're more of a social club than anything else. It's difficult to be a secret when everyone knows you exist."

Her eyes were focused intently on me, quietly processing every word I said. "So, what do you do that's so different?"

I gave a wry smile. "That's not easy to summarise. We have our fingers in a lot of pies. In a nutshell, we try to steer things in specific directions."

"What sort of things?"

"Whatever we think is important," I replied. "You have to understand, this isn't some two-bit little operation, Sophia. What you've seen here is the tiniest fraction of the group as a whole. We have people all over the world. Government, finance, entertainment, you name it. Each member is carefully selected for the influence they bring to the table and, through that network, we can pull whatever strings we want."

She closed her eyes briefly, pinching the bridge of her nose between two fingers. "I'm not sure I understand. I mean, I knew you had to be involved in something big, but this is some conspiracy theory stuff you're claiming." She shook her head slowly. "So, what, are we talking like rigging elections and starting wars?"

I licked my lips. "Those are pretty extreme examples. We tend to be a little more low key than that. I'd rather not go into the specifics — I'm breaking enough rules as it is — but everything we do has a larger purpose."

"And who decides on the larger purpose?" she asked, a hint of disapproval in her voice. "If what you're saying is true, aren't you basically just a group of people who conspire to use your connections to do whatever the hell you want?"

"It's a little more complicated than that. You're judging us without knowing anything about us."

"So explain it, because it seems to me that a group like this is basically corrupt by definition. No wonder you and your friends are richer than sin."

I sighed. It was almost impossible to make her understand in the space of a single conversation. People were normally brought in slowly, over a matter of months. It had taken me nearly a quarter of a year to fully wrap my head around it all. "It's not like that. Most people in the group are recruited *because* of their wealth and power, not the other way around. The group is fundamentally about doing good."

"In what way?"

Apparently I was going to have to give more details. I wracked my brains for an example that would get through to her. "Remember the town I told you I grew up in?"

She nodded.

"Well I made that my first project when I joined, before I came to Australia. The group worked wonders over there. We got the government to pave actual roads, had them install better water filtration, even got the town on the electricity grid. It's still dirt poor, but the people there actually have a chance now. Our work isn't all that overtly philanthropic of course, don't think I'm sugar coating it, but our overall goal is to fix glaring inequalities, to protect people who can't protect themselves."

"But those sorts of responsibilities belong to the government. You know, the people we actually *choose* to run things."

"Come on, Sophia. Someone as smart as you can't really believe in the effectiveness of the government when it comes to protecting the individual. There's as much corruption there as anywhere in the world. Look at the GFC. Millions of people were financially ruined, and yet nothing came of it. Nobody has really been punished, no changes have been put in place. And that's just the tiniest tip of the iceberg."

She pondered this. "Okay, that might be true, but if you're so concerned with the lives of the everyday worker, why didn't *you* do something about that?"

I grimaced. "That's a sore spot for us, actually. The truth is we just didn't see it early enough. We're powerful, but we're not omniscient, and the big banks are particularly hard for us to break into at a high level. The kinds of guys who are happy to swindle people for billions aren't generally the sort of members we want to recruit."

For a few seconds she sat in silence, her face impassive.

"You know me," I continued. "You know the sort of person I am. Is it so hard to believe we might actually have good intentions?"

Her expression softened, although she still seemed somewhat unsure. "Let's say I believe you," she said. "There's still a lot of questions unanswered. Like how are you not discovered?"

I shrugged. "We're very good at staying under the radar. We've had a lot of practice. The group is over two thousand years old."

Her eyes widened. "Two thousand?"

I nodded. "This sort of thing doesn't just spring up overnight. We started in ancient Greece — hence the name — as a way to keep the government in check, and it kind of grew from there. Democracy was new then, and there were... teething problems. When those problems didn't go away with time, we hung around. Anyway, with the amount of influence we've now got, keeping our activities out of the limelight is actually fairly easy, as long as we don't do anything too bold."

"So what about Fraiser Capital then?"

"It's a real company," I replied, "but it's also our main front, here in Australia. Venture capital firms throw money at all kinds of strange projects. Having it as a legitimate entity makes financing and directing our operations much easier."

"So that party I snuck into...?"

"A meeting for potential new recruits."

She nodded to herself. "Right." She was much calmer now that the initial disbelief had worn off, calmer than I'd expected.

Her eyes flicked to mine, and she hesitated. "So I'm guessing that a group like this probably has its share of enemies," she said slowly.

I could see where she was going with this, connecting the dots. "We do."

"Enemies that might do things like kidnap your members' girlfriends?"

My shoulders slumped. "It's possible." Instinctively I reached out to clasp her hand, but managed to stop myself. *No more mixed messages.* "Believe me, I've been wracking my brains trying to work out why this happened. I have no idea what anyone would hope to gain from taking you."

"Is there anyone out there that might want to hurt you personally?" she asked.

It wasn't like I hadn't been through that a thousand times too, both now and when Liv was killed, but I always came up empty. "Not that I can think of."

She pondered for a few more seconds. "What about whatever's going on here then? The other disappearances. Is there a connection there?"

I closed my eyes briefly, feeling a fresh surge of anger. With everything that had happened to Sophia, it was easy to forget that there was more at stake than that.

"Maybe. Those situations were a little different," I replied, struggling to keep my voice level. "They weren't disappearances. They were murders."

Her hand flew to her mouth. "Oh God," she said, and

this time she was the one that reached for me. That simple contact felt wonderful and, although I knew I should, I didn't pull away.

"The first one happened a few days ago. Charlie didn't show up for an appointment. We didn't think too much of it, until the next day, when someone went to his house and discovered his body."

"Jesus," Sophia replied.

"We were still trying to figure it out, but then yesterday, the same thing happened with Simon. At that point we knew we were under attack, so we followed protocol and gathered our senior members here." It felt strange to be saying this stuff out loud. It made it seem more real. I'd known Charlie and Simon for the better part of ten years. They were my friends, and although saving Sophia had briefly blotted out everything else, I felt their loss as keenly as anyone.

"I'm sorry," she said.

I nodded in thanks. "Perhaps there's a connection there," I said. "Perhaps it was the same people and we just got to you before..." I couldn't finish the sentence. "Anyway, we're using every available resource to work out who is responsible. And I swear to you, I won't stop until you're safe and you can leave all of this behind."

She stared at me for what felt like an eternity, her jaw set tightly, her eyes flickering with some emotion I couldn't identify.

Eventually, I heard the sound of a door closing upstairs. People were starting to wake up. Realising she still held my hand in hers, I reluctantly pulled away and got to my feet. "I have to go. There will be a meeting soon and I have to prepare. Just try to lie low, okay? I'll check in with you later."

She gave the barest hint of a nod.

I felt better, having told her the truth. Now she understood. It didn't make up for the pain I'd caused, but it was something.

On my way back to my room, I ran into Trey, who was just coming in through the front door.

"Just the man I wanted to see," he said. He wasn't part of our senior council, so he wasn't staying in the house. He was out on the street, working leads and keeping the rest of Alpha's ventures running smoothly.

"Oh yeah? What's up?" I asked.

He handed me a file he was carrying. "Just got these back from our team. None of those guys that took Sophia came back with any kind of match. Whoever they were, the computers of the world do not know them."

I let out a long sigh. Everything we'd run so far on Sophia's kidnappers had come back negative. Nobody should have been that hard to track. We had access to every database that mattered.

"Thanks," I said to him. "Keep at it. Something has to give eventually."

"Will do." He hesitated, like he was afraid to ask what came next. "How's Sophia doing?"

I gave a weary shrug. "I don't know. It's hard to tell. I think she might still be in shock, to be honest."

"Yeah, I can imagine all of this is pretty difficult for a civilian to process."

"That's one way to put it," I said heavily. I had no idea how she was going to react to everything I'd just told her once she had some time to digest it. It could go a thousand different ways. "Anyway, I should go. Meeting in a few minutes."

"No worries."

I turned to go, but then a thought occurred to me.

"How do you do it, Trey?"

He cocked his head to one side. "Do what?"

"Keep your private life and your professional life separate?" A few years ago, Trey had been just like me. One empty fling after another. But then he'd had his own Sophia moment. He'd met a girl who made him give all that up, but unlike me, he managed to keep her in the dark. I didn't think I'd even met her. He kept her totally separate from anything group related. I always wondered how he pulled that off.

He flashed me a half smile. "I just have a girl who understands me, I guess."

He made it sound so damn easy.

Chapter 4

Sebastian

I'd always known there were protocols in place for if a situation ever got really bad, but I'd never experienced them first hand until now. All of our key personnel were currently gathered here in lock down. It was part strategy meeting, part protection detail. We couldn't afford to leave ourselves exposed, not when we were completely on the back foot. Whoever was behind the attacks was clearly well connected. So far, they'd been like ghosts.

After a quick shower, I headed to the back of the house. We'd set up a makeshift board room in the study, and the bulk of the inner council was already there when I arrived. Thomas, and one or two others, nodded greetings, but the rest either ignored me or scowled pointedly before turning away. I hadn't done myself any favours rescuing Sophia the way I had. It went against several key group rules, and a good chunk of the room wasn't in a hurry to let me forget it. If the situation had been any less dire, I'd probably have faced disciplinary action; but, for now, they had to settle for dirty looks and snide comments. We had bigger things on our plate.

"How you holding up?" asked Thomas, coming over to join me.

I shrugged. "How do you think?" I tried to keep the frustration from my voice, but I didn't do a very good job.

He studied me for several seconds. "You got her out, man. That's what matters."

"Is it? Then why do I still feel like shit?"

"Hey, I don't blame you. I'd be angry too. But try to go a little easier on yourself. You couldn't have known."

I felt my hands contract into fists. "Of course I could have. You know, I really thought I was smart enough not to put anyone else in this position again, but apparently I'm a slower learner than I thought."

He flinched a little at my tone, but his voice remained calm. "I thought we were past this. You know as well as I do that the situations are completely different. What happened to Liv was a tragedy, but there's nothing tying it to any of this. It was a freak accident, that's all. You have to let it go. Stop blaming yourself."

I gave a bitter little laugh. It wasn't like I hadn't tried. Objectively, I knew he was right. Our investigation had never found anything to indicate that Liv's death was more than a standard break and enter gone wrong. But no matter how much evidence there was to the contrary, the heavy sensation I'd carried in my stomach since that day refused to dissipate.

From the moment Liv and I became something more than a casual fling, part of me had felt uneasy about it. There's no hard and fast rules about relationships within the group. As long as our secrets remain hidden, you're allowed to do whatever you want. Most Alpha members simply choose to forgo that kind of companionship to make their lives easier, and I'd been firmly in that camp. Then I met her.

Liv had a vibrancy to her that was completely infectious. I'd never known anyone like her. She was passionate and energetic, and she seemed to genuinely care about me for more than just my money. In retrospect, I could recognise more than a little youthful infatuation in our relationship, but at the time it felt like something deeper. A little voice in the back of my head constantly told me that I was leading her down a dangerous road, but I was too selfish to stop. I don't know why I was surprised when it blew up in my face. Even if her death *was* an accident, I still broke her heart, and I hated myself for that. I swore I'd never be responsible for that sort of pain again.

But now there was Sophia. If my attraction to Liv was the firm pull of a magnet, my attraction to Sophia was like gravity; unyielding and inescapable. Something about her just rendered me utterly powerless. From the moment I met her, I felt like I was trapped in a whirlpool, swimming in vain against the current as it gradually sucked me down. It scared me. It felt like only a matter of time before it drowned us both.

"Either way," I said, "I still put Sophia in danger. You're not going to try and absolve me of that one too are you?"

He sighed. "Just because you're involved doesn't make it your fault."

I wished I could believe that. He was just being a good friend, but no amount of support could fix this.

I gazed around at the roomful of men I'd given my life to. From the moment I joined the group, they'd been the world to me. Even when I was with Liv, I'd never considered a different path. "Do you ever regret all this?" I asked, my tone softening. "Because I have to say, right now, for the first time, I'm actually starting to doubt my choice."

He flashed a sympathetic smile. "I think we've all felt like that, at one time or another. This isn't an easy road, by any means. But you know how important it is."

I nodded, though it was more for him than me. Truth be told, I wasn't sure I knew what was important anymore. Nothing made sense now.

A few minutes later, everyone had arrived. We took our seats.

"So," said Ewan, "give me some good news." Although he wasn't in charge in any real sense, as the longest serving member, he ran the meetings. He was also the most visibly upset person in the room. Sunken eyes spoke of sleepless nights, and his hands roved restlessly across the table, as if just staying in motion might somehow speed things up. The two men we'd lost, Simon and Charlie, had been close friends of his.

Marcus, the youngest member of the group, grimaced. He was our point of contact for the investigation. "We don't know much more than yesterday, unfortunately. Our guys went over every inch of Simon's house, but it was the same as Charlie's. No signs of forced entry, security footage wiped. Whoever it was did one hell of a job."

"What about the autopsy?" asked Thomas.

"Still coming," replied Marcus. He glanced at Ewan. "He didn't go gently, though, I can tell you that much."

Ewan slammed his fist down on the table. "I'll make sure *you* don't go gently, you little shit."

"I don't mean to be disrespectful," replied Marcus, looking a little pale. "But it's important. This wasn't just about taking them out. Someone went to a lot of effort working them over, which means that, chances are, they wanted to know something."

"Were the two of them working on any projects together?" I asked. "Anything tying them together?"

But before Marcus could reply, Ewan cut in. "Well, look

who has decided to rejoin us," he said, making a big show of looking surprised to see me. "Does that mean you're ready to focus on what's important again?"

"I'm sorry about my absence last night," I replied, trying to remain calm. "I had other things on my mind." He was right to be angry, and if I'd been in his position, I'd have reacted the same way. I had an obligation to these men, an obligation that couldn't just be cast aside on a whim. But the suggestion that anything was more important than finding Sophia made everything inside me tense.

"That's exactly my fucking point," the older man replied. "We've got a major crisis going on, and your head isn't in the game. It's busy burying itself between a pretty pair of thighs."

Thomas' hand flew out, firmly holding me in my chair. He knew me well. Rage poured through me. "If you keep talking like that," I said, my voice sharp enough to cut glass, "the group will be down another member before too long."

"Is that right?" Ewan asked. He didn't look even slightly perturbed. "You'd put her before one of your own? You're even further gone than I thought."

Guilt and anger seethed in my stomach. Ewan and I had never gotten along, and I knew most of his aggression was just frustration at the loss of his friends, but there was a tiny part of me that thought he might be right. Perhaps my priorities really had changed. "Why do you care so much what I do?"

He laughed. "You flatter yourself. Honestly, Sebastian, I don't give two shits what you do. But what I do care about is you using Alpha resources to rescue your girlfriend when they could be out there finding the bastards that did Simon and Charlie in."

I opened my mouth, unsure exactly what I was going to say, but Thomas jumped in ahead of me. "You still don't think there's a connection there, Ewan? The people that took

316

Sophia were organised, efficient, and clearly backed by some serious money. Exactly the sort of operation that might have been able to take out our guys."

Ewan shifted uncomfortably in his chair. "That doesn't prove anything."

"That's true," Thomas said, "but it is a pretty big coincidence, and I, personally, don't care much for coincidences. In any case, we have very little idea what's going on here yet. Let's not lose our heads until we know more."

Ewan seethed in his chair for a few moments. "Maybe you're right. Maybe. But you want to hear what I know already? I know that the group is under attack, and yet there's a civilian girl walking around in our headquarters, seeing everything, overhearing God knows what." He turned his gaze to me and raised his eyebrows ever so slightly, as if to say, 'Or being *told* God knows what.'

"Where do you want her to go?" I asked, desperation creeping into my voice. "You know the kinds of people we deal with. Sending her back out there may well be a death sentence."

For a moment, I thought I'd gotten through, but then Ewan's expression hardened further. "I don't know, but she doesn't belong here."

"For now, I say she does," Thomas said. "At least until we know what we're up against. Someone wants her, and if it *is* the same people who did that to Simon and Charlie, then it's in our best interests to deny them what they want, wouldn't you say?"

Ewan glared around the table. Several others seemed to share his disapproval, but nobody could come up with a counter. It was hard to argue in the face of sound logic.

I shot Thomas an appreciative smile. "I'll make sure she stays out of everyone's hair," I said to Ewan.

He nodded curtly, and the meeting turned to other matters. Despite my best intentions, however, I couldn't focus. All I could think about were Ewan's words. In truth, he was right. Bringing her here had been a mistake. Even if I'd told her nothing, her curiosity would eventually have gotten the best of her. The moment she'd walked through those doors, everything had changed. But all other paths led to the unthinkable. I didn't know what other option I'd had. It was a no win scenario.

* * * * *

I spent the rest of the day alone in my room, trying a few more abstract methods to identify Sophia's kidnappers, but the truth was, it was mostly a waiting game at this point. All the information we had was already out there. We were just waiting for someone to get back to us with something positive. It was incredibly frustrating. We had all the power in the world at our fingertips, and we were still coming up empty.

At about five in the evening, there was a knock at my door.

"You got a minute?" asked Marcus, poking his head inside. It had ruffled a few feathers that we had promoted him to the council so quickly, but despite being relatively young, he was a really promising member; the perfect combination of smart and level-headed.

"Sure, what's up?" I said.

He stepped inside and closed the door behind him. "Well, I just got something back from the lab, and I thought you should be the first to know."

I felt a tingle of excitement. Maybe we'd finally caught our break. "Tell me you've got a name for me," I said.

He licked his lips nervously. "Not exactly. Our guys are

still trying to run down who exactly owns that house you raided. Whoever it is laid one hell of a paper trail. What we did get was a match on some blood we found in one of the rooms there." He hesitated ever so slightly. "It belonged to Simon."

I sank back slowly into my chair. Thomas had been right, the two situations *were* linked. I wasn't surprised — the coincidence was difficult to ignore — but knowing for sure only made our predicament more confusing. Why would anyone go to pains to kill two of my brothers, but then take Sophia instead of me? All I could think of was that they wanted leverage over me somehow, but I couldn't imagine what for. It was baffling.

"I appreciate you telling me first," I said.

"No problem. The others called a pre-dinner meeting, but I kind of figured you might not show."

I nodded. "Yeah, I might sit this one out. You've given me a lot to think about." As much as I wanted to be there to see Ewan's face when the connection was confirmed, I didn't particularly feel like wading back into that minefield just yet.

"No worries. I'll keep you posted."

"Thanks."

I sat for a while after he left, pondering the new discovery. As frightening as the situation was, in some ways that connection was a good thing. Whatever our enemies were planning, Sophia was obviously a part of it, and so rescuing her had likely thrown a spanner in the works. And since we now had just a single target, I could feel comfortable directing the full brunt of Alpha's resources at the problem.

It was little progress, but I knew Sophia would want to hear about it anyway. I found her in her room, curled up on the bed, nursing a cup of tea and staring at the wall.

"Hey," she said, as I entered.

"Hi." Our conversations were uncomfortable now, like the lies and secrets had piled up to form an invisible barrier in the air between us. It was what I wanted, it was what *we* needed, but it still hurt like hell.

"How are you holding up?"

She shrugged. "As well as can be expected, I guess. There's not much to do around here." She held up her mug and gave it a little shake. "Although this tea addiction I'm developing looks promising. This is my fifth cup today."

"That stuff will kill you," I said, managing a small smile.

She returned it, and something loosened in my chest. "So they tell me. Anyway, how's the big investigation? Assassinate any presidents today?"

"Not that I know of, although that's not my department," I replied. I was glad she was still able to find humour in the situation. Maybe she wasn't quite as damaged by it all as I'd feared. "I did get one small piece of info, though."

She gazed at me expectantly. "Yeah?"

"They found a few bloodstains in that house you were being held in. Our lab just matched it with Simon, one of my brothers who was killed."

Her expression grew tense once more. "I see. I guess the connection makes sense. Does that help you find out who's behind it?"

I shook my head. "We're still coming up empty on that, so far. But now that we know the investigations are linked, we'll be throwing everything we have at it."

She nodded, although she didn't look particularly comforted. "Okay."

"There's something else I wanted to talk to you about," I said, moving over to sit next to her on the bed. "I know this situation is awful for you, and God knows that being in this place isn't making it any easier."

"You mean the friendly Scotsman and his band of merry men?" she said.

"Yeah. I know they're not the most welcoming lot, so I was thinking, what if you went away for a while? We have the resources to get you a new passport, a new identity, and obviously money isn't a problem. You could go wherever you wanted, and nobody would be able to track you down. It would be kind of like a holiday."

Part of me hated the idea of sending her anywhere I couldn't watch over her, but my argument with Ewan had got me thinking about alternatives. Her presence here was certainly problematic, and it wasn't going to get any easier. In fact with everyone on such short fuses, it felt almost inevitable that something would explode eventually. This wasn't a world she belonged in, and taking a trip was the only way I could think of to extricate her while still keeping her safe.

"And how long would I be gone, exactly?" she asked, her expression unreadable.

"You know I can't give you an exact time frame, Sophia."

I thought she was going to blow up at me, but when she spoke, her tone was calm. "I appreciate the offer, but I have a life here, Sebastian. The idea of dropping everything and disappearing with no return date in mind doesn't sit well with me."

I closed my eyes, feeling a huge stab of guilt. Whether or not she went, her life was on hold. She could hardly wander back home in a few weeks if our enemies were still out there.

"Just think about it, okay?" I said.

"Okay."

She continued to stare at me. There was a sadness to her expression, but also a glimmer of something else, something questioning. I realised then how closely we were sitting. There was barely a foot separating us. Her smell — orange blossom and vanilla — suddenly seemed to be everywhere. All I had to do was lean in and my mouth would be on hers. I could already visualise how she'd taste, how she'd tremble, how her tongue would feel curled around my own.

I knew I should leave, but my muscles refused to obey. All I could do was sit there and drink her in. Fuck, I wanted to kiss her. I wanted to grab hold of her and push her down and show her that she was still mine. But, of course, that wasn't true.

I didn't understand why she hadn't sent me away yet. Instead she just sat with her eyes locked to mine, her lips hanging ever so slightly open, like an illicit invitation. There was something smoky lurking in her gaze now, something that shouldn't have been there.

It was almost enough.

Closing my eyes, I sucked in a shuddering breath and got to my feet. "I have to go."

She was still for a few seconds, then nodded slowly. For a brief moment, I almost thought she looked disappointed. It didn't make any sense.

I fled.

I needed to be alone with my thoughts, but as I headed for my room, I ran into the last person I wanted to see.

"Sneaking in a quickie while the rest of us are slaving away, hey?" said Ewan, who was waiting for me around the corner.

"I'm not in the mood, Ewan," I said, trying to swerve around him, but he stepped sideways, blocking my path.

"Maybe I am," he said.

I found myself fuming at his school boy antics. "Have you got something you want to say?"

He chewed thoughtfully for several seconds, as if working an invisible piece of tobacco around his mouth. "Marcus filled us in on what he'd found. Looks like your girl *is* involved in all this, somehow."

"Does that mean you're going to get off my back about it?"

He laughed. "Hardly. Just because you went and created a weak spot for yourself doesn't mean the group should have to clean up after you. Having her here is a liability. We don't know her and we don't trust her."

"I trust her."

"Do you?" he asked, bitter amusement evident in his voice. "Perhaps that's the problem."

I took a step closer, feeling something animal flare in my chest. "What's that supposed to mean?"

But Ewan was not easily intimidated. "It means that something here doesn't add up," he said, staring me right in the eyes. "Nobody outside of Alpha should even know the council exists. Yet a month or two after you start swapping promise rings with Ally McBeal in there, suddenly our guys start dying."

"You're joking, right? Did you forget that they took her too?"

He gave a little shrug. "Maybe they were just finishing the job. Cleaning up loose ends."

It took every fibre of my being not to knock him to the floor. My hands twitched at my sides, both balled tightly into fists. But I was already walking on thin ice as it was. Hitting him would only make things worse.

"This is ridiculous," I said.

"Maybe. Maybe I'm way off. But either way, there's no excuse for breaking the rules."

I stared at him with gritted teeth. There was nothing I could say. He was right and we both knew it.

Not knowing what else to do, I moved to leave again.

This time he didn't try to stop me. He'd gotten his message across. Sophia's presence here was more than an inconvenience, and it was only a matter of time before she was out on her own.

Chapter 5

Sophia

The second night was a little better than the first, but not much. More than once I woke flushed and sweating, the sharp tang of my latest nightmare still fresh on the back of my tongue. I wondered if this was post-traumatic stress. Based on what little I knew, it certainly seemed possible. I'd never understood how you couldn't just block that stuff out, but now I did.

Part of me expected Sebastian to magically appear once more and slip into my bed like a comforting ghost, but the door remained closed. I found myself disappointed about that. It seemed crazy to think about the prospect of 'us', in the context of everything that was happening, but no matter how terrified and out of my depth I felt, there was no denying the strength of my feelings for him. Not to mention my attraction. The energy that had sprung up between us when he'd visited earlier had nearly overwhelmed me. He had this way of looking at my body, like he was preparing to devour me, that ignited something deep in my stomach. I wanted to be angry — hell I *was* angry — but if, at that moment, he'd kissed me, I wasn't sure I'd have put up a fight.

I didn't know whether to be touched or offended at the 'holiday' he'd offered. It did feel a little like he was just taking the easy route and trying to sweep me under the rug, but at the same time, everything he said was valid. Things were uncomfortable here, and I knew it must be just as bad for him. I appreciated the predicament he was in, even if it was somewhat his fault. I just wished I wasn't in it as well.

More than once I considered agreeing to go. An all-expenses paid trip overseas was hardly the worst proposition in the world; but, truth be told, the idea of being out there all alone scared me. My life was here and it was under siege. I couldn't just run away while somebody else dealt with that.

After several hours of restless turning, I gave up trying to sleep and reached for my phone. Sebastian hadn't mentioned it, but when I woke up that morning, I found a few of my possessions waiting for me in the hallway outside. Apparently he'd sent someone to my house.

It was a good thing too, because there were already several texts from the girls waiting for me. Another day or two and they'd have started to worry.

Ruth: Hey Hon'. Hope the wallowing is going well. If you need another pick-me-up, I'm willing to take one for the team and suffer through a few more midday mojitos. Let me know.

I'd read them over and over today, relishing that tiny connection to my old life. It had been less than two days, but somehow that's what it felt like now: my old life. At a time where everything else was in ruins, it was nice to be reminded I still had someone waiting for me when this was all over. If it ever would be.

I'd already reassured them both I was fine, conjuring up some story about visiting my sister down in Melbourne for a little mental recharge, but as I stared at the screen now, I was nearly overcome with the desire to call them and tell them everything. It was a terrible idea, but curled up there, in the unfamiliar dark, surrounded by people I barely knew with agendas I couldn't even fathom, I felt so incredibly alone.

After staring for a few precarious seconds, my thumb poised over Ruth's number, I shoved the phone back into my bedside drawer and headed out in search of tea. What I really wanted was something a little more numbing — I figured a house like this had to have a wine cellar — but drinking away my problems probably wasn't the best option right now. I needed to stay alert. The world seemed to have turned into a much more dangerous place, virtually overnight, and in this dimension of secret societies and covert kidnappings, waking up with a killer hangover might have a different meaning entirely.

I had no idea how to process everything Sebastian had told me. Part of me wanted to laugh it off as an absurd joke, something dug out of a bad eighties espionage film, but taking into account everything that I'd seen, I believed it. I didn't know what it all meant yet, but I planned on remedying that situation. As unbelievable as it was, I was a part of this, now. I could either sit, awestruck on the sidelines, or I could try and work out exactly what the hell I'd gotten myself into.

The house was silent as I made my way to the kitchen. It wasn't until I put the kettle on and began hunting for a cup that I realised I wasn't the only person awake.

"Can't sleep?" said a voice behind me.

I nearly jumped out of my skin. Turning, I saw a familiar figure, cast in shadow, nursing a mug of his own at the breakfast table.

"Jesus, Joe. You scared the hell out of me."

He chuckled. "My apologies," he said, although he didn't sound particularly sorry. "Feel like some company?"

It seemed harmless enough. I wasn't exactly going to drift off anytime soon. I filled my cup and moved over to join him. "I take it you know what happened?" I asked.

He nodded. "I was there when Sebastian got the news."

"Then you know why I can't sleep."

He nodded again. "I don't blame you. I don't think anyone would rest easy after a thing like that."

I appreciated that he didn't offer any advice. Just understanding.

We sat in silence for a few minutes. Despite the lack of conversation, I was enjoying the company. He might not have been Sebastian, but his presence seemed to hold back the darkness a little nonetheless.

Eventually though, he spoke. "He told you." It wasn't a question.

Fear seized my belly. I turned my gaze to him slowly. He didn't look angry, in fact a ghost of a smile touched his lips, but I knew what he meant nonetheless. It hadn't occurred to me that Joe might be an Alpha member. He just seemed like hired help. But clearly there was more to him than that.

I debated denying it, but the certainty in his eyes said there was no point. He knew. The question was, what would he do with that knowledge?

I let out a long sigh. "He did."

Joe chewed his lip thoughtfully. "Well then."

"You don't sound surprised."

He shrugged. "Everyone likes to think they can keep their mouth shut when necessary, but the truth is, every man has his breaking point. The way he talks about you, the only thing that surprises me is that it took this long."

The way he talks about you. My mind instantly went back to Sebastian's letter, to all those heartbreakingly sweet things he'd said. And then to that look he'd worn when he first pushed his way inside my prison, the rapture that had lit his face when his eyes found mine. I wasn't the only one struggling to switch off my feelings.

You always hear stories about the purity of love, about the way it swells inside you until nothing else even matters. I never cared much for that perspective before — that kind of love typically isn't compatible with the sort of future I saw for myself — but now I found myself longing for it to be that simple. Every decision had turned into a conflict, a titanic battle between heart and brain, between logic and emotion. I couldn't deny my feelings for him, but whenever they rose inside me, they brought with them anger and betrayal. I knew it wasn't intentional, but he'd exposed me to this world, a world that was currently trying to chew me up and spit me out again. It was hard to forgive that, with the terror of my kidnapping still blanketing everything like a thick fog.

And even if I could get past it, there were other elements to the equation. Was he still the same man I'd fallen for? In light of everything he'd told me this morning, I didn't know. It was almost easier to just write him and his friends off as corrupt, power hungry monsters; but, try as I might, I couldn't see him being a part of something like that. Not to mention guys like Thomas, or apparently Joe. If Sebastian said their intentions were noble, then I believed him.

"This is a mess," I said, after a pause, not sure if I was referring to my relationship with Sebastian or the forbidden knowledge he'd shared.

Joe let out a laugh. "That it is, girl. That it is."

"So you're a member too then?" I asked, stalling for time. I wasn't sure where the conversation was going exactly, but he'd obviously brought it up for a reason. Something in my gut told me I could trust him, but Sebastian's warning loomed large in my mind nonetheless.

"Indeed."

"Well, I don't mean any disrespect, but isn't it a little demeaning having you drive another member around?"

He shrugged. "It's not so bad. I give him hell, but Sebastian's a better sort than most. Besides, it's not like I always did this."

"Oh?"

He grinned. "Alpha's not exactly in the business of recruiting chauffeurs. Not much to be gained by that. No, before this I served thirty years in the British Army."

I nodded. That explained the war wound he'd mentioned the first day we met. "In what capacity?"

"Infantry first, but they quickly shuffled me to the officers' path instead." He leaned in conspiratorially. "Didn't seem to care for all the questions I asked." He let out a short laugh. "Nope, there's not a lot of space for curiosity on the battlefield. I think they figured that if I was going to be doing all that thinking, I might as well be the one answering the questions instead of asking."

"I think that's fair enough," I replied.

"That's actually where I met Sebastian."

"Sebastian was in the army?" That revelation reminded me exactly how little I knew about the man who had stolen my heart.

"Briefly." He gave a rueful shake of his head. "He was a terrible soldier, just like me. Too headstrong, too stubborn. I was his commanding officer, and it got to the point where I was forced to discharge him, but it seemed like such a waste. There was something special about him. I knew he was capable of doing great things, and the characteristics that made him unfit for duty made him perfect for Alpha. So I released him from service and nominated him for consideration to join the group. He was accepted, and now here we are."

"I see," I replied, trying to picture Sebastian in mud spattered combat fatigues. It was difficult. The suit and tie seemed almost like his second skin.

"What about you? Why'd you quit?" I continued.

"Well, obviously I had more important things to do here," he deadpanned, nodding in the direction of the bedrooms.

I laughed. "Obviously."

"Honestly though, I just kind of got tired. You'd think gaining rank would be a good thing, but by the last decade of my career, I dreaded it. Every promotion meant a little more time spent behind a desk, a little more paperwork. There was nothing to look forward to, anymore."

"And so your solution was to drive your protégée around, day in and day out?" I asked.

He shrugged. "It may not seem particularly exciting, but the truth is, there's rarely a dull moment around here."

Thinking back on everything that had happened in the last few days, I could see his point. If this sort of stuff was a regular occurrence, I wasn't sure my heart could keep up. Another point against Sebastian and I ever having a real relationship. Thinking about it gave me a newfound respect for military wives. The prospect of my partner constantly venturing into indescribable danger was daunting, to say the least. I didn't know how they coped.

"Is it always like this?" I asked. "Kidnappings and secret lairs?"

He smiled. "Sometimes, but not as often as you'd think. These are pretty dire circumstances. Most of the time it's more like being a politician; lots of paperwork and meetings."

"So Sebastian just has impeccable timing then."

Joe stared at me for several seconds. "Don't be too hard on him, Sophia. He didn't mean for any of this to happen."

I let out a long breath and shook my head slightly. "I know, but it doesn't change the fact that it did."

"Not to downplay what you've been through at all, but to be honest, I think he's dealing with it as badly as you are. Like I said, I was there when he got the news. I've never seen anything like it before. He could barely speak. Everyone seemed to take it as anger, but I know him better than most. I knew it for what it really was. Fear.

"He wanted to throw everything we had at that house the moment they took you there, but that's not how the group works. You can't just use Alpha resources for personal situations, no matter how serious they may be." His lips compressed. "They argued for hours. Virtually the whole room was against him. Eventually, he realised they weren't going to budge, but rather than back down, he just stormed out and came for you anyway. Took an entire squad of our troops. To be honest, I'm kind of glad nobody physically stepped in to stop him. I have little doubt he'd have gone by himself, if he had to.

"For now, nobody is doing anything about it. We've got too much else to worry about. But if I know that group, he hasn't heard the last of it. Not by a long shot." His gaze bored into me. "I understand that this was hell for you, I really do, but Sebastian did everything in his power to make up for what happened. He put himself at risk to save you, so maybe cut him a little slack, hey?"

My mouth felt impossibly dry. I knew Sebastian had been distraught at my kidnapping, but this cast it in an entirely new light. He hadn't simply been cleaning up an Alpha group mess. If anything, he'd been doing the opposite. He'd actively put my safety above the interests of his brothers. He'd broken the rules for me. I didn't know what it meant — was it a temporary lapse or a permanent statement? — but it made me warm all over. My mind was suddenly racing with possibilities.

"I didn't know," I said eventually.

"Well, now you do," he said with a nod.

"Will he be in serious trouble?"

"I don't know. Time will tell. But, in the past, such actions have been... frowned upon, let's just say."

Something about the way he said gave me the impression it was more serious than he was letting on.

I weighed his words. Were Sebastian's actions enough to overcome all of the lies and the secrets? I didn't know. I still had so many questions.

"Liv's death," I said carefully.

His expression turned grim. "Now that was a hell of a thing."

"Sebastian said nobody really knows what happened. Is that true?"

Despite his age, he was still sharp. He saw my implication instantly. "You're wondering if he should have expected this?" He shook his head. "No, nobody could have seen this coming. He blames himself for Liv, but the reality is it was just a case of wrong place, wrong time."

"But if there was nothing to worry about, why did he leave someone outside my place?"

"Paranoia I suspect. You have to understand, Sebastian took that hard, harder than anything I've seen, until you disappeared. He feels like if he hadn't ended things with her, if he'd found some way to make the relationship work, perhaps things would have been different."

I blinked in surprise. "Ended things? He told me they

were engaged."

"Ah," he said with a wince. "I'm sorry. I assumed he'd told you the whole story. Technically he didn't lie; they were engaged. Several of us tried to warn him of the dangers of such big secrets in a marriage, but it's hard to argue with love. Of course, it became progressively easier as she began to get suspicious. She was a bit of a computer guru, you see. Was being headhunted by all kinds of A-list companies, but they wanted her to move overseas and Sebastian couldn't, so she turned them down. Anyway, one day, Sebastian left his laptop open at an Alpha login portal. To most people that wouldn't mean much, but to a girl like her, it was a beacon. Soon, she was digging up all manner of strange info. It wasn't enough to tell her anything concrete, but it told her he was hiding something."

He took a long sip from his mug. "So, she confronted him. They argued and she gave him an ultimatum."

"And he chose the group," I finished.

He nodded slowly. "Although 'chose' might be a little generous. This isn't the sort of thing you can just walk away from. A few people have managed over the years, but it requires an immense amount of planning and a willingness to drop totally off the grid. Not exactly an appealing prospect for an up and coming IT whiz."

"I guess not." It was a lot to take in. I couldn't help but notice all the parallels. As well as the one big difference. Sebastian had initially chosen the group this time too but, when push came to shove, he'd picked me.

"Anyway," Joe said, dragging himself to his feet, "it's time to take these old bones to bed. It's been lovely chatting with you, Sophia."

"Goodnight."

He moved to leave, but paused in the doorway. "I hope

that whatever comes of all this, you find some peace."

"Me too," I replied.

Chapter 6

Sophia

I intended to head back to my room but, instead, I found myself walking right past the door and continuing up the hallway. Something told me that Sebastian would still be awake. I didn't know exactly why I wanted to see him, only that I did.

My instincts proved accurate. I found him sitting at a desk in his room, hunched over a laptop screen. The door was open, but he didn't appear to notice me, so for a while I simply stood and watched. He looked tired. No, that wasn't the right word. Haggard was more appropriate. A man with the weight of the world on his shoulders.

Even now, just the sight of him sent a tingle curling through me. A surge of lust, but there was something deeper too, something comforting and strong that blossomed in my stomach like a sunrise. It made the prospect of seeing him again exciting, no matter how often it happened. I was beginning to think that feeling would never go away.

I tried to put myself in his shoes; impossible obligations

pulling at me from all sides. Would I have reacted differently? Would I have continued our relationship, knowing the world I was exposing him to? I didn't know. It felt like a position where there were no right moves.

"I know what you did for me," I said eventually.

He flinched at the sound of my voice, his hand darting towards the desk drawer, although he stopped when he recognised me. "Christ, Sophia. Sneaking up on people at four o'clock in the morning in this particular house is a really, really bad idea."

"Sorry."

He studied me. I could tell that part of him simply wanted to send me away. Every conversation between us now was difficult, strangled by guilt and uncertainty. But eventually he spoke. "What do you mean, what I did for you?"

"The way you stood up to your brothers when no one else wanted to help rescue me."

He waved dismissively. "Ah, that. It's not a big deal."

"That's not what Joe said. He said it was quite the argument."

I walked inside and sat on the surface of the desk. Sebastian was close enough to reach out and touch now, and I had to resist the urge to do just that. I was doing a good job of keeping my fear at bay, but that didn't mean it had fled. It still simmered inside me, waiting for another opportunity to boil over, and the prospect of facing that alone was almost too daunting to consider. Just being near him soothed my shredded nerves.

"You broke the rules for me," I continued. "In a pretty big way, from what I understand."

His gaze was hard, radiating intensity. I could almost feel the conflict playing out inside him. "What else could I have done, Sophia? I couldn't let them take you."

"I thought the group came first."

He hesitated, then shook his head slowly. "So did I."

We sat in silence for a few moments. I think we both knew what was coming. We couldn't avoid discussing our relationship forever. I was still afraid to do so, lest that wound tear open inside me again, but knowing what he'd done gave me a glimmer of hope. Maybe, somehow, there was a way through this.

"Sebastian, I—"

"Don't," he said, rising to his feet and putting some distance between us. "We can't do this, Sophia." His voice was sharp, almost pained.

"I have to know," I replied. "What does all of this mean for us?"

He stormed towards me and I jolted backwards. "There *is* no us. There can't be. You've seen the sort of life I lead. How can you even ask that?"

"I don't know," I said softly. "But I'm asking all the same."

He closed his eyes and swept a hand through his hair. "I nearly got you killed. I don't understand how you're even still talking to me."

A few days ago, I might have agreed with him. Logically I knew I still should. But logic had always taken a back seat where he was concerned. Yes he'd kept things from me, but I now appreciated the full weight of those secrets. Everything he'd done spoke of how much he cared for me, and I couldn't deny that my emotions burned just as strongly. I could hold the situation against him, or I could move on and try to build something to go back to, after it was over.

"I don't blame you, Sebastian. I did in the beginning, but I don't now. You couldn't have known. Yeah, if I hadn't met you, none of this would have happened, but then I'd never have met you and, the truth is, that thought terrifies me far more than any of this."

He stared at me with wide eyes, his expression hovering somewhere between anguish and awe. "How do you do that?" he asked. It was barely more than a whisper. "No matter what I do, no matter how sure I am, you say just the right thing to make me question myself."

A smile crept onto my face. "I'm just that talented, I guess."

His expression softened a fraction, but it didn't last long. "I can't keep making these mistakes, Sophia. It's too dangerous. Sure, I saved you this time, but what about next time? Or the time after? This life offers no guarantees. I won't give it another opportunity to claim you."

"So that's it, then? I don't even get a say?" Moisture rushed to my eyes. "Don't my feelings count for anything?"

"Of course they count," he lamented, although he didn't seem to know how to finish the sentence.

"So if we never had a chance, why tell me all those things then?" I asked. "Why bring me into your world? Why slip into my room at night and comfort me like nothing has changed?"

He shook his head desperately. "I don't know. I don't know."

For a few moments there was silence.

"Do you remember what you said to me over dinner, the first time we went out?" I asked eventually. "'Nothing worth having comes risk free.' Well, that's how I feel now." I got to my feet and moved over to him, taking his hands in mine. "I'm a big girl. I can make my own decisions. I understand the risks, and I'm telling you I'm okay with them. I love you, Sebastian, and if that's the price for being with you, then it's one I'm willing to pay. The question is, are you?"

The surge of emotion on his face mirrored my own. That

was the first time I'd said the L word out loud to him. It hadn't been intentional, but the moment it left my lips I knew it was true. It was so perfectly right. I could feel it down to my bones.

He closed his eyes momentarily. "You have no idea how long I've wanted to hear you say that. But not now. Not now!" Pulling his hands free, he turned away. "I don't know if I can keep fighting this, Sophia. It hurts too much. Seeing you every day, not being able to hold you or kiss you or love you. It's ruining me."

"So stop fighting."

For a few seconds, I thought I'd lost him again, but then he was spinning and his lips were crashing into mine.

I'd never been kissed like that, not even by him. In that gesture, I could feel every ounce of his guilt, his pain, his love, and I found myself kissing back just as ferociously, my own torrent of emotions thundering through my chest. The joy I felt was almost enough to make me weep.

In a few seconds, he'd worked my track pants free and lifted me back onto the desk. No words were necessary. Desperation and longing burned brighter than the sun in both of us. I needed that connection, that perfect affirmation that said more than words ever could.

I was dimly aware that the door was still open, but nothing in the world could have stopped us at that moment. We were utterly lost in one another. With raw hunger, he yanked his fly down, freeing his shaft, and then buried himself inside me. My skin burned with the suddenness of it, but I didn't care at all. I savoured the pain because it came from him, a stinging symbol of the bond between us.

He moved slowly, coaxing my body to life around him with gentle thrusts. I mewed softly against his mouth, feeling myself grow slick, but he didn't break the kiss. He devoured me, drawing my lips tenderly between his teeth and stroking them with his tongue. His hands found my legs, looping under my knees to lift them higher, allowing him to sheathe himself in me all the way to the root.

Finally he pulled away, only to bury his head against my neck. "Say it again," he whispered, teasing me with a slow rocking motion.

"I love you," I breathed.

"And I love you," he replied.

And then he was moving in me again, his mouth tracing fire across my collarbone, sending my capacity for speech spiralling away. His thrusts strengthened as the animal in him gradually broke free of its cage. He snarled against my chin, one hand slipping between my legs to find my clit, sending a new chord of ecstasy thrumming through me.

His lovemaking was different now. Every time before, I'd seen a new side of him; sometimes dominant, sometimes soft, sometimes hungry, but this was all of those things together; fierce strength combined with loving tenderness. I felt like I was finally getting all of him, no more shields, no more secrets, he was finally letting it all go, and it was the most beautiful thing I'd ever experienced. In that moment I knew that I was his and he was mine.

As his rhythm reached its crescendo, the pressure building in my core began to swell. I wrapped my hands around his neck, fingers digging into his flesh, his body tightening in time with mine as we came together.

"God, I've missed you," he said, laying his forehead against mine as we caught our breath. Standing there above me, dishevelled and bathed in sweat, he looked absolutely radiant.

I nuzzled my nose against his. "Me too."

We moved over to the bed and lay, for a while, in each

other's arms. The bliss I felt in that moment almost made it possible to forget everything that had happened; we were just an ordinary couple, snuggling together, after making love.

"I love you," I said again, turning to stare him in the eyes.

He smiled. "I'll never get sick of hearing that." His expression slipped a little, and I knew we were about to come hurtling back to reality. "I hate to break the moment, but we aren't done talking. If we're really going to do this, there's some things we need to think about."

"Okay," I replied cautiously, half afraid he was going to go off the deep end again.

He took his time choosing his words. "Even when we get through whatever is going on right now, I don't know exactly how we make this work." He raised his hand to cut off my objections. "I'm not saying we don't try. I can't deny this anymore, Sophia. I love you, and for some stupid reason you appear to return the feeling."

"I'm a slow learner, I guess," I replied.

He shot me a half smile. "The fact is, you're here and you're involved and you know things you shouldn't know. And my brothers... some of them are already worried about you. They're distracted now, but when things settle down, and we're still together, they're going to start asking questions of their own, and I don't think they're going to like the answers."

I'd been wondering about that. I may have been saved from immediate danger, but the longer I spent in the Alpha house, the more I realised that I wasn't as safe as I'd thought. I couldn't just forget everything I'd seen, and these people knew it. "So what do we do?"

He shook his head. "I don't know."

"You kind of make it sound like we're doomed, no matter what."

"No, no, that's not what I meant." He exhaled sharply. "I'll figure something out. For now, we just need to tread carefully. We both know a lot of people don't approve of your presence here, so let's not give them any reason to take it further."

Once again I felt an uneasy feeling settle in my stomach. "Are you sure about the people who kidnapped me?" I asked carefully. "Because if there's any chance it was someone here, we might wind up playing right into their hands."

"I'm sure," he said firmly. "These men are my brothers. Besides, whoever took you also killed Charlie and Simon. Nobody here would do that."

His certainty put my mind at ease; well, as at ease as was possible with some kind of rogue terror group trying to kidnap me. "You've used the word 'council' a few times," I said, spotting another chance to sate my curiosity, "is that like the Alpha board or something? I've been trying to work out how you make your decisions."

His jaw tightened a fraction. "I'm not sure I should talk about that."

"Oh come on. They're already going to be super angry if they find out what you've told me so far, right? So how much worse can it get?"

He hesitated, but eventually gave a resigned smile. "I guess you have a point. Yeah, in a nutshell, the council runs things in this area; it's in control of the Asia Pacific region. Other regions are run by different groups."

"And you're on it?"

He nodded. "Almost everyone here is, except the muscle, drivers, and house staff."

"So that makes you kind of a big deal, then?" I asked with a grin.

He laughed. "Kind of."

It made sense. I struggled to picture Sebastian anywhere but the top of the ladder, regardless of what he was doing.

"So it's like a democracy? You all just vote on everything?"

"Yes and no. For most decisions, the whole council has a say, but ultimately there still needs to be a figurehead, to settle disputes and keep the group operating smoothly. The official title is Archon."

"Archon?" I said, raising an eyebrow.

He shrugged. "Blame the Greeks. We're stuck with it now."

I laughed. "And who is this Archon?"

His face took on a strange expression. "I don't know."

"You don't know?" I said slowly. "How can you not know?"

"It's a secret, even amongst the group. The heads of each cell have an immense amount of power. For example, they're the only people with access to the full list of Alpha personnel worldwide. If that sort of power fell into the wrong hands, the damage would be catastrophic. So they stay hidden, just in case."

I licked my lips as I tried to process this. "But how does that work?"

"Well, the council has sixteen members, one of whom is in charge. By all appearances, they are just a regular member of the group. Anything that requires their attention as the Archon is dealt with through the Alpha computer network. The commands come anonymously, so nobody but the Archon and their lieutenant know the source."

"Lieutenant?"

He nodded. "The Archon chooses a second in command, someone to take over if anything happens to them. They're like a backup. Otherwise, there would be no way to choose a new leader when the existing one dies. The lieutenant is the only other person that knows who runs the show. It's a little eccentric, I know, but it works."

"I was going to say paranoid, actually."

"Maybe that too. We didn't always do things this way, but about five hundred years ago, one of our enemies managed to infiltrate the group and, through the Archon, they learned everything. We lost hundreds of members and years of progress. So we devised a system to stop that happening again."

It all seemed incredibly mysterious, but then again, that was true of the entire situation. Besides, on some level, that just added to the coolness of it all. I was basically living in a conspiracy theory!

I couldn't help but smile as the full implication of what he'd said sank in. "So, when you said you didn't know, was that you telling the truth, or you toeing the company line?"

"That was me telling you I didn't know," he replied, a twinkle in his eye.

"Right. But if you were in charge, I'm guessing you probably wouldn't tell me anyway, right?"

There was a twinkle in his eye when he replied. "Perhaps not. I need to keep *some* secrets, Sophia."

I sighed dramatically. "I suppose that's fair. Well then, mister councilman, what do we do now?"

I'd intended us to talk a little more about the problems we faced, but apparently he had something else in mind. In response he gently rolled me away from him, then pulling me close until we were spooning. Although I still wore my top, I was naked from the waist down, and the position pressed my bare ass against the growing hardness between his legs. I felt my body stir again.

"Now, we make up for lost time," he replied, his voice growing husky.

And despite the weight of the discussion we'd just had, he quickly convinced me that that was exactly what I wanted to do.

Chapter 7

Sophia

The next few days were a mixture of frustration and joy. By night, I had Sebastian back. We ate together, we talked, and we spent a great deal of time reacquainting ourselves with each other's bodies. Although it hadn't been that long since we'd been intimate, it felt like I was discovering him for the first time all over again.

However, while the sun was up, things were different. As much as we both wanted to just shut ourselves away and ignore everything, the fact was, Sebastian still had a job to do. The threat — whatever it was — wouldn't disappear on its own. If we wanted any hope for some kind of normality in the future, we had to take action.

Or should I say, *he* had to take action. Although he tried to keep me in the loop, my involvement was strictly second hand. There was no way for me to attend their meetings without putting us both at risk. He'd return to his room, which was now our room, and brief me on what had happened that day. They had a few leads, but so far they'd hit nothing but brick walls. Aside from that they apparently spent most of the time fighting about what the next step was.

I tried to amuse myself while he was gone, but it was hard. I wasn't used to being left to my own devices. I hadn't had more than a few days to myself since high school. It didn't help that I was confined to quarters. Until things were safe, Sebastian insisted I did not leave the building. I read a lot and watched more TV than I had in my entire life, but within a few days I felt dangerously close to breaking point. I began having visions of myself as one of those creepy old ladies in Victorian period dramas, who can be seen haunting the windows of ancient manor houses, but never venture out into open air.

Then there was the tension with the group members. Ewan and his cronies continued to make sure I was aware how unwelcome I was. It wasn't outright aggression, but the dark looks and biting remarks told me exactly how they felt.

"Have they said anything about us?" I asked Sebastian, after a particularly bad day.

He frowned and shook his head. "No, actually, they've been strangely silent."

"So that's good, right?"

"I guess," he replied, although he didn't sound convinced.

Most of the others didn't seem to know how to react to me, so they simply ignored my presence. And Joe, the only one I assumed might have talked to me, had gone overseas to attend to some family problem. I felt a little like a ghost, floating unseen and unacknowledged, around that buzzing house.

After several days, my boredom got the better of me and I went in search of a computer. I figured that if I had to kill time, I could at least do it laughing at cats with hilarious facial expressions. Sebastian had a laptop, but he carried it with him during the day. I'd seen a few desktops scattered around the building, and nobody ever seemed to be using them, so I didn't think anyone would mind.

Unfortunately, it wasn't as simple as just sitting down and turning the system on. The PC lit up when I hit the power button, but the screen only got as far as displaying a blinking cursor on a black background, and no amount of resetting or playing with the cables would fix it.

I'd seen Sebastian power up his laptop before, and at some point during the process he always swiped his thumb across the little biometric scanner that hung off the side. This PC had one too, sitting on the desk next to the keyboard. Perhaps the system wouldn't start without the right person in the chair.

Part of me wanted to swipe it myself just to see what would happen. I even got as far as poising my thumb over the pad, but then a voice from the doorway interrupted me.

"I wouldn't do that, if I were you."

I jolted back in my chair. It was Trey. I hadn't seen him since the night I arrived. Apparently he wasn't part of the inner council, so he wasn't holed up here with the rest of them.

"Sorry," I said.

"It's alright. No harm done. You're just lucky I found you when I did. A word of warning, though. Anything that needs a thumbprint you should probably stay away from."

In spite of my embarrassment, my curiosity was now peaked. "Why?"

He smiled. "If you don't have the right authentication, the whole system will shut down until someone comes and checks it out. I figure you could probably do without that attention."

Well, that answered that question. "Right. Thanks for the warning."

He stared at me for a few seconds, and I felt my skin begin

to prickle. It was another of those awkward moments where we were both aware I knew something I shouldn't, but we weren't discussing it. He didn't look concerned at all, but it still made me uncomfortable.

"So, what brings you here anyway? I didn't expect to see you around these parts," I said, trying desperately to fill the silence.

He shrugged and gave a conspiratorial eye roll. "Thomas needed something. You know how it is; the bosses call and we come a-running. Any idea where he is?"

"Actually yeah, I think I saw him chatting to Marcus in the kitchen, before."

Trey's expression darkened a little. Perhaps he and Marcus weren't on the best terms. "Alright, thanks." His smile returned. "Stay out of trouble, hey?"

I gave a little laugh. "I'll do my best."

In spite of how awkward I'd felt, it was nice to have an interaction with Sebastian's colleague that didn't involve any death stares. It made me feel like perhaps there was hope yet on that front.

But, the next day, Sebastian came to me with some news, and that theory promptly went to shit.

"We're leaving," he said.

I rocked back in surprise. "We are? Does that mean it's all over?"

He grimaced. "Unfortunately, no. Several of the council members simply feel like it would be better if you stayed elsewhere until we finish sorting this out." The words came out through gritted teeth. I got the sense it had been another long and bitter argument.

So, I was being exiled. On one hand, it was actually a bit of a relief. I was sick of being trapped here, constantly feeling like the awkward relative nobody actually wants around. But, on the other hand, the danger outside these walls was very real.

"I thought it wasn't safe out there," I said carefully.

He sighed. "It's not. But don't worry, they're not sending you home. I talked them into a compromise. This isn't the only secure facility Alpha owns. We've got several other places, scattered around the city, so we're going to move to one of the empty ones. It won't be as heavily guarded as this place, but it has all the same security measures. We'll be just as safe as we are now."

"Okay," I said, although there was a slight tremble in my voice. What other response could I give? There didn't seem to be any point arguing.

He gazed at me for a few seconds before lowering himself onto the bed next to me and taking my hand in his. "Hey, it'll be okay. Trust me. I'm coming too, and I'd die before I let anything happen to you."

I nodded. "I know. I just hate feeling so damn powerless, you know? I'm just a pawn, being shuffled around the board; only it's not a game, it's my bloody life."

"I know," he replied, offering me a sad little smile. "I know."

The next day, we left. There was no fanfare. Nobody even said goodbye. I guess that was to be expected.

We were met outside by two hulking rent-a-suits, who Sebastian introduced as Tony and Aaron. They were apparently going to be our daytime security team.

He was coming with me now to help me settle in, but he'd have to commute back to the main house every day to continue working on the crisis.

After about thirty minutes, we pulled up in front of a small but modern looking house on a quiet, leafy street. At first glance it appeared utterly normal, but the biometric scanner on the front door and the bars over the windows hinted that this was something more than an average residence.

"They're bulletproof," he said, following my gaze. "The doors too." Reaching out, he thumbed the touch pad by the front door, and the lock clicked open. "Nobody is getting in here without the proper authorisation. And to even try, they have to deal with Tony and Aaron first. The whole house will be under round the clock surveillance."

Some of the tension I'd been carrying around inside me dissipated. The place certainly seemed as secure as he'd claimed.

The two guards stationed themselves outside, leaving the entire house to Sebastian and I. It was nice to finally feel like we had our own space again. Despite its size, the main house had, at times, felt cramped, and the pervasive air of concern and hostility had made it a less than pleasant living environment.

Sebastian produced some takeaway food from somewhere and we ate it sprawled out in front of the television, mocking the terribleness of the reality shows that seemed to dominate every network. It wasn't a particularly interesting evening by most standards, but I found myself laughing harder than I had in weeks. Leaving the Alpha headquarters had lifted a weight from my shoulders that I hadn't even realised I was carrying.

After dinner, Sebastian disappeared into the back of the house for a minute and returned carrying a box.

"I have something for you," he said, his tone once again serious.

"Oh?"

He opened the container to reveal a petite silver gun. My breath caught in my throat. "I want you to have this," he said, removing it and holding it out to me.

"Sebastian, I don't know the first thing about guns." Just the idea of having something so deadly in my hands filled me with an uneasy energy.

"I know. I'm not expecting you to go take out our enemies all by yourself. In truth, I doubt that you'll ever have to use it. I meant what I said about this place being secure. This is just a precaution, nothing more." He reached out with his free hand and cupped my chin, his thumb grazing my cheek with the utmost tenderness. "I can't be with you all the time, and the thought of not being here to protect you myself... please, it would make me feel better."

The concern in his eyes was enough to allay my hesitation. Gingerly, I reached out and took the weapon from him. It's cliché, but it was surprisingly heavy. The metal felt cold against my skin.

"This is the safety," he said, indicating near the trigger. "Don't switch that off unless you mean it. The gun carries thirteen rounds and is already loaded."

Closing my hands more tightly around the grip, I raised it slowly in front of me. I didn't have any illusions about my ability to actually hit anything, but I did feel a certain sense of comfort with that weight between my fingers.

"Okay." Holding death in my hand, I suddenly felt the need to make a joke. "You know, I'm pretty sure none of my friend's partners have ever given them a lethal weapon before. I'm surely the luckiest girl in the whole world."

The tension eased on his face. "I'm glad I could be your first."

"So, what else is there to do around this place?" I asked, setting the weapon aside. "You know, besides play with my new firearm."

"Not a whole lot." He grinned wickedly and slid closer, looping his hands under my legs and lifting them over his lap until I lay cradled in his arms. "Although I have a few ideas about how we can take advantage of our newfound privacy."

"Oh? And what might those be?" I replied as sweetly as possible.

He leaned in to brush a soft kiss across my cheek. "Well, I thought perhaps I'd see how many different rooms I could fuck you in."

"I think I'd like that very much," I replied, already feeling my pulse quicken.

Suffice it to say that there were no rooms left unchristened by the time we finally collapsed into bed.

Chapter 8

Sophia

For a little while, the novelty of being somewhere fresh buoyed my mood. I explored the new house, and spent many hours pottering around with a glass of wine and a book. But soon enough, my frustration returned. Each morning, Sebastian would kiss me on the head and then disappear through the bedroom door, not returning until well after sundown. In many ways, he had little more freedom than me, but at least he had a mission. I, on the other hand, was left to simply float around, entirely without purpose.

I tried engaging the security guards in a little banter, but it quickly became apparently that all of the steroids must have burned their fun glands into oblivion. They were about as friendly as a pair of rocks, and even less interesting; I quickly abandoned all hope of alleviating my boredom through conversation.

At my request, Sebastian had brought me a laptop, so I turned to surfing job hunting websites online. I knew it was masochistic to taunt myself like that, but I couldn't help it.

After a decade of thinking about nothing but my career, I couldn't just switch off that part of my brain. To be honest, I wasn't sure there were many other parts anymore. It turned out there were several positions going at top tier firms, including one at Little Bell's biggest rival. Any one of them would have been perfect for me, and I knew I stood a good chance if I decided to apply.

I stared at the screen for a while, before closing the laptop and setting it purposefully aside. *Well, there you go. Who knows, maybe they'll still be available in a few weeks and all this will have blown over.*

But as I lay in bed that night, I couldn't stop thinking about what I'd found. Getting back to work was exactly what I needed. With all day to myself, I couldn't help but dwell on my situation. Being unemployed and trapped in a house, with mysterious forces plotting God knows what all around me, was hardly a recipe for inner peace.

"You know, I'm going a little crazy here," I said the next day, when we were sitting in the lounge room after dinner.

He shot me a sympathetic look. "I know it's rough. Hopefully we'll have something soon. In the meantime, try to relax and enjoy the time off."

"Have you seen me try to relax?" I replied. "It's a train wreck. Yesterday I actually rearranged every book in the study by author name, just to feel like I'd actually achieved something for the day."

He laughed.

"Incidentally, you have an awful lot of cook books from the fifties in there. Anyway, relaxation isn't my M.O," I continued. "I need to be out there, getting my life back on track. The longer I wait to find another job, the harder it's going to be. I get that the situation is dangerous, but I want something to come back to when it's all over."

He stared at me for several seconds, a strange smile playing on his lips.

"What?" I asked, realising that something wasn't right. He shouldn't have been smiling.

He opened his mouth, then closed it again, before standing up and walking over to his desk. "I was going to wait until after all of this was sorted out, but I guess there's no harm in showing you now."

"Showing me what?" I asked, feeling a rush of excitement.

He returned holding a small stack of paper.

"This," he said. "I know you have a thing about people helping you, but hopefully you can make an exception in this case."

With some trepidation I began to read, but before I'd made it more than half a page I found myself grinning like an idiot. "Oh my God," I said. "Where did you get these?"

"A friend of a friend," he replied nonchalantly.

"Well your friend struck gold," I said, flipping through several more pages. "My God, the partners are going to flip when they see this."

In my hands, I held a printout of a chain of emails that stretched back over several years. Sebastian and I were no strangers to a bit of written flirtation, but these took the idea of sexting to a whole new level. We're talking bad eighties porno script, and judging by the phrasing, it was just a prelude to what the couple were actually doing in the bedroom.

The email addresses weren't instantly familiar — they looked like personal accounts — but the signatures were.

Alan Beatie and Jennifer Smart.

"I thought you'd be pleased," Sebastian replied.

That was the understatement of the century. A long term relationship between an associate and her superior was already enough to land them in serious trouble, but this went a step further. Interspersed between the racier messages were numerous requests for favours and plenty of signs of preferential treatment. Judging by the dates, their arrangement had started before Jennifer was even promoted. It didn't take a genius to see how the other partners would view that. It felt like Christmas come early.

And then I spotted the coup de grace. "Holy shit." I held up one specific line for him to read. "Did you see this?"

He grinned and nodded.

Thank you for finally dealing with that little bitch Sophia. I'm sure I can think of a few creative ways to reward you ;)

It was morbidly gratifying to finally see her talk about me the way I always suspected she did. The prim, sweet girl that roamed our office building was nowhere in sight, here. These emails were Jennifer unfiltered, and it showed exactly what a nasty piece of work she really was. Although my name came up most frequently, she seemed to have a grudge against almost everyone who posed even a vague threat to her advancement up the ladder. For a brief moment, I actually felt bad for her, for being so insecure, but that was quickly crushed under a torrent of glorious satisfaction at knowing she was finally going to get what she deserved.

"I knew they couldn't have had a decent reason for firing you."

I nodded, still mesmerised by the words in front of me. "You think it'll be enough to get my job back?"

"Definitely. These make it pretty clear that there was more to your dismissal than the quality of your work."

I realised I was grinning like an idiot. "I'll go first thing tomorrow," I said, already playing the confrontation through in my head.

His expression dropped a fraction. "I'd rather you wait until we've dealt with our other problem. It's still dangerous out there."

For a second, I thought I'd misheard. "You seriously expect me to sit on this? Why give it to me at all?"

He shrugged uncomfortably. "You seemed upset. I thought it might make you feel better knowing you can wander back into Little Bell when this is all over."

"And what am I meant to do in the meantime? Keep twiddling my thumbs around here? Look, I'm not downplaying the risk. I know it's not safe, but the truth is, we have no idea how long this is going to take. Sure, it could be a week, but it could be a month, or two, or six. Who's to say they're even going to show their faces again, without an opportunity?" I closed my eyes briefly, trying to rein in my emotions. I felt like a hormonal teenage girl again, flitting from jubilant to angry to upset in the blink of an eye. "I need *something* Sebastian. Being stuck here is killing me — pardon the pun. Surely we can find a way to make it work? You go to and from work every day and you're still in one piece."

His jaw tightened and he glanced away. "That's true." He pondered for a while. "I'm sorry." Sliding closer, he pulled me against him and leaned down to kiss my hair. "I just find the idea of leaving you exposed terrifying. But you're right, this isn't fair on you. How about this: you go in there tomorrow and kick some ass, and once you have your job back, Aaron and Tony will take you to and from the office every day. As long as you don't leave the building, you'll be fine. Several thousand witnesses should be enough to deter anyone from trying anything."

I found myself grinning once more. "Not to mention building security. You, sir, have a deal." Snuggling in against his chest, I began reading over the emails again. "God, I can't wait to see her smarmy little face."

* * * * *

"Hello, Jennifer," I said in my sweetest voice, as I peeked my head around her door.

For a brief second, shock registered on her face, although it was gone in an instant. "Sophia. What a pleasant surprise. I thought you were still on leave."

"I was. I just dropped in to deliver something to Mr Bell."

Her brow furrowed. I think she could tell by my demeanour that something wasn't quite right, but she didn't know what. "That seems... unorthodox."

"Oh, I know. I wouldn't have bothered him, except I recently came into possession of some information that I knew he'd want to see."

"Oh?" She sounded uncomfortable, which only made my smile grow. I knew it was petty and childish, but it felt indescribably satisfying to finally be able to toy with her as she had so many times with me.

"Yeah. It's a bit of a scandal, actually." I leaned in close, as though sharing a secret with a friend. "Apparently, one of the partners has been fooling around with a senior associate. I got a look at the emails they've been sending each other. Some of the things they've been writing... well, graphic doesn't even began to describe them. But the worst part? He's been doing her all kinds of favours around the office. He even gave her a promotion after a weekend away together. Pretty shocking, right? You think your work is what's important, and then you hear about something like this. It's enough to make you sick."

The expression on her face was priceless. Her eyes were open so wide I thought they might pop out of her head, and her mouth worked soundlessly, as though she might somehow still be able to argue her way out of the situation. She looked like one of those rotating carnival clowns.

For a few seconds I simply stood and enjoyed. "Anyway, as you can imagine, Mr Bell is taking the matter very seriously. The partner is in with him right now I believe, and he should be calling the associate any moment. I can't imagine either of them have much longer with the company."

In a piece of spectacularly fortunate timing, at that exact moment, Jennifer's phone began to ring.

"Oh, you have a call," I said. "I'll let you go, then. Just wanted to share the news. Have a nice day."

I don't know how I did it, but I managed to turn around and leave without letting out a cheer, although internally I was giving myself a million high fives. Even Jennifer herself would have been proud of that performance. It had been as chirpy and fake as any act of hers.

I could have been the bigger woman and let that be the end of it, but after years of torture, the moral high ground was the last thing on my mind. This was my moment and I was going to enjoy the hell out of it. After a brief visit to see what had become of my office, I hunted Elle down and dragged her out into the main foyer to wait with me.

"Oh. My. God," she said, when I relayed what had happened. "You're my fucking hero. What did she say when you told her?"

"Nothing. She just sat there growing redder and redder, like someone was pumping her full of hot air."

She laughed. "Christ, I wish I'd been there to see it. That must have been the most satisfying thing in the world."

"It was pretty amazing," I replied.

"How the hell did you get access to her email, anyway?"

I shrugged. "I didn't. Some mysterious little bird forwarded them to me."

"You're kidding, right?"

I shook my head. It was a pretty flimsy lie, but ironically it was more believable than the truth. *Oh, yeah, my boyfriend is part of a secret society that hacked Jennifer's email.* That would go down a treat. "They just showed up in my inbox the other day."

She shook her head in disbelief. "Well, apparently you have a fairy godmother looking out for you."

I couldn't help but grin at the Cinderella reference. "You know, maybe I do."

At that moment, Jennifer appeared around the corner, escorted by building security. She was the picture of a sudden firing; eyes blank, skin deathly white, possessions clutched listlessly in a cardboard box against her chest. There had been no dancing around the issue with her, no feints involving temporary leave to ease the blow. She'd been summarily let go, and company policy dictated that she had to leave immediately. There was too much sensitive information at stake to allow ex-employees to linger.

She did her best to maintain the veneer of superiority, although the smeared mascara running below her eyes certainly detracted from the effect, and the moment she saw me her expression crumpled. I'd positioned myself perfectly, exactly where she'd stood during my walk of shame. There was nothing sweet about my smile this time. I let loose with everything I had. I even threw in my most sarcastic wave for good measure.

Elle was a little more direct. "Seeya, bitch," she said, as they swept past and into the lift. Jennifer flinched as if struck.

As the doors closed, Elle drew a deep breath and smiled. "Is it just me, or does the air smell a little sweeter in here all of a sudden?"

I sniffed pointedly. "You know, I think it does. Must be

the lack of bullshit."

She laughed. "So, please tell me this means you're coming back? This place is a bore without you."

"It will likely be a bore either way. But yeah, I'm back. Apparently they were getting ready to make my leave more permanent this week, so the timing is perfect. I'm still on the books, so we don't even have to do any paperwork."

Elle clapped. "Awesome. Surely this calls for a celebration?"

I winced, remembering Sebastian's rules. As appealing as an old-school office bender sounded, it wasn't safe. "Let me settle back in and then we'll talk. Okay?"

She looked a little disappointed, but didn't question. "Sure. Well, thanks for inviting me to the show, but I should get back to it. Wrights won't prosecute itself."

"No problem. Seeya round."

Once she'd disappeared around the corner, I took a moment just soaking in my surroundings. That might seem like a strange thing to do — I mean, for all its prestige, it was really just an office — but after having given the bulk of the last six years to Little Bell, sometimes it felt more like home than my own house. When Sebastian had handed me those pages, I'd been fairly confident it would be enough to get me back in the door, but I hadn't been certain until now. I was back. At least one part of the nightmare was over.

It didn't take me long to find my feet again. After letting everyone know I was available again, work quickly began to flow in. In just a few hours, I was once again neck deep in case files. Ordinarily that might have had me slightly frazzled, but today, I couldn't wipe the smile off my face.

Surprisingly, Sebastian was waiting for me when we got back. Most days he didn't return until well after dinner.

"I wanted to be here when you got back from your first

day," he said when I asked. He held a bottle of champagne in his hands, and there were two glasses laid out on the bench in front of him.

"Aww, that's very sweet of you," I said, leaning in for a lingering kiss. "But you didn't have to go to all this trouble. It's not like I got a new job. It's the same one I always had."

"That doesn't make it any less worth celebrating." He gave a wolfish grin. "Besides, I felt like champagne."

I laughed. "Ah, now the truth comes out."

He poured and then we settled into the couch.

"So, how was it? Everything went well?"

"You could say that. Evil was vanquished, order restored and all that good stuff."

"I'm glad to hear it. It must feel nice to be back."

I nodded. "Hell yes it does. I can honestly say, I don't think I've ever been so happy to be so busy in my life."

"I'm glad."

"Ernest also dropped a few not so subtle hints about 'recently vacated positions' that might need to be filled."

His face lit up and he pulled me in for a hug. "Congratulations! That's wonderful."

"It is, isn't it?"

"I bet you'd have been promoted years ago if not for those two," he said. "You'll be running that place one day, mark my words."

"Yeah, then maybe I'll have the credentials to join Alpha myself."

He gave a wry shake of his head. "You'd seriously want to do that, having seen what you've seen?"

"I don't know. It's not like it hasn't entered my mind. If you ignore all the guns and kidnappings and such, it is pretty cool." I took a sip of champagne. "Besides, it would certainly solve one of our current predicaments."

"I suppose it would."

"How exactly does one join anyway? Joe said he kind of just plucked you out of the army."

His smile gained a hint of nostalgia. "He told you about that, hey? Yeah, I'm not sure what I would have done if he hadn't found me. I was pretty lost, up until that point. Now I've actually got a purpose.

"As for recruitment, there's no one way. You get people like Thomas, who just work ridiculously hard in their chosen field until we can't help but notice them. He made an absolute killing working for one of the big oil companies, before we found him. And then you've got the guys like Trey, who just get in on their family name."

"Ooh, trust fund baby, is he? I had no idea. He doesn't seem like *that* much of a dick."

Sebastian laughed. "He's fine, most of the time, although to be honest, a bunch of us didn't want to accept his application. We like to recruit people on their merits, not their bloodline, but his dad was a member before him, and he desperately wanted his son to follow in his footsteps. I think it was one of those old money tradition things. Anyway, he pulled some strings and had enough friends that eventually he got his way. Keep that to yourself, though."

"Yeah, sure. I guess since my family has all the eminence of a McNugget Happy Meal, I'll have to go the hard working route."

His expression lost a little of its playfulness. "Let's cross that bridge if we get there, hey?"

I wasn't really sure if I was being serious, but the idea seemed to distress him, so I decided to drop it.

The next few days took on a strangely comfortable quality. If you ignored the nightmarish backdrop, Sebastian and I almost looked like an ordinary, wholesome, professional couple. Each day we'd race through a quick breakfast together before heading to our respective offices. We'd slave away for ten hours or so, occasionally calling each other to whisper sweet nothings, before returning home and spending a few hours in front of the TV or making love, and then collapsing into bed and doing it all again. I'd never really pictured myself being in a long term relationship, but if I had, that was basically how it would have gone. Only the occasional harried expression on Sebastian's face and the presence of our little security team managed to shatter the illusion of normality.

Of course, things were far from fixed. Work was a welcome distraction, but it didn't quite temper the edginess that I seemed to carry around with me permanently, now. In fact, if anything, it made it worse. Logically, I knew that nothing was likely to happen. My building was swarming with people until well past dinner time every night, and my bodyguards met me just feet from the front door. Someone would have to be incredibly bold or incredibly stupid to try anything there. But, nonetheless, I couldn't shake the sensation that I was constantly being watched. It made me jumpy and agitated.

Sebastian seemed to recognise that I was struggling, because he was really putting in a ton of effort. Between the sexy texts and cute little gifts he had delivered to my office — I'm not afraid to admit that I'm a sucker for a bunch of red roses — I was actually feeling rather spoilt. And then he delivered the coup de grace.

On Saturday, I arrived at home to find a note on the kitchen counter. Despite the fact that there was nobody else living there, he'd addressed it like all the others. *Sophia*. Unlike his last letter, this one sent a wave of excitement shooting though me. He was back to his old tricks.

With eager fingers, I unfolded it.

Dear Sophia.

I may be a little later than normal tonight. Hopefully you can excuse me. I know things have been a little difficult lately, so I've decided we need a nice romantic night together. I'd like you to set up a few things for me before I get home.

In the freezer you'll find a bag of ice. Take it into the bedroom and fill the bucket that's on the dresser. There's a bottle of champagne next to it which I'd like you to chill.

In the bedroom you'll also find a box of matches and several candles. There's nothing like a little mood lighting. Light them and scatter them around the room.

Finally, on the bed is an item I believe you will remember fondly. After you've removed everything else you're wearing, put it on and then wait for me on the bed lying face down.

I'll see you soon.

-S

I found myself biting my lip as I read, my skin already prickling with heat. The scene he described was basically the epitome of romance, but the heavy, commanding tone with which he wrote was unmistakable. There was more afoot here than was immediately obvious. It had been a while since one of his letters, long enough to make me heady with anticipation.

After ducking quickly to the freezer, I made a beeline for the bedroom, already suspecting that I knew what I'd find. I wasn't let down. If I'd had any doubts that tonight would be kinkier than our recent sessions, they vanished the moment my eyes fell on the bed. Lying on the quilt was the blindfold Sebastian had originally left for me in the hotel several months ago. Just thinking about that night sent something warm surging between my legs. The sting of his hand, the bite of the rope; that had been the night when everything changed. I'd gone in one woman and come out another.

Placing the champagne inside the bucket I buried it in ice, then lit the candles and dimmed the light. I had to admit, the scene did look incredibly romantic. After stripping, I knelt on the bed and wrapped the black silk around my head, knotting it firmly at the back. Last time I'd been hesitant, even a little frightened, but now could barely contain my excitement. Sebastian had taught me well the pleasure of sensory deprivation.

For a while I lay, enjoying the silence as anticipation rose inside me. I knew the wait was part of the experience. My wandering mind was winding me up as effectively as any foreplay. Would it be another spanking? More restraint? Or did he have other tricks up his sleeve?

It could have been fifteen minutes or an hour, I'm not sure, but eventually, I heard the tell-tale click of the front door unlocking. My body tensed. I assumed he'd come straight to me, but everything remained silent. I realised I'd left the bedroom door open and the floors here were carpeted, meaning I'd have no indication when he finally arrived. He could have been in the room at that very moment.

I squirmed a little, as some strange amalgamation of discomfort and desire lodged itself in my stomach. That was one of my favourite parts of discovering my submissive side; the realisation that other emotions besides arousal could be a turn on too. I felt more in tune with myself than ever before.

It doesn't matter if he's here yet or not. He told me to wait, and so wait I will. He'll come when he's ready.

I held my position.

Chapter 9

Sebastian

She flinched a little when I entered, although I hadn't made a sound. Perhaps some subtle shift in the air had given me away. Or perhaps she simply knew me too well. Regardless, she continued to lie still and silent.

I had no idea how she'd become such an amazing sub in such a short time. We hadn't delved into anything too kinky for a while, but seeing her like that made me desperate to do it more. There's something so erotic about coming home to a girl presenting herself for you, exactly as you instructed. She'd followed my directions to the letter: the champagne was chilling, the candles were lit, and the blindfold was in place.

I spent a few moments just taking in the sight of her. She was absolutely stunning; her hair was splayed out across her back like a chestnut river, her creamy skin bathed in candle light. I'd never seen a woman with a more gorgeous figure; perfectly proportioned curves but not an ounce more fat than necessary. Just being near her naked body had my blood rushing in my veins.

She didn't even jump when I spoke. "Well, isn't this romantic."

She gave a little laugh. "Is it? You'll have to fill me in. I'm having a little trouble seeing right now." It was funny, although my comment had been fairly innocuous, there was something different about her voice. It was softer, more compliant. The change occurred whenever we made love, whether there was kink involved or not. I don't even think she realised it was happening, as though she simply slipped from one persona to the other, automatically. I was amazed she'd never realised her predilection before. She was a natural.

I walked over and dragged a hand gently down her back. So soft, like stroking silk. She trembled a little, but otherwise didn't move.

"I have something special planned tonight," I said. "Something new."

"I suspected as much," she replied. "I don't suppose you're going to tell me what it is, though?"

I chuckled. "Now where would be the fun in that?"

I moved over to the dresser and withdrew a bottle I'd stashed there earlier. "Have I told you how gorgeous you are today?" I asked.

Her lips quirked up. "Not in at least ten hours."

"Then I have been remiss," I replied, moving closer. "I have to admit, I've been thinking about this all day. I could barely wait to get my hands on this body again."

"Your hands have been on this body a lot lately."

I slipped onto the bed and straddled her legs. "Not like this," I replied, popping the cap and squeezing a large drop of massage oil onto her back.

She twitched and let out a little noise of surprise, but it quickly morphed into a groan as my hands began to work across her skin. "God, a girl could get used to this after work."

She wasn't the only one enjoying herself. The sight of her skin, slick and shining, was like a shot of testosterone straight to my veins, and she felt magnificent between my fingers. I kneaded my way slowly up and down her back, paying attention to each individual muscle. In my younger days, in a spontaneous attempt to impress a woman, I'd taken a massage class, and while I was a little rusty, with a little trial and error I found the sort of pressure and pace Sophia liked. More than a few areas felt tight, so I spent extra time on them, enjoying the sensation of her gradually melting beneath me.

The lower I moved down her body, the deeper her noises became, the mood gradually shifting from sensual to sexual. Applying more oil I began working the firm globes of her ass slowly, occasionally dipping close to her sex but taking pains not to actually make contact. She shifted, letting out several little whimpers, but didn't voice any objection. Seeing that restraint got me so ridiculously hard. Only a month ago, she'd already be begging for me to touch her there. She'd beg eventually, I'd make sure of it, but the fact that she held back now showed how far her self-control had come.

I had no doubt that she knew there was more to the evening than a simple massage — we'd been together long enough for my surprises to be truly unexpected anymore — but I was still looking forward to what came next. I love that sense of unpredictability, of taking my partner into unknown territory. The uncertainty of it heightens everything. I could almost feel the anticipation vibrating through her body.

"You have magic hands," she said, when I finally pulled them away.

"I'm glad you enjoyed the warm up."

She paused. "Warm up for what?" Her voice was breathy, with the barest current of trepidation flowing through it. So fucking sexy.

Rather than answer, I leaned across to the side table and scooped up one of the candles. "Do you trust me?" I asked.

There was no hesitation this time. "Yes." After everything that had happened in the last few weeks, it was amazing to hear such certainty. I had no idea where she found the strength to forgive me, let alone trust me again. That trust was the most important thing in the world to me now, and I'd die before I breached it again.

"Good. I want you to extend your arms and press your palms against the headboard. I'm not going to bind you this time. It will be up to you to restrain yourself. If your hands move before I say so, there will be consequences. Understand?"

She nodded.

"Okay, this will be hot."

And before she had a chance to speak, I tilted the candle slightly, sending a small glob of wax tumbling onto the small of her back. Her body arched and she let out a short cry.

"Too hot?" I asked.

She assessed for a few seconds. "No, just unexpected." She let out a little laugh. "Is that wax?"

"Yes."

"I was wracking my brains trying to work out what you might do, but I didn't even consider the candles."

I grinned. "That was the plan."

"Well, it feels good," she said, as I poured again. Gradually, I worked my way across her body, varying the height and size of the drops to create different temperatures. There was something so artful about the act of covering her like that, the redness of the wax in stark contrast to the whiteness of her flesh. And the way she reacted, the little sighs and tremors that passed through her as the liquid hardened against her skin, had me aroused nearly to the point of pain. At the angle she was lying, I could see the lips of her pussy, nestled tantalisingly between those perfect cheeks, and in my head I was already playing through what it would be like when I was finally inside her. That divine warmth and maddening softness, the way her body would tremble and her voice would break as I took her, forcing her towards climax.

I began using my free hand to shape the wax, dragging my fingers through it, enjoying the heat and the sensation of her skin. She seemed to like that a lot. Soon, the whole bottom half of her back was a vibrant haphazard crosshatching of crimson.

"You must be making quite a mess back there," she said.

"You look beautiful," I replied. "But we're just getting started."

Setting the candle down and climbing free of her, I stepped over to the dresser and scooped up the champagne holder. Now that she was clued in to the game, she understood almost immediately.

"Oh god," she said, as I straddled her once more. Leaning down, I brushed a kiss softly against the back of her neck while reaching into the bucket.

"Now this, this will be cold."

She was trembling before I even touched her, but that first moment was like electricity, her body convulsing as I pressed the ice cube against her. Watching intensely for any sign of real discomfort, I began to trace the cube down her spine. She continued to wriggle, her breath hitching, but the noises slipping from her mouth were those of pleasure. Being a dom is always a bit like walking a tight rope; you're constantly pushing your partner's limits, trying new things, and it can be incredibly easy to accidentally slip across the murky line between enjoyment and genuine distress. Temperature play, in particular, is a sensitive activity, but Sophia appeared to be loving it.

The ice melted quickly, her body still radiating residual heat, so I took another piece and repeated the path, this time trailing my tongue behind on her chilled skin.

She let out a long sigh.

"You like that?"

She nodded. "The contrast is amazing. Keep going."

And so I did, slowly traversing the still clean portions of her body, savouring the taste of her, the texture of her skin, the feminine scent that filled my nostrils until she dominated my senses.

"Let's try both together," I said.

Her sounds grew louder as I began to alternate hot and cold, stroking with ice then chasing with wax. When the cube was nearly melted down I let it sit in place and tipped the candle directly over it, sending a stream of icy water swirled with crimson heat flowing down her side.

Now that she was in the zone, it was time for the main event. Stashing the candle again I took another cube, this time focusing on her ass. Slowly I circled each cheek, making no effort to ease the chill. The skin down there is more sensitive, and she shivered and twitched at my touch. Soon her entire ass was slick and goose pimpled.

"Should I go lower?" I asked.

"Yes," she breathed.

She inhaled sharply as I slipped my hand between her cheeks, rolling the tiny nub of ice softly around the puckered rosette inside.

"Jesus Christ."

"I still want to fuck you here you know," I said, slipping one chilled finger just half an inch inside her, drawing a short gasp from her lips. "Maybe tonight?" I left the question hanging in the air. I already knew it wouldn't be now. I'd have her there eventually — I intended to have all of her, everything she could give — but not tonight. Of course, that didn't mean I couldn't plant the seed, make her wonder.

I slipped the ice lower still. Parting her legs, I stroked it gently across her inner thighs, gradually working my way towards her pussy. She was incredibly turned on by this point. The scent of her excitement filled the air, and her lips were glistening despite the fact that I'd yet to use the ice there. I desperately wanted to slip my finger into that softness, to bury my tongue in it and lick her until she couldn't even speak, but I restrained myself. I found the act of forcing self-control extremely exciting. Waiting now meant more pleasure for both of us later. That said, I'd never found waiting so difficult as when I had her in front of me.

Every time my hand drifted closer to her sex, her hips bucked a little more wildly.

"Do you want me to touch you?" I asked.

"Yes," she replied, no longer making any effort to disguise the desire in her voice.

"You'll have to do better than that."

"Please, Sebastian, please touch my clit."

I poised my hand above the entrance to her sex, my fingers splayed around it, the ice pressed just above her entrance. I love the rush of power I feel at moments like that. For me, kink has never been about the pain or the taboo, it's about power and intimacy. This beautiful woman had given herself over to me. She'd put her pleasure entirely in my hands. Nothing is more intimate than that.

"You *have* done very well," I said, brushing the ice ever so gently along her slit. "But there's one more thing I want to do first."

She let out a groan of disappointment, but it quickly cut off as I began cupping and kneading her ass. God, it was so firm, so perfect. I could have played with just that part of her for hours. But I didn't want to lose the effect of what I'd just done. Her skin was still icy and wet, and it made a delicious cracking noise as I slapped my palm gently against it.

Instantly her body tensed. She knew what that symbolised, and although I'd spanked her once before, it was some time ago. I didn't blame her for being a little fearful.

"But I kept my hands exactly where you told me to!" she said.

I laughed. There was still plenty of vanilla in her. "I know. This isn't a punishment. It's a reward." I leaned in close, stroking her skin tenderly. "Remember how much you enjoyed being spanked last time? Remember how wet it made you?"

She swallowed loudly, her cheeks flushing pink, but after a few seconds she nodded.

"Good. You can lift up your hands now and get onto your knees."

She did as I asked, the smallest tremor evident in her movements. Sliding in next to her, I wrapped my hands around her hips and lifted her over my lap until she lay, bent over my knees, across the bed.

I took a moment to admire her in that position. I could feel the heat of her arousal radiating onto my thigh. She was so sexy and so strong, yet she allowed herself to be so vulnerable. It was one of the most erotic things I'd ever seen. "Wonderful. Are you ready?"

She drew a long breath, then nodded.

"Say it."

"I'm ready to be spanked." It was barely more than a whisper.

Those words were music to my ears. "Okay."

And without further ado, I pulled my hand away and

brought it whipping back against her left cheek. The crack was much louder this time, ringing throughout the room. She bit back a cry.

"It will sting more this time because of the cold," I told her, pausing to admire the small red circle that was blooming on her skin. "That's part of the fun of temperature play, it sets all your nerves into overdrive."

I started softly, easing her into it, alternating from side to side and soothing each cheek with a gentle rub before continuing. I kept my pace uneven, never pausing the same amount of times between blows, never allowing her to develop a rhythm. With the blindfold on, she was constantly guessing.

Her body flinched with every blow, her breath coming short and sharp, but the pitch of her cries and the quirk of her mouth told me all I needed to know.

"Are you enjoying that?" I asked, landing a slightly harder slap.

"Yes," she replied, her voice thick with lust.

"Shall I smack you harder?"

She nodded quickly, now utterly shameless.

My next blow was stronger, and she yelped as it landed, driving her crotch into my leg and sending a pulse of pleasure shooting through my own body as she pressed against my cock.

I sped up, losing myself in the moment. With every blow she grew more excited, and that in turn stoked my own arousal. There's something intoxicating about the connection I feel during a scene like that. The trust, the sensuality, the vortex of sensations; it's a potent cocktail.

Soon, her entire ass was rosy and glowing. I paused, parting her cheeks with my hand, mesmerised by the wetness between. Unable to resist, I punctuated my next smack by slipping a finger from my free hand inside her. She let out a long moan, a sound of pure animal pleasure, as all her muscles clenched tight around me.

"Christ, look how turned on you are," I said.

She writhed beneath me as I explored her, revelling in the way her body hummed as I stroked her G-spot. I'd been with a lot of other women, but none looked so perfectly alluring in their pleasure as she did. Something about her just sent all of my blood rushing south.

Slipping my finger free, I left it poised against her entrance, and then smacked her again. "Do you think I should keep going?"

"Please," she replied, sounding almost pained.

Stroking the outside of her sex softly, I leaned down close to her head, planting a slow kiss below her ear, letting her answer hang in the air just long enough to make her unsure.

Then, when the quick little breaths falling from her lips reached fever pitch, I whispered in her ear, "Okay," and plunged back in. Her whole body stiffened as I found that soft pad once more, savouring the way each tiny touch echoed through her. At the same time, I resumed spanking, trying to weave that pain in time with her pleasure.

The combination was nearly too much for her. In less than a minute her cries reached their crescendo.

"Are you ready to come for me?" I asked her.

"Oh God, yes!"

"Then do it."

And a few seconds later, her whole body stiffened. The sight of her, those trembling muscles and that perfectly flushed skin, was nearly enough to make me come too. I never tired of doing that to her. I could have watched her come all day.

When the room was finally quiet again, save for her little sighs of satisfaction, I lifted her off my knees and onto the bed and reached for my belt. The time for restraint was over.

In a matter of seconds I was naked and straddling her prone form. She said nothing, simply arching her ass up towards me and propping herself up on her elbows. So perfectly ready and willing. I paused a moment, to take her in, stroking my cock back and forward between her cheeks. The vibrant red of her skin had dulled now to a soft glow, although she still flinched a little at my touch.

A long moan escaped my lips as I pushed my way into her, her body welcoming me with a familiarity that set all my nerves tingling. She was incredibly wet from our games before, and I was able to bury most of my length in a single stroke.

"I swear you get bigger every time," she said, her voice low.

I responded by seizing her hips and pushing myself in further still, until I was pressed up against her. I started slow, giving her time to adjust, relishing her slickness and warmth. Our bodies quickly fell into sync, hers bucking gently beneath me, pressing upwards in time with my rhythm. Each stroke was almost torturous. Nothing had ever felt as good as she did.

Soon, that exquisite softness became too much. I longed to let go.

"Put your arms behind your back," I said.

She did as I'd asked, resting her head on the pillow in front. Somehow, that position made her look even hotter, the subtle angle of her back making her ass look good enough to eat. Crossing her wrists and pinning them behind her with one hand, I began to fuck her harder, using her arms as leverage to drive her against me. Her body was completely mine now, and the volume of her cries instantly increased. There was no doubt she loved being rendered so powerless as much as I loved rendering her so.

The wax on her back had hardened, and with every punishing thrust, little flakes broke off and drifted down onto the bed. I forced myself into her with a single minded urgency, as though by pushing deeper I could claim just a little more of her. There was nothing else in the world at that moment but her body beneath mine.

Her muscles tightened and her sounds became choked, and then another orgasm ripped through her. Then sensation of having her come around my cock drove me wild. I could feel every trembling contraction vibrate through her and into me.

It was too much. I felt the vestiges of my self-control shatter along with her. A mounting tension began building inside me as my hips took on a life of their own. It started low in my balls, radiating upwards and through my shaft then spiralling out further still.

"I'm going to come on you, Sophia," I panted, savouring the little sounds of encouragement the spilt from her lips.

As my pleasure reached its apex, I pulled myself free. There was a bursting sensation and my vision dimmed as I spurted liquid heat onto her back. Seeing her like that, coated in wax and water and me, was the perfect conclusion to the night's activities. It was so fucking hot seeing her marked in that way.

"Well now I *know* you've made a mess back there," she said.

I laughed. "I may have. Let me fix that." I went to get a towel and took my time wiping her clean. Thanks to the oil, everything fell away easily.

"Fuck, I love you," she said, as we lay there afterwards.

"That's the post coital hormones talking."

"Maybe," she said with a grin, "but it's still true."

"Well, I love you too." I reached out and gave her ass a squeeze. "Particularly certain parts of you."

She punched me playfully. "Now who's talking with their hormones?"

We snuggled together for a while, enjoying the come-down. Gradually, her breathing softened, and I assumed she'd fallen asleep, but then she spoke.

"I can't wait until this is all over."

"Me too," I said, running a hand through her hair. "I know this is rough, but you're dealing with it really well. I'm proud of you. And I'm so damn lucky you're putting up with it at all."

"You *are* rather lucky." She opened her eyes and gazed up at me, a playful little smile playing on her lips. "Then again, so am I." She let out a little sigh. "I'm just not much of a homebody, you know? Before all of this, if I wasn't at work in the evenings, I was out with Ruth and Lou, or Elle, or you. I can't wait to have that again. I want to be able to go out to dinner with you on my arm and watch all the other women in the place drool."

"If that's the case I dare say we'll be rendering the whole place incapacitated. You obviously don't see how most men look at you."

She laughed. "Perhaps in the interests of public safety we'd better stay here, forever, then."

"Perhaps." Some of my mirth slid away. "It won't always be like this, Sophia. We'll fix this, eventually."

"I know," she replied, but there was a hint of sadness in her voice.

I wished I could reassure her, but the truth was, I wasn't sure myself.

Chapter 10

Sebastian

Thomas intercepted me the next morning, as I was arriving at the house.

"Can I have a word?" he asked. He looked concerned.

I motioned him towards my office.

"What's up?" I asked, as he closed the door.

"I heard something last night from one of our guys overseas. It's just a rumour, nothing concrete, but word on the street is that The Syndicate might be planning something big."

My eyes widened. The Syndicate were one of the closest things we had to a rival. They were less tightly knit than us, more of a financial conglomerate than anything else, but that only made them more ruthless. Russia, China, Saudi Arabia - anywhere with big oil or natural gas production - those were their strongholds. We'd had an uneasy peace with them for decades, mostly because butting heads would cause both of us immense damage; but it certainly wasn't beyond the realm of possibility that they were behind the recent attacks.

"Any idea what?" I asked.

Thomas shook his head. "It's just whispers at this point. It may not even be connected to all of this."

"You don't sound like you believe that."

He smiled thinly. "You know me. I don't like coincidences."

"Me either. I can't see an end game in it for them, though," I said. "We're not remotely close to any of their power bases. Even if they did manage to somehow destroy us all down here, it wouldn't make any difference to their operations. If they were going to make a play, I'd expect them to go after Europe or America, not us."

"Maybe they're just sending a message?"

"Maybe," I replied, although that didn't feel quite right. These attacks felt targeted and meticulous. "If it is them, they've certainly upped their game. They're not exactly the most subtle group, but the people messing with us right now are like ghosts. They're always one step ahead."

Thomas nodded. "That's been bothering me too."

"Well, keep your ear to the ground. Maybe they'll slip up and give themselves away. We could use a gift like that, right now. This whole situation is really starting to wear on me. Not to mention the toll it's taking on Sophia."

My discussion with her had been on my mind all day. I desperately wanted her to be happy, and would have liked nothing more than to spend our nights out on the town, but that was a spectacular way to leave us both exposed. Leaving her alone at work was bad enough, but at least her office had door scanners and security guards and a thousand sets of watchful eyes. Bars and restaurants were a different story. They weren't contained, they weren't a known quantity. Even with our little rag tag security team, there were a million things that could go wrong.

But as the afternoon rolled around, I was struck by an idea. I tracked down Tony and Aaron, and organised for them to just go straight back to the house. Tonight, I'd be playing chauffeur.

A few hours later, I was waiting on the footpath outside Sophia's office. As she exited the building and caught sight of me, her face lit up with a curious smile.

"Hey you," she said.

"Hey yourself."

"To what do I owe this pleasure?"

I grinned and held up the bag I was carrying. "I thought maybe we could have a little dinner party in your office. Just because we can't go to a restaurant doesn't mean we can't eat out."

"Oooh, my office. How exotic!" Her voice was sarcastic, but her smile only widened.

"Well, we don't have to..." I replied, trying my best to sound put out.

She laughed. "I'm kidding. That's very sweet of you. And good timing. I'm starving."

I followed Sophia back inside, drawing a few strange looks from her colleagues, but we made it to the office without any awkward questions.

"It's still kind of early," she said, as I closed the door. "What happens if my boss decides to pop round for a chat?"

"Then I will politely ask him to leave."

"He might not appreciate that."

"Well I might not appreciate him interrupting our date."

She laughed. "I suspect you may just win that encounter."

I reached into the bag and cracked open a container. The room instantly filled with the smell of peanuts and garlic. "I hope Thai is okay."

She made an appreciative noise. "Thai is more than

okay."

"And the coup de grace," I said, pulling out the bottle of wine I'd brought.

She clapped. "You know me too well."

"Only plastic cups I'm afraid."

"What?" she replied, with mock haughtiness. "This is an outrage!"

We settled in, passing containers back and forth and shovelling food into our mouths with those thin, store provided chopsticks. We were ravenous, and within just a few minutes we'd both managed to drip sauce down the fronts of our clothes, but all it did was make us laugh. There was something so comfortable about this sort of sharing. I'd eaten at a lot of fancy restaurants in my day, and while they had their charms, none of them compared to this. This was a level of affection and intimacy I assumed I'd never have, but by some miracle of God or fate, or whatever you want to call it, I'd found a woman who seemed to be willing to take all of my baggage on board. And amazingly, with our lives currently wrapped up in conspiracy and danger, we could still share moments like these.

"Thank you for this," she said, as we were taking a breather.

I shrugged. "It's no Mi Casa."

She reached out to give my hand a little squeeze. "Maybe not, but it's perfect anyway." And she was right.

It was a little sad, heading back to our makeshift fortress, but that couldn't erase the joy of the evening. Sophia's eyes were sparkling more than any time since before she was taken, and that alone made me incredibly happy. She had such life in her, and at times I was terrified the situation would crush that to dust.

It was dark by the time we pulled into the driveway, but

I could still see the silhouettes of one of our guards sitting in his car on the grass to one side. The other would be around the back. It was encouraging to see that, even when we weren't home and they had every opportunity to slack off, they didn't. They were true professionals.

I parked the car and we hopped out. Thumbing the door scanner, I opened it and ushered Sophia inside.

"Home sweet home," she said.

I followed her, my eyes shamelessly glued to her ass. She turned her head and caught me. "And what are you looking at?"

"You," I replied. "Or rather, a specific part of you." I gave her a gentle little smack.

"What ever happened to look but don't touch?" she asked coyly.

"I plan on doing a lot more than touching."

I reached up to slip my jacket off, and then everything happened at once. There was a light, scraping sound from somewhere to our left. It was barely more than a whisper, a shoe catching a piece of furniture maybe, but my body had been on twenty four hour alert since this all started, so it was enough to set adrenaline exploding through my veins. If I hadn't already been removing my suit, I wouldn't have got there in time, but my gun was holstered in a shoulder strap that hung just below my armpit. As the two men appeared in the kitchen doorway, their own weapons pointed in our direction, I was already moving. My hand closed around my pistol grip as I lurched to one side, instinctively throwing myself in front of Sophia, knocking her into the room behind us. The air was suddenly thick with hot lead and the scent of gunpowder.

The first man missed his mark entirely, his bullets zinging into the plaster around me, and he paid the price as my first shot took him in the chest. However the next man was better. As his partner collapsed he took careful aim and fired a single round. I felt the wind of it plough past me as I threw myself behind the lounge room wall. Two inches to the left and I'd have been done.

I landed awkwardly and scuttled up into a crouch, then spun to check on Sophia. She looked over at me from the other side of the doorway, her face a mask of terror. I did my best to seem calm and collected, but blood was pounding in my ears. It had been a long time since I'd been in a real combat situation. I'd forgotten how sharp everything gets, how your heart feels like a fist pummelling the inside of your chest.

At any moment Tony and Aaron should have been bursting in through the doors, drawn by the sound of gunfire. But everything remained ominously silent. After a few seconds, I knew we were on our own.

I didn't understand how everything had gone so horribly wrong, but now wasn't the time to think. Now was a time for action. With every passing second, the situation grew more dangerous. Our opponent had gone quiet now. Probably holing up, to wait us out. He had a good position and a tiny space to watch. The moment I peeked out, I'd be done.

If I'd been alone, I could have simply looped around behind him through the lounge room's other doorway, but Sophia was essentially trapped in the corner. She couldn't go anywhere without exposing herself, which meant neither could I. I'd die before I left her alone.

I wracked my brains for some kind of plan, but nothing came. It would have to be a straight shoot out. That was the only way. He'd hit me, but maybe it wouldn't be lethal, maybe I'd still be able to take him out before I collapsed. I might not make it, but Sophia would.

She was still staring at me with those wide, beautiful eyes, her handbag clutched against her chest like a baby. I nodded reassuringly at her, trying to etch every line of that perfect face into my mind, then I crept to the edge of the doorway. She gasped as she realised what I was about to do, but I silenced her with a raised finger against my lips. There was no other option.

Taking a deep breath, I counted to three and then launched myself out across the doorway, the barrel of my pistol panning wildly for a target.

I expected to hear gunfire. I expected to feel that hot metal sting as he calmly picked me off from his perfect vantage. But instead, nothing happened.

The room across the hall was empty.

For a second I was confused, but then panic seized me, and everything suddenly seemed to slip into slow motion as I realised what had happened. I turned my head, catching sight of the man's profile in the lounge room's other doorway as he carefully took aim at me. I'd underestimated him. He hadn't been content to wait it out. Instead he was the one who'd looped around behind.

My gun was still pointed the other way. I tried desperately to bring it around, but my arm felt leaden and impossibly heavy, like I was dragging it through thick mud. His finger twitched toward the trigger. I wasn't going to make it.

And then, when he was surely just milliseconds from firing, a percussion of loud cracks rang out from the corner of the room. Plaster floured the air, and the man's expression went loose. As the red punctures on his chest began to blossom out across his shirt, his legs caved underneath him, and he fell limply to the floor.

For several moments, all I could do was stare. I'd been resigned. In my head, we were already dead, and it took a while for me to understand that that wasn't the case.

I turned slowly to Sophia. The gun I'd given her was still trembling in her hands. Every part of her was shaking in fact. She'd emptied the entire clip, only hitting him twice, but that was all it had taken.

The pistol dropped to the floor. "He was going to shoot you," she said woodenly.

That jolted me back to reality. Glancing over at each body once more to check for movement, I stumbled over and wrapped her in my arms. "I know. I know. You had no choice."

She nodded slowly, although her eyes were still distant. She was the strongest woman I'd ever met, but killing is something you can never be prepared for. It changes you. I couldn't believe I'd put her in that position.

I pulled her against me tightly, stroking her hair. She was in shock, and really needed time to recover, but that wasn't a luxury we had yet. For now I had to comfort her enough so we could move.

The fight felt like it had taken hours, but I knew from experience it was probably only about fifteen seconds. Still, we had to leave. There was a good chance that even through the solid walls someone had heard the shots. The police would likely be on the way, and spending several hours clearing up the mess would only serve to leave us more exposed. Then of course there were our assassins to consider. Things had just gone up to a whole new level, and I doubted that whoever was responsible would suddenly back down just because they'd lost this fight. More men could be on their way. We had to get somewhere safe.

"Sophia, look at me. We need to move now, okay?"

She turned slowly and stared for several seconds, before eventually blinking several times and nodding. "Okay. I'm okay. Let's go."

After scooping up our two weapons, as well as those of our assailants, I led her into the study. "Just getting some supplies," I said, removing my emergency duffel from the bottom of the cupboard.

She didn't reply.

Unzipping the bag I surveyed the contents; two changes of clothes for each of us, cash, phones, passports, and a laptop computer. I'd hoped to God we wouldn't have any cause to run, but I'd been prepared nonetheless.

I withdrew one of the phones and powered it on. It was a cheap, prepaid model, bought from a convenience store. In other words, it was utterly untraceable to me.

I guided Sophia back towards the front door, pausing briefly to snap pictures of the two men. Even as my brain struggled to process what had just happened, the logical part of my mind was still firing on some level. We couldn't stay, so I had to collect whatever evidence I could.

The air outside was warm and heavy. Raising my gun, I scanned the yard slowly, searching for any further danger. It was unlikely — it made more sense for our enemies to just stay together and ensure the job got done — but I wasn't taking any risks.

The garden appeared to be empty.

I started moving towards the gate with Sophia in tow. I could see how hard she was trying. The expression on her face was constantly shifting from frightened confusion to grim determination as she battled to keep her emotions in check.

As we passed the security guys' car, I couldn't help but glance over, already knowing what I'd find. From a distance nothing had looked wrong, but up close, it was Tony's shocked expression that greeted me. He wasn't moving. The red misting on his skin was lit up vividly in the moonlight like a poster for a horror film. Aaron would be around the back

390

somewhere, in a similar state. I felt a hollowness building inside me, but I shoved it to the back of my mind. Not now.

Sophia followed my gaze, and let out a little cry, but I reached out and seized her chin, pulling her eyes to mine. "Don't look." She trembled a little in my grip, her eyes glistening and impossibly wide. "Don't look," I said again. And after a moment, her expression hardened and she gave a curt nod.

"We're going to take a taxi," I said, as we headed up the street. The house was only a five minute walk from the main road. It would be easy to flag down a cab at this time of night. "We need to get somewhere private. For all I know, the car is bugged. I need your phone too."

Her brow furrowed slightly, but she pulled it from her purse and handed it over. I threw it, along with my own personal one, into a bush. "Can't be too careful." I handed her the second prepaid. "Use this instead. I've got one too. The number is already programmed in."

To her credit, she simply nodded again. I was partially awed and partially sickened at how quickly she was becoming used to this.

As I'd suspected, a cab was easy to find. I directed the driver towards Newtown, towards Sophia's house. That wasn't where we were really headed, but I had no idea how many resources our enemies had anymore. I wanted to keep them on their toes.

Once on King Street, we jumped out and hailed another taxi. "North," was all I said to the driver.

Sophia took my paranoia in stride, sitting and staring out the windows, hugging herself lightly despite the warmth. I didn't know what I could say, so I stayed quiet too.

The ocean fanned out in front of us, as we drove out over

the Harbour Bridge, but my mind was racing too fast to appreciate the view. When we arrived at the mini-CBD that is North Sydney, I ushered Sophia out once more and then, picking a random direction, we began to walk. I figured if I did everything as randomly as possible, it made the chances of someone guessing where we'd gone almost impossible.

Two blocks later we found a hotel. It wasn't particularly big, nor were the rooms particularly nice. Sterile was probably the best word to describe it. Cheap furniture, cream coloured linen, and the slightly sickly scent of lemon detergent in the air. People didn't come to this part of town to holiday. They flew in on rushed overnight business trips, their only requirements a clean bed and a well-stocked mini bar. The mere fact that we were a couple checking in together drew a raised eyebrow from the concierge.

The moment I closed the door behind us, something seemed to drain out of Sophia again. She sat down on the bed and turned to face me. "I thought you said that place was safe."

I exhaled slowly. "I thought it was. Nobody should have been able to get in there."

"So what does that mean?"

I could see she already knew the answer. I almost couldn't muster the words, words that had been playing in the back of my mind since the moment the fight ended. "It means you were right," I said slowly. "Someone in the group wants us dead." Despite how obvious it was, hearing myself say it out loud was like a punch to the stomach. One of my brothers had betrayed me. It was inconceivable.

Sophia closed her eyes briefly, like she'd just realised how little she wanted to be right this time. "So what do we do now?"

I shook my head, a sense of hopelessness clawing at my

stomach. "I don't know." And it was true. I had no idea what our next move was. Without knowing who to trust, I couldn't properly use the group's resources. I was effectively cut off. Before, it had been our team against theirs, but now, it was the two of us against the world.

She gave a little nod, like she'd been expecting that, then slipped off her shoes and curled up on the bed. I stood there, staring at this broken woman, feeling so completely ashamed. The signs had been there, but I'd been too blind to see them, and once again she'd nearly paid the price.

"Can you hold me?" she said, after a few seconds. The tremble in her voice was enough to break my heart.

Hurrying towards her I lay down, looping my arm under her neck to cradle her against me. "Hey, hey, it's okay." She didn't cry, she simply burrowed against me, as if she were trying to disappear beneath my skin.

I kissed her forehead softly. "Don't worry, we'll work something out." I filled my voice with as much confidence as possible. What else could I do?

"Okay."

We lay there like that for a few minutes, enjoying the security of each other's presence. Despite my calm facade, the night's events had shaken me. I'd had a little combat exposure back in the day, but nothing ever makes getting shot at any easier. I knew it would pass, but right now, every nerve in my body felt frayed and agitated.

"We should get some rest," I said. "We can deal with this tomorrow. We'll think better with a night's sleep in us."

"Okay," she said again.

I leaned down to kiss her goodnight. It was an instinctive gesture. I hadn't planned for anything to come of it, but the moment our lips touched, a massive current sizzled between us. The lingering adrenaline from our fight surged in my veins, driving my body against hers as though she might be ripped away from me at any second. She was hesitant for a moment, but then she was kissing me back with equal urgency, a fearful hunger that was heartbreaking and yet utterly beautiful. The air swirled, heady with our need; the need to feel each other, to affirm we were both here and safe and together. That somehow, we'd survived.

Our hands fumbled for each other's clothes, tearing them free, and I lowered my naked form over hers, sinking into her wet heat. She arched beneath me, drawing a long intoxicated breath as our bodies joined.

I pulled her against me, welding her form to mine, desperate to be as close to her as humanly possible. There was nothing sensual or controlled about our lovemaking. It was raw and desperate and devastatingly passionate. There were no words to express the way we both felt in that moment, but our bodies could say what our mouths could not. After the terror of what we'd just been through, I desperately wanted to feel something good, something pure, and I wanted her to feel the same.

We came together, our eyes locked, our muscles quivering in unison. We didn't speak when it was over. We just lay there, bathing in the tender glow that, at least temporarily, kept the darkness at bay.

Chapter 11

Sophia

For a few minutes after I woke, I actually felt really good. It was one of those lazy awakenings, where things come to you gradually; the sun through the window, the warmth of the blanket, the weight and scent of Sebastian besides me. Soon enough though, everything else made itself known.

Thinking back over it all, I felt strangely numb about the whole thing. I didn't know if that was normal or not. I'd killed a man. It seemed like I should have been balled up in a corner somewhere. But I wasn't. Maybe if I'd still been living my ordinary life, blissfully ignorant of this world, it would have been different. But given everything that was going on around us, it somehow didn't seem so shocking. He'd been trying to kill us, and I'd stopped him. That was all there was to it. I suspected it would come to haunt me, in time, but at that moment, I felt eerily calm. Perhaps it was just my body doing what it needed to, to get through this thing.

I glanced over at Sebastian's sleeping form, my eyes drinking in the taut coils of his back. It made me feel a little perverted that even now, the first thing I did was check him out, but the memory of our recent love making was blaring like fireworks behind my eyes. I had to admit, being shot at did have its perks. Our coupling had never been like that before; so raw, so desperate. He'd loved me like he might never get another chance, and my body had responded in kind.

He woke a few minutes later and rolled towards me, smiling through sleepy eyes. "Hey."

"Hey," I replied.

He leaned in to kiss me, and for a second I thought we might be taken by the same manic combustion that had seized us last night, but I had to settle for a little tingle in my belly instead. The crushing fear that had fuelled us appeared to be all burnt up.

"I'm starving," he said.

"Me too."

He slipped out from under the sheet and walked to the mini-bar. "Well, we can either have Snickers for breakfast, or we can venture out."

"You think that's safe?" I asked.

He shrugged and nodded. "It's going to be buzzing out there pretty soon. Finding two people in suits will be needle in haystack territory. Besides, nobody has any idea where we are. We're off the grid."

I glanced out the window. He was right. The streets were already thronging with people. North Sydney is the biggest business district outside of the actual CBD, making it a perfect disguise for people dressed like we were.

We found a little cafe in a side street and snagged a table in the back corner. We'd missed the breakfast rush and the place was starting to empty out, so if we talked quietly enough, we had a little privacy.

"So, what's our plan?" I said, when our waitress was out of earshot. She'd brought coffee, and I could already feel the sweet rush of caffeine wending its way through my brain. I was alert and ready as I was ever going to be to work out our next move.

He blinked several times, apparently taken aback by my directness. It was then that I noticed how tired he looked. The little lines that webbed their way out from his eyes were more pronounced than normal and his expression was slightly slack. I suspected he hadn't got much rest last night.

"I'm not entirely sure," he said.

"Well, let's work out what we know. We know that someone from Alpha sent those men to our house, correct?"

He closed his eyes briefly and nodded. "Nobody else could have gotten in there, let alone known where it was."

"Okay, so that gives us something to aim at."

"Kind of, yeah," he replied. "But whoever it is, they're smart. When they kidnapped you, we threw everything we could at them, and we came up blank. Property ownership, the identity of the thugs they'd hired, everything. It was like trying to track down a ghost. Assuming that they're still that competent, I doubt we're going to find them easily."

I knew this conversation was difficult for him, but there was no way to avoid it. "Well, surely some members are bigger candidates than others?"

He understood instantly. "You mean Ewan?"

I nodded. "It was pretty clear from the outset that he didn't exactly approve of me. What did you say he called me? A liability? If those aren't the words of a man who wants me out of the picture, I don't know what are."

His brow furrowed, and he let out a long breath. "I know he seems like the obvious candidate, but I just can't see it. Maybe he'd move against *us*, maybe, but even that's a stretch.

And Charlie and Simon? I'd bet a million to one he'd never do that. They were his closest friends. They'd been in the group together for decades."

"People can surprise us in the worst ways, sometimes," I said.

I could see him trying to make the pieces fit in his head, but eventually he shook his head. "You didn't see his face, hear his anger when he heard about their deaths. Besides, why would he be upset with you for endangering the group if he was also working to destroy it?"

He had a point. That didn't quite stack up. "So what about the others?"

He stared desolately down at the table. "I don't know. I can't really believe it of any of them. The group is a brother-hood, Sophia. I've known them all for years. I can't see any of them just turning power hungry all of a sudden."

"So that's what you think it's all about? Power?"

"Maybe. None of it really adds up. Taking out a few council members, sure, I guess I can see that as part of a larger plan, but then why go after you? That part still puzzles me."

I nodded. "Me too."

The waitress arrived with our food, and we ate in thoughtful silence for a few minutes.

"Let's try a different approach," I said eventually. "Who knew you were coming to my office last night?"

His eyes widened a fraction as he realised my implication. "Of course. I missed that. Whoever it was must have known we'd be out late. Every other night we arrived separately, and at different times. It would have been a nightmare to coordinate."

"Exactly. They saw an opportunity, and they jumped on it."

His expression slipped. "The only person I told was

398

Thomas," he said, a current of disbelief running through his voice. "I'm not exactly on friendly chatting terms with many people over there right now. But there's no way he'd... he's my closest friend." He closed his eyes momentarily, collecting his thoughts. "There were other people in the room at the time. We'd just finished a meeting. I didn't really pay attention to who might be listening in, but plenty of them could have overheard."

"So it could be any of them," I said.

He nodded. "That does limit it to the inner council only though. There was no one else in the room."

"Well, that's something." I weighed our options. "So, we obviously can't go back to the house and, I take it from the way you threw away our phones, using the Alpha network at all is also off the cards?"

"I'm afraid so. They'd find us in an instant."

"So do we have any options at all? Or are we destined to discard our identities and live out of hotels forever?"

"It's not quite that bleak," he replied. "There's a few things we can try. I've got pictures of the men from last night, as well as their weapons. I can send that info off to some of my contacts directly, without going through Alpha at all. Like I said before, I doubt the bad guys are sloppy enough to leave a trail, but it's worth a shot."

I nodded. "Okay."

"Also, Joe should be on his way back right now, and he might be able to help us."

I raised an eyebrow. "I thought we weren't trusting the group right now."

"Joe is a special case. I've known him for my entire adult life. He recruited me, for God's sake. I'm one hundred percent certain he's got nothing to do with this."

The firmness of his tone left no room for argument and,

the truth was, I trusted Joe too. "Fair enough," I said.

"We might be able to use his Alpha connection to see if whoever broke into our house left any evidence. Theoretically there should be security footage and a thumbprint record. I expect it's been cleaned up, but you never know."

"Okay," I said again. It seemed like a solid plan, given the circumstances. Then I had another idea. "Have you considered just announcing to the group that someone has gone rogue? Maybe you'll spook the spy and make him do something stupid."

"I thought about it. It might work, but it also might also have the opposite effect. If everyone suspects everyone, all sense of order will break down, and the chaos might help our enemy instead of hurt them. That's not a risk I'm willing to take unless we have no choice. The group is in enough danger already."

That made sense. "Alright."

We finished our food in contemplative silence.

"You know, a tiny part of me is regretting not taking those plane tickets right now," I said.

He managed a tiny smile. "I'm not surprised. The offer's still open, you know. I got you a passport made up just in case."

"Ooh, do I have a code name?"

"From memory, you're Lucy Page."

I made a face. "Makes me sound like a TV housewife from the fifties."

He chuckled. "Sorry."

"In any case, I'm certainly not going to go lie on any tropical beaches while you're stuck here, battling evil. You could come with me, though. Star crossed lovers fleeing to a foreign land together. It's kind of romantic."

He smiled wistfully. "I wish I could."

I'd said it like I was joking, but I'd be lying if I said the thought hadn't crossed my mind. Maybe running off together was the best solution. Would it really be so bad, starting over from scratch? "Have you ever thought about leaving?"

He didn't reply straight away. "I hadn't, but then I met you."

Such a short sentence, but it resonated through me.

"But it's daunting, you know?" he continued. "The group has been my life for so long. I don't know what I'd do without it."

I nodded. I understood that particular fear all too well.

"Anyway," he said, signalling for the cheque, "we should get back to the hotel. It will take a while for my contacts to get back to me, so the sooner we start, the sooner we might get some results."

A few minutes later we were back in the room. While he was sending off the info to his contacts, I fired through an email to my boss using my new phone, explaining that I'd come down violently ill and needed a few days off. He replied almost instantly saying it was no trouble. I got the sense he was extremely pleased to have me back at all, so a few more days made little difference. I didn't know what I'd do if our exile stretched into weeks, or longer, but I figured I'd cross that bridge when I came to it.

Once we'd both taken care of business, it was just a matter of waiting. I'd thought being penned up in the Alpha house was frustrating, but something about the cheap, cut and paste hotel decor made that room feel incredibly oppressive. We lay on the bed drinking wine from the mini-bar and watching daytime TV. I'd bought a few magazines on the way back, and I tried leafing through them, but I couldn't make myself focus. I was restless and frustrated at how powerless we were.

At some point, Sebastian fell asleep. Apparently he really

had been wiped out. I tried to join him, but my body would-n't cooperate. Instead, I found myself turning the situation over and over in my mind. I wished I'd paid better attention to Sebastian's colleagues. There were only a few who I'd even really talked with and, of that group, nothing stood out - besides Ewan's blatant dislike. Trey seemed friendly and relatively harmless and besides, he wasn't a council member. Then there was Thomas who, while being a little intense at times, appeared to care about Sebastian. Some of the other men had certainly seemed a little cold towards us, but I put that down more to Ewan's influence than anything else. Whoever the mole was, they were doing an amazing job of blending in.

At about six thirty, Sebastian woke up. "Sorry, I didn't mean to sleep."

"It's fine, you looked like you needed it."

He nodded and flashed me a half smile. "I'll make it up to you by getting dinner. There's a Chinese place just downstairs that does takeaway."

I glanced at the TV, feeling a tightness in my chest. The prospect of spending any more time here, stewing in the horror that had become our lives, was almost too much to bear. I already felt like I was losing my mind and, if I stayed here, all I'd be able to think about was how helpless we were. "What we should do is hit the town," I said.

I'd mostly been joking, but the moment the words left my lips, the idea took root in my head. The gradually blooming smile on Sebastian's face said he felt the same way. "Maybe we should."

I laughed. "Is that crazy?" It seemed ridiculous to consider going out on a date, given everything that was happening, but hell, if people were going to be constantly trying to kill me, I felt like maybe I should take advantage of the lulls in between.

Besides, I could desperately use the distraction.

"A little, maybe, but I can't see it being a problem as long as we keep it low key. If anybody had managed to follow us, they'd have made their move by now. A hotel is hardly going to provide much of an obstacle for one of my brothers. So we can assume they have no idea where we are. As far as they know, we could be anywhere in the city. Maybe anywhere in the country."

It made sense. "Low key hey?" I said. "Like pizza and a movie?"

"That sounds perfect."

A few minutes later, we were walking out through the hotel's front door. The streets were emptier at night, but there was still a steady stream of office workers who were clocking off late or heading home after a few end of day drinks.

It took us a while to find a pizza place, but when we did, we struck gold. A few blocks away from the main thoroughfare, we stumbled upon a tiny shop front with a giant neon pizza slice flickering above it. There was no other signage, not even a name, but it seemed to have what was important. It wasn't until we made our way inside that we realised what a gem we'd discovered.

The scene before us looked like it had been ripped straight out of a nineties sitcom. Dimly lit booths with red and white plastic table cloths, walls plastered with yellowed band posters and old advertisements for beer and motor oil. There was even an ancient pinball machine in the corner, it's warbling, high-pitched cries for attention fighting vainly against the throbbing rock music being piped through the speakers.

The place was relatively full, but the smiling, old, Italian-looking waiter didn't seem fazed, guiding us through the tables to an open booth, tucked to one side. Sebastian and I grinned at one another as we sat down. I could already feel some of my tension ebbing away, and I could tell he felt the same way.

We ordered a few pizzas to share, as well as a couple of the foaming mugs of unnamed beer that seemed to be the drink of choice.

"We might have another Mi Casa on our hands," Sebastian said to me once the waiter disappeared.

"We just might," I agreed. "It's almost enough to make you forget..." I trailed off, realising I was only going to kill the mood, but it was too late. His expression wilted.

"I didn't really ask before, but are you coping okay?" he said. "Yesterday... well, it was pretty rough."

Memories of the previous night appeared, unbidden, in my mind. The weight of the gun, the violent kick of it in my hands, the way the man's eyes grew wide as his legs collapsed under him. *Not now!* I pushed it all to the side. "That's one way to put it," I said, keeping my voice level. "But yeah, I think I'm doing okay."

He didn't look like he believed me, but he nodded. "I know the apologies are probably getting old, but I can't tell you how sorry I am that I put you in that position. I should have listened to you when you questioned my colleagues."

"You should have," I said, managing a small smile, "but, like I said, I stopped blaming you for all of this weeks ago. You can't shoulder the burden of everything that happens to the people you know, Sebastian. Proximity doesn't equal fault. I've forgiven you, but our relationship will never work unless you forgive yourself too."

Some of the tension drained out of his face. "You're right. The thought of you being in danger just tears me up, that's all. If I lost you..." he shook his head.

I reached out and weaved my fingers through his. "You

won't. The odds may be bad, but so far, we've survived everything they've thrown at us. We'll get through this, we just need to focus." I wasn't quite as confident as all that, but I knew that he needed to hear it. If, by some miracle, we were to beat this thing, we needed to keep our eyes on the prize.

It seemed to work. After a few seconds, his jaw tightened and he nodded. "That sounds like a plan."

"But not tonight," I continued. "We can't do anything until we hear back from everyone, so tonight, let's forget all about this and just be a couple, out on a date. I want to remember what it's like to feel normal again, even if it's just for one night."

His lips gradually curled upwards. "I can do that."

And so we did. For the next two hours, we talked about everything but the lurking danger. He seemed to enjoy hearing about my antics with the girls and, thankfully, Ruth provided enough material to base an entire sitcom on. Pretty soon we were both in hysterics, our stomachs aching from laughter.

The pizza was spectacular. Thinly cut and dripping with cheese, it tasted as delicious as it did unhealthy, and it was exactly the kind of comfort food I needed.

When we'd had our fill, we caught a cab a few minutes north to the nearest cinema. Out on the street, I found myself glancing over my shoulder a few times, but nobody was paying any attention to us. It appeared Sebastian had been right. We were off the grid.

None of the films playing really looked interesting, but I didn't care. It was more the act of going to the movies than the movie itself. Something about going on such a mundane date with Sebastian pleased me immensely. It felt like the kind of date I'd have gone on with a university boyfriend. There was no fanciness to it, no expectations or desire to impress. It was just the two of us hanging out and enjoying one another's company.

We settled on some big budget sci-fi title that seemed like it might at least look impressive on the big screen. It was a relatively quiet session, with only fifteen or so other people in the cinema. We took up residence somewhere towards the back.

Within about ten minutes, I was bored. It did look spectacular, but the script sounded like it had been written by an internet chatroom bot, and every member of the cast seemed to be too busy practising Blue Steel to actually display any other facial expressions.

Apparently, Sebastian felt the same way. "Is this what counts for cinema these days?" he whispered. "It's been a while since I've been to the movies, so I'm a little out of touch."

I shook my head. "I don't go much either, but this is definitely scraping the bottom of the barrel. I'm not sure I can take another hour and a half."

His eyes took on a wicked glint. "Perhaps I can find a way to make that time a little more bearable." Lifting the armrest so there was nothing between us, he slipped closer, burying his face against my head and breathing in deeply. "I wouldn't want you to be bored," he said, in a soft throaty voice, and before I knew it, his hand was skimming gently up my leg.

I laughed at his audacity and then glanced around. There was another couple in our row, about eight seats over, and a group of three guys just a few rows in front. Nobody was paying any attention to us so far, but it wouldn't take much to change that.

"Sebastian," I said, nodding at the couple and raising my eyebrows.

He grinned like a child who knew he was about to do something naughty and just didn't care. "They're not paying attention." Pulling away momentarily, he shrugged off his jacket and threw it over both our laps. "And if they are, now all they'll see is a cold girl and her chivalrous boyfriend."

Before I could argue, his hand was climbing my thigh once more. I felt like I should keep up the pretence of resistance, but the truth was, my heart was already beating wildly, and the closer he drew to my sex, the less fighting it seemed to matter.

His fingers inched upward until they found my panties, tugging them to the side. The first touch was soft, a gentle caress from my entrance all the way up, and I felt myself grow wet almost instantly. I let out a little sigh and sunk deeper into my seat to give him better access. Taking my cue, he slipped one long finger inside me, teasing and probing until he eventually settled on my g-spot. That sudden contact sent a spike of pleasure through me, drawing a sharp gasp from my lips.

"Uh uh, quiet now," he whispered. "We wouldn't want to alert our audience."

I swallowed loudly and clamped my mouth closed, glancing around the room once more. All eyes were still fixed on the screen, although the couple in our row both looked to be wearing tighter expressions than before. Was it just the film? Or were they onto our game and simply trying to ignore us? I felt an uneasy excitement settle in my stomach, the same kind of perverse thrill I'd experienced wearing the butt plug around my office.

Sebastian stroked me with a slow, rhythmic motion, and everything began turning to liquid inside me. A second finger joined the first, and I bit back another cry, curling my hands tightly around the arm rests for fear that my movements would betray us.

"Do you like that?" Sebastian breathed into my ear. "Do you like being pleasured in a room full of people?"

I nodded quickly, not trusting myself to do more than that.

"God, you feel so good around my fingers. I wish I had something else inside you. But I can wait. I'll fuck you soon enough."

For a moment, all I could think about was having his cock inside me, but then his thumb found my clit, and all other thoughts fled. There was just his hand and the exquisite things it was doing to me. The simultaneous stimulation was incredible. I had no idea how he was so dexterous, but every motion seemed to work together in perfect harmony. A tightness began to build in my core, beckoning, begging for release.

"I want you to come for now me, Sophia, and I want you to do it without making a sound."

I wasn't sure that was going to be possible. Even with my mouth firmly shut, there were shrill little noises escaping my throat. But I sure as hell wasn't going to stop and tell him that.

With the same relentless pace, he brought me over the cusp. I buried my face against his shoulder, my whole body shaking, as though all of the cries I wasn't letting out were bouncing around inside me.

"Fuck," I said when it was over.

He glanced around. "As tempting as that sounds, I think *that* might get us noticed."

I laughed, but the suggestion made my sex clench all the same. "Perhaps we should go somewhere where we won't be noticed then," I said, running my hand slowly along the bulge in his pants

He stiffened and let out a long breath. "And miss this fine excuse for a motion picture?"

I raised my eyebrows. "Well, hey, if you don't want to..."

The intensity returned to those emerald eyes. "You know

what I want?" he said, his voice a dry rasp. "I want you to watch the rest of the film and think about how hard I'm going to fuck you when it's over. I want you squirming in your seat, so wet for me I can smell it."

I swallowed loudly. Yeah, like there was any chance I could think about anything else now. "Okay," I said softly.

We did watch the rest of the film, but I'll be damned if I could tell you a single thing about it.

* * * * *

Sebastian's insistence on waiting had the desired effect. By the time we left the cinema, I was a flustered mess. Judging by the urgency in his walk, I wasn't the only one.

The moment we stepped through the door to our hotel room, I felt his body press up behind mine. My neck lolled to one side automatically, exposing the curve of my neck that I knew he was longing to kiss. He didn't disappoint, ducking his head to brush his lips softly across my skin. I let out a gentle sigh. It was an intimate position; sensual and tender. I used to think sexual familiarity was a sign that things were getting stale, but I loved those little moments with Sebastian, the understanding our bodies shared. If anything, that connection excited me more.

With reverent delicacy his mouth traced a path down one shoulder, and then the other, his fingers stroking my hips, before slinking upwards to toy with my dress straps.

"I want to look at you," he said.

"By all means," I replied.

With two gentle flicks of his wrist, my dress was tumbling to the floor. My bra followed moments later. There was a sharp intake of breath behind me, and then his arms were around me once more.

"Christ I love this position," he said, echoing my earlier thoughts. His hands moved up to cup my breasts, kneading gently, rolling my nipples between his fingers. The yearning in my veins surged, rushing to pool between my legs. "I love having your ass pressed against me while I play with you, knowing I just have to unzip myself and I'd be inside you."

I twisted my hips in response, grinding myself against him, causing his breath to falter. He was certainly ready. I could feel the strength of his excitement, hot and needy, pressing urgently through his pants. "Well I love feeling what I'm doing to you back there," I replied.

"Hmm, is that so?" he said in amusement. "Well, I would be remiss if I didn't check what I'm doing to you."

One of his hands stayed to roam my chest, but the other began to inch slowly, tantalisingly, down my stomach. He slipped inside my panties, parting my folds, my clit swelling with electricity at his touch.

"I do seem to be having the desired effect," he teased.

"That you are," I replied, squirming against him. Although there were no bonds involved, with our bodies arranged that way I was strangely helpless. I couldn't explore him as he explored me. My hands had nowhere to go but to curl around his powerful forearms while he pleasured me. He moved slowly, more a tease than anything else, but I still found my legs growing shaky beneath me.

He withdrew and spun me to face him, silencing my protest with a kiss. Now free to touch him, my hands began to roam, revelling in the coiled power of his body. I wanted to take my time, but I couldn't help but be drawn to the trembling bulge between his legs. I stroked him through the material, generating a deep vibration in the centre of his chest.

"Let's not get ahead of ourselves. There's something else I want you to do before I fuck you."

"Oh?"

"I want you to take a shower."

I gazed at him in bewilderment. "Do I really smell that bad?"

He favoured me with a small smile, but something in the air had shifted. This wasn't a request, it was a command. My skin prickled with anticipation.

"Not at all, I'd just prefer you were clean." There was a heaviness to his tone now, an edge I knew all too well.

"Okay," I said, the sudden rush of endorphins stealing the strength from my voice. I still found it amazing how he could do that with just a slight change in intonation, like a snake charmer mesmerising his cast.

Giving him one final squeeze, I slipped from his arms and sauntered to the bathroom, glancing back over my shoulder, enjoying watching him watch me. The lust in his eyes when he looked at my body never ceased to thrill me.

Once inside, I shut the door and removed my panties. I set the water running and adjusted the temperature before stepping inside. I knew he'd be joining me soon.

However, what happened next managed to surprise me. I heard the click of the door handle, but before I could even turn, the room was plunged into darkness. For a split second I felt a bolt of fear, but then Sebastian spoke. "On second thoughts, we're both rather filthy if you ask me. I believe we could both use a shower."

I laughed. "In the dark?"

"I don't need to see you to make you come, Sophia."

A shiver rolled down my spine. I wasn't sure I'd ever get sick of that dirty mouth. "We'll see about that," I replied, trying to sound coy. "Come on in, then. I'll wash you if you wash me."

"Deal."

In a moment, the glass door was opening and then his hard form was pressing against mine once more, only now he was naked too. The moment we touched, my confusion about the lack of light melted away. Feeling but not seeing him lent the experience a whole new kind of tactility. With my sight stolen, even the slightest contact seemed magnified a hundred times. It was like the blindfold all over again, only this time, both of us were blind.

His kiss was fiercer this time, hungrier, his hands seizing my shoulders while his tongue plundered my mouth. The pressure of his assault drove me backwards until I was pressed up against the wall, the coldness of the tiles contrasting wonderfully with the warmth of the water. He seemed at ease in the dark, but my heart was racing. Every movement, every brush of his hand, was an unexpected surprise. My body was thrumming, every nerve tingling.

Some indeterminable time later, he broke away. "I believe I promised to clean you."

"Oh, you did. You know how much of a dirty girl I am," I said in my best porno voice.

He chuckled. "That I do. Now hold still." I heard the squeeze of a lotion bottle and then something soft yet coarse began stroking my collarbone. Apparently the room came with a wash cloth.

He took his time, working his way gradually down one arm and then the other, scrubbing me with tiny circular motions. The cloth felt wonderful against my skin, a gentle scrape tempered by soap and water. I loved the sense of just being lavished upon. Sebastian may have called the shots in the bedroom, but he certainly never left me feeling neglected.

Soon, he turned his attention to my chest. "This area needs a more personal touch."

I made a little noise of encouragement, my body already

yearning for him to accelerate proceedings.

Squeezing more soap onto his hands he began to massage my breasts. The sensation of them sliding between his fingers, his slickened skin against mine, was exquisite. Judging by the low rumble emanating from the darkness, he was enjoying it too.

He picked up the sponge again to work my stomach, back, and legs, lathering me with a thick layer of suds that he made no effort to wash off. I soon learned why when the stream of water suddenly vanished from above, only to reappear moments later in front of me. I hadn't realised that shower head was detachable.

"I've heard it said that a shower head is a girl's best friend," Sebastian murmured.

"I've never had the chance to try one," I replied, although I was already beginning to believe it might be true. You'd think after a life time of showers, you'd pretty much understand what they're capable of. They're pleasant, soothing, warming, but that's about the extent of it. Only in Sebastian's hands, this became something else entirely. The way he danced the jet across my skin, constantly alternating the pressure, distance, and angle, was incredible. I don't know if it was just the sensuality of the experience, or the darkness, or Sebastian's expert technique, but it left my entire body tingling.

"Then allow me." With obvious relish, he began working his way slowly down my torso, meticulously washing every part. The closer he drew to my aching sex, the more I began to squirm.

"Widen your stance," he ordered, and then suddenly, the stream was between my legs.

"Oh Jesus," I cried. The warmth of it, the relentless rhythm, was like nothing I'd ever experienced before. It was like a thousand tiny fingers, all stroking me at once, and they weren't easing me towards orgasm, they were hurling me through the door as fast as humanely possible.

While the water strummed my clit, he leaned in close, bracing my ass with one hand and drawing my nipple into his mouth, swirling and sucking and nipping softly. I felt my knees begin to buckle, but he held me firmly, bringing the nozzle closer still. The stimulation was almost too much — it rode that impossibly thin line between pleasure and discomfort — but I was beyond caring. Already, everything was beginning to tighten inside me. It was like I could feel each and every drop of water vibrate all the way into my core.

"I'm coming, Sebastian. I'm coming."

He let out an affirmative grunt and sealed his mouth over mine as my climax took hold. Everything seemed to shrink away, then explode outward in a giant, rolling wave of ecstasy. I was glad he was supporting me, because I'm quite sure I would have ended up splayed on the tiles, if he hadn't been.

"So, there may be some merit to that rumour," he said, my body sagging against his.

"I believe so," I replied. "Especially if you're pressed for time. What was that, one minute?"

He laughed. "Something like that."

I felt utterly drained, but being pressed up against him again reminded me that only half our bargain had been fulfilled. "I think it may be my turn with that," I said, fumbling along his arm until I found the shower head. "I'm not the only one that needs a thorough wash."

"If you insist."

Partly out of a desire for revenge, but mostly because I wanted to savour his body, I took my time, painstakingly soaping and rinsing every inch of him. I was getting used to my blindness now, used to the amplified sense of touch it lent

414

me. In the past, with the blindfold, I'd always been in a position of submission, but here I was free to explore. I loved the way his body felt in the water, hard and soft and slick all at once. With only my hands to guide me I roamed across his skin, running them gently over the firm rises of his triceps, the thick slabs of his chest, revelling in every perfect ridge.

Even in the dark, I was constantly aware of his cock. Every so often as I shifted position it would graze against me, sending a bolt of lust shooting through my veins. I enjoyed those little moments of contact, the sharp breaths and soft noises they drew from him.

Soon, I abandoned soap and water all together, slipping in close until my face was against his chest. "I have a special cleaning implement I think would be very effective on you," I purred.

"Is that so?" he said, more than a little strain evident in his voice. I could tell he was close to breaking point.

"It is. Allow me to show you."

Wrapping my hands around the hard globes of his ass, I drew his nipple into my mouth. He gasped and rocked against me, pushing his shaft firmly against my stomach. I teased him like that for half a minute, but soon, I was unable to contain myself any longer. Kissing a trail down his stomach I dropped to my knees and seized his length in my hand. He felt impossibly thick, and seemed to be growing more with every passing moment. I loved how, even with no visual stimulation, he was utterly ready for me; a perfect picture of virility.

He let out a long groan as I took him into my mouth, pumping him from the base and sliding my lips up and down with painstaking slowness. He felt fleshy and soft and I took my time tasting every inch of him, dragging my tongue along the trembling ridge underneath. Heat rushed through his shaft as he swelled further still, but I took it in stride, gradually

415

easing him deeper down my throat.

"Your lips are fucking magic," he said.

I loved being in that position. It was submissive, yet utterly empowering. For the first time since we'd started, I wished the lights were on. I wanted to look at him, to see the pleasure I was giving, to watch his face contort as I gradually brought him undone.

His fingers found my head, tightening around my hair, guiding me and quickening my pace, and for a while I gave control over to him.

Eventually, an idea came to me. "I wonder if this is just for women," I mused, pulling back momentarily, and before he could reply, I aimed the jet of water at his balls and resumed sucking him. The effect was instantaneous. He sunk back against the wall, a long, throaty sound falling from his mouth. Continuing to stroke him with one hand, I began experimenting with the shower head, teasing every part of him as he had me.

"Fuck, Sophia, that's incredible. Don't stop."

Sensing that he was close, I focused my efforts, locking my lips just below his crown and stroking rapidly, keeping the shower head focused strong and close. His body stiffened and he let out a single guttural roar, then spurted down my throat. His orgasm seemed to last forever, and I pumped furiously, milking every drop.

"Jesus Christ," he said, his voice ragged. "That was a huge load."

I giggled and nodded, still tasting him on my tongue.

"I may have to have one of these installed," he said.

"You won't hear me object."

He reached out to take my arms, pulling me to my feet. "Put it back for now. I want to fuck you under the water."

I was only too happy to oblige. My exploration of his

416

body had left me aching for him.

Once the nozzle was back in place, he spun me around and positioned himself behind me. "Brace yourself against the wall," he said. "I'm done being gentle." The way he said that made my sex clench.

I did as commanded, laying my hands on the tiles, and in a moment he was pushing inside me. I let out a long breath. There was no initial sting now, no moment of accommodation. He fit inside me as though he'd always been there, as though he'd never left. There was a sense of completeness to that moment that I'd never felt with anyone else. A transcendence, where physical pleasure rose up and became something more.

From the moment he entered me, I could tell he was going to be true to his word. Each thrust of his hips was long and hard, and my body shook with the impact. After such exquisite foreplay, it was exactly what I wanted. An explosion of all of our pent up desire.

With my body angled upward, each punishing thrust stroked the bundle of nerves at my core, sending ripples of pleasure rolling through me. The air around us was heavy with steam, and I drew it into my lungs, savouring the warmth as it flowed through me.

Wrapping one hand around my hip, he seized my hair with the other, tugging my head backwards and sending a delicious sting through my scalp. There was something so raw about being fucked like that, standing up, darkness all around, my body trapped roughly in his grip. The ferocity of his movements hurt a little, but that only excited me more.

The sounds emanating from his throat were low, almost bestial, as he took from me what I'd been teasing all night. His size meant I could feel every pulse of lust, every firm ridge and soft edge.

"I promised I was going to fuck you hard," he said, pausing momentarily only to hammer back into me again.

"You did," I replied, although they barely sounded like words.

"Is this what you wanted?"

"You know it is."

The heat inside me continued to build. It was a raging fire. Impossible to ignore. My muscles began to contract, but there was nowhere for them to go. His hardness was everywhere, filling me, stretching me, claiming me. As my moans sunk lower in my throat there was a flooding sensation in my brain and that fire suddenly exploded. It shot out from my toes to my head, leaving me trembling and gasping for air.

A few moments later, he came too. There was a rush of heat, then a roar, and then his fingers were biting into my side as he slammed himself into me, forcing my whole body against the wall.

"Christ," he said, when his hips finally slowed.

"Mmmm."

He pulled out of me, and despite the slight sting of my now raw flesh, my body complained at the absence. Spinning me around, he trapped my lips in a kiss.

"And that is why we wait."

I laughed. "That's easy to say now."

His hands found my ass, and he gave a little squeeze. "I wouldn't worry too much. If I'm being totally honest I can never resist you for very long. And when this is all over, I plan on spending more time inside you than out."

"Well now, that's exactly what a girl wants to hear."

Chapter 12

Sophia

When I woke the next morning, Sebastian was already up. He was sitting in the room's only chair already fully dressed, idly thumbing his chin and staring off into space.

"Morning," I said.

He jolted a little. "Oh. Good morning."

"Everything okay?" I asked, stretching lazily.

"Yeah, everything's fine. Better than fine, really."

I slid down the bed and sat in front of him. "Oh yeah, how's that?"

He held up the prepaid phone that had been hidden in his other hand. "We've got something. My guy at the Federal Police ran our attackers' faces through their database and actually came back with matches."

The look on his face told me that perhaps this wasn't all good news. "Well that's great, right? Who were they?"

He gave a non-committal nod. "Our would-be killer seems to be working on his own, because he didn't use Alpha guys. It looks like he farmed the job out and basically hired two hit men. Those two guys were known muscle for Anton Silva, who is suspected to be one of the biggest crime bosses in the country."

"Wow. Okay. Just another small fish then."

He shot me a smile, but it was short lived.

"So what do we do with that info?" I asked.

His lips compressed and he let out a little sigh. "I'm still working that out. This guy is the real deal, Sophia. Drugs, weapons, prostitution; he runs it all. If we play it right, we may be able to use him to get to whoever wants us dead, but one misstep..."

He didn't need to finish the sentence. I could fill in the blanks. I felt a lump building in my throat, but I nodded anyway. "I get it. Bad guy."

"Bad guy," Sebastian confirmed. "Anyway, Joe is on his way, so we can talk about it more when he arrives, but I think our best bet is to just try and buy Silva off. He's a criminal, which means he has a price. Everyone has a price."

"But how do we get him to take the money without killing us in the process? I mean, he was hired to take us out and he screwed it up. We can't exactly just show up at his doorstep."

Sebastian stared me dead in the eye. "Actually, that's exactly what I'm thinking I might do."

I searched his voice for humour, but found none. "Are you insane?"

This time he smiled. "A little, maybe. But I think it will work. He's not going to just gun me down on sight, not if I give him the right incentive first. He may be ruthless, but you don't get where he is unless you're practical as well. He'll hear me out, probably figuring he can finish the job afterwards if he doesn't like what he hears."

"That's a lot of assumptions for us to risk our lives on."

He gave a heavy nod. "I know. But what other choice do we have? Joe's searches came back empty. Our enemy holds all the cards, and this is the only lead we've got. If we want our lives back, I don't see any other option."

I wracked my brains for an alternative. "I don't suppose we could just call Silva? Avoid putting ourselves in the firing line?"

Sebastian barked out a laugh. "I can call to set up the meet, but getting Silva himself on the phone will be all but impossible. You don't become a criminal kingpin by discussing organised murder over the phone."

My cheeks reddened. That made sense.

As much as it scared me to admit, I realised he was right. We'd been on the back foot for so long and we'd stay there, unless we took a chance. This might be our last opportunity. But, beyond that, I was sick of running, sick of being hunted. If I was going to be put in danger again, I wanted it to be on my terms.

"Okay, if you think we can pull it off, then I'm sold," I said. "But don't think for one second that just because you kept saying 'I' while I was saying 'we' that you're going in there alone."

His expression hardened. "There's no need for both of us to take the risk. I'm not going to let you put yourself in danger because of my mistakes anymore."

"Well I'm not letting you walk into that death trap by yourself," I countered. "You think it's any easier for *me* seeing *you* put yourself at risk? If you went in there and didn't come out, it would rip me open knowing that I might have be able to do something. I may not have much experience with this sort of thing, but last time shit hit the fan, I stepped up. Maybe I can be useful again." It amazed me how easily I was able to talk about that incident. Maybe I really was becoming desensitised.

I put a hand on his knee. "We're in this together, Sebastian. Whatever happens."

He stared at me for a full ten seconds, somehow managing to look touched yet incredibly anxious. Eventually, though, he broke into a sad little smile. "Together it is, then," he said softly, reaching out to squeeze my hand. And somehow it felt like an incredibly tender moment, instead of an insane suicide pact. Yep, definitely desensitised.

Joe arrived a short time later and we went out for breakfast to discuss everything. He sat, wearing an unreadable expression, while Sebastian recounted everything that had happened so far. He'd heard the short version, but now he was getting the gory details.

"If you have any other suggestions, I'm all ears," said Sebastian, when the story was over.

Joe pondered. He didn't even look surprised. "Nothing springs to mind," he said eventually. "Whoever this is, they're not making many mistakes. When I looked through our system, I couldn't find any loose ends. According to the database, nobody besides you and your team swiped into your Alpha house. They cleared everything. If we don't take this chance, we might not get another."

A scary thought suddenly occurred to me. "If you were using the Alpha system," I said to Joe, "doesn't that mean they could have tracked you somehow? Maybe picked up your trail?"

Joe smiled. "I wouldn't worry about that. I've got a few tricks up my sleeve."

I shot a questioning look at Sebastian, but he just shrugged. He certainly didn't seem concerned, so I let the issue drop.

He scooped up his coffee and threw back the last sip.

"Well, there's no time like the present." Reaching into his pocket, he removed his phone and tapped the screen several times before lifting it to his ear.

"Hi. My name is Sebastian. Your boss and I have unfinished business. Tell him I will give him a million dollars for five minutes of his time."

* * * * *

Everyone stayed silent on the trip to see Anton. Sebastian's million dollar offer had apparently been enough to buy us entry, but what would happen beyond that was anyone's guess. The closer we drew, the more heavy my stomach felt. I knew I wanted this, to be proactive and take matters into my own hands, but that didn't change the fact that we were driving straight into the lair of a man who, only two days ago, had been trying to kill us. When my brain phrased it like that, it just seemed like a really, really bad idea.

For his part, Sebastian wore a look of grim determination. That comforted me a little. To anyone who was paying attention it said 'fuck with me and you'll regret it,' and I hoped Anton would get the message. I suspected we'd need every little edge we could get.

We were meeting him in the back room of a Kings Cross strip club, which he undoubtedly owned. I'd never really spent much time in the Cross. It's as close to a red light district as Sydney has, and thus the people there are most certainly not my sort of crowd. Between the metric fuckton of makeup that made all the women look like drug addicted clowns and the rather scandalous skin to clothes ratio on display, whenever I visited I wound up feeling trashier just by proximity.

The sight outside the window was no different than I remembered. Even on a weeknight, the main strip was seething with neon light and fake tan. We pulled up outside the club. We'd hired a limo and made a big point of being seen stepping out of it by the two bodybuilders, with sleeve tattoos and steely expressions, who stood guard out front. For appearances, Joe was once again relegated to the role of driver. We had to look calm, in control, and dangerous, rather than desperate and out of options.

"You ready for this?" asked Sebastian.

I took a deep breath. "As ready as I'm going to be."

"Good." He shot me a reassuring smile. "And don't worry, we'll be fine."

I nodded, trying to let some of that confidence seep into my skin.

The men looked us up and down as we approached. They were both as tall as Sebastian, but much wider, which made them incredibly intimidating, by any standards. They looked like someone had taken two plastic bags and crammed them full of walnuts. The larger of them smirked as his eyes rolled over my body, which gave me the sudden urge to go home and take a long shower, but that leer fell away once he turned to Sebastian. My partner was practically radiating danger now, and it was enough to make even these guys pause.

"My name is Sebastian and this is Sophia. We're here to see Anton." His voice betrayed no emotion. 'Just business as usual,' it said.

"Who is Anton?" said giant number one, a look of mock confusion appearing on his face. "I think you must have the wrong place, my friend."

Sebastian didn't even miss a beat. "I don't have time to play games. You know as well as I do that your boss is expecting us."

The man glanced at his partner, who gave a little nod and disappeared upstairs.

The first guy stared daggers at us for several seconds. Apparently he didn't like having his little power trip interrupted.

"I need to search you," he said.

"We're not stupid enough to be carrying here," Sebastian replied.

The guy shrugged. "Then you've got nothing to worry about."

Sebastian waited a few beats then gave a curt nod and stretched his arms out to the sides, gritting his teeth while the guard patted him from head to toe. He wasn't gentle. He almost looked disappointed when he came up empty-handed.

"They'll probably check for these," Sebastian had said to me earlier, nodding towards our guns. "I'd never get one past them, but you just might. Most men struggle to see women as a threat. They never check as carefully."

That had made sense at the time, but as the guard stepped towards me, suddenly the pistol holstered against my inner thigh felt like it weighed a thousand kilogrammes. What would he do if he found it? Laugh and take it away? Or flip out and call his buddies?

He reached out and gave my shoulders and back a cursory check, before moving down my front. He lingered a little below my breasts, the smirk returning to his face, and I had to stop myself from dry retching in his face. I could almost feel the primal frustration simmering below Sebastian's skin, but he restrained himself.

My cheeks started burning as the goon's hands gradually drew closer to the weapon. Despite what Sebastian had said, his search seemed very thorough. He made it as far as the top of my thighs, just inches from the butt of the gun, but as he began to dip between my legs, Sebastian let out a dangerous

425

little growl. "If you want to keep that hand for more than the next three seconds, I suggest you stop there."

The man hesitated, eyes locked with Sebastian. It felt like that night, at my work function, all over again where he'd sent Taylor fleeing with a simple stare. I wasn't sure it was going to work this time — the guard looked like he had something to prove — but after a few moments, he pulled away. I let out a silent sigh of relief. He finished the search in a matter of seconds.

By that point the second thug had reappeared, and he gestured for us to follow him inside. It was early by strip club standards — about six in the evening — so the show hadn't even started yet. The only people in the place were two bartenders milling behind the counter, and a couple of bored looking, scantily clad girls that I brilliantly deduced were strippers. The lack of activity meant that every set of eyes was on us as we crossed the room, which only added to my discomfort.

We were led past another two action movie extras and up a narrow staircase. Unlike the unapologetically tacky stage area, the room we wound up in was fairly inoffensive. It was basically an office, with several chairs, a filing cabinet, and a large desk. The man behind it stood as we entered.

"Welcome," he said. At first glance he didn't appear particularly frightening. He looked to be in his early fifties. Lebanese maybe, or Mediterranean, and with his balding head, slightly retro clothes, and easy smile, he seemed like the kind of guy who'd be found taking his kids to soccer practice on the weekends or playing nine holes with his friends. But the longer I looked, the more I realised how wrong that impression was. It was the eyes, mostly. There was something cold flickering there, something calculating. I got the sense that his friendly appearance was well cultivated, and it could drop away at any moment.

Then, of course, there were the two extra men who had melted across the doorway as we stepped inside. They were doing their best to look bored, but the way they stood, with their jackets casually thrown open to expose their weapons, said that was an illusion too. The message was clear. We weren't leaving unless Anton wanted us to.

"Thank you for seeing us," Sebastian replied.

Anton smiled wider and spread his hands. "When someone makes an offer such as you did, the least a man like me can do is hear him out, wouldn't you agree?"

Sebastian nodded. "I was hoping that would be the case."

"Besides," Anton continued, "it's not often I get a chance to sit down and talk with two people I condemned just days earlier. I had men out there looking for you when you called, you know. And now, here you are. I must admit, I'm curious." The lightness of his tone sent a shiver down my spine. Oh yes, this was a man for whom killing was of no consequence.

But Sebastian appeared unshaken. "Well, like I said, I appreciate it."

"Did you bring what you promised?" Anton asked.

Taking my cue, I lifted the duffel bag I was carrying and dumped it on the table. I'd been quite surprised to find out that a million dollars in cash really did only occupy a few square feet. I thought that was just in the movies.

He didn't even bother to count it. He just unzipped the top and glanced inside. "Wonderful." I figured most people were too afraid to actually try and rip him off.

He gestured for the two of us to sit. "So, what brings you here? I have to say, this is a little unconventional. I'm not conceited enough to say I've never messed up a hit before, but those few lucky souls are usually eager to get as far away from me as possible. You and your lovely lady, on the other hand, have strolled right into my lap."

This was all part of the plan. Intrigue him enough to hear us out, then throw so much money at him that he couldn't resist. I just wished he didn't sound so amused by it all.

"It's simple, really," Sebastian replied. "You have information we want. We're willing to do what's necessary to get it."

Anton laughed. "Nothing is ever that simple in this business. This information, I take it, relates to the people who want you dead?"

Sebastian nodded. "Indeed."

Anton leaned back in his chair and laced his fingers together. "And what's to stop me simply refusing and then having Shawn and Iman here finish the job?" I glanced behind us and saw that the two men now had their hands resting on their pistols. I knew that if Anton gave the order, there would be no hesitation. We'd be dead in seconds. Despite how futile it seemed, I found my hand inching towards the hem of my dress.

"Money, mostly," replied Sebastian.

Anton shrugged. "I already got paid a lot of money to take you out, and that was only half. Now that you have kindly brought yourselves to me, I can get the rest when I report you dead. Not to mention the million you brought along. This has already been an incredibly profitable transaction for me."

"I'm sure we can come up with a sum that will convince you."

The other man studied us for several seconds. "And what about my existing client? I don't know him personally, but I'd hazard a guess that he'll be none too happy with me if I help you. Not to mention the damage he could do to my reputation; client confidentiality and so forth."

Sebastian's gaze turned ice cold. "If you tell us what you

know, I assure you that he won't be around to cause you any problems."

Anton nodded slowly, like he'd just gotten the answer he was expecting. "And what do you think about all this, sweetheart?" he said, turning to me. "You haven't said a word, so far."

That had been part of the plan too. Sebastian was much more familiar with this game than I was, so while I wasn't willing to let him leave me behind, I agreed to let him do all the talking. But I couldn't exactly ignore the question.

"I think it would be in your best interests to take the deal." As soon as the words left my mouth, I realised how they sounded. I hadn't intended to threaten him.

But apparently I wasn't as intimidating as I'd feared, because Anton just burst out laughing. "Is that right? I have to admit, when Leo told me you'd tracked me down, I was a little surprised. That must have taken some serious pull. It makes me wonder." He had that calculating look in his eye again, like he was trying to decide whether we were dangerous or stupid. I realised then that we were dealing with a very smart man. Callous, relentless, but also incredibly shrewd.

Sebastian seemed to recognise an opportunity. "There is more at stake here than you realise, Anton. You don't want to be caught up in the middle of this."

He cocked his head to one side. "Why don't you let me be the judge of that?"

He stared intently at us, weighing our case, our lives reduced to little more than dollar signs on a hypothetical page. Now that we'd played our hand, he knew how much money was really at stake. I assumed he was debating whether to contact his client and start a bidding war. If he knew how powerless we really were, it wouldn't even be a question, but thankfully he was still wary of exactly what we might be capable of.

I did my best to look calm, but my heart was raging like a jackhammer in my chest.

After what felt like a lifetime, he spoke. "Ten million."

"Done," replied Sebastian instantly.

I let out the breath I hadn't even realised I was holding. It was a ludicrous sum — cocktails on a tropical island for all eternity kind of money — but the truth was, we were desperate. We needed him more than he needed us. Besides, I was fairly sure Sebastian could afford it.

Judging by the look in Anton's eye, I think he realised that too. He seemed to be considering if he could get even more.

"I don't have a name for you," he said. "I make it my business to know as little as possible about my clients. It's safer that way, if anyone comes looking." He shot us an ironic grin. "What I do have is the phone number that he originally contacted us on to organise the meet."

Sebastian grimaced. "He won't be using his real phone for this. It's too easily tracked. What about a description? Anything that might help me identify him? I have reason to believe it's someone I'm familiar with."

Anton chuckled softly. "I don't meet them myself. Too risky." He nodded to one of the men in the doorway. "Iman organises the hits."

Sebastian and I both turned to the thug, but he simply shrugged. "He was man. Business man. It was dark, I don't see much." His voice was heavily accented, and it was clear English wasn't his first language. We weren't going to get much out of him.

"Sorry," said Anton.

Sebastian brought his hand up to cover his mouth and

stared into space for several seconds.

"I don't suppose we could just call him? See if you recognise the voice?" I asked.

"Maybe," Sebastian replied. "But then we give away our hand. And he might not answer at all. You said you guys used text messages?"

Anton nodded.

"Then yeah, a call will probably just scare him off."

And then I had an idea. "What does your client know?" I asked Anton. "Did you tell him we got away?"

Anton looked surprised for a moment, but he recovered quickly. "He knows. We had to go in and clean up your mess." He didn't sound even slightly upset about the two men we'd killed. He might as well have been discussing spilt juice. "He was not pleased, although we assured him we were doing everything we could to find you."

"Can you organise another meet?" I continued. "You said he still owes you half on completion of the contract, right? So tell him you've taken us out and you want the rest of your money."

Anton licked his lips. "This is not part of our deal. I would be exposing myself for you."

But Sebastian was nodding now, a hint of a smile on his face. "Fifteen million," he said. "And five more when we have him. Plus you get to keep whatever money he brings."

Anton's eyes widened a fraction. I could practically feel his sense of greed and self-preservation squaring off inside him. He got to his feet, and for one brief terrifying second, I thought he'd changed his mind, but then he extended his hand. "You have a deal."

The tension drained out of Sebastian's face, and he reached up and shook. "I'll have my guy drop the money off." He glanced at the two men behind us. "We'll need to borrow a few of your men."

Anton nodded. "I expected as much. Go with these two. They'll make the necessary arrangements. It's been good doing business with you."

Sebastian stared at him for several seconds, before inclining his head ever so slightly and turning towards the door.

I followed, doing my best not to break into a grin. Somehow, we'd pulled it off. The light at the end of the tunnel had suddenly grown that little bit brighter.

Chapter 13

Sebastian

The meet was set for early evening, in an old warehouse in Macdonaldtown, on the outskirts of Sydney. The location couldn't have been more of a movie stereotype if it tried. Cracked windows, rusted girders, piles of industrial detritus littering the floor. It certainly was empty, though. The roads nearby were completely devoid of people or cars. Movie stereotypes are stereotypes for a reason.

At this point, things were basically out of our hands. Sophia and I sat in the back seat of Anton's car, waiting for the trap to be sprung. Whoever was on the other end of the phone didn't seem to suspect anything. Their text message just sounded relieved. If everything went to plan, in a little while, we'd have our traitor in custody.

I looked over to Sophia, who was staring out the window. She'd handled herself well with Anton. Part of me had wanted to burst out laughing when she'd threatened him, but I'd restrained myself, and somehow we'd bluffed our way through it. We made a good team. She saw the things I missed and she wasn't afraid to speak up when she did.

She glanced up and caught me looking, and a smile lit her face. "Show time, soon." That smile was like a drug to me now. It was my reason to get up each morning. And every time I saw it, I wanted just a little more. When this was all over, I was going to make it my mission to put that smile there as often as possible.

I nodded.

She gazed at me for several seconds, a question poised on her lips. "Do you think this will be the end of it all?" she asked.

I exhaled slowly. I didn't want to dampen the mood of the victory we were about to win here. "I'm honestly not sure," I replied. "Whoever the traitor is, they have a lot of questions to answer. Once we know his motives, and who he's working with, we can plan our next move."

Her shoulders slumped a little, but she tried to remain stoic. "That makes sense."

"Hey," I said, reaching out to brush her cheek with one knuckle. "This is a big step forward. With any luck, they'll crack quickly and tell us everything we need to know. I suspect you'll be back burning the midnight oil at work and getting tanked with Ruth and Lou again in no time."

The smile returned. "I have missed excessive quantities of wine."

"You're allowed to drink more than a glass or two with me, you know."

"And be that embarrassing drunk with the begrudgingly tolerant boyfriend? I don't think so."

"So maybe I'll have more than one or two as well."

She raised an eyebrow. "I didn't realise you did messy drunk."

"I haven't for a few years. But I'm willing to make an exception for you."

She laughed. "That might just be the most romantic offer you've ever made me. It's settled then. When this is all over, we will drink to excess!"

"Deal," I replied.

Another minute passed. "You know, something about this still doesn't sit quite right with me," she said.

"In what way?"

"Well, when you rescued me, you fought your way through a whole house of guards, right?"

I nodded.

"So why did they hire out the killing this time around? Why not use their own people?"

"That's been bothering me too," I replied. "So much of this still makes no sense. Obviously they had their reasons. Maybe we hurt them worse than we thought when we raided that house?"

"Maybe," she replied, although she didn't sound convinced.

"We'll have some answers soon."

"I know," she said.

At that moment, another car appeared at the gate. It was one of the fleet of black Alpha BMWs. I felt something heavy settle in my stomach. Behind those doors was one of my brothers. A man I would have trusted with my life. A man who had betrayed me. I took a deep breath and tried to remain calm.

Through the tinted glass window I watched as the car pulled slowly into the empty lot and stopped about thirty meters away. Iman was standing off to one side, flanked by two of Anton's thugs. He was doing a good job of playing the part. He looked impatient, perhaps even a little bored. Just a guy on another routine pickup.

For a few moments, nothing happened; then the back

door opened and out stepped a man.

Ewan.

Something hot surged in my chest. Until that moment, I think part of me had still refused to accept it. A tiny voice in the back of my head, arguing that there was some other explanation for the way those assassins had surprised us; a hacked security system, or a building flaw we didn't spot. But seeing Ewan there, delivering payment for our deaths, meant that I couldn't lie to myself anymore. The group had been compromised.

It made me feel so damn stupid. I'd always believed the group rhetoric, those wonderful tenants that spoke of using power for the greater good, but now I realised how naive that was. The Alpha Group wasn't some last bastion of nobility. We were as susceptible to greed and self-interest as anyone. I still didn't understand what would possess Ewan to do these things, but I was going to do everything in my power to find out. He would pay for the pain he'd caused.

I looked to Sophia. She had every right to be wearing an 'I told you so' expression, but she seemed to understand the gravity of the situation. Instead, she just shot me a sympathetic smile and reached out to squeeze my knee.

Two Alpha security personnel followed Ewan out of the car, but after a few seconds of hushed conversation, they stayed in place while Ewan began to stride purposefully over the dust towards us. I wondered if the guards had turned on us too, or if they were just doing their job and simply had no idea of the traitorous deal going on right under their noses. I suspected the latter. In our line of work, you naturally see a lot of strange things, and they were taught not to ask questions. Besides, Ewan had kept them purposefully out of earshot. If he had nothing to hide, he'd have brought them in with him. They were probably just here to stop Iman and his men trying anything shady. Only a fool wouldn't tread carefully around Anton Silva.

It felt like it took Ewan forever to cross the empty yard. The animal inside me was raring to simply charge out of the car and let loose with all my rage, until he was just a bloody wreck on the ground, but I knew I needed to hold back. The situation could get messy in a heartbeat, if not handled carefully, and we needed Ewan alive if we wanted any chance of ending this.

When he was a few feet away from Anton's men, he stopped. In his hand he held a plain black briefcase that no doubt contained the rest of Anton's money. "You had me worried," he said. I had the window down ever so slightly, so we could hear everything clearly. "When they escaped the house I thought we'd lost our shot."

Iman smirked. "We find them. Or rather, they find us."

Ewan's eyes narrowed, but before he could react, all three of Anton's men had guns trained on him. The Alpha guys were good. In a split second they were both charging forward and reaching inside their jackets, but they froze as two more thugs emerged from the shadows behind them with weapons raised.

"What is this?" Ewan asked, but there already was a sense of understanding in his voice.

I nodded to Sophia, and we both reached for our door handles. I was expecting fear, but all I saw in his eyes when they fell on us was surprise, followed by resignation. The anger inside me flared. I didn't want him to be okay with what was coming. I wanted him to feel the same terror Sophia had, when he'd taken her from her house. That raw hopelessness of knowing that there was nothing left for him, beyond pain and death.

"This is you, getting what you deserve," I growled, and

before I could stop myself, I clocked him with an enormous uppercut that lifted his body from the ground. I was on top of him, moments later, my fists a blur in front of me, my vision clouded red. There were people yelling behind me, but they were muted and distant. All that mattered was Ewan and the pain I wanted him to feel.

It wasn't until Sophia grabbed my face and yanked my gaze up to hers that the rest of the world came back into focus. "Sebastian, stop! You're killing him!"

I looked down at the crumpled form below me. Ewan's face was a mask of blood and dirt. His hair was matted and his breathing shallow. He wasn't moving.

I closed my eyes and flung myself to my feet. I'd never lost control like that before. It was frightening. And scarier still, it had felt good. I wanted someone to blame for everything that had happened, someone that wasn't myself. And now that someone had finally presented himself, I could finally unleash some of the guilt that was devouring me from the inside. "I'm okay," I said. "I'm okay."

The adrenaline was already fading from my veins. My skin felt hot and my lungs burned. I'd hit him with everything I had.

Sophia leaned down to check Ewan's pulse. "He's alive."

"He's a tough old bastard," I replied.

"We need to get him somewhere soon, though, and check him out. You did quite a number on him."

I nodded. "I'll call in the cavalry."

I walked off towards the corner of the lot, just to put a little distance between Ewan and myself, and pulled out my phone.

"Thomas, I'm going to need a little help here."

* * * * *

"Doctor says he's alright," said Thomas, appearing in the doorway. "You certainly did a number on him."

I grimaced. "That's what Sophia said."

He pulled up a chair and sat down next to me, pouring himself a scotch from the bottle in front of us. It was about two hours since I'd called him, and we were inside a small Alpha complex in the Inner West, which had a couple of rooms fitted to keep prisoners. Holding people wasn't something we did often — we pulled strings, we didn't arrest people — but we liked to be prepared, nonetheless.

He threw back the entire glass in one sip, wincing with the burn, then shook his head. "I never suspected he could do something like this. I mean, he was a bit of an asshole, sometimes, but still. Not this."

"I know," I replied. "Is he talking yet?"

"Not yet. He's awake, but still pretty groggy. It won't be too long, I imagine." Something in the way he was looking at me told me what was coming next. "You could have called, you know. When you disappeared, we all assumed the worst."

I hated that I had to have this conversation, but there was no avoiding it. "I know, but at that point I didn't know who to trust."

A look of hurt crossed his face, and I didn't blame him. He was my friend and he deserved my trust. Then again, I'd thought Ewan deserved it as well. Would I ever be able to fully trust these men again? I wanted to think so, but I suspected there would always be a niggling doubt. I didn't know what to do with that. Maybe I could have lived with it a few years back, but I didn't just have my life to consider anymore. Sophia claimed she was okay with the risks, but that didn't mean I was. I couldn't stand the thought of ever putting her in jeopardy again. She deserved the happiness that came with a normal life, a life of not constantly looking over your shoulder. No matter how hard I tried, I didn't know if I could provide that anymore.

I took the scotch and refilled both our glasses, and we drank in silence for a while. I suspected there would be a lot of this over the coming days. The news of Ewan's betrayal had hit the group hard.

"How's Sophia coping?" Thomas asked eventually.

I felt a ghost of a smile creep onto my face. "She actually seems okay. She's a hell of a lot tougher than she looks."

"I can believe that. Is she still floating around here? I haven't had a chance to talk to her."

"No, I sent her back to the main house with Trey. She wanted to stay, but it was obvious how wiped out she was. Besides, there was no reason for her to be here. At this point, it's just a waiting game." With Ewan in custody, much of the danger had passed, but I wasn't willing to let Sophia go back out into the real world just yet. Now that we knew who the traitor was, she'd be safe in the Alpha house until we could unravel the rest of Ewan's operation. Soon, this whole nightmare would be behind us.

A few minutes later, Marcus walked into the room. "He's awake."

"Does he have anything to say for himself?" I asked.

"Not yet. He wants to speak to you, Sebastian. Said he won't talk to anyone else."

It wasn't a good idea. Despite having had a little time to process his betrayal, I still didn't trust myself to be in the same room as him. Just thinking about it turned my blood to lava. But Ewan was a stubborn son of a bitch. If he wanted me there, he'd hold out until it happened.

"Take me to him," I said with a curt nod.

I followed Marcus into the prison area, and he buzzed me through into Ewan's cell.

He was slouched on the bed in the corner of the room. Thomas and Sophia were right, I really had done a number on him. His face was a mottled collage of purple and yellow. Most of his features were barely recognisable behind the swelling and broken skin. He stared up at me, through his one good eye, still managing to look unafraid.

"So." My voice could have frozen water.

He sighed heavily. "So."

"Let's get this over with. You wanted to see me. Well, here I am."

There was a pause. "I'm sorry, Sebastian."

He couldn't have surprised me any more if he'd tried. My hands clenched tight and I took two big steps towards him until I was close enough to feel his breath on my skin. "Sorry? That's why you brought me in here? To apologise? I don't want your apologies, Ewan! I want answers!" I realised I was shouting, but I didn't care. I needed some outlet for all the anger seething inside me or it was going to come out through my fists again.

He flinched, but his expression remained stoic. "I appreciate that. I'm not going to pretend like that makes it better. All I want is for you to understand; everything I did, I did in the best interests of the group."

"You don't get to decide what's best for the group. That's not your call alone," I spat.

"Maybe not, but I didn't see any other way. She's a liability, Sebastian. And now you are too. The way you reacted when she was taken, well, the council can't afford to have that kind of weakness. Especially not with everything else that's happening. So I did what I thought was necessary."

A trickle of discomfort flowed down my spine. "What do

you mean everything else? You're responsible for everything else."

His eyes widened. "You can't be serious."

"I'm deadly serious. You just admitted to trying to take both of us out, but you expect me to believe you weren't the one who tried to kidnap Sophia?"

He sat up taller, raising his head as close to mine as possible. "I may have been concerned about you for a while, Sebastian, but I didn't do anything about it until that night with Anton's men in the safe house. And as God is my witness, I fucking certainly had nothing to do with Charlie and Simon. They were my friends."

His voice was louder now and full of conviction. It made my head spin.

"So if it wasn't you, who was it?"

"I don't know, but they're still out there."

"You're lying," I said, but I think it was more for my benefit than his. The certainty in his eyes rippled through me.

He studied me. "Maybe I am. Believe what you like, I guess. It makes little difference to me at this point." His eyes narrowed. "But when all of this comes crashing down around you, don't say I didn't warn you."

I stared at him for several seconds, my mind and stomach churning as one. I desperately wanted not to believe him, but what reason did he have to lie? Even if he did convince me, he couldn't think that would earn him clemency. There were no excuses for trying to assassinate a brother. Perhaps he was just messing with me, a last little 'fuck you' for good measure, but if that were the case, he was the best actor in the world. Besides, the sinking feeling in my belly was growing more powerful with every passing second.

The truth was, everything he said made sense. Ewan and I had never seen eye to eye, but his dedication to the group bordered on zealous. Even with what we thought was proof, right in front of us, I still hadn't really been able to see him doing all of this. Add that to the inconsistencies Sophia had raised earlier in the car, and the doubt only grew.

If he was telling the truth then someone else out there wanted to hurt the group. And that meant we were all still in danger.

Including Sophia.

I was out the door before I knew it, my phone already in my hand. *She's safe. By now she's probably asleep back in the house with armed guards stationed all around her.* But as the phone continued to ring out, a chill rolled through me unlike anything I'd ever felt before.

Ten rings. Twenty.

No answer.

With desperation clutching at my lungs, I hung up and called again. Nothing.

She's not answering because she's passed out. That's all.

I tried Trey's number, but it went straight to voicemail. With my heart beating like a wild drum in my chest, I raced back to find Thomas.

"Who's still at the house?" I asked.

He recoiled as I drew close, like he'd seen something horrifying in my face. "What the hell? What happened?"

"The house," I repeated, barely even hearing his questions. "Who's there?"

He licked his lips. "Jav should still be I think."

I was dialling before he even finished his sentence, and within a few rings, Jav picked up.

"Where's Sophia?"

There was a pause. "Sebastian? What do you mean? She's with you, isn't she?"

I closed my eyes and drew a ragged breath. *This can't be*

happening. "She was coming back to the house with Trey," I said slowly, my voice trembling. "She should have been there an hour ago."

"Trey hasn't been here since he left to meet you."

My hand shot out to clutch the wall as the room spun around me. There could have been other explanations, flat tires and empty phone batteries, but I knew that wasn't the case. I could feel the truth of it right down to my bones. They had her. Again. And it was my fault.

All the signs had been there, and I'd ignored them. And now... oh Christ. I had all the power in the world at my hands, and it wasn't enough. I couldn't even protect the one thing I truly loved.

Trey. He was responsible for this. Whatever destructive plan he had for the group, Sophia was somehow involved. And I'd handed her right to him.

Thomas' expression had slipped even further. "What is it, Sebastian? Is Sophia okay?"

But I couldn't respond. I couldn't even breathe. I felt like I was drowning, like the air around me had suddenly thickened into something my body could no longer process.

Last time I'd had a tail on Sophia from the start. I knew where they'd taken her, and I used that purpose and direction to hone my fear into focus. But this time she could be anywhere. The chance of finding her was next to nothing.

I collapsed against the wall and buried my head in my hands. I realised I was sobbing. I wanted to die. I wanted to curl up into a ball so tightly I just disappeared. My mind was racing, desperately searching for any kind of next move, but it was like trying to catch the wind in my hands. I had no clues. No information. No hope.

And then, my phone vibrated in my hand. The caller ID listed Sophia's number.

Barely breathing, I swiped the screen, and a picture of her flashed before my eyes. She was bound to a slim wooden chair, her mouth gagged, her eyes wide with fear. The caption simply said, "Come alone." It didn't give any directions, but it told me all I needed to know. The room in the background was instantly familiar. It was one of the control rooms in the old Alpha headquarters. The place the two of us had first met.

Trey had Sophia, and he wanted me to come for her.

I felt an icy calm descend over me, a sudden sense of clarity that was almost painfully sharp. Despite how stacked the situation looked, he'd made a mistake by inviting me. I didn't know how yet, but I was going to end this tonight. I'd failed Sophia too many times already.

I wouldn't fail her again.

Chapter 14

Sebastian

There was plenty of muscle waiting for me when I arrived at headquarters; at least ten men wearing suits and impassive expressions. No one commented as I approached, they just stood by with their hands on their holsters as the two closest moved in to search me. The gun strapped under my arm was commandeered without even a frown. I hadn't expected to actually get it past them, but I had to try anyway.

I'd nearly called in the cavalry. Thomas had been flipping out trying to work out what was going on, and it would have been so easy to explain the situation and bring the whole team down here with me. But I took Trey's warning seriously. He wouldn't hesitate to kill her if he got even a sniff of Alpha activity, and I had no idea how far his eyes and ears reached. If he had the right alerts set up, she could be dead before our cars made it a block. I couldn't take that risk.

When the guards were sure I was unarmed, they stepped back and I continued inside. I reached the door that led to Sophia's prison, but I took a moment before opening it to draw a deep breath. I still had no idea how I was going to get us out of this, but I had to remain calm. Blacking out, like I did with Ewan, would get us both killed in a heartbeat. If I wanted Trey and his friends to pay, I had to keep my wits about me. I refused to believe this was the end. After everything Sophia and I had been through, an opportunity would present itself. It had to.

I turned the handle and stepped inside.

Sophia sat towards one side of the room, bound to the chair exactly as she had been in the photo. Her face was puffy and red.

She cried out through her gag when she saw me, a visceral, frightened sound that seemed to echo inside my head. Without even realising what I was doing, I began rushing towards her.

"Uh uh," Trey said, stepping into view and pressing the barrel of his gun right up against her temple. "That's far enough."

Sophia seemed to be trying to tell me something. She'd gone quiet, but her eyes flicked continuously between Trey and the door behind me. I had no idea what it meant. It seemed like all the cards were pretty much on the table at this point.

I turned my gaze to Trey. My anger reared like a rabid dog in my chest, but I kept it leashed. *Focus.*

"You," I said, my voice sharp enough to cut glass.

He blinked a few times, then gave a shaky little bow. "Me."

The room was empty, apart from the three of us. Not that it mattered. He was armed and his goons were just a few steps away.

I studied him for several seconds. He mostly looked like himself. His smile held the same playfulness it always had, but there was something dark seething behind his eyes now too, something off. I had no idea how he'd kept that hidden for so long. "Why?" I asked.

He grinned. "That's the million dollar question, isn't it?"

"Million dollar? So it's money you want?"

"Oh, God no," he replied with a laugh. "Bad choice of phrasing, I guess. No, I may not be worth as much as you, Sebastian, but I'm perfectly comfortable. This is about so much more than that."

The motive behind the attacks had bothered me constantly. I'd never quite been able to make the pieces fit. "You killed Charlie and Aaron."

Trey nodded. "Guilty." He didn't show even the slightest sign of remorse.

"How could you do that? How could you kill your own brothers? We took you in, made you part of the family, and this is how you repay us?"

Trey's expression darkened. "I was never part of the family, Sebastian. I may have the tattoo, but I never had the respect."

I gave a sour laugh. "Respect? Seriously, that's what this is about? Poor little Trey is feeling under-appreciated?"

His jaw tightened. "Even now, you laugh at me." He gave the pistol a little shake. "Not wise to mock a man with a gun."

For a moment, I thought maybe I'd gone too far, but eventually he relaxed.

"You know, my dad used to tell me about you guys, back when I was a kid," he continued. "I know he wasn't supposed to, but he did. He used to tell me the kinds of things you did, the kind of power you had. I used to dream about the day I'd be a part of that. Then you finally invited me to join, and it was the best day of my life. I finally had a chance to prove myself. I spent the next three years busting my ass for the group, but in the end, you know what I had to show for it? The same shitty jobs and cruel jokes as when I started."

"The group is a lifelong commitment, Trey. Things don't happen overnight. You can't just waltz in and expect to be running the show."

"You did. You were, what, twenty seven when they invited you to the council? And dad was just twenty five. Not to mention Marcus. You promote *that guy* over me?" There was something wild in his expression now, something broken. Clearly this wound had been festering for some time. "Dad didn't invite me to the group to be a fucking errand boy. I'm capable of better. I *deserve* better."

"Yeah, well your dad would be turning in his grave if he could see you now." The words left my mouth before I realised I'd said them.

Trey's mouth parted in a snarl and he flung the gun upwards at me, his arm trembling. "You take that back," he hissed. "You take that back! He'd understand. He'd be proud I finally stepped up and did something. He wasn't the sort of man who let other people walk all over him, and neither am I."

"So what is all this then? Revenge? Kill a few group members and make yourself feel better?"

The smile returned to Trey's face, but it was off somehow, crooked, like I was looking at a reflection of it in a splintered mirror. "A little, maybe. But there's more to it than that. That's the problem with the group now. You don't think grand enough. Besides, I'm not the one you should really be talking to about revenge."

I cocked my head. "What's that supposed to mean?"

"Well, as much as I'd love to take all the credit for everything, I have to confess I didn't do it alone. I had a little help from someone who had a slightly more personal stake in all of this." He raised his voice. "You can come in now, babe."

My eyes darted to the door just in time to see a woman step through.

"Hello, Sebastian," she said.

My jaw dropped. It had been years since I'd seen her, but those perfect features and golden locks were unmistakable.

Liv.

For about ten seconds, nobody spoke. She merely smiled, radiating satisfaction while my mouth worked wordlessly. The sight of her made me feel like I was falling, like everything else was zipping past around me. My stomach heaved, my skin prickled, my lungs seemed frozen in my chest. A million thoughts crashed through my head. For a few moments I was actually certain I was dreaming.

"You're alive," I said finally.

Liv let out a little giggle. "As observant as ever, I see." She seemed to have actually dressed up for the occasion. Between the long black gown she wore and the elegant clutch under her arm, she looked like she'd come directly from some kind of fancy charity dinner.

I took a step towards her, my arm twitching forward ever so slightly before I stopped myself. "I saw your body."

"You saw *a* body. Some poor girl they found in an alley in The Cross. OD'd, from memory. A bit of decoration, some creative police reporting, courtesy of Trey, and poof," she made a fist then popped it in front of her, "I was dead."

I felt like my eyes were about to pop out of my head. Turning away, I forced them closed. "Do you know what that did to me?"

Her voice was impossibly cold. "It hurt, I imagine. I hope it did. After the way you left me, you deserved to hurt." She had the same callousness to her demeanour now that Trey did. It changed her. That feminine allure was still there, but it was hardened, tempered by years of bitterness. Two people with huge chips on their shoulders; in a morbid way, they made the perfect couple.

"I left to protect you, Liv." I gestured to the room. "To protect you from all of this."

"I didn't want your protection," she spat. "I wanted you. But apparently that was too much to ask."

I had no idea how I was supposed to be dealing with this. I'd never been so confused in my life.

"So now you're with him?" I asked. "You can't have me, so you take this insecure, traitorous little shit instead?"

Treys snarled and lifted the gun once more, but Liv raised her hand. "Easy, Trey."

She turned back to me. "Yes, I'm with him. After you left, it felt like the world had ended. I gave up my life for you, Sebastian. My dreams. Everything. And then you dropped me without so much as an explanation. When I ran into Trey one day, I was desperately looking for a friend, and at first, that's exactly what it was. But soon enough it turned into something else. He was there for me when no one else was, and so I was there for him too."

She shot Trey a smile, but even that seemed to lack true joy. I wondered how much of their relationship was real and how much was simply fuelled by spite. "Unlike you, he's not afraid to be himself with me. He doesn't treat me like a child who can't handle the truth. He told me who he was, who you were, the way you all treated him, and soon it became clear that our goals overlapped. I realised what we had to do."

I glanced at Sophia, hoping the sight of her would steady me a little. She looked almost as surprised as I felt.

"Well, it looks like you succeeded," I said heavily. "You've got me. Whatever it is you want, Sophia has nothing to do with it. You can let her go now. This is between you two, me, and the group."

Sophia let out a high pitched squeal and shook her head rapidly. I loved that she wasn't willing to leave me behind, but I wasn't going to let her throw her life away for my sake. I'd cost her so much already.

"Well, isn't that touching," Liv replied, her voice dripping with scorn. "Trey told me you two had fallen hard for each other." For the first time, she turned her attention to Sophia. Walking closer, she dipped a hand under her chin, stroking it with one finger. Sophia tried to pull away, but Liv's grip closed around her face, angling her head upwards. Every fibre of my being wanted to stride over there and tear those hands away but, somehow, I restrained myself. We were still poised on a knife's edge. All I could do was watch as Liv appraised Sophia, envy and hatred blazing in her eyes. "To be honest, I'm not sure I see what all the fuss is about."

She turned back to me. "You want us to let her go? Well, that's entirely up to you. Let's see exactly how much you love her." She nodded to Trey.

"It's simple really," he said, gesturing to the Alpha computer terminal at the end of the room. "You log me into the system, we release her."

"I don't understand," I replied. "You want council access to the network?"

He grinned. "Remember what I said about thinking big? No, council access won't be enough I'm afraid. I want the main international database. My employers want access to everything."

"Your employers?"

He spread his hands. "The Syndicate. You don't think we hired all those men ourselves, do you? No, we've had a little support. Once I told them what we could bring to the table, it wasn't difficult to convince them to give me a position in their organisation. A *senior* position."

So The Syndicate *was* involved. I shook my head. The level of betrayal was beyond anything I could have imagined. Trey was quite happy to destroy the entire group, all two thousand years of history, to feed his desperate ego. And Liv, my God. I knew I'd hurt her, but I never dreamed she'd be capable of something like this. Then again, one look at her and it was clear that the woman I'd fallen in love with was nowhere in sight. All that was left was a bitter parody.

I needed to focus. Something he'd said didn't make sense. "Only the current Archon can give you that kind of access. You know that."

He gave a little laugh. "This isn't the time to play games, Sebastian. What do you think we've been doing for the last two years? We've been working out who runs the show. We couldn't see the actual orders of course, but you might be aware that Liv is a little handy with a PC. She actually managed to get a few bits of software piggybacking on your system, while you two were still together, so between that and my basic Alpha access, we've been able to build a pretty accurate picture of the way information in the group flows."

I felt a glimmer of hope, the tiniest hint of light at the end of the tunnel. "And you think it comes from me?"

Trey nodded. "Until a few weeks ago, we had it narrowed down to three. You, Simon, or Charlie. At that point we decided it was more effective to just ask. After giving the others a little more... incentive to tell the truth, they still denied it. Which just leaves you. I have to admit, I was pretty pissed off when you managed to find Sophia the first time. That set us back several weeks. Not to mention Ewan's little stunt." He gestured to the room around us and smiled. "But I guess it all worked out in the end, and that's what counts."

I let my shoulders sag a little, trying to play along. "And

what do you get out of all of this?" I asked Liv.

"Oh, my aspirations aren't nearly as grand," she replied. "Revenge will do me just fine. I'm so glad it turned out to be you. We had our suspicions, even from the start, but we couldn't rely just on those. Now we get to take care of everything all at once. It's so much neater this way."

"And if I refuse?"

"Then we kill both of you, drag you over, and swipe your thumb on the scanner anyway." Her voice was ice cold.

"So why not simply do that to start with?" I asked. "Save yourself all this hassle?"

Liv's expression twisted even further. "I'd rather you were alive to watch it happen."

She'd obviously intended to sound like she was talking about the downfall of Alpha, but the way her eyes narrowed fractionally and darted to Sophia as she spoke said it was more than that. I suspected that the moment I gave them what they wanted, Liv was going to have Trey shoot her in front of me and let me watch her die. My group and my girl in one single move. The ultimate payback for the pain I'd caused her.

Judging by the expression on Sophia's face, she realised the truth as well. Whatever flimsy mask of self-control she'd been maintaining so far had crumpled. She looked absolutely terrified. My mind was madly scrabbling for a way to let her know that we weren't totally out of the game. We were only going to have a tiny window of opportunity and I needed her to be ready, but anything I said would tip our hand. And then it came to me.

"You promise you'll let her go?" I asked.

Liv smirked. "Cross my heart."

My death, on the other hand, was apparently a given, but I'd anticipated that the moment I walked through the door.

I nodded slowly and began moving over to the computer

terminal. Trey followed, gun trained on my chest. "Don't try anything clever. I'm going to bring up the root Alpha portal, and you're going to swipe your thumb for access, then back away. Understand?"

"Yep."

He opened the program. "All yours."

I reached out, and then paused with my thumb over the pad. "You know this is really sweet," I said, gesturing between the two of them. "A real Cinderella story."

A look of confusion crossed both their faces, but I wasn't really paying attention to them. I was staring at Sophia. For a second, she looked perplexed too, but then her eyes lit up as she recognised the safe word she'd picked the first time we were together. Bingo. I tried to draw a line between her and the floor with my eyes, and she gave a tiny nod. It would have to be enough.

"Whatever. Get on with it," Trey said.

I took a deep breath, and pressed down.

And the room was plunged into darkness.

There were two brief cries of surprise, and then the crack of gunfire, but I was already diving to the right. Unfortunately I wasn't fast enough. Heat exploded through my arm and I stifled a scream. It was just a graze along my bicep, but it hurt like hell, and blood was already seeping through the ragged slash in my sleeve. I forced the pain away. I couldn't think about that now. If I went down, so did Sophia, and that was not an option.

A few more bullets slammed into the darkness around me, one passing close enough that I could feel the wind of it on my face. I scuttled along the floor, fumbling blindly for the edge of the desk and pulling myself around it. I hadn't been sure it would work. I'd heard rumours about what happened when someone without authorisation tried to log into the central database, but nobody had ever been stupid enough to try. As I understood it, the whole system, lights, door locks, computers, was now locked down, and an alert had gone out over the network. In a few minutes, Alpha would be showing up here in force. Of course we still had to survive until they arrived.

For a moment I thought that perhaps Sophia hadn't understood my message, but a split second later there was a loud crack, the sound of wood splintering. She'd thrown herself to the ground.

"What the hell, Trey?" It was Liv's voice, and there was a tremble running through it now.

He let out a howl and fired blindly again. "We checked everyone. It had to be you. It had to!" He sounded as though he was talking mostly to himself.

There was a distant commotion outside. No doubt Trey's guards were trying to leap to his defence. But with the system down, all doors into this room had sealed themselves. They weren't getting in any time soon.

Trey had gone quiet now, apparently realising that sound was everything when you were fighting in the dark. Sophia, however, was still audible. Judging by the noise it had made, the chair had broken when she fell, but she still had to extricate herself from the remains. If I didn't distract them, it wouldn't be long before they found her.

It was incredibly disorienting being in pitch darkness. My mind's eye knew roughly where I'd landed, but with no point of reference I felt lost, like I was swimming in a sea of nothingness. I groped behind me where I thought the bookshelf should be, but all I snatched was empty air. I could still hear Sophia struggling to my right somewhere.

"Trey?" said Liv again.

"Quiet," he hissed. His voice had moved now. It was in

the centre of the room. I was running out of time.

Finally, my hands found something solid, the leather spine of a book. I slipped it from the shelf as quietly as I could and then hurled it towards where I'd last heard Trey. I don't know if I struck anyone, but there were two startled screams as the book collided with something, and another bullet zinged into the furniture to my right.

I threw several more, sliding softly along the ground, never staying the same spot. Judging by the yelp of pain, at least one of my projectiles hit its mark, but it wasn't enough. At best I was just delaying them by a few moments. Trey had stopped firing now, knowing the muzzle flash gave him away. I debated simply charging the area where I'd heard him cry out, but I doubted he was staying in one place, either. All that would do is make me an easy target.

I wracked my brain for a way to locate him in the darkness. His mistake had given us a chance, but he still had the advantage. He was armed and I was wounded. Even through the endorphins flooding my brain, my arm was burning like crazy. It wouldn't kill me, but I was already feeling woozy and light-headed. I needed to end this soon.

I fumbled through my pockets looking for anything that might give me an edge. Keys, wallet, phone.

Phone.

And just like that, something clicked into place in my head.

Burying it beneath my jacket, I took a moment to steady my quivering thumb, then I swiped the screen. I had to be quick. I was shielding the light as best I could, but in the pitch darkness it could still give me away. Fortunately, on this unit I only had one number in my favourites list. Sophia's.

I mashed the call button, then locked the screen once more, stuffing it into my pocket to hide the noise. Trey had used her phone to text me just half an hour earlier. I hoped to god he was still carrying it.

After a few agonising seconds, I was rewarded with a chime just a few meters to my left. It was one of those abrasive, pre-programmed ringtones, and it sounded impossibly loud in the blackness. Someone gasped, and I prepared to charge towards the noise, but then another gunshot rang out.

For a moment, I was overcome with confusion. Trey had the only gun, and the shot hadn't come from the same place as the call sound. But then Liv spoke, and I understood.

"What?" Her voice was soft, but full of disbelief, the phone still ringing by her side. There was the sound of something heavy dropping to the floor.

Trey let out a long shriek, and the pain of it was nearly enough to pin me in place. In spite of everything they'd done to us, and the years I'd already thought her dead, I still felt a burst of anguish myself, knowing that she'd been shot. But this was my opportunity, and Sophia's life still hung in the balance. I had to act.

I launched myself into the darkness, hurling my body towards the source of the cry, praying that he was frozen in shock. My shoulder contacted something soft, and there was a grunt, and then we were tumbling to the ground. I wrestled blindly for his arm and two more shots sprayed into the darkness. The sound was loud enough to set my ear ringing. I was bigger than he was, but I was injured, and he was filled with the mad fury of a man with nothing left to lose. My wound was like fire, spreading all across my left side, as I wrestled him for control of the gun. Sophia must have removed her gag. I could hear her calling to me now, desperate and frightened, but I didn't have the oxygen to reply. Every ounce of me was going into this fight.

Somehow, I pulled myself on top of him, wrapping my

hand around his fingers and twisting, sending the gun skidding off into the blackness. He clawed at me with his free arm, snarling wordlessly, but with his body beneath mine, my superior weight came into play, and I managed to keep him at bay. But it wouldn't last. I could feel myself tiring.

With one final surge of energy, I forced my way through his guard, seizing his hair and pulling it up before slamming his head back onto the floor. His body went limp.

And just like that it was over.

As the adrenaline faded, the rest of the world came back into focus. Sophia was still calling for me. "Sebastian? Please, answer me."

"I'm okay," I replied hoarsely. "I'm okay."

She let out a little sob. "I thought he'd shot you. I didn't understand what was going on. Are they...?"

"I don't know." Dragging myself off Trey, I reached out to check his pulse. He was alive. I suspected I'd just knocked him unconscious. I turned towards where I'd heard Liv fall, searching for any sounds of life, but the darkness stayed silent. I couldn't bring myself to try and confirm it. I'd already felt her death once. "I think we're safe," I said.

"What about them?" she asked, and I realised I could still hear the faint rattling of Trey's men trying to break their way inside.

"These doors are deceptively strong. We'll be fine in here until the cavalry arrives."

I searched until I found the gun. It was unlikely Trey or Liv would trouble us again, but I wasn't taking any chances.

By the time I reached her, Sophia had shed the rest of her bonds. She was shivering and, as she burrowed into me, I ran my hand up and down her arm, despite knowing it wasn't the cold that chilled her.

"What happened there?" she asked. "With the lights I

mean? One moment I was sure we were dead, the next you were signalling at me, and then everything just went crazy."

"They had the wrong guy."

"So you're not the leader?"

I shook my head. "Nope."

She actually laughed. It was a tiny sound, but glorious too, and it seemed to release something inside me. "Then who the hell is it? Because I have to say, I was pretty sure it was you, too."

At that moment, there were several gunshots outside. Sophia tensed.

"It's okay. That'll be the good guys."

The door opened, and in stepped Joe, flanked by several guards.

"Well, aren't you two a sight?" he said.

It took her a few moments to understand. "No. Way. *You're* in charge?"

Joe grinned in amusement. "That's perfectly ridiculous, Sophia. After all, I'm just a driver."

But she wasn't having any of it. She turned to me. "Does that make you second in charge?"

"What happened to letting me keep some secrets?" I replied, but I kept my voice light. There was little reason to hide anything at this point.

Soon, the room was swarming with people. Once it had become clear how stacked the odds were, The Syndicate soldiers outside had thrown down their weapons and surrendered. We hadn't lost a single man.

Trey was still out cold, but nonetheless his stretcher was escorted out by an entire team of our best guys. I wasn't sure what exactly would become of him, but I was certain it wouldn't be pleasant. In our laws, the only crime worse than trying to kill a fellow brother is trying to hurt the group itself, and he'd committed both to extreme levels.

Liv, on the other hand, wouldn't have the chance to be punished. Trey's bullet had taken her through the neck, nicking an artery, and she'd bled out, there in the dark. I couldn't even stomach to look at her body. My mind was still reeling from discovering she was alive. Dealing with her death for a second time was the last thing I needed.

At some point, while everything was being dealt with, Sophia slipped away. I found her sitting alone, on a stool, in the crumbling old bar at the front of the complex.

"This is where it all started," she said as I approached. "If I hadn't snuck through the door that night, all of this would have played out differently."

I nodded. I'd never believed much in fate or destiny. The idea of having no control over my life terrifies me to my core. But it was hard not to feel the divine hand of providence in all of this. How else could I have found the soul that so perfectly matched my own? The person that healed the wounds I'd thought were beyond repair?

"Do you regret it?" I asked. "That night?"

One side of her mouth curled up. "Not even for a second."

Part of me thought that made her crazy, but it was exactly what I needed to hear. I pulled up a stool and joined her.

"Is it over then?" she asked.

"I'm almost scared to say yes, but I think, this time, it actually is. We still have a lot of cleaning up to do. I expect once Trey tells us what we need to know, the group will be moving against The Syndicate ASAP. It will be messy, but it needs to be done. With any luck, things will be back to normal in a few weeks."

She nodded, and for about thirty seconds we sat in silence. "I'm sorry about Liv," she said eventually.

I exhaled slowly. "Now *that* was a surprise."

She reached out and took my hand. "Are you okay?"

I didn't answer straight away. After all of the betrayal and deception, and with all of the hurdles still to come, I felt like I mostly definitely should not be okay. But sitting there, with her fingers laced through mine, the worst of our problems finally in the rear view mirror, all I felt was a strange sense of contentment.

"You know, I actually am."

Epilogue

Sophia

The period after it was all over was a bit of a blur. Having learned my lesson, I stayed close to Sebastian for a few days, making sure all the loose ends were tied up.

When we were confident it was well and truly over, Sebastian moved back into his apartment and I went with him. He'd organised a crew to come through and fix the damage to my place, but I wasn't ready to go back there yet. Maybe I never would be. Sleeping alone still held a lot of terrors for me. I doubted I'd fully get over my experiences for some time.

Surprisingly, it was kind of difficult to adjust to a normal life again. After the constant adrenaline, the daily grind felt a little muted, a little dull. I wasn't stupid enough to actually miss all the peril and the betrayal and the men with guns, but there was a certain mystique to having been involved in that clandestine world that, in retrospect, I could almost romanticise.

Despite the fact that we were living together, Sebastian and I didn't get much time alone for the next few weeks. The

Alpha Group was in turmoil over everything that had happened, and there was an awful lot of cleaning up to do. I missed him. After everything we'd been through together, that powerful sense of 'us versus the world', it felt strange to suddenly be apart once more. But I tried to use that time to focus on getting back into my old rhythm. My boss was pleased to have me back, and I assured him that this time it was for good. A few days later, the promotion he'd hinted at officially came through, and I became a senior associate. There was something extra satisfying about the idea of not just being promoted, but stepping into Jennifer's shoes. I had no doubt I'd be up to the task.

I even managed to fit in a little pre-hens night with the girls, which left me with a headache to rival anything Trey had injected me with.

"I knew that skank had to have a secret!" said Ruth, when I filled her in on what had happened with Jennifer.

"Yeah, talk about sleeping your way to the top," agreed Lou.

"The worst part is that it was with Alan," I said, suppressing a shudder. "No promotion under the sun is worth that."

"Well, I'm glad things are back on track," said Lou.

Ruth's smile turned playful. "Speaking of back on track, you hinted on the phone that Sex-On-Legs had a change of heart too."

I grinned at the nickname. "It looks that way."

"Well, that's awesome," she replied. "If any other woman is going to have him, I'm glad it's you."

"You never had him at all!"

Her smile widened and she tapped the side of her head. "Up here I did."

I laughed. "I choose to take that as a compliment."

"And so you should. Just don't go getting any ideas about

diamond rings and screaming toddlers, like this one here," she said, nodding to Lou, "or I may have to disown you both."

"Oh don't be so dramatic," replied Lou. "Once Soph squeezes one or two out and settles down in the burbs, you can come around on Fridays and play charades with us!"

Ruth's face twisted in mock horror.

"I'm not sure there will be much settling in our immediate future," I told them. "After all, I have a partnership ladder to climb."

In truth, I had been feeling a little uncertain about the future, but not for that reason. It was one thing Sebastian and I had yet to talk about. The events of the last few weeks had shown the depth of his feelings for me, and I returned them just as strongly. But now that things were returning to normal, and the adrenaline was fading, the reality of that commitment was sinking in. For better or for worse I'd fallen for a man with some rather unique obligations, and I didn't know exactly what they meant for us. I had no objections about the way our life was now; in fact, it felt a little like I was living in some kind of dream, but was that going to be our life forever? Were the things Ruth joked about permanently out of reach?

All I knew was that I loved him and wanted to be with him, and I figured we'd work it out as we went along.

A week or so later, Sebastian surprised me with another trip to Mi Casa. It was every bit as warm and welcoming as I remembered, with several waiters I only dimly recognised welcoming me like an old friend. The food was incredible again, and since I knew what was coming, I buzzed with anticipation for the entire meal.

As the plates were cleared, and the music started, Sebastian stood and held out his hand. "May I have this dance, my lady?"

This time there was no hesitation. "Certainly, sir," I replied with a giggle.

We danced for what felt like hours, our bodies slowly igniting each other with sensuous rhythm. I half expected him to pull me aside again, to relieve the tension, but much to my disappointment, he restrained himself.

Eventually, he guided me to the edge of the crowd, and then towards the door. I didn't have to ask where we were going.

It was much warmer outside than the last time he'd brought me here, and even up on the headland, utterly exposed to the elements, there was only a soft sea breeze. We settled on the grass, just a few metres from the cliff's edge, and nestled against one another, gazing out over the dark water.

"This really is a spectacular view," I said.

He nodded, but didn't reply, his brow slightly furrowed in contemplation.

"Is everything okay?" I asked.

He blinked several times, then turned to me, his lips curling into a smile. "Everything is perfect." He planted a kiss on the top of my head. "I do want to talk to you about something, though."

"Oh? Let me guess. Thomas has gone rogue and is hunting us even as we speak!"

He laughed. "Not quite." His expression slipped to something that almost looked like nervousness. "I was hoping you'd like to make our living arrangement permanent."

"For real?" We basically were already living together, but nonetheless, the formal acknowledgement was a big step.

"For real," he confirmed. "I love knowing that I've got you to come home to every night. I want to know that I've got that forever."

The word 'forever' sent a warm tingle rolling through my

chest. "You make me sound like a kept women," I replied. "What about the nights where *I* come home to *you*?" I was going for a little sass, but it was somewhat ruined by the sickly sweet smile I couldn't seem to wipe off my face.

He chuckled. "I love those, too."

I made him sweat it for a few seconds, but the truth was he'd had me from the moment he opened his mouth. Hell, he'd had me almost from the moment we met. There was no want left in our relationship now, only need. I needed him like I needed air, and I couldn't imagine going home to a house without him either.

"Of course I'll move in with you."

He let out a long breath and his face lit up like a Christmas tree. "That's what I wanted to hear."

"Although I have to say, Ruth's probably going to have an aneurysm. I'm the last domino standing, and I have no doubt she'll see this as a sign that the end is nigh."

"The end?"

"You know, marriage, kids, impractically fluffy pets. To Ruth that stuff is the end."

He laughed. "I see."

"No pressure from me — these hips won't be passing any little bundles of terror for at least a few more years — but if you plan any more big changes, give me a little notice so I can ease her into the transition, okay?"

His expression lost a little of its amusement. "Well actually, there is one other thing I wanted to mention."

"Oh?" I said cautiously.

There was a long pause. "I quit."

Something shifted in my stomach. "Quit? What do you mean quit? I thought that wasn't allowed."

"Well, maybe that's not quite the right word. Rather, I asked Joe to fire me."

"He can do that?"

Sebastian shrugged. "He's in charge. He can pretty much do what he wants. Call it a perk of knowing the boss."

"And he was okay with it?"

Sebastian gave a surprised little smile. "Yeah. He actually seemed happy to do it."

I shook my head slowly, trying to come to grips with what he was saying. I couldn't deny that the idea of having Sebastian all to myself filled me with joy, but I didn't want that at the expense of his happiness. "Wow. I appreciate the gesture, Sebastian, but are you sure? I mean, we're doing okay now, aren't we? Things don't need to change."

"I'm not worried about the ninety nine percent of the time things are going fine," he said. "I'm worried about the one percent that they're not." There was pain on his face now. "Everything that happened recently has made me realise a few things. I'm not sure I'll ever trust the group like I used to. Those men are my friends, and they'll remain that way, but they also swim in dangerous waters. You know that as well as anyone." He took one of my hands in his and raised it to his mouth, brushing soft kisses across each knuckle. "Maybe nothing like that will ever happen again. But I'm not willing to risk it. I'm not willing to risk you."

The look on his face, the fierceness, the fire, the love, it rippled through me. But still, this felt like too much. "I don't know, Sebastian. I mean, this is who you are, this is what you do. It may not make for an ideal relationship, but we can make it work. I never expected you to give up your life for me."

"This isn't me giving up my life, Sophia," he said. "This is me beginning it."

I could only shake my head and grin like an idiot as my heart melted into a puddle in my chest. "Well, how can a girl argue with that?"

He pulled me in for a kiss and, for a while, I lost myself in his lips. There was a strange sensation blossoming in my chest, one that took some time for me to recognise. Hope.

He was right.

Everything was perfect.

Thanks!

Thank you so much for reading. I hope you enjoyed the story. Writing this series has been an amazing journey, and I have each and every one of you to thank.

When I was writing the series, I was considering a couple of options for the epilogue. Basically, I saw Sophia and Sebastian's HEA going one of two ways when the dust had settled. One of them was a lot of fun, but I ended up deciding that they just wouldn't make that decision after everything that happened. So in the final version of the story, I went with the more believable (and sweeter) option.

But since the other option was fun to consider, I decided to release it for people on my mailing list as an exclusive little bonus. It doesn't in any way impact the real end. It's just a deleted scene that I thought some people might enjoy. If you want to see how Sophia and Sebastian's lives could have been, all you have to do is sign up to my newsletter (just go to my website, http://mayacross.com, and click 'newsletter'). Once you've put in your email address, it will send you a confirmation link. Click that and you'll receive an email with a link to the bonus scene. If you're already on my mailing list, the link was included in the mailout I sent when Unlocked launched, so look back through your inbox. It would have arrived around the 18th of August.

I'll be releasing several bonus scenes exclusively to my email list over the coming months (I really want to write the Mi Casa dance scene from Sebastian's POV), and I am also planning to start a monthly gift voucher giveaway for my mailing list fans, so there's lots of reasons to stay in touch! I promise not to share your email with anyone else, and I won't clutter your inbox (I'll only be mailing when there's something important like a book launch or sale).

Also just a friendly reminder that if you did like the story, the best way you can show thanks and help me keep producing more work is to leave a review on the site you bought from. You don't have to compile an epic three page analysis; even just a single line and a star rating helps. Anything that lets other people know you enjoyed it. It's a little thing, but it makes a big difference to writers like me.

Thanks again!

About the Author

Maya Cross is a writer who enjoys making people blush. Growing up with a mother who worked in a book store, she read a lot from a very young age, and soon enough picked up a pen of her own. She's tried her hands at a whole variety of genres including horror, science fiction, and fantasy, but funnily enough, it was the sexy stuff that stuck. She has now started this pen name as an outlet for her spicier thoughts (they were starting to overflow). She likes her heroes strong but mysterious, her encounters sizzling, and her characters true to life.

She believes in writing familiar narratives told with a twist, so most of her stories will feel comfortable, but hopefully a little unique. Whatever genre she's writing, finding a fascinating concept is the first and most important step.

The Alpha Group is her first attempt at erotic romance.

When she's not writing, she's playing tennis, trawling her home town of Sydney for new inspiration, and drinking too much coffee.

Website: http://www.mayacross.com
Facebook: http://facebook.com/mayacrossbooks
Twitter: https://twitter.com/Maya_cross

16275771R00290

Made in the USA
San Bernardino, CA
25 October 2014